MAYBE <u>NOW</u>

A novel
by Dave Hughes

Prickly Pair Publishing
Chandler, Arizona, USA

Previous books in the "Gay Tales for the New Millennium" series:

Maybe Next Year
Instant Adult
Open Books, Closed Sets
If I Seem Quiet...
Karma Train from Kansas

Visit AuthorDaveHughes.com to learn more about Dave, gain background information and insights into Dave's books and the writing process, and receive advance notice of upcoming book releases and subscriber discounts. You will receive Dave's short story, *Cruise Virgins*, free when you subscribe to his newsletter.

If you would like to contact the author, please send an email to Dave@AuthorDaveHughes.com.

Cover photo: EpicStockMedia (licensed from depositphotos.com)
Cover design: Dave Hughes

Library of Congress Control Number: 2024915750

ISBN: 978-0-9970018-2-2

An Advancement Opportunity

Tuesday, January 8, 2019

At 2:50 p.m., Ryan Robertson pulled open the heavy glass door leading into the Regional Headquarters building of Technovations. He entered a modern, opulent lobby that was bathed in sunshine thanks to the two-story floor-to-ceiling tinted glass windows. He scanned the well-maintained potted plants, the beautiful artwork, and the waiting area with comfortable seating. Ryan flashed his employee badge to the security guard at the front desk, who nodded and allowed him to pass. He walked over to the elevators. When he pushed the Up button one of the cars immediately opened for him. He stepped into the elegant wood-paneled cube and pressed 4 – the building's top floor. The doors closed with a quiet whoosh and the elevator smoothly began its ascent.

The Regional Headquarters building, or RH as it was known, was one of five buildings on Technovations' Scottsdale campus. It was the one Ryan had been in the least since he rarely needed to meet with anyone in the company's upper echelon. But yesterday, he had received an invitation to meet with Richard Caldwell, Senior Vice President of Human Resources and Workforce Development. He had no idea why.

Technovations was a casual workplace. A polo shirt and nice jeans or casual slacks were the norm. For today's meeting, he wore a light blue freshly dry-cleaned dress shirt and a nice pair of dark slacks. He had debated wearing a tie, but even the higher-ups rarely wore ties around the office.

The elevator eased to a gentle stop and the doors slid open. Ryan stepped into a lavishly-appointed foyer, with elegant dark wood paneling, high-grade maroon carpeting, and plush chairs. He approached the large desk, where a well-dressed middle-aged woman sat with perfect posture in front of her monitor. She looked up and smiled. "May I help you?"

"My name is Ryan Robertson. I have a 3:00 appointment with Mr. Caldwell."

The receptionist glanced at her monitor and nodded. "I'll let him know you're here. Please have a seat over there. If you would like coffee, iced tea, or water, please help yourself." She gestured toward a small table that held a Keurig machine and two 5-gallon glass dispensers, one with iced tea and one with water. Several lemon slices floated atop the water. An assortment of snacks was pleasingly arranged in a small basket. Ryan wasn't sure how long he would be waiting, so he didn't want to get too invested in refreshments. He poured himself a glass of water and sat down.

While he waited, he couldn't help but think, *Why am I here? It probably isn't for a bad reason – if that were the case, I'd get called into HR or escorted out by security. Am I dressed well enough? Maybe I should have worn a tie.*

After the longest five minutes of his life, he heard an alert sound on the receptionist's computer. She glanced at the monitor, clicked on something, and stood up. "Mr. Caldwell will see you now. Right this way, please."

She led Ryan through a wooden double door and down a hallway. Ryan recognized most of the names on the nameplates as he passed. Although Technovations' main headquarters was in Silicon Valley, many executives chose to be based in Scottsdale, where real estate prices were lower and the surroundings were still serene and upper-class. She reached an open door and took a few steps inside. Ryan followed her in.

A middle-aged man with salt-and-pepper hair stood and walked around his large desk. He wore an expensive-looking dress shirt, but no tie. As he approached Ryan, he smiled and extended his hand. "Rich Caldwell."

Ryan shared a firm, manly handshake with Mr. Caldwell and tried to look confident. "Ryan Robertson. Pleased to meet you, Mr. Caldwell."

"Rich! Please call me Rich. Would you like water or iced tea or anything?"

"No sir, I'm fine. Thank you."

Rich nodded to the receptionist, who took that as her cue to leave. She closed the door behind her. Rich walked back to his chair and gestured toward the guest chair facing the desk. "Have a seat."

After they exchanged a few pleasantries, Rich said, "So, Ryan, it looks like you've been with Technovations for about six and a half years." Ryan nodded. "Where do you see yourself in the next five or ten years?"

Ryan paused for a moment to compose the best possible answer. "With Technovations, if at all possible. Given that, I'd like to look for assignments in other divisions so I can learn more about what Technovations does. In terms of advancement, I hope I can make it at least as far as Project Manager." Rich nodded but didn't say anything. *Is he waiting for more?* Ryan let out a nervous chuckle. "I know that's not too specific. But with everything moving so quickly, it's hard to know what new technologies will exist in five or ten years. Like with AI. Who knows what kind of opportunities that will bring? I'm grateful to work at a company where I can be part of advancing technology, whatever that ends up being."

Rich smiled. "You're right. Things change quickly. Hell, five years ago most of us would never have anticipated some of the projects we're working on today."

"I guess you just have to be flexible and adapt to whatever comes along."

Rich's smile was disarming and Ryan was starting to feel less nervous. Rich seemed satisfied with the answers Ryan had given. "So, let's get to why I invited you here today. At Technovations, we're committed to developing our talent from within. Whenever we have an opening at the VP or Division Manager level, we prefer to elevate someone with a proven track record who understands our culture and our methodologies, rather than hire someone from outside. To that end, we created the Leadership Development Program, or LDP as we often call it. Every year, we select twenty individuals who have displayed leadership potential. We put them through a series of training courses and give them a variety of assignments throughout the company. Each person is paired with a mentor – someone at the Division Manager or VP level. The program lasts four years. By the time you're through you will have gained the skills and experience to perform well at higher levels in the company. Of course, there are no guarantees for what positions might become available and where you might end up, but you'll be well-positioned for advancement and career success. And of course, the skills you gain will be a great benefit to Technovations as well."

"Sounds like a wonderful program."

"Thank you. This program has been in place for ten years and we're pleased with the results. It's my baby, so to speak. It earned me my promotion to VP." He smiled proudly. "Each year, we ask everyone from Department Managers on up to identify individuals within their organization who might be good candidates for advancement. You have been nominated. I've looked over your past years' performance evaluations, and they're quite impressive."

"Thank you, sir."

"I see that you've been a first-level manager for the past two years. You've received some of the highest Manager Feedback Survey scores in the company. That's quite an accomplishment for someone who's only been managing people for two years. Your direct reports think very highly of you."

"Thanks. I have a really great team. They're very dedicated and they work well together."

"And that's a reflection on you. You have created a work environment where people flourish and succeed in their roles. With that said, I'd like to offer you a spot in the LDP. Now, before you say yes, you should be aware that this will involve extra work in addition to your regular responsibilities. Your manager will do her best to give you some bandwidth for this, including covering for you while you're taking training classes."

"Sounds good so far."

"One aspect of this program involves putting you on a rotation of assignments in various organizations within the company. At least one of those assignments will be at one of our overseas sites so you can learn about the international aspects of our business. That means you'll have to live somewhere else for a year. We provide the housing and a generous per diem to cover food and other incidental expenses. Are you married?"

"Yes, I am."

"Any kids?"

"No."

"Well, if you and your wife decide to have her move with you, we would cover her airfare and increase the daily per diem. If not, we'll pay for a round-trip ticket for you to visit home every three months. Or if you prefer, you can use that ticket to have your wife come visit you."

Rich's assumption that Ryan was straight threw him off balance. *What should I do now? Should I say something or let it go? Technovations includes sexual orientation and gender identity in their non-discrimination policies and I haven't had any issues up to this point, but now what?* Before he could figure out if or how to address that issue, Rich asked, "Do you have any questions about the program?"

Ryan thought quickly. "Yes. Tell me more about having a mentor. What sorts of things would we talk about?"

Rich smiled. "A mentor is a more senior person who is willing to give you advice, whether that's long-term career guidance or help with day-to-day matters such as navigating workplace challenges. They may introduce you to people that would be helpful for you to know or provide other resources. Think of them as a role model or a trusted advisor. Every mentoring relationship is different. It depends on the people involved and the mentee's needs."

"How will my mentor be selected?"

"We'll host a kick-off event for this year's LDP class in a couple of weeks. You'll meet the others from this site who will be part of this year's class. The higher-level managers who have volunteered to be mentors will be there too. They'll introduce themselves to the group and talk about their backgrounds and interests. Then there will be some social time where everyone mingles. You can chat with the ones who seem like they might be a good fit. You'll probably find that you click with one or two people. Then you will indicate your top few choices for your mentor, and we'll do our best to match you up accordingly."

"It sounds like having a mentor involves forming a personal relationship as well as a business relationship."

"Yes, it does. You'll get to know each other pretty well. If you decide that you and your mentor aren't clicking or you aren't getting what you want from the relationship, it's okay to say that and select a different mentor. It happens sometimes."

Ryan thought for a moment. He remembered the promise he made to himself when he left home at 17 and began his adult life on his own in Los Angeles: He would be openly and proudly gay. Hiding his gayness from his parents had taken a toll on his happiness and self-esteem, and he vowed he would never hide again. "Are there any people in your pool of available mentors who identify as LGBT?"

Ryan studied Rich's face to gauge his reaction. Rich's expression conveyed surprise, but not shock or disapproval. "Well... uh... there are none I'm aware of. It's not something we ask."

"Okay."

"But I'm sure most of our senior managers wouldn't have any problem with it. Having an inclusive culture is one of our corporate values."

"Well, I'm sure I'll be able to find a mentor who would be a good match."

"So... Are you interested in participating in the Leadership Development Program?"

"Yes! Definitely! It sounds like a very special opportunity."

"It is. Do you have any other questions for me?"

"No, none at this time."

"Very well. You'll receive an invitation to the kickoff event I mentioned earlier. I believe it's scheduled for Friday, January 18th."

"Great! I'm looking forward to it." They both rose from their seats. Rich extended his hand across the desk and Ryan shook it. "Thank you for giving me this opportunity!"

"You've earned it. We'll be in touch soon."

Ryan turned and left the office. As he walked down the hallway toward the lobby, he glanced into some of the other offices. *I could sure get used to working in these surroundings!*

***

Ryan walked across the parking lot to return to his building, elated by this development. He decided to stop by his friend Eddie's cubicle. Ryan rented a room in Eddie's house during his summer internship while he was in college. They remained good friends. As Ryan thought more about having a mentor, he realized that Eddie had been an informal mentor since that summer.

When Ryan arrived at Eddie's cubicle, he was catching up on his emails. "Hey!"

"Hey! What's up?"

"Got a few minutes?"

"Sure."

"Let's see if there's an empty conference room."

Eddie locked his computer and stood up. Since it was late in the afternoon, they found an empty room easily.

Ryan said, "I just got some great news! I've been selected for the Leadership Development Program!"

"Wow! That's fantastic! Congratulations!"

"Thanks. I'm really excited about it. I just came from a meeting with Rich Caldwell. There was one thing he said that got me thinking. He said I'd have a mentor. And he said the mentor and I would develop a pretty close relationship. I asked him if there were any LGBT people in upper management positions, and he said he didn't know of any."

"That's true. There aren't any – at least none who are out. We've talked about that in Techno-Pride, our LGBT employee group. Everyone in that group is an individual contributor or a first- or second-level manager. No higher-ups are in the group and no one knows of any."

"I wonder why that is. There are dozens of VPs, Division Managers, and Principal Engineers. Statistically, there must be a few who are gay."

"You would think. But either people have decided they need to stay in the closet if they want to advance, or there's a lavender ceiling. Maybe you'll be the first one to break through it."

***

When Ryan arrived home, he planted a juicy kiss on his husband Aaron's lips and gave him an enthusiastic hug.

Aaron said, "Well, you must have had a good day."

"I had a fantastic day. I'll tell you all about it over dinner. How was your day?"

"Not as good as yours. Just another day in paradise, if you consider the Food World pharmacy paradise. At least it was a little slower than usual."

"I feel like going out for dinner. How about you?"

"Yeah, sure. You pick the place."

"How about Kahuna's Tiki Paradise?"

"Your day was that good, huh?"

"It was. Anyway, let me change and we'll get going."

Forty-five minutes later, they were sitting in Kahuna's, Mai Tais in hand and dinner orders placed.

Ryan said, "Okay. So today, I was invited to a meeting with the VP of Human Resources and Workforce Development. He told me I've been identified as someone with leadership potential and he offered me a spot in their Leadership Development Program."

Aaron said, "That sounds exciting!"

"Yeah. So I told him I was definitely interested and grateful for the opportunity. Then I asked what was involved. He said I'll be assigned a mentor and we'll meet once or twice a month. There will be training classes they'll send me to every so often. Later, they'll put me on a rotation of assignments in different parts of the company so I get exposed to a broader view of how the company works."

Aaron said, "That sounds amazing! I'm really happy for you!"

"Thanks! I'm still trying to wrap my head around it. Anyway, just so you know, at least one of those rotation assignments will be in a foreign country."

At that moment, their server appeared and delivered their entrees. "Is there anything else I can get for you? Maybe another round of Mai Tais?"

Ryan was in a celebratory mood. "I'd like a Tropical Itch."

Aaron felt like he needed another drink. "I'll have a Doctor Funk."

When the server left, Aaron said, "So, you're going to have to work someplace else?"

"Just for a year. But I'm not surprised. Almost everyone who's made it to the upper ranks of our company has worked overseas at some point during their career. They say it's important to learn about the international parts of our business."

"When would that happen?"

"I don't know. Not right away."

"So, what about me? Does that mean we have to be apart for a year?"

"Not necessarily. Usually, when someone takes an overseas assignment they move their spouse and kids there too. Since we're married, you could come along. They'll pay for it and give me a higher per diem."

"What would I do for a year? Just sit around in some apartment?"

"You could get a job at a pharmacy for a year, couldn't you?"

"No. It doesn't work that way. I'd have to sit for that country's board exam and pass it before I could get a job. And that would interrupt my career path here, such as it is."

Ryan thought for a moment. "Well, okay. Maybe it would make more sense for you to stay here. But they'll pay for visits home once a quarter, or I could use that funding for you to come and visit me."

Aaron sighed.

"We can chat on Zoom every day or at least several times a week. Anyway, we'll cross that bridge when we get to it. At this point, I don't even know if I'll make it that far in the program or where they might send me."

"Well, okay. But I'm not crazy about having to spend a year apart."

"I get it. I don't like that part either. But it's still a ways off. We'll figure it out. But this is a great opportunity! Very few people get a chance at this. And those senior-level people make at least a half-million dollars a year. At least! Think about the traveling we could do! Think about the house we'd be able to buy!"

"Is the money really that important to you?"

"It's not just the money. It's also the challenge and the opportunity."

Aaron said, "I'm happy enough with what we have." He took another bite of food and chewed it thoroughly. "But if it's that important to you and it's something you really want, I'll support you."

Ryan's face lit up. "Thanks, honey!" He reached across the table and squeezed Aaron's hand. "I love you."

Aaron tried his best to smile. "I love you too."

The Kick-off

Friday, January 18, 2019

A few minutes before 3:00, Ryan returned to the RH building for the Leadership Development Program Kick-off. This time, two other passengers joined him in the elevator. They were dressed much like him – neat dress shirts and slacks – so Ryan assumed they were heading to the same function. The riders glanced at each other and smiled but nobody said anything.

The elevator doors opened on the fourth floor. This time, double doors at the other end of the foyer, opposite the receptionist's desk, were propped open. A sign by the door announced, 'Welcome LDP Class of 2022!' Ryan headed toward the open doors and the other two followed.

Rich Caldwell was standing inside the door greeting the arrivals. He was brimming with enthusiasm as he shook each person's hand. "Welcome! Glad you could make it. We'll start in about ten minutes, so feel free to get yourselves something to eat and drink and find a place to sit."

Ryan scanned the room. Along the back wall was a buffet table, covered in a dark red tablecloth. It offered hors d'oeuvres including jumbo shrimp, taquitos, meatballs, bacon-wrapped scallops, sandwich rolls, fresh fruit, and a large cheese-and-cracker assortment. White plates were stacked at the beginning of the buffet, along with a basket of rolled cloth napkins containing real silverware. Ryan picked up a plate and a rolled napkin and took a little bit of everything.

In the corner beyond the buffet table was a portable bar. Two bartenders wearing white shirts and black bow ties were serving cocktails, beer, wine, and soda to the attendees.

Ryan decided to choose a seat at a table and place his plate and napkin there before returning to the bar. There were four round eight-person tables, with several unclaimed seats at each. Ryan saw a lectern near the front of the room opposite the buffet table, so he chose a seat facing forward. He walked over to the bar and got in line behind two others. He was impressed by the selection of liquors and wines on offer, and the bar was well-stocked with mixers. The bartenders seemed to know what they were doing. Normally at such a set-up, he'd play it safe and order something basic like Jack and Coke. But he took a chance and asked for a Mai Tai. It wasn't quite as good as the Mai Tais at Kahuna's Tiki Paradise, but it was decent enough.

He returned to his table and sat down. There were four men seated at the table already. Two were older men, presumably executives who would be part of the mentor pool. Ryan guessed the other two were in their mid- to upper-30s, so he assumed they were fellow LDP participants. Nobody seemed to know each other except the two executives. Everybody focused on eating their hors d'oeuvres. They exuded a combination of nervousness and anticipation. Ryan smiled at the others and said, "Hi. I'm Ryan Robertson." He extended his hand to the men seated on each side of him, and they replied with their names. Ryan stood and walked closer to the other two and shook their hands. That broke the ice at the table and the others relaxed a bit.

Ryan scanned the room and counted 24 people. There were four women among the participants, one of whom was African-American. He spotted a couple of Asians and Latinos. Ryan, at 29, was probably the youngest person in the room. Most of the other participants were in their 30s or early 40s. He assumed those over 45 were the executives.

A few minutes later, Rich Caldwell closed the double doors and approached the lectern. He stood in front of it and addressed the gathering without a microphone. "Good afternoon and welcome to the kick-off for this year's Leadership Development class. As I look around the room at the bright young faces here, I think, 'You are the future of Technovations.' And I feel good because that means the future of Technovations is in excellent hands!" People politely clapped. That seemed a little over the top to Ryan, but he admired Rich's optimism.

Rich gave a brief overview of how the program would work and the types of training the participants would receive. He went over the schedule for the rest of the year. Ryan noticed a small table with some swag bags bearing the Technovations logo. As Ryan would soon discover, they contained several books about management and leadership, a notebook embossed with the company logo, a coffee mug, a lanyard, and a leather RFID-blocking passport cover.

After Rich concluded his overview, he asked each executive to come forward and state their name, describe their position, and share some information about themselves. Before long, they all sounded the same. Many of them seemed rather stuffy and uninteresting.

Then Rich asked each participant to come forward and state their name, job title, department, and something interesting about themselves. Everyone seemed so mindful of the first impression they were making to company executives that nobody allowed much of their personality to shine through. As each person finished, Rich handed them a swag bag.

By the time it was Ryan's turn, there was no energy left in the room. Everyone was tired of hearing people introduce themselves. Each introduction sounded about the same, and it was unlikely that anyone would remember any details about anyone else an hour from now. He stood quickly, walked briskly to the front of the room, and flashed a big, friendly smile. At 6'6", he was a commanding presence, but he was determined to present himself as a friendly, confident, and interesting person. "Hi, everyone! I'm Ryan Robertson and I'm thrilled to be here! I'm a manager in the Quality & Reliability Department. As for something interesting about myself, I play the trumpet. I love jazz. I play in Desert Jazz Connection and Desert Pride Wind Symphony."

Ryan scanned the room. The last statement elicited no response. People looked like they had never heard of either band, which wasn't surprising. The word 'Pride' had not registered with most people. He added, "Those bands are made up mostly of members of the LGBT community."

Ryan scanned the room again. That last statement woke people up. The younger people seemed not to care, but the older people looked surprised that someone had dared to say that.

He reminded himself to keep smiling and stand tall as he walked confidently back to his seat.

As the last three people introduced themselves, Ryan looked around the room to see if anyone was looking at him. He wondered how his introduction had landed with the others – especially the executives.

After everyone finished, Rich said, "Thanks for sharing a little bit about yourselves. Now, I'd like you all to stand, circulate around the room, and mingle with others. I'm sure you'll find a few people who have common interests. Help yourself to more refreshments if you like. When we reconvene in half an hour, you'll have an opportunity to indicate your preferences for a mentor on the form you'll find in your packet."

Everyone stood. Ryan waited to see what other people would do. Most people headed back to the buffet table and bar. He selected some more food and asked for a Coke. He observed whether the other participants were approaching the executives or vice versa. He decided to start with Rich Caldwell. Rich hadn't specified whether he was among the available mentors or not.

After they shook hands, Ryan said, "This is quite an event you've put on! Now I'm more excited than ever to be part of this program."

Rich smiled. "Thank you. Your enthusiasm showed during your introduction. And by the way, I appreciate that you mentioned the nature of the bands you play in. Even though we have all the right policies in place, I still get the impression that LGBT people are reluctant to mention their status at work. I want that to change. And that will only happen if people start doing it."

Ryan said, "I agree. I decided a long time ago I'm not going to hide. But yeah, I think a lot of LGBT people at work still censor themselves to some extent. We've talked about that in the Techno-Pride group."

"How pervasive do you think that is? I'd hate to think that people still don't feel comfortable bringing their full selves to work."

"It's not so much of an issue among the people in the group. But I think it says a lot that only a small percentage of the LGBT people at work even belong to the group."

Rich frowned. "What do you think we can do about that?"

"Well... Another thing we've noticed is that there are no higher-level people in the group. Everyone's an individual contributor or a low-level manager. Maybe if more people at higher levels were visible, people wouldn't feel like there's a lavender ceiling."

"Let me think about what we could do to change that. Like I said in our meeting, I'm not aware of any LGBT people among our executives. In fact, after our meeting, I emailed all the local managers who are department heads or higher. I asked if anyone identified as LGBT and would be willing to serve as a mentor. I didn't get any responses."

"Perhaps you could visit a Techno-Pride meeting and have a roundtable discussion with the members. You'll get a better feel for people's experiences and it would mean a lot to the group to see that you're interested."

"That's an excellent idea. Well, I suppose I should circulate some more. But I'll definitely be in touch."

"Thank you. Thank you so much!"

Ryan and Rich shook hands, then turned to see who they might talk with next.

Ten seconds later, a 50-ish man excused himself from the person he was chatting with and approached Ryan. "Hi, Ryan. I'm Bob Fordham. I'm the Division Manager for Government Affairs and Community Relations."

"Hi, Bob. Nice to meet you." By now, Ryan had learned that these executives preferred to be called by their first names. They shook hands. "Tell me more about what you do."

While the executives were introducing themselves, Ryan decided he'd prefer a mentor from one of the technical divisions. But Bob seemed interested in meeting him so he was okay with chatting for a few minutes.

Bob said, "It's my organization's job to maintain good relations with the federal, state, and local governments where we have locations. At the federal level, we focus on tax laws, import and export laws, and winning government contracts. At the local level, we deal with tax issues, our involvement with local schools, and deciding which charitable organizations the Technovations Foundation contributes money to."

"That sounds interesting."

"Oh, it is. But that's not why I wanted to introduce myself to you." Bob's demeanor changed. He seemed a little nervous and he began speaking more softly. "Our 17-year-old son recently came out to us. Of course, we love him and we want him to be happy. We want to be supportive parents. But... well... this kind of came at us from left field, so we're still processing this information and figuring out the best way to deal with this. Do you think maybe we could meet sometime and talk about this some more? I'd love to get your advice on how to handle this situation."

Ryan smiled. "Sure. I'd be happy to. My calendar is up-to-date, so whatever works for you is fine with me."

"Thanks. I'll find a day to take you to lunch sometime soon."

"That would be great. I'll look forward to it."

Bob seemed like a nice guy. He presented himself as a real person, not just a business figure. And indirectly, they had something in common. At least Ryan knew his orientation wouldn't be an awkward subject with Bob.

Neither of them had anything else to say at the moment, although they knew they'd have plenty to talk about soon. Bob glanced at his watch. "We have about ten minutes left, so why don't we mingle a little more?"

Ryan nodded and they shook hands.

Ryan found a couple more people to chat with during the remaining ten minutes. Then Rich called for people to return to their seats and he made some closing remarks. He reminded people to indicate their choices for a mentor or mentee and leave their forms in a tray on a small table near the door. Ryan listed Bob Fordham and Rich Caldwell as his choices.

***

On Tuesday the following week, Ryan received an email notifying him that Bob Fordham would be his mentor. It occurred to him that this mentor relationship would work both ways.

Looking Ahead

Sunday, March 24, 2019

Desert Pride held its spring concert on Sunday afternoon. Aaron and Ryan played in the concert, and Ryan's younger brother Brandon, a junior at Arizona State University and a player on their basketball team, came to watch. After the concert the guys helped load the instrument truck, then they headed home for their Sunday dinner. In the interest of time and minimal effort, they stopped and picked up Chinese food.

Once they had settled in, Brandon said, "The concert was awesome, guys! I'm looking forward to playing with the band again now that basketball is over and I'll have Thursday nights free."

Ryan said, "They're taking this Thursday off, but they'll be starting up again the first week of April."

Aaron said, "You had a pretty good season. And you got a lot of playing time."

"Yeah, starting the season with eight straight wins was pretty amazing. Too bad it didn't last. For a while, we were having fantasies that we could go undefeated all season. That really motivated us."

"Still, going 22-9 in your regular season and getting to play in the NCAA tournament is pretty decent. I'll bet it's a relief to be through with it, though. It must be challenging to balance your classes with daily practices and traveling to games."

Brandon said, "Yeah, but it's gotten easier every year. I'm used to it now. Since they offer some classes that are a half-semester, I'm taking more classes during the second half so I can take fewer classes during the rest of the year. And I took a couple of classes last summer."

Ryan said, "Speaking of summer, you'll be a senior next year. Are you going to take classes this summer, or have you thought about getting an internship?"

"I've been so focused on basketball and midterms, I haven't thought about it."

"I think it's a good idea. My internship at Technovations paved the way for me to get a job there. Regardless of whether you end up working at the same place where you intern, it's a valuable experience and it will look good on your resumé. It pays well, too."

"Yeah, that makes sense. I'll start looking into it."

"Technovations has a Public Relations department. They have a department that handles internal communications, too. They might have an opportunity for someone who's majoring in Communications. I know the guys who are in charge of those organizations. If you're interested, I could see whether you could get an internship there this summer."

"That would be awesome! And if I stay here this summer, I'd be close to work."

"Cool. I'll check into that tomorrow."

"Thanks! So what else is happening with you guys?"

Ryan said, "Well, I got some exciting news. Remember how I told you about the Leadership Development Program I've been accepted into?"

Brandon said, "The one where they might send you overseas for a year at some point?"

"Yeah. So I just found out I'll be going to Auckland, New Zealand for a year starting in September."

"Auckland?"

"Yeah. A couple of years ago, I got to go to our office there for two weeks, and I really liked it. I'm excited about it."

Brandon glanced at Aaron. He was unusually silent and not smiling.

Brandon said, "Won't it seem weird being away from home for an entire year?"

"Yeah. But they'll pay for three trips home, and I can use one or two of them to have Aaron fly there instead of me flying home. Anyway, it's part of what I have to do to stay in the LDP. I'm looking forward to it. It'll be interesting to learn what it's like to live someplace else and see how their society is different from ours."

"And that means you won't be able to play in your bands."

"That's true. Although I guess I could take my trumpet with me. But it won't be too hard to get my chops back after a year off."

There was a lull in the conversation. Aaron hadn't said anything up to this point. Ryan seemed oblivious as he dug into his Chinese food. Brandon glanced at Aaron again. Aaron glanced back. Finally, he spoke. "So what about me? Have you given any thought to how this will impact me?"

"Well, of course. I'll miss you. But as I said, we'll get to see each other three times during the year. And we can talk to each other on Zoom anytime we want."

"That's hardly the same. So I'm supposed to stay here and take care of the whole house by myself. And be lonely."

"You lived alone for two years before you moved in with me."

"Yeah, and I was miserable. One of the benefits of marrying you was that I'd have someone to share my life with ... not to mention my bed. This will be like being married and being single at the same time."

"Oh, come on. It'll only be for a year. And you have all your friends in the band you can hang out with."

"It's not the same thing."

The escalating tension in the room was making everyone uncomfortable.

Brandon said, "Couldn't you go too? What do they do for straight people who are married and have kids? Maybe you could get a job as a pharmacist there."

"Ryan suggested the same thing when this first came up. But it's not that easy. For one thing, I'd need to get a work visa. And I'd have to sit for exams again to get licensed to practice there."

Ryan said, "I read somewhere that they have a list of occupations that are in demand. If you work in one of those fields, that will qualify you for a work visa." He pulled out his phone and started searching for information. After typing, tapping, and scrolling for half a minute, he said, "Here it is! Retail Pharmacist is on the list."

Aaron said, "Let me see." Ryan handed him the phone and Aaron read the information surrounding the listing. "It says you must have a job offer from a New Zealand employer to get this visa. You can't just enter the country and start looking for a job once you get there."

"You should be able to stay for a while as a visitor as if you were on vacation."

"Maybe, but... No. I'm not interested in quitting my job and disrupting my career. Besides, we'd have to leave the house vacant for a year. Who would take care of the pool and the hot tub and mow the grass and stuff?"

Brandon said, "I could do that. I come up here once or twice a week as it is."

Aaron said, "Thanks, but what if you get a job somewhere else after you graduate? And once basketball season gets underway, you won't have much time. It's probably best if I just stay here and be lonely for a year."

Ryan was visibly annoyed that Aaron was so fixated on the negative aspects of this arrangement. "Okay, okay. I'll turn it down. I'll drop out of the LDP and stay here with you."

Aaron let out a huge sigh. "No. That's not right either. I don't want to be the one to quash your opportunity for advancement. I know this is important to you and I need to support you."

Brandon said, "I could live here with you during my senior year. I'm getting tired of living in the dorms."

Aaron said, "Thanks, but would you really want to drive back and forth to campus every day from up here in Scottsdale? That's like, what? A 20-minute drive each way? And isn't your scholarship paying for your dorm? Besides, part of the experience of going to college is the social life. You'd miss out on all that."

"Yeah, I guess..."

Ryan said, "We'll figure out how to make it work. It'll only be a year. So anyway, I was thinking I'd come home for Christmas–"

Aaron interrupted him. "And would you still go to Ohio with me to see my folks?"

Can't he go for Thanksgiving or some other time? I guess I need to give a little too. "Yeah, we can do that. And then you could come to New Zealand in the spring, which would be autumn there. Maybe you could come for your birthday in March!"

"I'd have to see when Desert Pride's spring concert is. But yeah, going there in the spring would be nice."

Ryan turned to Brandon. "And then I could come home for your graduation. Do you know when it is?"

Brandon checked his phone. "Monday, May 11th."

"Wow. That's earlier than I thought. UCLA's was in mid-June, but I guess since you're on semesters, it's earlier. But anyway, I want to be here for that. So there we have it. Then I'll be back for good in September."

Aaron still wasn't happy about it, but he'd deal with it. There was nothing more to say.

Welcome to Auckland

Friday, September 6, 2019

Ryan's flight from Los Angeles arrived in Auckland at 6:35 a.m. Friday morning. He managed to sleep for about four hours on the 13-hour flight. When he added in the two hours in the airport in Phoenix, the 90-minute flight to LA, and the 90-minute layover, his travel adventure lasted over 18 hours. When Aaron dropped him off, it was 5:15 p.m. Wednesday. Now Ryan's body had no idea what time it was. He only knew that he was exhausted.

Thankfully, he didn't have to wait too long for his luggage and he made it through Customs quickly. When he exited the secured area, he spotted a cluster of people holding signs with names. Someone from Technovations had volunteered to meet Ryan and drive him to the corporate apartment that would be his home for the next year. He smiled when he spotted a sign that read, 'Ryan R.'

The person holding the sign was a handsome, smiling man whom Ryan guessed was in his early 30s. Ryan approached him and said, "Hi. I'm Ryan."

"Michael." Michael extended his hand and Ryan shook it. "Welcome to Auckland!"

"Thanks. I've been looking forward to being here."

"Let me grab one of your suitcases. Come, follow me to the car."

Ryan thought, *Michael is obviously a morning person. There's no way I could be this perky and cheerful at 7:00 in the morning.*

Once they were in Michael's car heading north on Route 20A, Michael asked, "How was your trip?"

"Long. Very long. Fortunately, both of my flights were on time and it was a smooth flight, but still... I'm exhausted. My body still thinks it's 1:00 in the afternoon yesterday."

"Well, you'll have three days to get yourself acclimated here before Monday morning rolls around. Have you been here before?"

"Yes. I was here back in 2017. Two weeks for work, and then I tacked on two weeks of vacation so I could see some of the country."

"I think I may have spotted you in the office when you were here before."

"Yeah, you look familiar too. Since I'm 6'6", I tend to stand out in a crowd."

They merged onto Route 20 and continued north. Ryan caught himself nodding off a few times. "Sorry I'm not saying much. I'm really tired."

"No problem. Quite understandable. So... aside from work, what are you hoping to do while you're here?"

"I'd like to get out and do some hiking and see more of the country."

"Well, you're in luck. There are plenty of good hiking trails within an hour or so of the city."

"I want to check out the music scene, especially if there are any jazz clubs around."

"Again, you're in luck. The apartment where you're staying is right in the heart of the city's nightlife. You'll be close to Karangahape Road, or K Road as we call it, and Queen Street. And Ponsonby Road's not too far to walk. There's every kind of bar and restaurant you could possibly want. And it's only a couple of blocks to the office. Quite an ideal location, really. I'd live there if I could afford it."

"Yeah, I remember the area from when I was here before. The hotel where I stayed was in the same neighborhood. There's a lot going on."

Michael exited Route 20 and turned right onto Dominion Road. "It's a straight shot from here into downtown. We might encounter a bit of traffic since it's rush hour. But as I was saying, the area around K Road attracts quite a diverse group of people. It happens to be popular with the gay community, as well."

"Oh. Okay." *I wonder how he knows? Gaydar? Or perhaps he would say that to anybody.*

Michael asked, "Have you a family back home?"

Is he just making small talk or is he trying to figure me out? In any case, I'm proud of who I am and I'm not going to be dishonest or evasive about it. "Just my husband and my brother. My mother has passed away and I'm not in touch with my father."

Michael smiled. "Ah. It's too bad your husband couldn't come with you."

"Yeah, we talked about it. But we decided it would be disruptive to his career. And we didn't want the house sitting empty for a year."

"Well, we have a few other gay people in the office and I have a nice network of friends I can introduce you to if you're interested. And there's a gay hiking group that meets once a month. I can put you in touch with them if you like."

"Thanks. I'd appreciate that."

"Hopefully that will make your stay here a bit more enjoyable."

Fifteen minutes later, Michael turned onto a narrow street that sloped downhill. At the end, he pulled into the parking lot of Paramount Apartments, a modern 16-story building. He parked the car near the front entrance. "Here we are. They should have your keys waiting for you at the front desk. Would you like help with your luggage?"

"Sure. Thanks."

After Ryan received his keys, he said, "Thanks, Michael. I really appreciate you driving me here from the airport. I could have taken a cab or a bus, but this made it a lot easier."

"You're certainly welcome. There's a small convenience store at the corner of Symonds and K Road. On Queen Street and K Road, you'll find some larger markets. Do you know how to get to the office from here?"

"I'm sure I'll be able to find it. I'll probably sleep for about 24 hours, but I'll get out later this weekend and walk around a bit."

"Well, then, I'll see you in the office on Monday morning. Here, let me give you my cell number. Call me if you have any questions."

"Thanks. One of the first things on my list is to get a SIM card for my phone."

"Very well, then. See you on Monday."

"Thanks. Bye."

They shook hands, and then Michael turned and left.

Ryan hauled his suitcases to the elevator and rode it to the 12th floor. When he opened the door to his apartment, he was amazed. It was nicely furnished and offered a spectacular view of a large bridge spanning a wooded ravine, with several tall buildings in the distance. He pulled out his phone and sent Aaron a text.

Ryan brushed his teeth, stripped off his clothes, and collapsed onto the comfortable king-sized bed. He didn't set an alarm.

Brandon and Aaron Fix the World

Sunday, January 19, 2020

On Sunday, Brandon visited Aaron as usual. With Ryan in New Zealand, Aaron appreciated the company. Aaron and Brandon wanted to continue the Sunday night dinner tradition, even if it was just the two of them and the meals weren't as expertly prepared as Ryan's. Tonight's menu was a store-bought supreme pizza and beer.

Over dinner, they caught up with each other.

Aaron said, "Great game last night. You made some nice shots!"

"Thanks. I'm just glad we won. We did pretty well with the pre-season games, but until tonight we were 1-4 in the Pac-12."

"You'll turn it around. I think the team looks pretty solid this year." Aaron took a bite of his pizza. "Sorry I couldn't make it Thursday night, but that was a band night."

"Yeah, I know. It's cool. We lost that game anyway."

"I know you'd rather win than lose, but I enjoy watching you play either way."

Brandon asked, "So how's band?"

"It's fine. I wish Ryan was there, but otherwise, it's okay. It's our second week of rehearsing tunes for our spring concert, so there's a lot of stopping and starting while Lee fixes things. But it's always like that at the beginning of the concert cycle. So you just finished your first week of classes. How's your semester shaping up?"

"Pretty good. I can't believe this will be my last semester and I'll graduate in May. In a way, it's dragged on forever and I'll be happy to be done with it. But on the other hand, I'll miss it."

"I know what you mean. It's like you want to be done with all the studying and tests, but keep the fun parts."

"Exactly. Like I'll miss the basketball and the parties. Even going to classes is all right, at least the ones where it's interesting and I'm learning something."

Aaron said, "Yeah. When I think back to my years at Ohio State, I think about the marching band, my friends, and campus life in general. I never think about all the hours I spent studying, especially after I got into pharmacy school. But anyway, life changes and you move on. So enjoy your last semester as much as you can!"

"I'll try. There's this one class I'm taking that looks like it'll be fun. It's all about how to use social media and the internet to build a customer base for clients. That should be useful. The professor told us what our project for the semester will be. We're supposed to design a media campaign and see how much we can grow it by the end of the semester. It can be a podcast, a YouTube channel, a website and blog, articles on LinkedIn or Medium, or whatever. And he issued a challenge: if we can meet certain goals, we won't have to take the final and we'll get an A in the course."

"Sounds interesting. What are the goals?"

"For YouTube or a podcast or a blog, it's 100 subscribers and an average of 500 views per episode or article. I forget what it is for Medium and LinkedIn. And you have to put out at least ten episodes or articles."

"That's pretty ambitious for one semester."

"I know, right? I don't think he expects anyone to actually hit those numbers, but it gives me something to shoot for. Even if I make good progress, I will have learned things and I should get a good grade. Fifty percent of the grade is based on this project."

Aaron asked, "So what do you think you'll do?"

"I've been thinking about that. You know, there's so much going on in the country and the world now. But most of the news is geared toward older audiences. Kids in my generation are tuning it out because so much of it is bullshit, you know? But I don't want my generation to tune it out, I want them to get involved. But most of the information out there isn't speaking to us."

"Well, I'm ten years older than you so I'm a Millennial, but I know what you mean. I read the other day that the percentage of Gen Z people who vote is smaller than any other age group. If we could get more young people engaged and convince them to vote, we could finally put a lot of these old conservative Republicans out of office."

"Exactly."

"So how do you think you're going to do that?"

Brandon thought for a moment. "I've been going back and forth between doing a podcast or starting a YouTube channel."

"Why not do both? Record a video of each episode for YouTube, then release the audio as a podcast."

"It would be more work, but I'd reach a wider audience."

"And what would you do in each episode?"

"Pick some current event and talk about it."

Aaron said, "With 2020 being an election year, there should be plenty to talk about."

"True. But I don't want to talk about only politics. People won't tune in for that. I want to talk about social issues facing young people, like the environment, racial justice, the job market, and that sort of thing. I want to deal with it from a younger person's perspective. And I want to make it fun and kind of irreverent. You know, tell some jokes and poke fun at situations, like they do on the Daily Show."

"Are you going to do all the talking yourself or have guests on?"

"I'd like to have someone else so it's not just my voice. I think it will be more interesting if I have someone to go back and forth with."

"Yeah, you're probably right. Anyway, I think that's a great idea. How do you think you'll publicize it?"

Brandon said, "That's where I have an advantage. Since I'm a basketball player at ASU, I have a lot of name recognition on campus. I have several thousand Twitter and Instagram followers. I have a Facebook page, but I don't really focus on that. But I can publicize this podcast on Twitter and Instagram, and some of those people will check it out. Then hopefully, some of them will share or retweet it and it will grow."

"You're right, you've got quite an advantage. Like you have a ready-made audience."

Brandon took a few more bites of pizza. "I have an idea. Why don't you and I do it together? It's like you can be the Millennial voice and I can be the Gen Z voice. We joke around with each other all the time anyway, so we can do that on the show."

"Really? I've never thought of doing anything like that. Hmmm..." Aaron took a swig of his beer. "Why not? That sounds like fun. And it will give me something new to focus on since Ryan's not here."

"I think you'd be great! You have a nice speaking voice and you're good-looking, which always helps on camera."

Aaron feigned a bashful smile. He was mildly surprised that Brandon would comment on his looks. "Awww... you really think I'm good-looking?"

"Of course you are. I totally get why Ryan married you."

"Well, I hope he didn't marry me just for my looks."

"You know what I mean. Anyway, here's another angle. You can also be the voice for the LGBTQ community on the show. A lot of young people are pro-gay and pro-trans."

"Yeah, I guess. And with Pete Buttigieg running, that'll give us some things to talk about."

"So you're in?"

"Yeah! Let's do this! So what are we going to call it?"

They both thought for a moment.

Aaron said, "Well, it's your project. It should be 'The Brandon Bauer show.'"

"Nah, that's too generic. It doesn't tell people what it's about. Plus, I want your name to be on it."

"Well, if we want the title to tell people what it's about, then maybe something like, 'How Gen Z and Millennials See the World.'"

"Close. But we need something catchy that people will notice and remember. Maybe even a little edgy." Brandon paused. "Wait! I've got it! 'Aaron and Brandon Fix the World!'"

"I like it! Except your name should go first. It's your project and you have the name recognition."

"Okay, 'Brandon and Aaron Fix the World.' It's catchy and a little outrageous. Besides, I don't want to just complain about things or make fun of them, I want to talk about what people can do to make things better."

"Cool! So what do we do next? When do we get started? How are we going to work this into our schedules?"

Brandon said, "Well, I need to do most of the work because it's my project. But you could come up with a list of topics we can cover in each episode. We can record it in Ryan's office. His two-monitor set-up will be helpful and I think his webcam will be good enough to use – at least for now. I'll look into buying a couple of good-quality microphones."

"I can help you pay for them."

"Thanks. Let me see how much they are. As to when, well... I come up here every Sunday for dinner and most of my games are on Thursday and Saturday nights. We can do it here after dinner." Brandon reached for his phone and checked his schedule. "I have an away game at California on Sunday, February 16, but otherwise Sundays look good."

"Sounds like a plan."

"Maybe we can find another time during that week or do two episodes the week before. Remember, I've got to get at least ten episodes done before the semester ends."

"Yeah, we'll probably be more successful if we put out episodes regularly."

"And every week we miss will be a week we don't get new followers."

They finished their pizza and beers and got up from the table. Aaron said, "I'm excited about this! Thanks for letting me be part of it."

"I'm excited too. We're gonna be great together." Brandon gave Aaron a nice hug.

In Like a Lion

Wednesday, March 11, 2020

At 10:00 p.m., Aaron logged onto Zoom for his weekly video chat with Ryan. It was 6:00 p.m. Thursday in Auckland. Moments later, Ryan joined. "Hi, Honey. What's up?"

Aaron sighed. "It's getting crazy around here. Everyone's starting to panic about this Coronavirus thing. Just today, Arizona State announced they're moving classes online for two weeks starting Monday."

"Really? How's that going to work?"

"I don't know. I guess they'll set up a Zoom meeting for every class."

"Wow. I wonder if Zoom has the bandwidth to handle all those simultaneous calls. Especially if colleges and universities across the country will be doing the same thing."

"I guess they'll find out. Anyway, Brandon wants to come and stay here. Already, three guys on his dorm floor have it."

"Yeah, sure, of course. Speaking of Brandon, what does that mean for his basketball team?"

"Well, the regular season ended last Saturday. But they've canceled the Pac-12 tournament. I don't know about the NCAA tournament, but I'll bet it gets canceled too – or at least postponed. I guess it depends on how long this thing lasts."

"Wow. It sucks that his last season has to end like this."

"Yeah. They finished 20-11, so they may not have even made it into the tournament, but still... Oh, and Desert Pride just canceled their concert this coming Sunday."

"Seriously? After you guys have spent the last two and a half months rehearsing for it? Is it really spreading that much there?"

"Well, it wasn't our choice. Maricopa Cultural Center canceled all events in their venue for the next month. So, what's it like there?"

"We've only had five cases so far. All of them are people who had just returned from either Italy or Iran, and so far they've only infected a couple of people in their immediate families. The government is watching it closely. But so far, people aren't very concerned."

Aaron said, "God, I can't wait to come see you next week. It will be so nice to escape this craziness for a couple of weeks."

"Maybe after two weeks, you'll want to stay."

"After spending two weeks with you, I won't want to come home anyway. But who knows? If it gets much worse here, I might change my mind."

"I'll do my best to convince you. And with Brandon living there, the house won't be empty."

"Well, hopefully, this will all be over soon. If everyone stays home as much as possible and wears masks when they go out, we can probably nip this thing in the bud."

"I hope so too, but it's spreading like wildfire in Italy and Iran. And there was that cruise ship that got quarantined in Japan. Almost 700 people got it."

"But enough of all that happy talk. What have you been up to?"

"Well, we're on the tail end of summer here, so it's still warm and sunny. Last weekend, the gay hiking group I belong to went for a hike up to the top of Mount Donald McLean. It was kind of strenuous, but man! The views were amazing!"

"Sounds nice. So, they have good hiking in New Zealand?"

"Oh, yeah! All over the place. Michael connected me with this group right after I got here, and they haven't gone to the same place twice. And they're all within an hour or so of downtown Auckland."

"Sounds nice. Maybe you can take me on one of those hikes while I'm out there."

"Definitely! I'll add it to my list. I've already got a lot of things I want to show you."

"Do they have a gay running group there, too?"

"Yeah, they do, but it's not like ours. Their runs are a lot more leisurely. They go for about an hour, then they go someplace for brunch. For many of them, it's more about the brunch than the running."

"Sounds like it's not quite your speed."

"Yeah. It's nice from a social perspective, but it's not the kind of running I want to do to stay in shape."

"They probably gain more calories at the brunch than they lose with their running.”

“Exactly.”

“Well, sounds like you’re meeting a lot of people and you have plenty of things to do.”

“Yeah. I guess after six months, I’ve gotten pretty well acclimated.”

“Well, don’t get too acclimated. You’re coming home in six months.”

“I’ll make the most of it and enjoy it while I can. But yeah. It’s hard to believe I’m at the halfway point already.”

“Yes, I know. Believe me, I’m counting the days. It’s been six lonnng months. And the next six are going to seem even longer.”

Ryan smiled playfully at Aaron. “You’ve never complained about things being too long before.”

Aaron rolled his eyes. “Yet another reason I can’t wait to see you. I hope one of the things you have on your list of things to do when I visit is *me*.”

Ryan grinned. “Every day. And twice on Sunday.”

Aaron and Ryan gazed longingly at each other. Aaron reached down. It was already starting to grow. As soon as the call ended, he would head to the master bathroom as usual.

Ryan looked like he was having the same thoughts. “Well, honey, I should probably let you go.”

“Yeah, I guess.”

“Just think! In ten days, we’ll be together again!”

“Ten long, slow days. I can’t wait!”

“Well... give Brandon a hug for me. And tell everyone in band I said hi.”

“I’ll post that to our Facebook group. Remember, rehearsals have been canceled.”

“Oh yeah, that’s right. I forgot. Sorry. Anyway... I love you!” Ryan puckered his lips and kissed the air in front of him.

Aaron air-kissed him back. “I love you too!”

“Bye!”

“Bye!”

They ended the call. Aaron walked briskly to the master bathroom, his cock tenting his shorts.

Canceled

Friday, March 13, 2020

At 4:00, Aaron took a quick break. He stepped into his tiny office at the back of the pharmacy and popped open a can of Diet Dr Pepper. He checked his phone and saw a message from Ryan.

> Hi Sweetheart. Terrible news. The New Zealand government just announced that starting March 16, everyone entering the country must quarantine for two weeks. Shit! XOXOXO, Ryan.

Aaron yelled, "SHIT! ... FUCK! ... GODDAMMIT! ... GOD! FUCKING!! DAMMIT!!!"

He cocked his right arm but stopped himself an instant before he hurled his phone into the wall. He dropped the phone onto his desk and started pacing back and forth, uttering more swear words under his breath.

In the pharmacy, the techs glanced at each other apprehensively, wondering what had just happened. Most of their faces were covered by masks, but their eyes conveyed fear and uncertainty. They hoped that none of the customers, who were waiting on the other side of the Plexiglas shields that had recently been installed at the registers, could hear that. They tried to go about their business and deal with customers as if nothing was wrong, but they were filled with dread about what might happen when Aaron emerged from his office.

Aaron picked up his phone. He saw a notification from United. His flight had been canceled.

He took a couple of chugs from his soda, then walked out the door. As he passed his staff, he muttered, "I'm going for a walk. I'll be back soon."

Aaron paced up and down the rows in the parking lot, brainstorming possibilities for how he could overcome this obstacle. Maybe he could get a flight out tonight that would arrive in Auckland on March 15. Maybe they could meet in Hawaii or Tahiti or Australia or something. Maybe Ryan could come here. He should be able to get back into New Zealand when he returns.

Aaron realized he needed to get back into the pharmacy. There were probably customers he needed to consult with before he could release their prescriptions. As he headed for the entrance, he texted Ryan.

> Can we talk on Zoom tonight as soon as I get home? 6:15 my time.

He entered the pharmacy and tried to remain courteous and level-headed as he spoke with the customers.

He could sense the uneasiness among his staff. When no customers were waiting at the counter, he pulled everyone together and said, "I just found out that if I go to New Zealand I'll have to quarantine for two weeks. That means there's really no point in going."

Everyone shook their heads. Lauren, the lead tech, said, "Wow. That totally sucks. I'm sorry."

Others muttered, "I'm sorry," and returned to their tasks.

Aaron retreated to his office. The hopelessness of it all was settling in. Hopefully, he could hold it together until 6:00 without crying on the job.

When his shift ended, he drove home quickly. At 6:15, he logged onto Zoom. Ryan was waiting for him. "Hi, Honey. I'm really sorry."

"Hi. Yeah, me too. So anyway, I was thinking. What if I can get a flight out tonight? It would arrive in Auckland on March 15. Or how about this? Is there someplace else we could meet? Like maybe Hawaii or Tahiti? What if you came here?"

"Well, maybe, but if I left the country, I'd have to quarantine for two weeks when I got back. And do you really think it's a good idea for either of us to be getting on an airplane at all? Let alone for a long flight."

Aaron sighed. "Yeah... I suppose you're right. Shit. I was looking forward to this so much."

"Me too. But it should all blow over in a few weeks. Hopefully, I can still come home for Brandon's graduation on May 11. And we can rebook your flights for sometime in the summer."

"Yeah, I guess. But it sucks. And not in the good way."

"I know. But we should do what we have to do now and stay safe."

"That means my birthday is going to suck, too."

"At least you'll have Brandon there. How's he doing?"

"Okay. He moved his stuff in last night. Today's his last day of in-person classes."

"He's wearing a mask, isn't he?"

"Yeah, but I don't know how many other kids are. We've run out of them at the pharmacy. I pulled the last few boxes off the shelves so my staff would have some for a little while longer. Just in time, too. People were starting to hoard them. They're telling everyone to wear cloth masks."

"It's better than nothing."

"True. Okay, well, it's 6:30 and I'm hungry."

"Hang in there, honey. We'll get through this. Tell Brandon I said hi."

"I will. I love you."

"I love you too. Bye!"

"Bye!"

Ryan disappeared. Aaron stared at the blank screen for a few seconds longer, then walked into the kitchen and chose a frozen entrée from the freezer.

Disappointing News

Wednesday, August 5, 2020

At 7:00 p.m., Aaron launched Zoom for his weekly video call with Ryan. Ryan was already online.

Aaron forced a smile. "Hi, Honey."

"Hi. How's everything in Scottsdale?"

"Same shit, different day. More COVID cases than ever. More people refusing to wear masks. More BLM protests."

"I'm really sorry. I know it's been five months now. It must be getting old."

"Yeah, and there's no end in sight. Remember when we thought this would blow over in a few weeks?"

"Yeah."

"Anyway, how have you been?"

"Pretty good." By this time, Ryan had learned not to talk much about his life in Auckland. New Zealand was still minimally impacted by COVID aside from being isolated from the rest of the world. Whenever he talked about how well work was going or what he did with his friends, it made Aaron feel worse about his situation. So he didn't say much about that. "How's Brandon?"

"He's fine. He likes his new job. I'll get him in a few minutes and you can say hi."

"I've been keeping up with your podcast episodes. You guys keep getting better and better."

"Yeah, well, Lord knows we have a lot to talk about. Between the podcast and YouTube, we just hit 10,000 subscribers."

"Wow! Good for you!"

Aaron said, "I can't wait for you to come home next month. Have you scheduled your flight yet?"

"Well..." Ryan was dreading the conversation that was about to take place. "As it turns out, they want me to stay another couple of months. The guy who was supposed to rotate in and take my place just quit. And the project is at a critical juncture right now. They need me to continue in my role until they can find a replacement."

Aaron stared at Ryan in disbelief. "Did they ask you or tell you?"

"Well, technically, they asked. But it seemed like the only acceptable answer would be yes. But I told them I needed to check with my husband."

"Can't you work from here? The rest of the world has learned how to work remotely."

"No. There's too much hands-on testing."

As this new information sank in, Aaron became irritated. "So I have to be the bad guy. I mean, I want you home! I wish you were home right now! But if I say no, I'll make you look bad at work and endanger the success of your project – and by extension, your career."

"That pretty much sums it up. I'm sorry."

Aaron sighed. "Well, okay. I guess another two months won't be that bad. But I really want you to be home in time for your birthday on October 14th and our anniversary on October 21st."

"So I do. Believe me, so do I. I miss you, honey. I wish, more than anything, that we could be together. Thanks for being so understanding. I'm sorry."

Aaron frowned. He was still reeling from this development, but he knew there was no way he could change it. Nothing he could say would help the situation. "Well, let me get Brandon so you can say hi to him."

Aaron got up from his desk and walked into the kitchen where Brandon was fixing dinner. "Wanna say hi to Ryan?"

Aaron's unhappiness was obvious. "What's wrong?"

"He just told me he has to stay there another two months."

They looked at each other. Their expressions conveyed their shared annoyance and disappointment. Brandon walked back to the office and sat down in front of the computer. "Hi."

"Hi! How's it going?"

"Okay. Aaron just told me the news."

"Yeah. I feel really bad about it. But it can't be helped. Anyway, Aaron tells me your new job is going well."

"Yeah. I've been there for two months. I've been taking a lot of online training, so that's been okay. And all of our meetings are on Zoom. It's weird not being able to meet my co-workers in person, but I'm kinda getting to know them anyway."

"Yeah, I know what you mean. I work with people at our other sites around the world, and the only way I ever communicate with them is through email and conference calls. At least with Zoom, I get to see them."

"How's New Zealand?"

"The same. Thankfully, they're keeping COVID at bay, so we can still live normally."

"Must be nice. I'm getting tired of sitting around the house all the time. We've been using the pool a lot and sitting out back in the evenings, so that helps."

"Yeah, I guess the only thing worse than having to work from home is having to go in to work. According to Aaron, it's really stressful having to deal with the public at the pharmacy."

"Yeah, he's constantly testing himself to make sure he doesn't have it. He's only gotten it once. Thank God I haven't gotten it yet."

"I'm really glad you're there to keep Aaron company. I know that's a big help."

"Thanks for letting me stay here."

"Of course. Well, I guess I'll let you go. Does Aaron want to say goodbye?"

"Let me go ask."

Brandon returned a moment later. "He says he doesn't have anything else." He lowered his voice. "He's pretty upset. Maybe the less said, the better at this point."

"Okay. Well, tell him I love him."

"I will."

"And I love you too. Bye."

"Love you. Bye."

Brandon walked back out to the kitchen to resume dinner prep. Aaron was fuming. "God, I can't believe it. And you know what? He says he's sorry and he wishes he could come home, but I think he wants to stay. He's having too much fun there. No COVID, no isolation, no Trump, no BLM protests... Hell, no wonder he doesn't want to come home."

"Then tell him no. Tell him to tell them he needs to come back. He committed to a year, and now a year's almost up."

"I can't do that." Aaron was seething. "I can't fucking believe it. I just can't. Even. Fucking. Believe it. And the hell of it is, I really don't have any choice. According to him, it would throw a big wrench in the project and make him look bad. And that would make me look bad, like I ruined his chances for career advancement."

"Well, if you don't have any choice, then I guess you have to accept it and learn to deal with it." Brandon hugged Aaron. "I'm sorry. I want him home too. But I guess if we've lasted this long, we can last a few more weeks."

Conflicting Emotions

Wednesday, October 21, 2020

Ryan was still in New Zealand on their third anniversary. They agreed to call each other on Zoom at 10:00 p.m. Arizona time, which was 5:00 p.m. the next day in Auckland. Ryan stayed in his office after work and made the call from there.

Ryan greeted Aaron with, "Happy Anniversary!"

Aaron forced a smile. "Happy Anniversary to you too, even though it was yesterday for you. Thanks for the flowers. That was very thoughtful."

"I'm glad they arrived on time, with all the supply chain issues. Did they look okay?"

"Oh yes, they're beautiful. Delivery seems to be the one thing that's working well here. Did you do anything special?"

"I went out for a nice dinner. Just by myself. I imagined you were with me and we were enjoying it together. I thought about some of the things I've seen and done here, and I imagined you coming to visit and me taking you around to show you all those places."

"That's really sweet. I wish I could do that."

"It was kind of weird eating dinner alone on my anniversary, but I didn't want to let the day go by without doing something. I went out to eat by myself before I met you."

"Yeah, I did too."

"So did you do anything?"

"Yeah. Earlier this evening I got out our wedding video and watched it with Brandon. That brought back a lot of fond memories."

"I bet it did. Just think – three years!"

"Yeah. In some ways, it seems like it has sped by. But this year seems like it's going on forever. So anyway, on to something else. What did you do last weekend?"

"It was nice out. It's starting to get warmer here. Michael knows these guys named Reed and Gavin who have a sailboat. Last Sunday, they invited us and a couple of others to go out with them."

"I'm sure that was nice."

"It was! The view of the Auckland skyline from the bay is incredible! There were lots of other boats out on the water. We spotted several others with rainbow flags, so we'd sail over and say hi to them. Reed and Gavin usually knew them. Anyway, it was great."

"Well, I'm glad you had fun. I so envy you. There's not a damn thing to do here, other than walking or running outside. Pool season is over now. When I'm not at work, I spend way too much time on the computer."

"I'm sorry it has to be this way. I really wish you could be here."

"Or that you were home for good. Anyway... You wanna say hi to Brandon?"

"Yeah, sure."

"I'll go get him."

Aaron returned a moment later with Brandon. Brandon pulled up a chair and shared the screen with Aaron. "Happy anniversary!"

"Thanks!"

"I enjoyed watching your video. You guys had the best wedding!" *Except for that moment when Dad showed up and you lost your shit.* "So, how's New Zealand?"

"Great. It's springtime here, like March in the States. So the weather's getting nicer and everything's coming to life."

"Sounds nice. I hope I get to go there someday."

"How's everything where you are?"

"Work's going okay. But it's weird that I've worked at Technovations for five months and I've never actually met anyone in person except my boss. How's your work going?"

"Really well."

"Good. Well, it's great to see you, as always. I'll let you get back to Aaron."

"Okay. I love you."

"I love you too." Brandon waved, then scooted his chair off to the side. He got up and left the room.

Aaron said, "So... When does it look like you'll be able to come home?"

"I'm hoping by Christmas."

Aaron sighed. "I was hoping for Thanksgiving."

"Yeah, me too, but they still haven't found my replacement. And we uncovered an issue during our testing that pushed our schedule back. So things are rather critical right now."

"Damn you for being so good at your job that they can't do without you."

"Yeah, I know. But I still think Christmas is possible. I mean, it's not like we can go to Ohio or anywhere else, but I want to be home with you."

"Yeah, me too."

Aaron and Ryan looked at each other to see if they had any more to say. Aaron didn't, so he said, "I guess I should let you go. You're probably getting hungry, and it's getting late here."

"Yeah, okay. Well... I love you."

"I love you too."

After the call ended, Aaron sat in his chair. He didn't feel like getting up or doing anything. He needed some time to process his thoughts.

There he is, down in New Zealand, having the time of his life. No COVID, no Trump bullshit, no racial injustice protests. He's able to go out with friends. They go sailing in the bay, drinking cocktails and sunning themselves in their swimsuits.

And here I am, trapped at home. God, I miss him. I'm so over these fucking Zoom calls. It's just so unfair. And let's face it... Who knows when he'll actually come home?

Tears started running down Aaron's cheeks.

About ten minutes later, Brandon stuck his head in the door. "Are you through with your call?" Aaron turned to face him, and Brandon saw him crying. "What's wrong?"

Aaron stood up. "Everything's wrong. He's down there having the time of his life. He loves his job, he loves New Zealand, and he's got all these gay friends he hangs around with. And that Michael guy... I don't know, but I think something is going on. Ryan says nothing's happened, but it's only a matter of time. And here we are, stuck in this house. No band, no running club, no parties, nothing. And I can't work from home. I have to go into the fucking store every day and wear a fucking mask all day long and test myself constantly. And you know it's only a matter of time before I get it again. It's so fucking unfair."

"Yeah, it definitely sucks."

"And I have to admit, I'm angry about it. I'm jealous. And I feel guilty for even feeling that way. I know, I should be happy for him. I should be the supportive spouse. I should be glad he doesn't have to put up with this shit. I should be happy he has a job he loves and his career is advancing. I mean, he didn't know COVID would happen when he took the assignment. But still, I'm angry. I resent it. I can't help it. It's how I feel."

"I don't blame you. And you're entitled to feel what you feel."

"But most of all, I feel lonely. I feel abandoned. Don't get me wrong. You're wonderful and we get along great and I'm happy you're living here. If I was here by myself, I'd go insane. But I miss seeing him. Seeing him on a fucking screen isn't the same thing. I miss holding him. I miss kissing him. I miss having someone to snuggle with at night before I fall asleep. And... okay, I'm just going to say it. I miss fucking him! Thinking about him when I jerk off got old a long time ago. And... okay, I probably shouldn't say this, but... every time I see you, I think of him. You're both tall and you look so much alike except, of course, you're younger. And I know that's wrong. You can't help it you look so much alike. And you're not him, you're you. But still, whenever I see you, I think of him. It's like you're a constant reminder."

Aaron started crying again. Brandon stepped up and wrapped his arms around him. Aaron buried his face in Brandon's chest and hugged him back.

God, this feels good. This is what I've been missing – just being held by someone. I know, he's not Ryan, but he's tall and he feels like Ryan.

After a moment, Aaron stopped crying. *I'm so glad Brandon is here. He's not Ryan, but he's the next best thing. And I love him too, just in a different way. I know, I've probably hugged him enough, but... this feels so comforting. This is what I've been missing for over a year. I just want to hold another human being for a while. I want to bask in the loving warmth of another man's arms. Just a moment longer.*

Okay, Brandon's probably starting to get weirded out. But... he's not letting go. He's still holding me too. Maybe he feels the impact of being shut in too. Maybe he needs to be hugged as much as I do.

Finally, Aaron pulled his face out of Brandon's chest and looked up at him. Brandon looked down at Aaron and smiled. Aaron looked into Brandon's eyes and saw empathy, compassion... and love. Instinctively, he leaned up and kissed Brandon on the lips, as he had done hundreds of times before when he hugged Ryan.

OH MY GOD! WHAT DID I JUST DO?

But then he realized Brandon had kissed him back. Neither of them was letting go. Brandon kissed Aaron, and Aaron let him. Aaron stopped thinking about what was happening. He opened his mouth and locked lips with Brandon. A year of pent-up emotion and desire poured out, and Aaron let himself get swept away in the moment.

After five minutes of increasingly intense, passionate kissing, they stopped and took a step back from each other. All kinds of thoughts and emotions swirled in Aaron's head. He couldn't make sense of any of them. Finally, he looked up at Brandon. "What just happened?"

Brandon gazed into his eyes. "I think we just confronted our truth."

"What do you mean?"

"C'mon, let's sit down and talk." Brandon led Aaron into the family room and motioned for him to sit on the couch. "Wine?"

"Yes, please."

Brandon poured two glasses of Chardonnay, carried them over to the couch, and sat down next to Aaron.

Aaron looked distressed. "I'm sorry. I never should have done that. I don't know what came over me. I just–"

Brandon gently pressed his finger to Aaron's lips. "I enjoyed it as much as you did."

"I don't get it. You're not even..."

"Gay? Well... I've never been into labels, but I seem to be attracted to another man."

"You mean..."

Brandon nodded.

"But... How? When?"

Brandon took a generous sip of his wine, swirled it in his mouth, and then set the glass down on a coaster. "It started the first time I saw you, on that day you came up to me after basketball practice and told me you knew my brother. You were so cute! You were nervous, but it was an excited kind of nervous. And you were so nice. At first, I thought I just liked you because you reunited me with my brother. I kept telling myself that's all there was to it. And besides, you were dating him, and then you married him. So I've always told myself you're off limits and I can't let myself go there. But this past year, when we've been cooped up in this house together and it's been just you and me, well... It's been harder and harder to fight my feelings. I mean, look at us. We're so comfortable together. We like the same things, we laugh together, and we even finish each other's sentences now. And the way we interact on the podcast feels so natural. We've bonded."

Brandon paused to take another sip of wine. Aaron had no idea what to say.

Brandon continued. "And maybe it's just me. Maybe it's wishful thinking on my part. But I think you feel the same way."

Aaron stared at the coffee table, not looking at anything in particular. He knew Brandon was right. He muttered, "Yeah."

For a moment, neither of them said anything. Then Aaron said, "So, you're attracted to me. Is it only me, or have there been other guys you've felt attracted to?"

"During the four years I was at ASU, I thought a lot about who I am and what I want. It's a huge campus, and I would see hundreds of people every day. I realized I was checking out the cute guys a lot more than the cute girls. And meeting all your friends and getting to know the people in the band... I felt so comfortable around other gay people. I finally realized it was because these are *my* people."

"Since you were away from home, couldn't you have been more open about being gay on campus?"

"Not when I was on the basketball team. Homophobia and toxic masculinity were alive and well in the locker room. Everyone was hyper-masculine and uber-straight. There's no way I could let my teammates find out. And of course, being a basketball player made me stand out on campus. Believe me, I met plenty of guys I would have liked to get together with, but I just couldn't go there. I figured once I graduated and I was through with all that, I could be more open to getting together with guys. That's one reason I wanted to join Desert Pride. I figured I might meet someone there."

"Okay, that's all well and good, but why you didn't tell us?"

"I don't know. It's hard to explain. It's like, I didn't want anything to get in the way of you and Ryan, you know? I knew I was attracted to you, but you belong to him. So I figured if you didn't know I'm gay and you assumed I'm straight, I wouldn't be a temptation. It's like we could be good friends and brothers-in-law and live together and everything, but none of that stuff would get in the way. And I didn't know whether you felt any attraction to me. I kinda thought you did, but as long as you thought I was straight, nothing would happen. Does that make any sense?"

"Kinda. But wouldn't you have told us sooner or later?"

"Yeah, maybe after I had met some other guy, or maybe after I wasn't living here anymore. But despite all my efforts to hide it and not act on it, here we are. It happened anyway."

Aaron finished off his wine. "So now, what are we going to do?"

"I don't know. On the one hand, I feel relieved to have this out in the open. On the other hand, this is going to make living together more awkward. And I feel rotten."

"Yeah, me too."

"What do *you* think we should do?"

Aaron thought for a moment. "I think for now, let's not do anything. I need some time to process this."

"Yeah, you're probably right." Brandon stood up. "I'm gonna go back to my room until it's time to go to bed."

Aaron stood up. They looked at each other, wondering what they should or shouldn't do at this moment. Aaron took a step toward Brandon and gave him a quick kiss on the lips, then hugged him for only a few seconds. He pulled away before it went any further. Then he picked up his wine glass and headed into the kitchen. Brandon retreated to his bedroom.

Aaron refilled his wine glass and walked out to the back patio. It was a beautiful night. He plopped down onto one of the padded chairs and gazed up at the heavens as if there would be some kind of cosmic answer for him.

For the next hour, he replayed many of his interactions with Brandon over the past four years.

He thought back to the first time they met, a day before Ryan's birthday. He remembered going to the arena where the basketball team practiced and approaching Brandon as he walked to his dorm. At the end of their initial encounter, they shook hands. But then, Brandon hugged him. Aaron didn't think much of it at the time since young guys are typically more open to hugging other men. But tonight, Brandon said he felt attracted to Aaron the first time he saw him. Was there more to that hug?

Aaron thought back to that day in May, three and a half years ago, when he and Ryan were in the pool naked and Brandon came home from work early. He remembered how quickly Brandon shed his shirt and shorts. He vividly recalled staring at Brandon as he bounded down the steps into the pool with his pendulous cock swinging from side to side. He remembered sneaking glances at his cock once he was in the pool. It seemed as if he was semi-erect at times. He didn't seem to care. And he recalled the brief discussion they had while Ryan went in to make more mojitos, when Brandon said, 'I don't get hung up about this gay-or-straight thing. People are people. If two people feel the desire and they want to do it, fine!'

Aaron thought about all the times they hugged hello and goodbye. They seemed innocent enough. After all, they're close and they're brothers-in-law. He's family. Even the occasional kiss didn't seem awkward. Brandon hugged and kissed Ryan the same way, but they're brothers. Aaron had no idea how many grown brothers kiss, but he guessed not very many. But now that he knew Brandon was gay, label or not, it made more sense that he'd be comfortable kissing guys.

Dozens of other moments flashed by. He remembered the day this past January when they talked about starting their podcast. At the end of the discussion, Brandon said, "I think we'll be great together," and gave Aaron a nice hug. Now, that statement seemed prescient.

After contemplating everything that had happened up to this moment, Aaron still didn't know what to do. He walked back inside. He poured a half-glass of wine, even though he knew he probably shouldn't. It wasn't going to help him gain any more clarity about the situation, but it might relax him and help him fall asleep.

He walked down the hallway toward the master suite. As he passed Brandon's bedroom, he saw a line of light below the bottom of the door. *He's probably doing post-production on our latest podcast. Either that, or he's watching porn and beating off.*

Aaron brushed his teeth, shed his clothes, and climbed into the large empty bed. A familiar wave of loneliness swept over him. He reached down and idly stroked his cock – not that he was in the mood for masturbating, but just because it was there. Sure, it would be great to put it to use, but he wanted as much as anything to snuggle and fall asleep in another man's arms.

Ten minutes later, he got up. He put on his shorts and walked into the hallway. He knocked on Brandon's door.

"Hang on a sec!"

That was different. Usually, Brandon would say, 'Come in!' About ten seconds later, he opened the door about six inches. He stood behind the door, hiding his body, leaned to the right, and looked at Aaron through the gap. "Hey, what's up?"

"Can we talk for a few minutes?"

Brandon paused. Then he stepped back and pulled the door open further. He was wearing only shorts with a massive pitched tent.

Aaron glanced down and smiled. "Obviously, you're still *up*."

Brandon chuckled. "Yeah, I was... having a moment with myself."

"I'm sorry I interrupted."

"I'm not."

Aaron glanced down at the throbbing mound he wanted so much, then looked into Brandon's eyes. "I think we can find something better to do." He reached for Brandon's hand and led him to the master suite.

The Morning After

Thursday, October 22, 2020

At 6:30, the sun peeked through the blinds and bathed Aaron's bedroom with soft light. Aaron awakened to the touch of a tall, slender man spooning him from behind with his arm draped over his body. He smiled as he recalled the many times he had awakened to the sweet comfort of Ryan snuggled behind him. That was one of the things he missed most about Ryan being in New Zealand. But if Ryan's in New Zealand... Aaron's eyes popped open. He suddenly remembered his passionate tryst with Brandon last night. He felt Brandon's morning wood pressed against his taint and scrotum, just below where it had been the night before.

Aaron lay motionless in bed. Thoughts raced through his head and emotions pulled him in every direction. He glanced at his alarm clock; he had 15 minutes until it went off.

What should I do now? Just lay here? Get up quietly and try not to disturb him? Wake him up too? Several other possibilities occurred to him as well. He felt so conflicted that he did nothing. He continued to lay there with Brandon pressed against his back, arm wrapped around his waist, erection pressed against his crotch. Aaron couldn't move. Then he realized he didn't want to.

Aaron was filled with grief, regret, and shame over what he had done. But for over a year, except for Ryan's visit at Christmas, he had been deprived of love and love-making. He was stressed, lonely, and unfulfilled. Intellectually, he knew last night was wrong, but on the other hand, it was exactly what he needed. Being held by another man was what he needed most – especially a man he loved and who reminded him so much of Ryan.

Being held was only part of what Aaron needed right now. He glanced at the nightstand. The bottle of lube sat right where they had left it the night before. He leaned forward and reached for the bottle. He popped open the lid, squeezed a generous puddle into his left hand, and pressed the lid shut. He reached behind his butt, smeared the lube up and down Brandon's cock, and guided it inside.

Brandon awakened to the thrilling sensation of penetration. It took him a few seconds to realize he wasn't in his bed and who he was now entering. His mind tried to process the conflicting emotions over what took place last night and what was happening at this moment. He was getting laid, and like any 22-year-old male, that was his most desired state. And obviously, Aaron wanted it. Oh well... the deed had already been done. The boundaries had been crossed. Doing it a second time would hardly make things worse. He leaned forward and kissed Aaron on the side of his neck. Aaron pressed his butt back against Brandon, sending him deeper inside.

The alarm went off and Aaron slapped the snooze bar to silence it. Work, and the rest of the world, could wait a while.

***

After two more snooze bar delays, Aaron said, "We really need to get up now." He wished they could lay in each other's arms for another hour, but they needed to get to work.

Brandon sighed. "Yeah." He kissed Aaron and climbed out of bed.

They showered separately, silently agreeing that taking a shower together would surely lead them into further naughtiness and make them late for work.

Aaron arrived in the kitchen first. As he opened the cupboard to get a bowl and glass, Brandon walked in. Aaron asked, "Toast or cereal?"

"Cereal."

Aaron got out two bowls and two glasses and set them on the table. "Orange juice?"

"Yeah, sure." Brandon opened the pantry. "Raisin bran or shredded wheat?"

"Shredded wheat."

Brandon carried the cereal box to the table. Aaron walked to the refrigerator and returned with a carton of milk and a bottle of orange juice. He set the milk on the table and poured orange juice into their two glasses. "Would you get the spoons?"

Brandon walked to the silverware drawer and returned with two spoons. They sat down to eat. Brandon let Aaron pour milk into his cereal first, then Aaron handed the carton to Brandon.

They took a few bites in silence. Neither one looked the other in the eye.

Finally, Aaron said, "We must never say anything about this to anyone. Not Ryan. Not anyone. Ever."

Brandon took a few more bites. "So does that mean we're never going to do it again?"

Aaron thought for a moment. "I don't know."

"We probably shouldn't."

"We probably shouldn't have done it last night either."

"Or this morning."

They ate a few more bites in silence. Knowing they shouldn't didn't stop them last night, and they both knew it wouldn't stop them in the future.

Finally, Brandon said, "I guess time will tell."

Aaron rushed through his cereal and orange juice and got up from the table. "I'm running late. I need to get going. But we need to talk about this more tonight." He started to pick up his bowl, spoon, and glass.

Brandon said, "Just leave it. I'll take care of it." He stood up and stepped away from the table. "Have a good day!"

Aaron rolled his eyes. "From your lips to God's ears." He picked his insulated lunch box up off the counter, pulled a frozen entrée out of the freezer, and stuffed it into the lunch box. He hurried toward the door to the garage. Brandon called out, "Hey."

Aaron stopped and turned to face Brandon.

Brandon stepped up and gave him a quick goodbye kiss on the lips. "See you tonight."

Aaron forced a half-smile, then hurried out the door.

The Evening After

Thursday, October 22, 2020

At 6:00, Brandon heard the garage door open. He walked into the kitchen to greet Aaron. The door to the garage opened and Aaron walked in. He looked frazzled. He tossed his lunch box onto the counter and sighed.

Brandon walked up and hugged him, a little longer than usual. Then Brandon said, "How was your day?"

"It sucked, as usual. I swear, I don't know how much longer I can do this."

"That bad, huh?"

"Yeah. Those goddamn Snottsdale rich bitches think they're so fucking entitled. They come into the store not wearing masks, and I know if I say something to them, they'll tell me off. Hell, one of them slapped the produce manager the other day. And everyone's so goddamn rude. They look down on me and my techs like we have no inherent worth and we're just there to serve them. Hell, I have a Masters, which is probably more than they have, but they treat me like shit. Irrelevant, expendable shit. No please, no thank you, no smile, just a buttload of fucking attitude."

"I'm sorry." Brandon hugged Aaron again. "What would you like for dinner?"

Aaron sighed. He was in no mood for making decisions about dinner. "Oh, I dunno. Let's just have pizza. I know, we had pizza last night. If you want something else, that's okay."

"No, pizza's fine. It's the perfect food! As long as you have meat and vegetables, you've covered all four basic food groups."

"And there you have it."

"I'll get started on it. Why don't you change into comfy clothes and catch up on Instagram and Facebook? I'll let you know when it's almost ready."

"Thanks." Aaron forced a weak smile to let Brandon know he appreciated him. Then he headed for the master bedroom.

Twenty-five minutes later, they sat down for dinner. Brandon made them each a Long Island Iced Tea. He knew it would help Aaron relax a little. And he figured it might relax them both for the conversation he knew would take place sometime this evening.

Aaron had calmed down. He wasn't in a happy mood, but at least he wasn't so upset. He seemed distant, like he had a lot on his mind.

After they had eaten a few bites, Brandon asked, "Anything new on Facebook?"

Aaron perked up a little. "Yeah, I chatted with Chris for a few minutes."

"How's he doing?"

"Okay. He's looking forward to the election being over."

"Aren't we all?"

"No shit. God, I hope Trump loses. I don't think I could take another four years of this."

"If he wins, maybe we should all move to New Zealand."

"Yeah, maybe. Anyway, the senator he works for is up for re-election too. And they're hoping the Democrats can take over the Senate."

"That would be nice."

"Yeah. It's looking pretty good for Mark Kelly here in Arizona, and several states are really close, like Iowa and Maine. Chris says it'll probably come down to whether the Democrats can take both seats in Georgia."

"That seems like a tall order."

"Yeah, but we can always hope. Anyway, he's all caught up in that." Aaron took another swig of his Long Island. "Oh, and I asked if he and Seth are coming to Glendale for Christmas. They're not, because of COVID."

"That sucks. I guess it's the right thing to do, though."

"Yeah. I don't think I – or we – should go to Ohio either. I don't want to put my folks or Grandma at risk by traveling there on an airplane."

"God, I can't wait for this to be over."

This conversation was doing nothing to lighten Aaron's mood. He took another bite of his pizza. "Great job on the pizza. You put a lot of stuff on it."

"Thanks. I know how much you like toppings." Brandon hoped his attempt at humor would make Aaron smile. It didn't.

The double entendre was not lost on Aaron. "Okay, so that brings up something we really need to talk about. Wanna do that now?"

Brandon's smile disappeared. "Yeah, I guess so. Now's as good a time as any."

Aaron took a deep breath. "We must never tell anyone about what happened last night. And this morning. Not a word to anyone."

"Don't you think we should tell Ryan at some point? We can wait until he gets back, but don't you think he'll find out sooner or later?"

"He won't find out if we don't tell anyone."

"Don't you think he'll suspect something when he sees how we interact?"

Aaron thought about that. He wasn't sure what to say.

Brandon continued. "And what about us? What are we going to do until he comes home? Are we going to do this again or not?"

"I don't know. Good question."

"I mean, if we never do it again, then maybe I could see never telling him. But we're cooped up together, we get horny, and let's face it – we want each other."

Aaron said nothing.

"I guess what it comes down to is this. In hindsight, do you wish we hadn't fucked last night or are you glad we did?"

"I don't know. I've been thinking about this all day. On the one hand, I know what we did was wrong. Ryan and I are supposed to be monogamous. We don't have an open relationship. And I know that if he ever finds out, he's going to be hurt. And angry – which I wouldn't blame him for. So I guess that means we shouldn't have done it and we should never do it again. Except for one thing: I want to. I really, really want to. I don't think I could last however long it's gonna be until Ryan gets home and not do it with you again."

"Well, then, maybe I should move out."

"But then I'd be here all by myself, and I'd be even more miserable than I am now. And that would raise the question of why you moved out. The truth is, I love having you here. You're the one thing in my life that keeps me sane. You're the one thing in my life that doesn't suck."

Brandon resisted the urge to say, "And as of last night, now I suck too." Instead, he said, "Whether we have sex again is one thing. But there's another thing we need to deal with that runs much deeper. I think we're genuinely attracted to each other. Well, I'll speak for myself. I'm attracted to you. I'm in love with you. And I know you have feelings for me too. So regardless of whether we have sex, we still need to deal with our feelings for each other."

Aaron knew Brandon was right. "Yeah. God, I feel like such a horrible person. But you're right. You and I click. I mean, I love Ryan and everything. And I know he loves me. And he's been very good to me on so many levels. He doesn't deserve this. But as much as he and I love each other, it's like... I don't know... It's like we're not 100% compatible. With him and me, it's like most of the pieces fit. Whereas, with you and me, all the pieces fit. I mean, you're more upbeat. You've got your naughty sense of humor, which I love. And... Well, I'm just going to say it. You're constantly horny. You have sex oozing out of every pore. With Ryan, we have great sex and everything, but he's more reserved about it. He's more reserved about a lot of things."

"Yeah. When we were growing up, he was quiet and shy. Reserved, as you put it. I was always talkative and excited about everything."

"Yeah. You're more positive and outgoing. I really like that about you."

"Thanks. But I feel like a horrible person too. I mean, he's my brother. He's always been my hero. I looked up to him so much when we were kids, and I still do now. Like you said, he's been very good to me on so many levels. He's so generous about letting me stay here and cooking meals for us all the time and always having drinks on hand. And this is how I thank him? I mean, I love him more than anyone else in the world." Brandon paused. "Well, except for you now, I guess."

Aaron sighed. A tear escaped from his right eye and rolled down his cheek. "Last night, when I was on the Zoom call with Ryan and you came in and sat next to me... I looked at him on the screen and then I turned and looked at you. And in that moment, I realized I love you more than I love him." A few more tears ran down his face and he sniffled. He stood up, retrieved the box of tissues from the pantry, and brought it back to the table. "I feel so awful. So slimy."

Brandon reached across the table and put his hand on top of Aaron's. "Me too."

After Aaron regained his composure, Brandon said, "So what are we going to do?"

"Well, now that everything's out in the open, there's no use pretending this isn't what it is."

"I guess not."

"Hmmph." Aaron shook his head. "A couple of minutes ago, you and

I both said we love each other more than anyone else in the world. Isn't that supposed to be a joyful, happy moment? Isn't that supposed to be, like, really romantic? And yet, here I am crying and we're all sad and depressed."

"Yeah, it's not exactly the best circumstances."

They stood up and hugged. There were two slices of pizza left, which was unusual. They carried their plates and glasses to the kitchen counter. Aaron wrapped the remaining pizza in foil. Brandon put the plates, glasses, and pizza cutter in the dishwasher.

Aaron said, "Let's get in the hot tub later tonight. I don't think I'll be in the mood, but I want to hold each other and maybe talk some more."

"What time do you want to get in?"

"Around 9:00."

Brandon nodded. "I'll come out and turn it on at around 7:30."

"Oh, and one more thing. I really enjoyed having you in bed with me last night. Can we sleep together from now on?"

Brandon nodded.

"Thanks. That would really help."

They kissed. In some inexplicable way, their kisses felt different now.

You Have My Permission

Friday, November 27, 2020

Aaron wasn't looking forward to this week's Zoom call with Ryan. Yesterday was Thanksgiving, and he and Brandon had cobbled together dinner for two with turkey slices, a container of ready-made mashed potatoes, store-bought stuffing, green beans, and dinner rolls. It was a poor substitute for the gourmet feast Ryan would have prepared had he been here. He didn't feel like he had much to be thankful for.

When 7:00 p.m. came, he called Brandon into the office, sat down, and launched Zoom. Ryan was waiting for him. He seemed to be in a particularly upbeat mood. "Hi, Honey! How are you?"

"Okay, I guess."

"And how are you, Brandon?"

"Going stir-crazy, but otherwise okay. How about you?"

"Great! How was your Thanksgiving?"

Aaron said, "Honestly? It was kinda lame. I mean, we can't get together with anyone else. We went for a walk on the path around the lake just to get out of the house. But it was chilly and overcast, so we didn't stay out long. We had a mediocre dinner since none of the restaurants that would normally be open for Thanksgiving are open this year, or else they're only doing carry-out and delivery. And it's been an absolutely shitty year and you're not here. So yeah... Thanksgiving kinda sucked."

"I'm really sorry. I should have called you yesterday, but it was a regular work day for me."

"I get it. It's okay. Today is fine."

"Did you call your parents? How are they doing?"

"They're okay, all things considered. Dad's still having trouble breathing some days. He has what they're calling Long COVID. That means he no longer has the virus, but he's going to suffer the effects of his illness for months to come."

"That's too bad. But I'm thankful he's doing somewhat better."

"Thanks. So what have you been up to?"

"Work's going well and the weather's getting nice again. It's spring here. I went out running this morning, and Michael and I have theatre tickets this evening. It's supposed to be sunny and warm tomorrow. Remember me telling you about this older couple Michael knows, Reed and Gavin? They invited us to go sailing on their boat."

"I'm sure that will be nice."

"Yeah. I've been out with them a couple of times before. The harbor here is beautiful! It seems like everybody and their brother owns a boat, and on weekends like this lots of people are out on the water. There are colorful sails everywhere you look! And the Auckland skyline is so beautiful from the harbor."

"Well, good. Take a few pictures for me." Aaron turned and nodded at Brandon. Brandon said, "Okay, well I'll leave you two to talk amongst yourselves. But it was great seeing you! Love you!"

Ryan said, "Love you too. Take care."

Brandon left the room.

Aaron said, "So... you seem to be hanging out with Michael a lot."

"Yeah, we've become good friends. I met him at work, as you know, and I've met all kinds of nice people through him. The people out here are so welcoming and friendly!"

"Is he interested in you?"

"What do you mean? Like romantically?"

"Or sexually."

"Well, maybe a little, beneath the surface. But I told him about you – and us – right up front, so he knows I'm not available. Trust me, we're just friends."

"If you were single, would you be interested in him?"

"I don't know. I don't even think about that. I'm not single, and I'm only going to be here a little while longer."

Unless your assignment gets extended again, Aaron thought.

Ryan continued. "But yeah, he's a nice guy. We get along great, we have a lot of common interests, and yes, he's attractive. But don't worry, nothing's going to happen."

A wave of nervousness swept over Aaron. *Here goes.* "Well, you know, I've been thinking. Originally, your assignment was going to be for one year, and we were going to visit each other three times. Now, your assignment's been extended and who knows how much longer we won't be able to see each other. It's been a long time to be apart and... well... to go without sex. So, as far as I'm concerned, if you want to have a little fun while you're over there, you can."

Ryan was stunned. He studied Aaron's face on the screen, trying to figure out what was up. "Did you just say what I think you said? That we should stop being monogamous?"

"Just for the duration of your assignment. And you don't have to. But if you want to, you have my permission. No harm, no foul."

Ryan looked confused. "Okay, this is a surprise. I totally didn't see this one coming. What prompted you to suggest this?"

"Just what I said before. We've been apart for a long time, you're enjoying your experience in New Zealand, and it seems like Michael is someone special to you. So I want you to have fun."

"Okaaaaay..." Then another thought occurred to Ryan. "So, is there another reason you're suggesting this? Do you want to have sex with other people while I'm gone?"

Aaron shrugged. "Well, it's not like I should be seeing anyone else right now because of COVID. And I have no desire to get on Grindr and start hooking up with strangers. I just wanted to give you options, if you want them."

Ryan shook his head. "I'm not sure how I feel about this."

Neither of them had anything else to say on this subject.

Finally, Aaron said, "Well, I'll let you go for now. Have a fun evening tonight at the theatre and a great day sailing tomorrow!"

"Thanks, I will. I love you."

"I love you too. Bye."

Aaron quickly clicked the button to end the conversation. He got up from his chair and walked out to the family room. "Well, that's done."

"How did it go?"

"I don't know. He seemed really surprised, like he wasn't sure what was up."

Brandon said, "Yeah, that's what I'd expect. So what do you think he'll do?"

"I don't know. He said he would think about it. He may or he may not."

"Would you want to know?"

"Kinda. I wouldn't want to know the details, like how often they did it or what they did, but I'd kinda like to know if they did something. But that will be awkward to talk about on our calls."

"Probably the less said about that, the better."

"Yeah. Well, anyway... you wanna get in the hot tub tonight?"

"Definitely! I'll go fire it up now."

The Travel Bubble

Monday, April 19, 2021

On April 6, the government of New Zealand announced that effective April 19, people could travel between Australia and New Zealand without quarantining for two weeks upon arrival.

On Monday, April 19, Ryan boarded a Qantas flight from Auckland to Sydney to visit his college buddy Ted. Ted was already a year and three months into his two-year assignment there, but the pandemic had made visiting him impractical until now.

As Ryan approached the security zone exit, he spotted Ted waiting on the other side. He ran into Ted's open arms and almost knocked him over. They held each other tight for half a minute and kissed a few times. None of the passersby seemed to care.

Finally, they released each other. Ryan said, "Aw, man, it's so good to see you again. I've been waiting a long time for this."

"Me too. How do you like Auckland?"

"I love it. I totally love it. But even so, it's nice to be able to leave. In many ways, it's the best place in the world to be right now, but still..."

"I get it. You want the freedom to come and go as you wish."

"Yeah, that's it. It's like I've been trapped. And as far as the rest of the world is concerned, I still am."

"Well, let's get outta here. I can't wait to show you all around Sydney."

"Can you start by showing me a good restaurant? I'm starving."

Ted chuckled. "Yeah. Let me take you to my place. There are a few good cafés near my apartment."

Once they were seated at a table on the sidewalk and had ordered their food, Ryan asked, "How do you like Sydney?"

"I love it. It's by far the nicest place I've lived so far."

"You think you might stay here?"

"I'm seriously considering it. It's stunningly beautiful. There's lots of art and culture. And there's a huge gay community. This area, Darlinghurst, is one of our gayborhoods. I've met a lot of nice guys and made some friends."

"Any special friends?"

Ted paused and smiled. "There's two or three who have potential. It's too soon to tell. I guess a lot depends on whether I decide to stay here. There's no sense in investing too much into a relationship if I'll be moving in less than a year."

"That sounds like a chicken-and-egg thing. If you met a guy you liked enough, you'd stay. But if you're not going to stay, you won't find out whether you like him enough."

Ted thought about that. "Yeah, that pretty well sums it up. But I like it well enough that I might stay either way."

"Sounds like you have a good social life here."

"Yeah, probably the best social life I've ever had. As I said, they have a great gay community here. The fact that there's no language barrier helps a lot, too. So yeah, I've made some good friends."

Ryan wasn't sure whether he should ask the question he really wanted to ask. But then, he and Ted had always been open with each other. They could talk about practically anything. So why not? "Any... shall we say... friends with benefits?"

Ted chuckled. "Oh, yeah. I've definitely gotten some good action here. But no commitments yet. And how are things going with you and Aaron? How are you managing with not getting to see each other?"

Ryan sighed. "I don't know. It's weird. During the first few months after I left, we'd have Zoom calls every week and text each other pretty often during the rest of the week. But after the COVID pandemic hit, he started getting stressed out and angry. All he'd do during our calls was vent and complain. I know it's part of my job as a spouse to listen and be empathetic. But then when I would tell him what was going on with me, he'd get all upset because I wasn't having to suffer through the same shit he was. It's gotten to the point where I'm hesitant to mention anything for fear that it will make him jealous or angry – or suspicious. And there's this one guy at work named Michael who's also gay. He and I have become good friends. He's introduced me to his friends and we have a lot of fun together. Aaron asked me a few times if I was having sex with him. I'm not, but now I don't feel like I can talk about him and me doing stuff together without Aaron wondering whether we're fucking. So our Zoom calls aren't much fun anymore. And he cancels them sometimes. He says he has other stuff going on, but I don't think he does. Most activities, like band, still aren't meeting in person yet. And for the last six months, he's seemed kind of distant."

"Sounds like, after this much separation, you're growing apart. And it seems like there's some suspicion going both ways."

"Yeah."

"And that's not healthy. Looks like you have some relationship repair work to do."

"Yeah. In hindsight, I probably shouldn't have let them extend my assignment. He wasn't thrilled that I took the assignment in the first place – and we had no idea COVID would come along. But things definitely got worse after I had to stay longer."

"Well, you know, I can't blame him. After all, he married you so he could spend his life with you, not be separated from you."

"Yeah, I know. But here's another thing. Back in November, we were on our call and he asked whether Michael was interested in me or I was interested in him or whatever. Then he said that since we've been separated for so long, it was okay with him if we fucked. And I told him once again that I had no intention of doing anything physical with Michael."

"So, wait... He gave you permission to have sex with Michael, even though you said you didn't want to?"

"That's right. And actually, he didn't limit it to Michael. He said it was okay with him if I, quote, 'have a little fun over there.'"

"Wow... That's fucked up."

"I know, right?"

Ted thought about it for a moment. "So then, is the assumption that he has permission to have sex with others while you're gone, too?"

"I asked him that. And he kinda deflected the question. He said he couldn't get out and meet other guys now because of COVID, and he had no desire to start using Grindr. He said he just wanted me to have options if I want them."

"But you didn't ask for that."

"No."

Ted thought some more. "That doesn't seem right. There's something else going on."

"Yeah. I keep trying to convince myself that's not it, but it probably is."

"Could you ask Brandon?"

"Ehh... Maybe. But I don't want to put him in the middle of this. That would be awkward for him. But anyway, yeah... Things aren't great with me and Aaron right now."

"I'm sorry to hear that."

"Thanks. But on to other things! What do you have planned for the next couple of weeks?"

"Well, you can't visit Sydney without seeing the Opera House and the Harbour Bridge. They have lots of good art museums. Then there's the Royal Botanic Garden, Taronga Zoo, and either Manly Beach or Bondi Beach."

"Manly Beach. I like the sound of that! Is there a Feminine Beach somewhere else?"

"Ba-dum-dum. Manly is a suburb in the northern part of the city. It's a lot of fun. Then there's the Blue Mountains National Park west of town which should be good for at least a day. And we can take a day trip up to Hunter Valley for wine tasting. And I thought we'd go down to Melbourne for three days. How does that sound?"

"Like a lot. But it all sounds good. Have you been to all those places?"

"Most, but not all. I got some recommendations from my friends – especially for places to eat. And I haven't been to Melbourne yet, so that will be new for both of us. My friends have recommended some stuff there, too."

"Sounds good. Man, if you ever get tired of business and finance, you could do well as a tour organizer."

Ted chuckled. "Yeah, maybe that could be a semi-retirement gig someday."

They finished dinner. Since it was a lovely fall evening, Ted said, "Let's go for a walk. Hyde Park is a few blocks to the west, and I can show you a little bit of my neighborhood."

When they reached Park Street, they looked west and saw some of the tall buildings in downtown Sydney. Ted pointed to one of them. "See that tall building with the slanted wall? That's where my office is."

"Oh, wow. So you can walk to work."

"Yeah. And this park connects to a couple of other parks, so I have plenty of places to run. They have really good public transit here, so I don't need to own a car. In fact, I haven't owned a car since I left the US. I've gotten to the point where I don't miss it. There are several car rental places in the neighborhood so I can rent one for a day or two if I want."

"Auckland has good mass transit too. My apartment is near my office, and everything else I need is within a few blocks. There are tons of restaurants. Whenever I do stuff with Michael and our other friends, he drives. So I haven't driven a car since I've been down here. What's it like to drive on the left side of the road?"

"I got used to it pretty quickly. It's not as hard to adapt as you might think."

They walked through the parks and Ted's neighborhood for over an hour. They talked about work. Ryan talked about his bands and Ted described some of the friends he had made. At one point when nobody was nearby, Ted put his arm around Ryan's waist and pulled him closer. "It's great to see you again."

"Yeah, you too! It's been, what? Four years? And we can just pick up right where we left off."

When they returned to Ted's apartment, Ted said, "How about a glass of wine before we turn in?"

"Yeah, sure. What are the wines like here?"

"They're pretty good. Maybe not quite as good as California, Spain, or France, but still good. They have some good wine regions throughout New South Wales, Victoria, and Tasmania. We'll do some wine-tasting up in Hunter Valley. When we go to Melbourne, we can check out the Yarra Valley."

"What kinds do they produce here?"

"A little bit of everything, but a lot of Shiraz, Malbec, and Merlot for reds, and Chardonnay and Cabernet Sauvignon for whites. Here's a Shiraz I like." Ted opened a bottle and poured them each a glass.

Ryan swirled the glass, inhaled the bouquet, and took a sip. "Nice! That *is* good."

"I thought you'd like it. Australia is the seventh largest wine producer in the world and the fourth largest exporter."

Ryan took a couple more sips. "I can tell you like it here."

"I do. The weather is mild year-round. In January and February, it gets up to around 80, and 65 at night. In July, it's like mid-60s during the day and upper-40s at night. So it's never too hot or too cold. It rains a little more than I'd like, but it's not too bad."

"What are prices like?"

"It's cheaper than LA, but more expensive than many other places. Since I don't own a car, I don't have that expense. And my apartment is a little smaller than what's typical in the US. But I'm doing fine."

"Sounds like you might be ready to settle down."

"I'm seriously thinking about it. I'd have to see what permanent positions are available with my company. Or I could get another job. With my resume, I shouldn't have any problem." Ted took another sip. "But you know, the biggest thing is the people. The society. Everyone's really nice here. And you get used to the accent after a while. But they don't have all the gun violence and religious extremists like they have in the US. And they're very gay-friendly, at least in the major cities. So yeah, it's a much nicer environment."

"Yeah, I like New Zealand for the same reasons."

They finished their wines. Ted asked, "Another glass?"

"No, I'm ready to turn in. It's been a great day, but I'm fading fast."

They stood up. Ted said, "Okay, so... About sleeping arrangements. This is just a one-bedroom apartment. When you've visited me in the past, we've always shared a bed. But since you're married now, I guess there's the couch."

"I'm okay with sleeping with you. That is, if you are."

Ted grinned. "No problem here."

Ryan could tell Ted was hoping it would turn out that way. They said nothing as they cleaned their teeth and stripped down to their underwear. They both wondered whether they should leave their underwear on. Ryan waited to see if Ted would drop his shorts, while Ted waited for a cue from Ryan. A moment later, they climbed into bed with their underwear on.

Ryan leaned over toward Ted and Ted turned to face him. Ryan planted a quick kiss on Ted's lips and said, "Good night."

Their eyes met and they smiled. Ted kissed Ryan and whispered, "Good night."

Neither of them closed their eyes. They remained with their faces inches apart, neither wanting to move in any direction except forward.

Ryan said, "Can we snuggle? I've slept alone for the last year and a half, and it would be so nice."

Ted scooted a few inches forward and Ryan slid his arm under Ted's neck. Moments later, Ted's right arm was stretched across Ryan's body and his right leg was resting on Ryan's thigh. Their lips were inches apart. They kissed some more.

Moments later, their underwear was on the floor. It would be at least an hour before they got any sleep. After all, Ryan had Aaron's permission.

Such Sweet Sorrow

Sunday, May 1, 2021

Ryan and Ted's twelve days together flew by all too fast. They managed to check off most of the items Ted had planned for them to do. It rained for a couple of days, so they visited museums. Thanks to Sydney's extensive Metro and train network, they could minimize their time outdoors on rainy days.

On Sunday morning, Ryan's last day, they began with yet another energetic romp in bed. After they showered and got dressed, Ted cooked a spectacular brunch.

They sat down, toasted their friendship with mimosas, and took a few bites. Ryan said, "Ted, this brunch is outstanding!"

"Thank you. It's nice to have someone to cook brunch for."

After a couple more bites, Ryan said, "You know, I think showing us how to cook a nice meal is one of the greatest gifts Hal gave us."

"Yeah, I'd have to agree."

"When I first moved to Scottsdale, I decided I'd cook a nice dinner on Sunday nights like Hal did for us. At first, I'd invite a friend or two over now and then, but most of the time it was only me. And that was okay. That meant I'd have leftovers for later in the week. And it made me feel good to do something nice for myself."

"It's nice that you kept that tradition alive."

"Yeah. And then when Aaron and I started seeing each other, I'd invite him up for dinner on Sunday almost every week. Then later, Brandon came along, and occasionally we'd have other friends from band or work or the running club over. So gradually, it became a Family Night again."

"That's sweet."

"You know, this reminds me of that time after you graduated but you still lived in LA. You invited me over to your apartment to celebrate my 21st birthday. You took me to that super-nice restaurant there at the edge of the ocean. That night I stayed over and... we got to know each other better."

Ted smiled. "That was our first time together. I'll never forget that night."

"Me neither. And then the next morning, you made brunch for me. It was a lot like this. So yeah, this got me thinking back to that weekend. You really made me feel special."

"You *are* special."

"And you've made me feel special now. Well... you do that in many ways, but good food and good wine are definitely two of them."

"I wanted to make this visit as nice as I could."

"And you succeeded! Seriously, man, these last two weeks have been fantastic. I totally see why you love Sydney so much."

"Yeah, it really resonates with me. I've enjoyed living in the other places I've been, but when it came time to move on, I was ready. I've lived here for over a year, and I don't want to leave. Playing tour guide for you has driven home how much I like it here. When I go back to work next week, I'm going to meet with a few managers who might have some positions open."

Ryan said, "I hope Biden can turn the country around again. But Trump's not going away any time soon. And if somehow, God forbid, he ever gets back in office ... well, I don't even want to think about it."

"If that happens, you oughta move here."

"Either here or New Zealand. But I've got Aaron to think about. He's not so keen on the idea of leaving the US. I don't think he'll be willing to move as long as his parents are still around. When I took this assignment, I got the impression he thought I was doing it to scope out New Zealand as a place to live."

"Were you?"

"Well, yes and no. I thought living there for a year would satisfy my curiosity. And maybe the luster would wear off and I'd have a more realistic vision of what it would be like. But as it turns out, I really like it. And when my assignment got extended ... well, I have to admit that I wasn't totally disappointed."

Ted hesitated before he asked his next question. "So... What do you think will happen with you and Aaron?"

"Well... I'm hoping that we'll be able to pick up where we left off. I know we'll have to work through some things. But I think once we're together and we get back into our routine, everything will be fine again."

They took a few more bites without talking. Both of them had a lot on their minds.

Ted asked, "Are you going to tell Aaron you visited me? Or more to the point, that we fucked?"

That question had been on Ryan's mind throughout their visit. He took a moment to choose his next words. "Yeah. I should be honest with him. I mean, I'm not going to walk in the door and say, 'Hey guess what? I visited Ted in Sydney and we fucked like rabbits for twelve days.' But I'm sure at some point we'll talk about why he suggested that we could have sex with other people, and I'll mention it then."

Ted debated what he should say next. He didn't want this to get awkward or mushy, but he had to say something. "You know how the first time you're with someone, it's all passion and fireworks – you know, like the thrill of discovering someone new?" Ryan nodded. "Well, with us – at least as far as I'm concerned – every single time we've been together it's been like that. Seriously! It's like we never have an off night. Every single time it's amazing. Every single time I ask myself, 'Is it even possible for it to be any better than this?'"

Ryan wasn't sure where this was headed, but Ted was right. "Yeah, I'd have to agree. No matter who's doing what to whom or what position we're in, it's pretty incredible."

"I keep telling myself, this is everything man sex is supposed to be."

"I think part of it is that we don't get to see each other that often. So when we do, there's all this anticipation. It's like we have to make the most of the limited time we have."

"Yeah, there's that, but... What we have is special. We're tuned into each other on a much deeper level."

They ate a few more bites. The silence started getting awkward.

Finally, Ted said, "Do you remember the last night on the cruise, back in 2013, when we sat outdoors at the back of Deck 12 and shared that pitcher of sangria?"

Ryan smiled. "I sure do. That was a great trip. It's hard to believe that was almost eight years ago."

"Remember how, at one point in the conversation, we talked about whether we could have made it as a couple?"

Uh-oh, Ryan thought. "Yeah...?"

"At the time, there was too much difference in what we wanted to do with our lives. You wanted to settle down in Scottsdale, and I wanted to keep moving around from place to place in the world."

"Yeah, I remember that."

"Well... We've already talked about this a couple of times, but I think I'm ready to settle down. I think I've found my place." He paused. Ryan didn't say anything, so Ted continued. "And uh... I was thinking that if things don't work out with you and Aaron, and if things keep getting worse in the US... well... maybe you could come here. Maybe we could give it a try."

Ryan said nothing.

Ted said, "You have to admit, we're perfect together. And I don't just mean the sex. We have such a deep connection. We get along so well. And... well... I love you more than I've ever loved another human being."

Dozens of thoughts were swirling in Ryan's head. He knew he had to say something. He took a deep breath. "First, thanks for telling me all that. That took courage. And I can't really argue with anything you just said. We get along great, the sex is fantastic, and we have a deep connection. That connection is love. I've loved you since we first started getting to know each other back in the house. But... I love Aaron too. And I'm married to him. When you marry someone, you're promising you'll stay with them. You're promising you won't dump them when somebody better comes along. So yeah, I suppose if our marriage ever fell apart, I could consider that. But, as close as we are and as much as we've talked about all kinds of things, we've never discussed being in a relationship. There are other conversations we'd need to have. But in any case, you shouldn't wait around for that to happen. It might not. Earlier, you said there are a lot of nice guys here, and some whom you're interested in. I think you should focus on that."

Ted was looking down at his plate, obviously crushed with disappointment. A tear ran down his cheek. Ryan couldn't recall ever seeing Ted cry before. He reached across the table and placed his hand on Ted's. With his other hand, he gently lifted Ted's chin so they could look at each other eye to eye. "I love you. You're the best friend I could ever want, but I think that's the best way for us to be. When we had that conversation on the last night of the cruise, we agreed that even if you love someone a lot, it doesn't mean they're the right person for a relationship."

Ted sniffled and another tear ran down. "Yeah, but—"

"But no. If it ever happens that we're both single at the same time, then we can talk about it. But don't count on that happening. You need to move forward with your life. You're obviously happy here, so stay. There are plenty of nice men here, so get out and meet them. Put yourself out there. Don't sit at home waiting for a 'someday' that may never come."

Ted picked up his napkin and blotted his cheeks. "Yeah, I guess you're right."

Ryan glanced at his watch. "We need to leave for the airport in the next fifteen minutes or so." They stood up. "Or I can go by myself. I know which train to take."

"No, I'll go with you."

"Can I help you clear the table and put things away?"

"Just leave it. I'll take care of it when I get back."

Ryan wrapped his arms around Ted. They held each other tight. Neither of them wanted to let go right away.

Ted whispered in Ryan's ear, "I'm sorry. I shouldn't have gone there. I just... Well, I guess I hoped that maybe..."

"That's okay. We needed to talk about it. I think that's been on both of our minds the past several days."

"But now I feel bad that our time together has to end this way."

"Don't worry about that. I'll always remember this visit fondly. It's been incredible. And *you're* incredible. You'll always be one of my best friends."

One of, Ted thought.

They released each other and stepped back. "So, I guess if you ever come to Australia again, it will be with Aaron."

"Yeah, probably. I don't know when that will be, but it will happen sooner or later."

It dawned on Ted that their passionate sex this morning would probably be the last time they'd ever do it.

Ryan said, "Next time you come to the US, I hope you'll visit us in Scottsdale. I'd like you to meet Aaron and my brother Brandon."

Ted nodded. He wasn't sure he wanted to. And it might be awkward, depending on how Aaron reacts when he learns about the twelve days they spent together. He glanced at his watch. *Maybe, if we do it quickly... No. There's not enough time. I'd want to lay there and hold him for hours afterward. And besides, after what just happened it would probably be weird.* "Okay, well, let's get you to the airport."

Ryan sensed what Ted was feeling. He hugged him again. "Thanks for everything. *Everything!* It's been amazing. I'll never forget it."

They continued to hold each other, and Ryan could feel the tension melt.

Ted spoke softly. "I love you."

"I love you too. I always will."

They separated, and Ted smiled at Ryan. Ryan smiled back. He picked up his suitcase and they headed for the door.

Go West, Young Men

Saturday, August 7, 2021

At 10:55 a.m. Saturday, Ryan sat at his computer and eagerly launched Zoom. He was filled with excitement and anticipation for the call that was about to take place.

Moments later, Chris joined. He wore the same friendly, adorable smile Ryan remembered from the first time he saw him at band camp in 2004. Of course, they were 31-year-old adults now, not 14-year-old high school freshmen. Although Chris's face had aged from a cute teenager to a handsome young adult, his smile and the twinkle in his eyes still conveyed a youthful spirit.

A wave of happiness washed over Ryan. "Hi!"

"Hi! How are you?"

"Great. And how are you?"

"Fantastic!"

"Yes, you are."

Chris smiled at the compliment and the underlying affection it conveyed. "I'm glad we got the time zone thing figured out. It's what? 11:00 a.m. Saturday morning there?"

"Yes. I live in the future. But yeah, it's complicated because the US and New Zealand go on and off Daylight Savings Time at different times. But whatever... we figured it out."

"What's the weather like there?"

"August here is like February in the US. So it's still winter here. But it's not bad. Our highs are usually around 60 degrees Fahrenheit and our lows are around 45. It doesn't change that much year-round. In our summer, the highs are around 75 and the lows are around 60. So it never gets too hot or too cold."

Chris said, "Sounds nice. It's so hot and humid here. If I'm outside for more than 15 minutes I start sweating like a whore in church. But anyway... You look really happy and relaxed. Looks like New Zealand is treating you well."

"Is it that obvious? But yes, I love it here. Auckland is amazing! From my office window, I can look out over the harbor. It's so beautiful with all the sailboats and the hilly islands in the distance. And my apartment is in a cute neighborhood. Everything I need is within a few blocks, so I walk everywhere. The bus system is excellent, so I don't have a car. I take an Uber if I need to, and occasionally I rent a car if I want to take a day trip or something."

"Sounds awesome! It's kinda like that where I live in Arlington, but I still drive a lot. I take the Metro to work every day, but that's a pain when it's crowded."

Ryan said, "But the biggest difference is the vibe. People here are so much nicer. Like in the US, it's gotten so angry and divisive. Based on everything Aaron's told me, between the pandemic and the BLM protests and the whole Trump thing, everyone's more hateful and angry than ever."

"Yeah, it's gotten really bad the past couple of years. In some ways, things have gotten better now that Trump's out of office, but in other ways, they haven't. It's like he just won't go away."

"Yeah, I think that's the biggest thing I like about being here. We don't have to deal with any of that shit. And like, there is no gun violence here. No one owns guns. No one even wants them. And we don't have right-wing religious nuts here, either. Well, maybe a few, but they don't have much influence. And there's not much racism, either."

"Wow. Sounds great. I can see why you like it there."

"Yeah. To be honest... In some ways, I wish this assignment would never end. I wish I could stay here. But I miss Aaron, I miss my house, and I miss band and all my friends. So it will be nice to go home."

"And that's when?"

"Next month. My last day here is Friday, August 27th. My flight is on Wednesday, September 1st, and because I'll cross the International Date Line, I'll get home on the 1st, too. It's funny... my flight leaves Auckland at 3:50 in the afternoon and arrives in Phoenix at 12:13 – four and a half hours earlier!"

"Sounds like a long day!"

"Yeah. Auckland is 19 hours ahead of Phoenix, so Wednesday will be a 43-hour day."

"Yikes! How long is the flight?"

"Over 16 hours, counting a two-and-a-half hour layover in LA. Thankfully, I don't have to be at work until the day after Labor Day, so I'll have the rest of the week to adjust to Arizona time. Aaron's planning a welcome home party on Saturday of Labor Day weekend, but I should be okay by then."

Chris smiled. "Can I come?"

"Huh? Are you visiting Seth's folks in Glendale that weekend?"

"No! That brings me to why I wanted to have this call. I'm moving out there."

Ryan lit up. "What...? Really? When?"

"Next week. The closing on our condo is Monday morning. I'll finish packing my stuff this weekend, and on Sunday a couple of friends will help me load it into a rental truck. I'll stay with them Sunday night. Then after the closing, I'll hit the road. I'll stay with my parents in Prairie Village Tuesday and Wednesday night, then I should get into Glendale late on Friday night."

Ryan asked, "What about Seth? Everything you just said seemed like it was only about you."

"He's already there. He moved back in May. He already has a job and an apartment. Once I get there I'll move into the apartment with him and we can start looking for a house."

"So he moved without you?"

"We agreed that I should stay here until the condo sold. Plus, I wanted to wrap up all my work with Senator Snelling. The Senate usually takes August off, so that seemed like a good time to quit. We put the condo on the market Memorial Day weekend, and we had an offer by the second week of June."

Ryan thought about this some more. "So, what about you? Do you have a new job lined up?"

"Not yet. I'm not sure what I'll do. I've looked into jobs with the Democratic senators and representatives in the Arizona legislature, but there aren't nearly as many positions for attorneys. Maybe there are other jobs within the government I could get."

"Why limit yourself to government work?"

"Mostly because it's what I've done so far. It's where I have experience. And it's important to me to have a position where I can help affect change through better legislation."

"I get that. But wouldn't you have a lot more opportunity to do that in Washington?"

Chris sighed. "Yeah."

"So it sounds like you're moving because Seth wanted to."

"Yeah, that's pretty much what it boils down to."

"I remember when you guys visited five years ago. I could tell back then he wanted to live out here and that was a source of conflict between you two."

"Yeah. He was ready to move to Arizona back then. So I guess I got five more years of living where I want, and now it's time to let him have what he wants. Besides, I can see the advantages of living there. And I have to admit, it's time for a change. The Trump years were terrible. And even though he's out of office now, he's still in the news all the time. Washington has become really toxic. And on top of all that, there's the pandemic."

"Well, we have crazy government and the pandemic in Arizona too, y'know."

"Yeah, but still, I'm ready for a change. And I'll be close to you guys! That's a big plus."

"That's true! It will be great to have you out here! And you can join the band! You'll make lots of new friends. Some of us go out to dinner before band, so we'll see each other all the time. And we can hang out together whenever we want!"

"That'll be great. But I'll need to start practicing again before I try to join the band."

"Don't worry, it will come back quickly. Trust me! Their next concert is on the first Sunday in October. October 3, I think it is. So you can come and listen to it with me. The first rehearsal for the holiday concert will be the following Thursday, October 7. So that will give you almost two months to get back in shape."

"Cool. And depending on how long it takes me to find a job, I'll have lots of time to practice."

"Speaking of that, if you want, I can see if they have any openings for attorneys at Technovations. They have a legal department at my campus in Scottsdale. They deal with stuff like patent infringement, immigration, HR stuff, and government affairs – you know, legal compliance, lobbying, that sort of stuff. In fact, my mentor is in charge of government affairs and community relations. So send me your resumé! I'll send it to him and put in a good word. It would be a lot less pressure and more regular hours."

"Yeah, go ahead and look into that. It's not quite what I had in mind, but I'd be willing to consider it."

"It's a great company. I really like working there. Brandon works there, too, in their Employee Communications department."

"Okay, thanks. I appreciate it."

For a moment, neither of them said anything. Then Ryan said, "Wow! This is still sinking in. You'll be living in Glendale! We'll be in band together again! We can hang out!"

"I know! It's gonna be great!"

"Already, I'm feeling better about my assignment ending and moving back to Scottsdale."

"I know what you mean. This is the part of moving to Arizona I'm looking forward to the most."

"Well, okay. I should probably let you go. You have boxes to pack."

"Yeah. Plus, some friends are throwing a going-away party on Saturday night. It's kind of overwhelming, but I guess it'll all get done somehow."

"I'm sure it will. Anyway, it's been great catching up with you. And thank God for Zoom. It's nice to see you while we talk."

"Yeah, same here. And just think! A month from now, we won't need Zoom!"

"I can't wait. Anyway..." Ryan thought, *Should I say 'I love you?' I mean, I do, and I know he loves me too and he'll say it back. But I don't want to give the wrong impression. Oh, hell with it! Everyone says you should tell people you love them more often. And we said 'I love you' that time we had lunch at the restaurant in Glendale.*

They looked at each other expectantly. Ryan realized Chris was probably having the same internal debate. "I love you."

Chris's look of anticipation changed to relief. He smiled. "I love you too."

"Well... Good luck with your move."

"Thanks. I'll need it."

"See you soon!"

"Yeah... In person!"

Ryan realized they were both delaying the inevitable. "Bye."

Chris sighed. "Bye."

Ryan willed his hand to move the mouse to the red button to end the call. He clicked and Chris disappeared.

Welcome Home!

Wednesday, September 1, 2021

When Ryan exited the secured area at Phoenix Sky Harbor Airport, he was exhausted but excited. He scanned the cluster of people waiting to greet the arriving passengers. Brandon, at 6'7" tall, was easy to spot. Seconds later, Brandon saw him and they rushed toward each other.

Ryan released his grip on the handle of his rolling carry-on and threw his arms around his brother. They hugged for several seconds and Brandon said, "Welcome home!"

Ryan kissed the side of Brandon's neck and Brandon kissed him back. They stepped apart and Ryan gazed at Brandon's face and smiled. "It's so great to see you!"

"Great to see you too!"

They exchanged another quick hug.

Ryan asked, "Where's Aaron?"

"He couldn't get off. One of the other pharmacists is on vacation and another called in sick. They couldn't get a floater, so he had to work the whole day by himself."

"That sucks." *Both for him and for me.* "But hey, let's head to the carousel and get my luggage. I can't wait to get home!"

As they walked, Brandon asked, "How was the flight?"

"Long. Really long. But at least the company sprung for business class, so it was a lot more comfortable."

"Really? Technovations pays for business class?"

"Not usually. But since I didn't get to take the trips home as I was promised, I felt they owed me something. My manager didn't complain when I asked for it. Speaking of work, how's your job going?"

"Pretty good. Everyone's still working from home most of the time. I've only been in the office, like, ten times. But I've seen everyone on Zoom calls so much, I feel like I know everyone."

"Yeah, I think most people in my group are still working from home.

In Auckland, I went into the office most of the time. But I still had plenty of Zoom meetings with people in Scottsdale and other places."

They retrieved Ryan's suitcases and hauled them into the parking garage adjacent to Terminal 4. After they left the airport, they drove east along Loop 202 past Tempe Town Lake. Ryan gazed at the modern glass and steel buildings on the opposite side of the lake. "Man, I never thought I'd appreciate seeing Tempe Town Lake as much as I do right now. Looks like they've built several new buildings in the past couple of years."

"Yeah, I guess so."

"I suppose when you drive past it often, you don't notice the changes day-to-day. But when you're gone for two years, it's easier to see the difference."

"Yeah. Plus, when I'm driving I have to pay attention to the road."

"Hey, can we stop somewhere for lunch? I'm starving. Dick's Pork Pit would really hit the spot."

Brandon paused. "Well, okay, but can you get it to go? I have to dial into a meeting at 2:00."

Ryan thought for a moment. "Never mind. I'll just eat something at home."

"We've got plenty of frozen entrees in the freezer."

"Okay, I'll have one of those. I'll probably crash pretty soon anyway. My body thinks it's 9:00 tomorrow morning."

A few minutes later, Ryan asked, "So how is everything?"

"Oh, all right, I guess. They started having band rehearsals back in July. Everyone has to show proof of vaccination to participate. We're all a little nervous about being in a room for two hours with people blowing instruments, but so far we haven't had any COVID outbreaks."

"That's good. I'll bet it's a relief to get out of the house and see people again."

"Yeah."

A few more minutes passed.

Ryan asked, "So how is Aaron doing? I know the pandemic has really stressed him out."

"He's a little better. But now more and more people aren't wearing masks so he's still nervous about going in to work."

"He's had COVID, what? Twice?"

"Yeah. Mild both times, thank God. The second time I got it too. But at least it's easier for me to stay home."

After they arrived home, Brandon disappeared into the office to dial into his meeting and Ryan ate lunch. Then he headed for the bedroom.

He entered the walk-in closet and stripped off his clothes. Unpacking could wait until tomorrow. He closed all the curtains, pulled back the covers on the right side of the bed, and plopped down. Moments later, he was fast asleep.

***

At a few minutes after 8:00 that evening, Brandon came into the bedroom and gently jostled Ryan's shoulder. Ryan slowly opened his eyes. "Huh...?"

"Hey. Aaron should be home in ten or fifteen minutes. You wanna get up and join us for dinner or would you rather sleep some more?"

Ryan yawned, stretched his arms to each side, then rubbed his eyes. "I'll get up. Give me a few minutes to take a quick shower and throw something on."

Brandon left and Ryan climbed out of bed. When he stepped into the shower, he noticed a different kind of shampoo on the ledge where they kept their body washes and shampoos. In addition to the Costco brand he and Aaron always used, there was a bottle of Tea Tree shampoo for men. Ryan opened the cap and sniffed it. He decided to try it. It had a nice fragrance and left his hair feeling clean and full-bodied. He noticed a different brand of body wash, too.

When he stepped out of the shower, he reached for the towel on the right half of the rack. It seemed like it had been used. He felt the other towel, and it felt used, too. He went ahead and dried off with the towel on the right.

Ryan put on gym shorts and a T-shirt and headed toward the kitchen/family room. Brandon was plating some salmon fillets he had just pulled from the oven. He smiled at Ryan and said, "I just heard the garage door open." He spooned some mixed vegetables onto each plate.

Seconds later, Aaron entered from the garage. Ryan hurried up to him with his arms spread wide. "Hi!!!"

Aaron looked physically and mentally exhausted. He forced a weak smile and said, "Hi."

Ryan threw his arms around Aaron and hugged him tightly. Aaron hugged him back but with less enthusiasm. Ryan kissed Aaron several times and said, "Aw, honey, it's so wonderful to see you again!"

Aaron tried to look enthusiastic. "You too. Welcome home!"

"Thanks! I'm so happy to be back!"

Ryan's enthusiasm dimmed slightly. "You must have had a rough day at work."

"Yeah. I was the only pharmacist available, so I had to work all day, 9 to 8, with only a half-hour off for lunch at 1:30."

"That's what Brandon said. I'm sorry! At least it's better than the 14-hour days you had to work at HealthPro."

"Yeah, there's that." He turned to Brandon. "I'm starving. What's for dinner?"

"Salmon and mixed vegetables." He smiled at Aaron and Aaron smiled back. "It'll be on the table in less than a minute. Do you want wine?"

"Definitely." Aaron took a couple of steps toward Brandon, then stopped. "Lemme go wash my hands."

Ryan asked, "Would you like me to pour the wine?"

Brandon nodded. "Would you? Thanks."

Once they were seated at the table and everyone had taken a few bites, Ryan asked, "How's band been so far?"

Aaron said, "Okay. I'm still a little nervous about getting COVID. But it's nice to be playing again."

"Did everyone come back?"

"Yeah. In fact, we have a bunch of new people. I think people are eager to get out and do things with other people again."

Brandon added, "I like the music Lee has picked. Since we're doing an outdoor concert in a park, he's picked lighter, more recognizable stuff. The audience will love it."

"Well, cool. I can't wait to hear it."

They ate in silence for a moment. Then Ryan asked, "How's the party on Saturday shaping up?"

Aaron said, "Fine."

"Who's going to be there?"

"Oh, the usual suspects – Kent and Justin, Rob and Eddie, some of the other guys from the band."

"How about Chris and Seth?"

"Chris is a definite, Seth is a maybe. He said there might be something going on with his family."

"Cool. Chris said he plans to join the band after the concert on October 3rd."

"Yeah, that's what he told us."

A moment later, Ryan turned to Brandon. "How was the rest of your day?"

"Fine. In that meeting I dialed into after you got home, we started laying out the roadmap for the employee communications campaigns for the rest of the year. There's the United Charities drive in October, then Open Enrollment in November, then Adopt-a-Family for the holidays."

"Sounds like they're keeping you busy."

"Yeah, it's always something. But I like it. I'm really glad you got me the gig there."

"Well, I put in the employee referral, but you got the job on your own merits."

Brandon smiled.

Ryan turned to Aaron. "You've been pretty quiet. Your day was that rough, huh?"

"Yeah. So... Brandon and I have an agreement. He doesn't ask me about work. It's up to me whether I want to talk about how my day went, and usually I don't."

"It's that bad, huh?"

"Yeah. It's very stressful. I'm really getting tired of it."

"I'm sorry to hear that. Have you thought about doing something else?"

"Oh, yeah, I think about it all the time. But as I see it, I don't have many options. But I don't want to talk about it now, okay?"

Ryan let it go. They finished the rest of their meal without saying much.

After they had cleared the table and loaded the dishwasher, Aaron poured himself another glass of wine and said, "I need some time to chill out. I'm gonna go catch up on my email and Facebook."

Ryan said, "Okay. I'm gonna head back to bed. Lemme think... It's 4:00 in the afternoon tomorrow in New Zealand. My body has no idea what time it is. Hopefully, I'll be back on schedule tomorrow."

"I'll try not to bother you when I come to bed."

Ryan smiled at Aaron seductively. "Oh, you can 'bother' me all you want. I wouldn't mind at all."

Aaron rolled his eyes. "Not tonight. I am sooo not in the mood."

Ryan didn't bother to hide his disappointment. "Alrighty, then... goodnight." He gave Aaron a quick kiss and turned toward the bedroom.

Trying to Get the Feeling Again

Thursday, September 2, 2021

When Ryan awakened the next morning, he was alone in the bed. He glanced at his alarm clock. 8:45. Aaron was, no doubt, on his way to work. He got up, used the bathroom, and put on the same shorts and T-shirt he wore last night. He ventured into the kitchen and found no one. He stuck his head in the office and saw Brandon sitting at his computer, checking his email. "Good morning!"

"Good morning!"

"Have you already had breakfast?"

"Yeah, I ate with Aaron half an hour ago. There's bread and cereal and part of a quiche. Help yourself!"

"Thanks."

After breakfast, Ryan went back to his bedroom and took a shower. The Tea Tree shampoo and the new body wash he saw yesterday were gone, and he had a fresh towel.

****

At 5:20, Aaron arrived home. He seemed to be less tired and irritable than yesterday.

Ryan and Brandon emerged from the office to greet him. Ryan reached him first and gave him a long hug and a kiss. "Hi, Sweetheart! How was your day?" Then he remembered what Aaron had said yesterday. "Sorry. I'll try to remember not to ask."

Aaron's hug was a little more enthusiastic today. "That's okay. It was better than yesterday. We had another pharmacist come in and work 12 to 8 today, so it was a lot less crazy."

Brandon stepped up, and Aaron and Brandon hugged. Ryan marveled at how close and comfortable they seemed with each other. But then, Brandon has been a full-time resident since the spring of 2020.

Ryan asked, "So, what do you guys want to do for dinner?"

Aaron and Brandon looked at each other as if they were surprised to hear this question. Aaron said, "It's band night. They're meeting for dinner at Ann Quesada's Enchiladas at 5:45."

"Oh, that's right. I forgot about that. I guess it'll take me a couple of weeks to get back into the routine."

Brandon said, "You can come if you want."

Ryan thought, *It would be nice to see my band friends again, not to mention eating with Aaron and Brandon. But then...* "Hmmm... That means I'd have to drive separately since I won't be re-joining the band until October. Ehhh... It's probably not worth battling rush hour traffic."

Neither Aaron nor Brandon said anything.

Ryan asked, "Are you guys going out to Raise! The Bar after rehearsal?"

Aaron said, "Nah... We went the first week, but we were uncomfortable being around so many strangers in an enclosed space."

"But you're okay with going to a restaurant."

Brandon said, "That's different. Ann Quesada's has some outdoor tables. And the other places we go have larger dining rooms so there's plenty of space. They're usually pretty empty because a lot of people still aren't eating out much. They get carry-out or delivery, or they cook at home. Sometimes the band people are the only ones there."

Ryan sighed. "Okay, well then I guess I'll see you when you get home from rehearsal."

Aaron and Brandon nodded. Aaron glanced at his watch. "We'd better get going. We'll probably be a little late as it is."

Aaron and Brandon grabbed their instruments and headed toward the garage. Aaron gave Ryan a quick kiss as he passed.

Ryan fixed dinner for himself. Then he got out his trumpet and played it for the first time in over two years.

***

When Aaron and Brandon returned home after rehearsal, Aaron seemed to be in a better mood. Ryan asked, "How was rehearsal?"

Aaron said, "Great! The music's coming together really well. We could probably do the concert next week."

"Cool. So... I want to hear all about it. You guys want something to drink?"

Aaron and Brandon looked at each other and silently communicated, 'Why not?'

Brandon said, "Sure. I'll have a Long Island."

Aaron added, "Me too."

"Three Long Islands coming up."

Soon, they were sitting in the family room. Aaron and Brandon had loosened up. They talked about the music they were playing and gave Ryan updates about various people in the band. The awkwardness that had been present since Ryan arrived home seemed to be evaporating.

After half an hour, Aaron stood up. "Well, I should probably get ready for bed."

Brandon stood up. "Yeah, me too." He hugged Ryan and Aaron and headed off to his bedroom.

A few minutes later, Ryan and Aaron stood side by side in front of the dual sinks in their master bathroom. After they brushed their teeth Ryan sidled up to Aaron and put his arm around his shoulder. "Sooo... You think maybe we can celebrate me being home?"

Aaron thought, *It's a reasonable request. He's my husband and he's been gone for two years. I can't keep saying I'm tired. I guess we need to start trying to get things back on track.* He turned to face Ryan. He looked up at him and smiled. "I think that can be arranged."

Ryan grinned. He pulled Aaron close, closed his eyes, and went in for a kiss. Upon contact, Ryan opened his lips and Aaron opened his. He extended his tongue into Aaron's mouth and brushed it back and forth against Aaron's.

He flashed back to their wedding day almost five years ago. He recalled the moment Rob pronounced them husband and husband and said, 'You may now suck face.' He had practically lunged for Aaron, and for at least ten seconds they kissed passionately in front of everyone present. Ralph, Aaron's father, said, 'Get a room!' They probably overdid it a little, but what the heck? It was their wedding – still the most special day of Ryan's life.

As he recalled the passion of those newlywed kisses, he couldn't help but notice that Aaron wasn't displaying that passion now. He was going along with being deep-kissed but wasn't quite reveling in it. Ryan knew how to turn the heat up a few notches. He stopped kissing Aaron long enough to whisper, "Let's get more comfortable."

He led Aaron into the bedroom, pulled back the covers with one grand, sweeping motion, and leaped onto the bed. Aaron climbed on and they scooted together until they faced each other a few inches apart – Ryan on his right side and Aaron on his left.

Ryan resumed kissing Aaron and caressed his back with his upper hand. Aaron followed suit.

Soon, Ryan moved his hand to Aaron's chest, running his fingers up and down and circling Aaron's nipples. Aaron did the same for Ryan.

Ryan's cock was hard as a hammer. He slid his hand down Aaron's stomach. He felt the bristly sensation of Aaron's pubes on his fingertips, then he reached for his manhood.

Aaron was half-hard, at best. Ryan began stroking it, and it started to respond. Aaron reached for Ryan's rigid cock and began stroking it.

Ryan pushed Aaron onto his back. He lovingly kissed the sides of his neck, then lowered his lips to Aaron's nipples. He flicked one nipple with his tongue while he teased the other with his fingertips, alternating back and forth. Then he kissed and licked his way down Aaron's torso, following his treasure trail from his navel to his cock. His cock had relaxed a bit since Ryan stopped stroking it. *No problem,* Ryan thought, *I know just how he likes it.* Ryan began applying his talents, and soon Aaron was showing results. He could get him off this way if he wanted to, but Ryan didn't want third base, he wanted a home run.

When Ryan thought Aaron's cock was hard enough to insert, he stopped sucking and reached toward the bedside table. He opened the drawer and pulled out their pump bottle of lube and a hand towel. The bottle seemed light, like it was almost empty. Ryan recalled buying a new bottle before he left for New Zealand. *Aaron probably jacked off a lot during the time I was gone.*

He pumped the bottle three times, depositing a generous dollop of lube into his palm. He reached for Aaron's cock, only to find it was already deflating. He coated it with lube and started pumping it to bring it back to attention.

Twenty seconds later, he gave up.

"I'm sorry," Aaron said. "I probably shouldn't have had that Long Island if we were going to do this."

Ryan thought, *A drink or two never stopped you before.* But he didn't want to ruin things by saying anything that could be the least bit off-putting.

He couldn't think of anything to say to salvage this awkward situation and turn things around.

Aaron reached for the towel and wiped the lube off his cock. "But I can still give you what you want." He rolled onto his stomach, arched his back, and spread his legs slightly.

With Aaron's face now pointed down, Ryan didn't need to hide his disappointment. *Well, okay, better only this than nothing at all, I guess.* One of the things he loved about their relationship was that they were both versatile. To Ryan, one of the biggest advantages of being gay was that he could enjoy the best of both worlds. As far as he was concerned, it was more blessed to give *and* to receive.

Ryan reached for the lube again and coated his cock. He applied some to Aaron's opening. As he straddled Aaron, he thought, *It's been a year and eight months since we've done this. I'd better take some extra time to get him ready. I know ten inches is an awful lot to take.*

As it turned out, Aaron accommodated him with no trouble at all.

Aaron made some effort to move in coordination with Ryan's motions, but it soon became clear that he was engaging in this act only for Ryan's benefit. Ryan finished quickly, then wiped them both off. Then he lay on his side of the bed and turned toward Aaron, hoping they could snuggle for a while. But Aaron got up to use the bathroom, and when he returned he laid down near the edge of the bed, at least a foot away from Ryan. Ryan rolled onto his side facing away from Aaron and tried to go to sleep.

The Party

Saturday, September 4, 2021

Guests began arriving for Ryan's welcome home party at around 3:00. Ryan greeted people as they entered. Most people were comfortable with light hugs, but since COVID was still a factor, nobody kissed.

Chris arrived alone. They broke pandemic protocol and hugged each other for at least ten seconds. Ryan gave him a light kiss on the cheek. "It's so great to see you! It's been, what? Three years?"

"Yeah. I think the last time was when we came out here for the Fourth of July in 2019. You guys went to Ohio for Christmas that year and we went to Kansas."

They hugged again. Ryan said, "I'm so glad we live in the same city now. Just think, a month from now we'll be in band together."

"I've been practicing. I can't wait!"

"So where's Seth?"

Aaron sighed. "He went to Vegas for the weekend with several friends. But there was no way I was going to miss this. I'm not a big fan of Vegas anyway."

"Me neither. Well, let me take you back and introduce you to people."

Aaron and Brandon had done a good job planning and executing the party. A 'Welcome Home' banner stretched across the passage from the living room into the family room, flanked with balloons. They bought matching paper plates, napkins, cups, and disposable tablecloths, all with a 'Welcome Home' motif.

People were socializing in the family room and kitchen, munching on chips and salsa and pub mix while they chatted. When everyone had arrived, Aaron encouraged the guests to move out to the back patio. Most guests brought swimsuits and got in the pool. Now that it was September, the pool water had dropped to 88 – ideal for a warm, sunny day.

Around the tiki bar were coolers with ice, sodas, bottled water, and beer. The beverages of the day were white and red sangria. Two 5-gallon dispensers sat on the counter of the tiki bar with their spigots hanging over the edge. The sliced fruit had been marinating in the wine mixture for several days and today, with the addition of sparkling water, it was ready to serve. It was a huge hit.

Ryan wore a sexy but not salacious swimsuit that provided adequate coverage from just below his waistline to his crotch. It was tailored with a generous pouch in front which he amply filled. He had debated wearing something more conservative, but he decided that these were his friends and his generous endowment was no secret. Some of them had, no doubt, seen him in videos he had appeared in a decade ago when he did porn to pay for college. He wasn't sure who among his friends had seen those videos and who had not, and it was just as well.

Brandon, who closely resembled Ryan both in outer appearance and anatomically, wore a more loose-fitting gym-short-type suit that provided coverage from his navel to halfway down his thighs.

The mood was celebratory and upbeat. It became even more upbeat as people partook of the sangria. Even Aaron seemed happy once the party was underway and he could set aside his hosting duties and enjoy the guests. Ryan regaled people with stories about his two years in New Zealand. Everyone agreed that today was not the day to bring up unpleasant topics such as COVID or Trump.

As the party progressed, people shifted from one conversation group to the next. At one point, Ryan got out of the pool to refill his sangria at the same time as Chris. As they refilled their cups, Ryan asked, "So how do you like living in Arizona so far?"

"Arizona is fine. I've been out here to visit Seth's family plenty of times so I knew what to expect. I'd like it better if I had a job and it wasn't at least 110 degrees every day."

"But it's a dry heat! And you moved here at the worst possible time of the year."

"Yeah, I know. But it is what it is. Speaking of jobs, I have an interview at Technovations on Thursday."

"Cool! Will it be on Zoom, or are you going there in person?"

"In person. They said masks are strongly encouraged, but no longer required. I'm going to wear one, though."

"Good. It will show them you're considerate of others and follow guidelines. Since we have a highly educated workforce, we don't have many science deniers. Anyway, since you'll be in the area, wanna come over for a drink afterward? You can tell me all about how it went."

"Yeah, that would be great. And thanks so much for referring me! I'm excited about it."

"Depending on what time it is, you could stay for dinner. Aaron and Brandon have band rehearsals on Thursdays, and they always go out to eat with the band folks before that. So it would be great to have company."

"Cool!"

Someone else approached the bar to get more sangria, so Ryan and Chris stepped aside. They looked at everyone in the pool talking, laughing, and having a good time. Brandon and Aaron were talking to Kent and Justin and a couple of others.

Chris said, "Brandon sure seems comfortable being around so many gay people."

"Yeah, and I'm glad. After being separated for nine years, we both want to stay close for the rest of our lives. So it helps that he's so comfortable with me being gay – and with my husband. But you know, back when we were in high school and he was in third grade, he had already figured us out. He knew we were gay and it was fine with him. We talked about that when we were reunited back in 2016. He and Aaron became friends right away. And it helped that Aaron was the one who got us back together."

"I can tell they have a connection."

"Well, they lived through the pandemic trapped in the house together."

"I suppose after that, two people would either be really close or be totally sick of each other."

"Yeah. Anyway, we should probably get back to the party."

***

At around 5:30, the guests were getting hungry. Brandon got out of the pool and changed into dry clothes. Then he fired up the grill and began grilling hamburgers and hot dogs. Aaron changed, then went into the kitchen to arrange the buns, condiments, and the side dishes everyone brought into a buffet line on the kitchen island. The other guests took turns in the bathrooms and bedrooms to change out of their swimsuits.

Grilling was usually Ryan's domain. But Brandon and Aaron insisted that since Ryan was the guest of honor, they should do all the work. Brandon did a masterful job, and soon all the guests were enjoying dinner at the kitchen table and the outdoor tables and chairs.

The Party's Over

Saturday, September 4, 2021

Shortly after 8:00, the party began winding down. By 8:30, almost everyone had left. Chris stayed to help clean up since he would be returning to an empty apartment and he wanted a little more human contact. Ryan insisted that Aaron and Brandon let them help. They were exhausted and didn't argue. Thankfully, the crowd had been responsible and there were no messes. They only needed to gather and discard the remaining cups and plates, empty the coolers, and put the remaining food in storage containers.

Half an hour later, they were done. They finished off the sangria and relaxed in the family room. For a few minutes, they dished on trivial things like what people wore, who seemed to be flirting with whom, and the food people brought.

Finally, Brandon said, "Well, I think everyone had a good time."

Aaron said, "Yeah. And you did a fantastic job with the hamburgers. I heard a bunch of compliments."

Ryan said, "Guys, the party was terrific. I really appreciate everything you did. I know it was a lot of work."

Brandon and Aaron smiled, but it was obvious they had a full day.

Chris sensed it was time to depart, so he said goodbye, hugged everyone, and left.

Brandon disappeared into his bedroom to check his email and social media.

Ryan hugged Aaron and whispered, "That was wonderful. It was nice to see everyone again." He paused as he continued to hold Aaron. "But it's really great to be back in your arms." He gave Aaron a gentle kiss.

Aaron knew what was on Ryan's mind, and he couldn't blame him. Ryan had been home for three days, and they had only attempted sex once – and that didn't go so well. Wanting to make love was a perfectly reasonable expectation. But...

Ryan released his hug and gazed lovingly into Aaron's eyes. "It's a lovely night. Would you like to get in the pool – just you and me? It would be nice to lay on the big raft in each other's arms and look up at the stars."

Aaron recalled the many times they had done that before Ryan left for New Zealand. *Those were such blissful and carefree times. We were so in love. We'd be lying on the raft naked, our bodies touching, with the warm breeze blowing lightly across our skin. Gazing up at the stars while the raft slowly rotated around the pool. Saying little but communicating so much. And of course, it would always end with lovemaking – either in bed or in the water or even right there on the raft. It was so idyllic ... so why don't I want to do that now? How can I say no? What can I say?*

Aaron looked at Ryan, who was anxiously awaiting an answer. He smiled. "Sure." *Maybe once we're out there lying naked together in the calm, quiet evening, I'll get in the mood.*

"Would you like a glass of wine?"

"No, I think I've had enough already."

"Yeah, me too."

Ryan turned the back patio lights off and pulled the curtains across the sliding glass door so the light from the house wouldn't wash out their view of the stars and so Brandon wouldn't see them if he came into the family room.

They walked back to the master suite in silence. They shed their clothes and passed through the door from the master suite onto the patio. Ryan pulled their large, round, two-person raft out of the storage shed and threw it onto the pool. Then he walked over to the steps. The extra wide top step made a perfect place to climb onto the raft. Ryan held the raft steady while Aaron climbed on, then he climbed on next to him and shoved the raft toward the center of the pool. He extended his right arm. Aaron scooted closer and rested his head on it, as they had done so many times before. Ryan bent his arm at the elbow and rested it along Aaron's right side.

It was a lovely evening. Aaron gazed into the clear night sky and tried to convince himself that there was no logical reason why he shouldn't be enjoying this.

Ryan let out a contented sigh. "This is so nice. This is one of the things I missed most while I was in New Zealand. My apartment building had an indoor pool, but it wasn't much fun to hang out at."

"Yeah. Having our own pool is great."

"I'm glad I got home in time to enjoy it for a few more weeks." He paused. "But then, pretty soon it will be hot tub weather, and that's fun too."

Those statements didn't require a response. Still, Aaron wondered whether he should say something. He couldn't come up with anything. Maybe this was a moment best suited for silence.

A few minutes later, Ryan turned his head and kissed Aaron's cheek. He shifted his position so he was now turned slightly toward Aaron. He paused, expecting Aaron to turn his head so they could kiss on the lips.

Aaron knew that's what Ryan wanted. He glanced down and saw that Ryan's cock was hanging to the right, pointing toward him. It was still flaccid but enlarged. He knew that with the slightest encouragement, it would grow harder.

Aaron realized that the only thing more uncomfortable than kissing Ryan and launching the inevitable sequence of events would be not kissing him and the conversation that would follow. He turned his head and kissed Ryan on the lips.

Ryan smiled. He extended his left arm across his body to Aaron's and began playfully stroking Aaron's chest. He placed another kiss on Aaron's lips, then another. Ryan parted his lips and Aaron could feel his tongue pressing into his mouth. Ryan turned a little more toward Aaron, and Aaron felt the tip of Ryan's hardening cock land on his thigh.

Ryan was turning the heat up quickly. Aaron tried to get into it, but he couldn't.

Ryan stopped kissing Aaron and pulled his head back a few inches. He opened his eyes and looked at Aaron's uncomfortable, passionless face. "What's wrong?"

Aaron turned his head away from Ryan and looked up at the cloudless sky as if the words he needed to say would be written among the stars. He sighed. "I don't know. I'm just... I don't even know what to say. But... for whatever reason, I'm just not getting into this. I don't know. I'm physically tired, I'm mentally exhausted, I'm ... I guess I'm just not in the mood."

Ryan didn't say anything.

Aaron glanced down. Ryan's dick had deflated. "Can we go inside?"

Ryan remained silent as he pulled his right arm from under Aaron's head. He reached his left arm into the water and paddled several times to send the raft back toward the steps. He climbed off the raft and onto the top step, then held the raft while Aaron did the same. Ryan shoved the raft back into the storage shed while Aaron headed for the master bedroom.

When Ryan entered the bedroom a moment later, Aaron had already put on a T-shirt and a pair of gym shorts. It was only a few minutes after 10:00, so it was too soon to go to bed. Aaron headed toward the door into the hallway. Ryan said, "Can we talk?"

Aaron turned to face Ryan. "Yeah, I guess we need to."

Ryan looked at Aaron with an expression that conveyed annoyance, disappointment, and concern. "What's going on?" He paused and waited for a response, but Aaron averted his eyes downward and said nothing. "Things haven't been right from the moment I got back. It's like there's this huge gap between us. You seem to be avoiding me. And not only for sex – all the time. It's like you're just going through the motions of being my husband."

Aaron debated how he should respond. After a moment, he said, "Yeah, you're right. Things aren't the same. So much has changed. Can we sit down?"

Ryan nodded. They sat down on the side of the bed. Ryan sat facing Aaron, with his left leg crossed in front of him on the bed and his right leg hanging over the edge with his foot resting on the floor. Aaron sat with both feet on the floor, facing away from the bed. He looked at the entrance to the bathroom in front of him as he spoke, not at Ryan. "The last two years have been difficult, Ryan. At first, being separated wasn't too bad. Seeing you and talking to you on Zoom calls was all right for a while, although not having sex and just jerking off got old pretty quickly. But then the pandemic hit, and everything got canceled. No more band. No more getting together with friends. No more eating out. And then add in everything that was going on with the Black Lives Matter protests and Trump and all his bullshit and January 6 and... well, everything went to hell in a handbasket. And it didn't stop. It didn't let up. And you weren't here. No, you were lucky enough to be living in a place that seemed to be shielded from COVID, and you didn't have all the other political stuff to deal with. No, your life was just peachy keen. You were making new friends and spending your Sundays on sailboats sipping cocktails with other gay guys. And I'll admit – I resent you for it. For the last year and a half, I've been angry and jealous and resentful and, most of all, lonely. I felt abandoned. You remember at our wedding when we said, 'for better or for worse?' Well, worse came and you weren't here."

Ryan scooted closer to Aaron and put his hand on his shoulder. Aaron shuddered ever so slightly, so Ryan took his hand away. "I'm sorry. I get that. I really do. I'm sorry you had to go through all of that. But what did you expect me to do? Ditch my assignment and come home and go through all that stuff too? Would that have changed anything in the world around you?"

"It wouldn't have changed anything in the world, but it would have made a big difference at home. At least I would have had you. And yeah, I guess if you came home it would have ruined your chance to get promoted. But what really pushed me over the edge was when your assignment kept getting extended and ended up being two years. It's like, during the first year, at least I could tell myself, 'Just hang on. He'll be home in a couple of months.' But then, I didn't even have that anymore. And technically you asked me, but I knew that saying no wasn't an option."

"Yeah, that was wrong. But they didn't give me much choice, either. Since I was already so deeply involved, it made sense for me to continue until the project was finished. If they brought a new person in, it would have taken several months to get them up to speed."

"Okay, so it worked out well for you and your company. So what if I had to suffer? So what if our marriage suffered? None of that mattered to Technovations. And apparently it didn't matter to you, either."

Ryan took a deep breath. "Okay. I admit, it was a mistake. I should have come home after the first year. I guess I didn't realize how bad it was. But anyway... So here we are. How do we move on from here? How can I make things right again? How can we work through this and get back to normal?"

There was more Aaron had to say, but he decided this wasn't the time. He had laid out enough issues for the time being. He debated how he wanted to answer Ryan's questions. He knew, but he wasn't sure which words to use. He sighed. "I don't think things will ever get back to normal. We can't go back to how things were before the pandemic like none of this ever happened." He turned to face Ryan. "Earlier this year, after the huge surge of cases from the Omicron variant started tapering off and it looked like the worst of the pandemic was over, people started talking about getting back to normal. Some articles written around that time said things wouldn't ever return to how they were before the pandemic. We're forever changed. We won't get back to the way 'normal' used to be. Instead, things will settle into a 'new normal.'

"Okay. So what does this 'new normal' look like to you?"

"I don't know." *Well, I do, but...*

Ryan took a moment to process everything he had heard. "So, let's see if I have this right. You're angry and resentful that I went away for two years and left you to deal with the pandemic by yourself." Aaron nodded. "You say we're forever changed and we can't go back to how things were before I left." Aaron nodded. "You say we need to settle into a 'new normal,' but you can't describe what that is. And you can't identify anything I can do to make up for it or improve our situation."

"Yeah, that pretty well sums it up."

"Well then, if we can't come up with any solutions, maybe we need counseling."

Aaron seemed surprised by the suggestion, but he couldn't argue with it or object.

Ryan asked, "Is that something you would be willing to do?"

"Yeah, I guess so. What's it going to cost?"

He guesses so. And he's concerned about the cost. "Counseling is included in our benefits package at work. I think there's a small co-pay, like $10 or something. I'll get online tomorrow and check out the counselors in our network and see if any of them specialize in same-sex relationships."

"Okay."

"And I don't know about you, but I don't care what it costs. Saving our marriage is worth it." Ryan paused. "To me, anyway."

After a moment of awkward silence, they both realized that this was enough for one evening. Aaron stood up. "Well, I'm gonna go check my email and Facebook." He turned toward the door.

Ryan put some clothes on and went out for a long walk.

Nothing Seems Right

Thursday, September 9, 2021

At 4:30 on Thursday, Chris texted Ryan after he had finished his last interview.

Ryan hurried across the parking lot to the RH building. He arrived in four minutes. They shook hands, then exchanged a light hug. They talked as Ryan led Chris back to his building.

"So, how did it go?"

"Oh, man, what a long day! I am mentally and physically exhausted! I had two interviews in the morning, and then someone else took me to lunch, which was basically another interview. Then two more interviews and a meeting with someone in HR who went over all the benefits. Man, I am totally spent."

"Sounds pretty intense."

"It was! Like I had to be 'on' all the time! I felt like they were evaluating me every second I was in their presence. Everything from how I shook their hand, how I sat in the chair, and even how I asked if I could go to the bathroom."

"Well, I'm sure you made a very favorable impression. How do you think it went?"

"Pretty well, overall. A couple of times they'd ask me a really off-the-wall question and I'd have to take a minute to think about how to answer. But I think I did okay."

"That was the right thing to do. That's better than just blurting something out. So what did you think of the company? Interviews work both ways, you know."

"I'm impressed! It's totally different than working at the Capitol. Everyone was so organized and professional. In Washington, it's chaos all the time. And I guess I got used to it. Heck, I probably became part of it. But this seems so much different. It even looks different."

"Yeah, I'll bet it is."

They arrived at Ryan's building and he led him through the dining room. It was mostly empty, but a few people sat at tables having one-on-one meetings. "You want a soda?"

"Is the cafeteria still open?"

"No." Ryan led Chris to a restaurant-style soda fountain.

His eyes popped open. "You get free soda???"

"Yeah."

"Okay, then, I'll have a Diet Coke."

Once they had their sodas, Ryan led him to the second floor. "Welcome to Cubicle World." They arrived at Ryan's cubicle. He motioned for Chris to sit in the guest chair while he sat down in his swivel chair. "I have a few emails to finish before we can go."

"No problem. I need to chill for a bit anyway."

Fifteen minutes later, Ryan shut down his laptop, disengaged it from the docking station, and slipped into its carrying case. "Okay! Let's go."

As they walked toward the door, Chris said, "I can't get over how quiet it is here."

"Well, a lot of people are still working from home. I'm going to be working from home most days. But this is my first week back after being gone for two years and I'm starting on a new project. So I want to meet people in person whenever I can. Plus, you were going to be here today for your interviews."

They reached the parking lot. Ryan turned to Chris and asked, "Hey, you wanna go out somewhere for dinner?"

"Sure. Do you have a place in mind? I have no idea what's in this part of town."

"Yeah. Let me take you to my favorite place. It's called Kahuna's Tiki Paradise."

"Sounds exotic."

Ryan tapped on his phone for a few seconds. "It's in downtown Scottsdale. You can follow me. I just sent you the address in case we get separated."

Once they were seated in the restaurant and had placed their order for Mai Tais and the ceviche appetizer, Ryan asked, "So tell me honestly, and there's no wrong answer. If they offer you the job, do you think you'll take it?"

"Probably. Unless they give me a real low-ball salary offer."

"Oh, don't worry... They pay well and the benefits are great. Even if it's not quite what you were making in DC, remember that the cost of living is much cheaper here."

"Yeah, I got the whole rundown on the benefits when I met with the HR person. That was pretty impressive."

"But do you think you would enjoy the work?"

"Yeah, probably. It will be a lot different. But I'm ready for something different. It'll be good for my career. My biggest concern is the commute. It was almost 20 miles from our apartment to here."

"How was the traffic this morning?"

"It wasn't bad, but it was after morning rush hour. And a lot of people still work from home. After the pandemic ends, assuming it does, and traffic gets back to normal, I could see it taking me 30 to 40 minutes each way."

"Well, you and Seth are staying in an apartment he picked. Where does he work?"

"In Deer Valley, up in the north end of Phoenix."

"Maybe when you start looking for a house, you can find someplace in between. There are plenty of nice neighborhoods between here and there."

Chris's demeanor turned serious. "I don't know. Something tells me we should hold off on buying a house for the time being."

"Well, for one thing, we don't know if you're going to get a job offer from Technovations. And he moved out here, when? Back in May? So he probably has a one-year lease. So you have plenty of time to look."

"That's not what I mean."

Their food arrived, so they took a minute to enjoy the first few bites.

Chris said, "This is awesome! I can see why you like this place."

"Plus, the drinks are great. I always try to come while it's still happy hour and the drinks and appetizers are cheaper." Ryan glanced at the time on his phone. "It's ten 'til six. Do you want another drink before happy hour ends?"

"Definitely." *I may need it.*

Ryan made eye contact with their server and waved him over. The server asked, "How is everything?"

"Everything's great. We'd like two more Mai Tais."

"I'll get that order in now." The server smiled and hurried away.

Chris said, "Anyway, as I was saying... Things are kind of weird with Seth and me. I'm not sure what's going on. It's like ever since I got here I get the feeling he wishes I wasn't there." He paused while he finished the rest of his first Mai Tai. "It's like after living on his own for three months, he's decided he likes that better."

"Have you tried talking about it?"

"A couple of times. But he's like 'yeah, whatever.' Like he's okay with things the way they are, so if I have a problem I need to deal with it. It's like he's got himself all set up with an apartment and a job, so he's good."

"So it's all on you to adapt to what he wants."

"Exactly."

"So... it's none of my business, but... How's your love life?"

"What love life?"

"Well, okay. That answers that question."

"We haven't had much sex for the past several years. Of course, part of it was me being tied up with work so much. But now that I'm out here and I'm not working and we have more time together, I thought we'd time for that stuff. But I guess not."

The server delivered their second Mai Tais. Ryan tried to think of something to clink their glasses to, but he realized this wasn't the right moment. Chris picked up his drink and took a generous swig.

Ryan said, "I'm really sorry to hear that. I'm going through the same thing with Aaron. Things have been weird between us since I've been home."

"Yeah, I picked up on that at the party."

"You'd think after being apart for two years we'd be fucking non-stop for a week, but no. The two times we tried it, he couldn't even get it up. It's like I have to force him to even kiss me."

"Do you suppose he's having trouble with ED?"

"Maybe, but I doubt it. He's not in the mood."

"Is there something else on his mind, like work?"

"Yeah, he complains a lot about work. Either that or he's tired. But again, that's a result of work. But last Thursday night when he came home from band he was in a good mood so I thought, 'Okay, maybe tonight.' Things started out okay, but then he couldn't keep it hard. He rolled over onto his stomach and let me fuck him, but I could tell he wasn't into it. I was hoping it would be passionate and romantic! I wanted to make love to him! I didn't want to just use his asshole to get off."

Chris looked uncomfortable. Ryan suddenly remembered they were out in public. He glanced around. The nearest diners weren't that close and nobody was giving him the stink-eye, so he assumed nobody heard it. He lowered his voice and continued. "And last Saturday night after you left, we went out back and floated on a raft for a while. That's always gotten us in the mood in the past, but not that night. We ended up having a really painful conversation. He said he was angry and resentful toward me because I took that assignment in New Zealand and then it got extended for another year. I apologized over and over and said, 'Okay, what can I do to make it up to you?' And he couldn't come up with anything. He said things will never be the same again and we have to try to find some kind of 'new normal.' But he couldn't tell me what that would be. So I suggested that we go for counseling and he agreed. Our first appointment is tomorrow."

Ryan realized he had probably shared too much personal information with Chris. This was supposed to be a celebratory occasion and he had ruined it. He took a bite of his food and tried to think of how he could change the subject.

Chris looked at Ryan with empathy. "I'm really sorry to hear that. But at least you talked about it and you're getting counseling. I haven't had much luck getting Seth to talk. Everything seems okay to him."

"Maybe you two should try counseling. Do you know if counseling is part of Seth's benefits?"

"Probably, but I don't know."

"Well, if you get hired by Technovations, it's in their benefits. The guy I found lists same-sex relationships among his specialties. I guess we'll find out whether we like him tomorrow."

Chris sighed. "That's great, but I don't know if I could even get Seth to go to counseling. I guess I could ask."

They didn't say much as they finished their food.

The server brought their check. While Ryan was reaching for his wallet, Chris snatched it away. "This one's on me."

"Are you sure? I can at least pay for my half. Besides..." Ryan was about to tell Chris he shouldn't be expected to pay since he wasn't working, but that seemed awkward.

Chris sensed this was what Ryan was about to say. "I have plenty of money. I'm not down to my last dime. Besides, I want to thank you for referring me. I want to celebrate getting the interviews."

"Okay, but let me pay when we celebrate you getting a job – either at Technovations or somewhere else."

Chris handed the server his credit card. While they waited for him to return, Ryan said, "I'm sorry I dragged down our celebration with my tales of marital woes."

"Well, I did too. I think we both needed to vent."

The server returned with Chris's credit card and the charge slip. Chris added a tip and signed it. They left the restaurant and headed toward their cars.

Ryan said, "I know things haven't been going well since you moved out here. But I'm glad you're here."

Chris sighed. "Thanks. At least that makes one person."

"I'm glad that after all these years, we still feel comfortable enough that we can talk about stuff like this."

"Yeah, me too. I guess that's the sign of a true friendship – when years go by and you can pick up where you left off."

They reached their cars. While they hugged, Ryan whispered, "I really appreciate you."

"You too."

When they released each other, Chris said, "Don't worry. We'll get through this."

"I sure hope so. Call me anytime you want to talk."

"You too. I'm here for you."

They hugged and kissed each other again, then got in their cars and drove away.

A Concert in the Park

Sunday, October 3, 2021

On a perfect Sunday afternoon, Desert Pride Symphonic Band presented their first concert in a year and a half. Lee Parker, the Artistic Director, had selected a light, upbeat program of show tune medleys, pop tunes, and classic concert band literature – music that would have wide appeal to a diverse audience.

Ryan rode with Aaron and Brandon to the city park on the north edge of downtown Phoenix. The band members were required to be there at 3:00 for the 4:00 performance, but Ryan didn't mind getting there early. After the band finished warming up at 3:30, he circulated among his friends whom he hadn't seen in over two years and said hi. Nobody was kissing, but most people were comfortable with light hugs since everyone had to be vaccinated to participate in the band.

By 3:55, a considerable crowd had gathered. Most of the 240 folding chairs the city had provided were filled. Ryan had claimed three seats near the front – one for him and two for Chris and Seth. He stood up and scanned the walkways leading up to the large cement slab that served as the band's stage. He spotted Chris and Seth approaching and waved enthusiastically. They saw him and made their way to the seats he was holding for them.

Ryan and Chris hugged. Ryan hugged Seth, who returned his hug willingly if not enthusiastically.

Ryan asked Chris, "How was your first week at Technovations?"

"Great. I mean, I'm still meeting people and getting settled in. The first day was New Employee Orientation and I've been taking some online training courses since then. I'll get started on my first assignments next week."

"Yeah, I remember my first week. It was information overload! But you'll get into the swing of things quickly."

Chris looked around. "This is exciting! The band is bigger than I thought it would be. And look at this crowd!"

Ryan replied, "Yeah. They were surprised at how many people

showed up when they started having rehearsals back in July. I guess everyone was eager to see their friends, play music again, and get on with their lives."

Chris said, "I can't wait to hear how they sound. I've been practicing for two months and I don't sound too bad!"

"See? I told you it would come back. Seth, are you going to join the band too?"

"I dunno... I guess I'll see how they sound first."

All the band members had taken their seats. Lee was standing to the side, ready to make his entrance. Ryan, Chris, and Seth sat down.

***

After the concert, Chris was ecstatic. "Man, they were fantastic! I'm going to love this!"

Ryan said, "Yeah, they were really good, especially after not rehearsing for 15 months. But you know, the music's great and everything, but what I enjoy most is the people. You're gonna make so many good friends. C'mon, let me introduce you to some people."

Ryan led Chris and Seth up to the front. The band members were circulating among the crowd saying hello and accepting compliments from their friends. They headed for Aaron and Brandon first. Chris hugged them both and said, "That was awesome! You guys sounded great!"

Aaron said, "Thanks. I'm glad you came."

Brandon said, "So, does that mean you're going to join us?"

Chris grinned. "I can't wait!"

Ryan said, "Seth, I'd like you to meet my younger brother Brandon. Brandon, this is Chris's partner Seth."

They shook hands. Seth deadpanned, "I'd never guess he's your brother. Seriously, the resemblance is uncanny." Seth looked up at the 6'7" Brandon and smiled.

Aaron turned to Ryan and said, "We volunteered to help load the instrument truck. Meet you back here in fifteen minutes?"

"Sure. I'll probably help."

Aaron and Brandon excused themselves. Ryan introduced Chris and Seth to Lee Parker, who said he looked forward to seeing Chris at the next rehearsal. Ryan introduced them to Rob Chilcott, his friend and the trombonist who had invited Aaron to attend his first Desert Pride concert and subsequently guided him on his journey out of the closet.

Then Ryan heard a familiar queeny, campy voice call out, "Well... Look who's here! If it isn't our long-lost trumpet star, finally back from the land down under! Of course, I can only imagine *who* you've been down under."

That last comment took Ryan aback. Had Aaron told others about their temporary pause from being monogamous?

Ryan forced a smile. "Guys, this is Petunia. Petunia, this is Chris and his partner Seth. Chris is going to join the band on alto sax. We're still working on Seth."

Petunia curtsied and offered his hand to Chris, palm down and wrist limp. "Dahling, my pleasure. Any friend of Ryan's is a friend of mine." Chris gently shook his hand.

Then Petunia made eye contact with Seth. Suddenly, his demeanor shifted and the scene turned awkward. Petunia shed his effeminate persona and said, "Nice to meet you." He extended his hand and Seth shook it. Neither of them said anything else.

Petunia smiled and returned to character. "Well! I'll leave you boys to socialize. I need to say hi to some of my other fans and put my French horn away." And with that, he flitted away.

Chris turned to Ryan and said, "Petunia? What kind of name is that?"

"A self-inflicted one, apparently. His real name is Stephen. When Aaron went out to Raise! the Bar with the band after his first rehearsal, he commented on how many guys in the band were named Stephen. Then he said, 'Well, let me make it easier. You can just call me Petunia.' Since then, everyone has called him Petunia. He doesn't seem to mind."

"He's certainly, shall we say, *fabulous*."

"That he is. He's also the band gossip, so be mindful of what you say around him. But once you get used to him, he's a nice guy. And he's a great French horn player."

Most of the crowd had dispersed by now and the band members were putting their instruments away. Some were departing with their friends and others were loading the instrument truck.

Chris said, "Well, I guess we'll be on our way. Thanks for inviting us!"

They hugged and Ryan said, "I'm glad you came. And I'm looking forward to being in band together again!"

Ryan gave Seth a light hug. "Give it some consideration. It's been a great experience for me."

"I'll think about it." He seemed uncomfortable.

Chris and Seth headed back to their car and Ryan walked over to the instrument truck and pitched in to load it.

The Truth Will Set You Free

Thursday, October 7, 2021

At the next Desert Pride rehearsal, the band began working on their repertoire for the holiday concert in December.

As was the band's custom, the director asked the new members to stand up and introduce themselves. When it was Chris's turn, he stood and said, "I'm Chris Robertson. I moved here from Arlington, Virginia last month. I haven't played my sax since I graduated from college in 2012, so I guess it's been nine years. Anyway, I've been practicing, so I hope I don't sound too bad. As for something interesting about me, well... Ryan and I were best friends in high school. He and Aaron convinced me to start playing my sax again and join the band. And I have a partner named Seth. We've been together for 13 years." Chris sat down and people politely applauded.

During the break, Petunia approached Chris and said, "Hi. Welcome to Desert Pride. So you knew Ryan back in high school!"

"Yeah. He and I were best friends. Actually, we came out to each other and kinda turned into boyfriends."

"Kinda? How do you kinda have a boyfriend?"

"I don't know. I mean, we never really labeled ourselves, it just kinda turned into that."

"So what happened?"

Chris didn't want to get into the whole story with this person who Ryan said was the band gossip. "He moved away. Then we went to different universities and lost touch for a while. And once I got to the University of Maryland, I met Seth, and we've been together ever since."

"Is he the guy you brought with you to the concert last Sunday?"

"Yeah, that was him."

"Oh. How nice. Well, I need to visit the little boy's room before rehearsal starts again. We'll chat some more soon."

Chris sensed there was something Petunia wasn't telling him, but he had no idea what it might be. Petunia seemed a little strange anyway.

***

After rehearsal, Petunia walked up to Ryan. "Hi, Sweetie. I have an off-the-wall question for you. Do you know whether Chris and his partner have an open relationship?"

"I doubt it, but I don't know for sure. Why? Are you interested in him?"

"Oh, no, no. I was just curious."

Ryan frowned. That seemed like an odd question to ask, even for Petunia. He said, "If you really want to know, you could ask him."

"I just might." Petunia sauntered over to Chris. "Sweetheart, can we chat for a moment?"

Chris looked puzzled. "Yeah, I guess."

Petunia motioned for Chris to follow him into the courtyard. He led him to the opposite side where they could speak privately. "So did I hear you correctly when you said you and your partner just moved here last month?"

"Actually, Seth moved here several months ago. I stayed in Arlington until our condo sold and I got my work wrapped up. His family still lives here. He's wanted to move back for a long time."

"Ah. I see. So uh... I know this is an odd question to ask someone I've just met but... Are you and your partner in an open relationship?"

"No. Why?"

Petunia pulled his phone out of his pocket. He touched the screen a few times and then showed the phone to Chris. "Is that him?"

"Yeah. So... What's this about?"

Petunia sighed. "Honey, that's his profile on Grindr. When I saw him at the concert last Sunday, I recognized him from a few weeks ago when we hooked up."

"WHAT??? You had sex with my partner???"

Petunia took a deep breath. "I'm sorry. I would never have done it if I knew he was in a relationship. I never hook up with guys who are cheating on their partners. But his profile said he was single, and of course, I didn't know you yet."

Chris started pacing back and forth. Then he turned back to Petunia. "Do you have any idea if he's been hooking up with others too?"

"Grindr doesn't tell you that, but I've seen him online for two or three months. In fact, when I checked Grindr at around 6:30, he was on."

"So he was looking for someone to hook up with while I was here at rehearsal."

"It sure looks that way." Petunia put his hand on Chris's shoulder. "Honey, I am so sorry. I hate to be the one to break the news to you. But I figured if it was me and I had a partner who was cheating on me, I'd want someone to tell me."

Chris didn't say anything while this new reality set in.

Petunia said, "And again, I would never have hooked up with him if I knew he had a partner."

Chris said, "That's okay, I'm not upset with you. And yeah... I guess I should know."

Petunia walked back into the band room to pick up his French horn.

Most of the other band members were gone and the director was about to shut off the lights. Chris headed back into the band room to get his sax. Aaron, Ryan, and Brandon were waiting outside the door. Ryan asked, "What did Petunia want?"

Chris said, "Apparently, during the time Seth has been out here without me, he's been hooking up with guys on Grindr."

Ryan asked, "How did he know that?"

"He hooked up with him. Then he recognized him when he was with me at the concert last Sunday."

Aaron said, "That slimy piece of shit! Hooking up with someone else's partner?"

Chris said, "He didn't know. Seth said he was single. He didn't know until we met after the concert and I introduced him as my partner."

Ryan said, "Wow. That really sucks. I'm sorry."

"Yeah, me too."

Brandon said, "What are you going to do?"

"I guess I'm going to go home and confront him about it."

Ryan said, "Well, I hope it goes well. Or at least as well as such a conversation can go."

"Thanks. Suddenly, I'm not looking forward to going home."

Ryan hugged Chris. "Keep me posted. And you can call me anytime. I mean it. Anytime."

Aaron and Brandon hugged Chris and they all said goodbye.

Suddenly Single

Friday, October 8, 2021

At around 8:45 on Friday morning, Ryan received a text from Chris.

***

Chris's office was in the Regional Headquarters building, so it took Ryan five minutes to walk there. When he entered the room, Chris looked tired and despondent, almost on the verge of tears.

Ryan approached Chris with his arms open. Chris stood up and they hugged. Then they sat down and Chris began talking.

"I don't think I told you this last night, but Petunia said he saw Seth on Grindr before rehearsal yesterday, so he was looking for someone to hook up with last night. And apparently, he found someone, because when I got home he wasn't there. When he got home, he was surprised to see me. He said, 'Oh, I thought you and your friends would go to a bar or something afterward.'

"So I asked him where he had been. He said, 'Oh, just out with a friend.' And I said, 'Did you happen to meet this friend on Grindr?' He looked kinda surprised, but he said 'Yeah.' And he was like 'So what,' you know? So then I asked, 'Have you been hooking up with guys since you moved out here?' and he said, 'Yeah.'

"I said, 'What the fuck, man? Since when do we have an open relationship?' And he just laughed and said, 'I've had an open relationship for years. You've been too busy – or too blind and dumb to see it.' So yeah. For, like, the last five years, he's been whoring around on me."

Ryan said, "Aw, man, that really sucks. I can't believe he did that to you. Did he ever talk about wanting to have an open relationship?"

"There were a couple of times he wanted to have someone over for a three-way, but I always said no. So apparently he went ahead and hooked up with them on his own. After the first couple of times, he quit asking."

"Wow. I'm really sorry. But if he was that unhappy with your relationship, at least the sexual part of it, why didn't he talk to you about it? Maybe get counseling?"

"Well, even if we talked about it, my answer still would have been no. I'm just not interested in open relationships. I guess he figured, why bother? So he did it behind my back."

"Do you think it would have helped if you had cut back on work so you could be more available for sex?"

"I don't know. I think he was tired of me anyway. The spark hasn't been there for a long time. I think he wanted some fresh meat."

Ryan shook his head. "It must be tough to learn about all this stuff now and realize he's been dishonest with you for so long."

"You have no idea."

"If he was that dissatisfied, why didn't he just break up with you?"

"'Cause he's too much of a chicken shit. And why should he? I still served the purpose of paying half of the mortgage and the bills – more than half, actually, 'cause I made more money. And since I wasn't there much, it was a convenient living situation. But get this! That's why he wanted to move out here. Everything's cheaper out here. He could afford to have a place of his own here. He told me last night he didn't think I'd actually quit my job and move out here."

"So he was hoping you'd end the relationship because you didn't want to give up your career and move out here?"

"Exactly. And that way, I'd be the one to break up with him, not the other way around."

"Wow. What a shithead."

"I know, right? And now that I know everything he did, I wonder why I stayed with him as long as I did."

"Well, we all have 20/20 hindsight."

"I guess I was so committed to making the relationship work, I never considered breaking up to be an option."

"Sounds like he was a lot less committed than you were."

"Yeah. Now I know that's why he didn't want to get married. That should have been a big warning sign."

Ryan said, "Well, as painful as it is, I think breaking up with him was the right thing to do. I think you'll be a lot better off."

"Oh, definitely. But it still hurts."

"So what are you going to do? Are you going to stay here or move back to DC? Or something else?"

"I don't know. It just happened last night. I need some time to think about it. I like my job here, but it's only been two weeks. And I'm grateful to you for helping me get it. But I don't know, I might miss being part of the political scene. Although it's kind of nice to have a break from it. I suppose I shouldn't make any big decisions right away. I guess I'll stay in one of those extended-stay hotels for a few weeks until I decide. Then I'll either move back to DC or find an apartment here, closer to work."

Ryan frowned. "No, you won't."

"What do you mean?"

"Don't stay in some hotel for several weeks. That'll cost a fortune. Come stay with us."

"Thanks, but I couldn't impose on you like that. Besides, you already have Brandon living with you."

It's a four-bedroom house. It's over 2800 square feet. There's plenty of room for four people. We'll make it work."

"But what would we do with all my stuff?"

"We'll either store it in the garage or rent a storage unit."

"Well..."

"I insist. Seriously. Come stay with us. It will be good to have friends around you for support."

"There is that." Chris paused. The more he thought about it, the more appealing it sounded. "Well, okay. We'll give it a try. But if it gets too crowded or I'm too much of a downer for everyone, I'll go somewhere else."

"It'll be fine. So you'll stay at our house tonight. I've got an air mattress and a sleeping bag, and you can sleep in the music room. Tomorrow we'll rent a truck and get your stuff from Seth's place."

"Sounds like a plan." Chris stood up and walked around to Ryan's side of the table. Ryan stood up and they hugged. "Thanks for being so nice to me."

"I'm glad I can help."

"You know, it's funny. We were separated for so many years. Now, after only a month, you're already treating me like we're best friends. Like nothing ever changed."

"I never stopped caring about you."

They hugged again.

Ryan glanced at his watch and said, "Well, I'd better get back to my desk. I've got an 11:00 meeting I need to get ready for."

As they headed for the door, they looked at each other and smiled.

Family Night for Four

Sunday, October 10, 2021

It was a busy weekend. On Saturday, Chris rented a truck, and Ryan, Aaron, and Brandon helped him move his possessions out of Seth's apartment. Chris and Seth discussed who would get what in a surprisingly agreeable conversation. It was pretty clear-cut. Most of the things Seth brought with him when he moved earlier in the year would remain his, and Chris would keep the things he brought with him a month ago. Much of it was still in boxes.

Seth remained in his apartment while Chris, Ryan, Aaron, and Brandon loaded Chris's possessions into the truck. He wanted to make sure Chris didn't take anything that was supposed to remain with him, but he didn't lift a finger to help. Nobody said much.

Chris decided to rent a storage unit for most of his possessions. Brandon offered to let Chris store his boxes in the third garage stall. But Chris didn't want to displace Brandon's car so he declined.

Sunday, Ryan cleared some space in the music room closet. Chris unpacked his clothes and other things he would keep in his room.

For dinner, Ryan chose a menu of pulled pork with Kansas City barbecue sauce, cole slaw, and sweet potato fries. He figured that would be a welcome nod to their Prairie Village roots.

When Ryan told Chris dinner would be at 6:00, Chris said, "No way! You've gone to enough trouble for me already. I was planning to take everyone out for dinner to thank you for helping me move."

"Dinner on Sunday night is a tradition around here. It's like a family night. It's a chance for everyone to be together and catch up."

"Okay. But I'd like to take everyone out some other night."

"Deal. See you at around 6:00."

***

After everyone sat down and started eating, Chris said, "This is delicious! Just like Bateman's Barbecue back home."

Ryan said, "Thanks. It does lack a certain ambiance, though, like not having the employees screaming, 'May I help you?' every thirty seconds."

Aaron set his fork down. "Are you serious?"

Chris said, "Yeah. Whether there were customers at the counter or not. It was part of the charm, in its own weird way."

Brandon said, "And we wouldn't be drinking Jack and Gingers at Bateman's."

"There is that. Still, it's a nice throwback to home."

Ryan said, "I stopped calling Kansas 'home' a long time ago. Home is here now. But yeah, Bateman's was one of the few good things about living there."

Chris's mood lightened. "Remember that time we went into KC and visited those used record stores? Then we went to Bateman's for lunch and after that, I dragged you to the gay pride festival."

"How could I forget? You were like a kid who had just discovered Gay Disneyland, and, well, let's just say I didn't share your enthusiasm. Especially when we encountered those protesters."

"Yeah, you got pretty shaken up by that. But you have to admit, it was our first introduction to all the things the gay community had to offer."

"It's hard to believe now, but back then, I wasn't even ready to say I was gay, let alone be part of some community. You were all into getting gay T-shirts with rainbows on them and I wanted no part of that."

Aaron said, "I remember what it was like when I went to my first gay pride festival in San Diego. God, that was what? Five years ago? Hard to believe so much time has passed."

Ryan said, "Yeah, but San Diego Pride is a hundred times bigger than Kansas City's. KC's was pretty tame in comparison. There were only around thirty booths and they had this tiny stage. And there were probably no more than 300 people there. While we were there, this lesbian folk singer with a guitar was performing and they had a drag queen for the MC. I totally wasn't into it."

Another memory flashed into Chris's mind and he smiled. "That was a special day for another reason, too."

It took Ryan a moment, but then he remembered. "Oh, yeah." *Please, let's leave it at that.*

Brandon said, "And...? What happened?"

Chris blurted it out. "We were at my house, and my parents and older brother were out somewhere. We gave each other our first blowjobs."

Brandon said, "Cool! Did you guys ever do it at our house?"

Ryan said, "Oh, hell no! I was scared to death Mom and Dad would find out."

Aaron said, "That's funny. Earlier in the day, you weren't ready to say you were gay, but by the end of the day you were giving him a blowjob."

Brandon said, "I guess you can't say you're gay with your mouth full."

Everyone laughed except Ryan, who at least made a weak effort to smile.

Brandon asked, "How come you never told me?"

"Are you kidding? You were nine years old then."

"So? I already knew you and Chris were gay. And we talked about everything else."

"You've got to draw the line somewhere."

"Did you guys go all the way?"

Ryan sighed. "Only once. And then I had to run away. Now can we move on?"

Chris glanced at Brandon. "You know, I'm still trying to wrap my head around the fact that you're all grown up now. You're 6' 7" and a college graduate. I still look at you and remember you when you were nine years old. You were so cute back then."

"And I'm not cute now?"

"Of course you are. But now it's a more young adult kind of cute. I bet when you were in high school and college, you had girls hanging all over you."

"Yeah. You could say that." Brandon sensed this was not the right time to bring up his high school exploits, so he left it at that.

Chris didn't understand why the conversation had suddenly ended, so he tried to think of another topic to move them beyond the awkward silence. "Guys, I really appreciate all your help this weekend. I wanted to take you out for dinner tonight, but I didn't know about your Sunday dinner tradition until today. So I want to take you guys out sometime soon. How about Tuesday?"

Aaron said, "I have to work late that day. Wednesday would be better."

"Okay, Wednesday it is!"

Aaron said, "Thursday is Ryan's birthday, but that's band night. So this could be kind of a pre-birthday dinner."

Chris said, "And don't you two have an anniversary coming up? I know you got married in the middle of October. What was it, the 21st?"

Aaron said, "Yeah, the 21st. Good memory."

Chris said, "I'll never forget that day. I'm glad I came."

For a moment, nobody said anything. Then Chris said, "So do you have any plans?"

Ryan said, "Not yet. We'll think of something."

Everyone ate a few bites. Then Chris said, "Guys, I really appreciate you letting me stay here and making me feel so welcome. I know it's an inconvenience, but I expect it will only be for a few weeks until I decide what I want to do next."

Aaron said, "No problem. Glad we can help. What do you think you're going to do?"

"I don't know. Part of me wants to go back to Washington and continue my career there. But if I went back, I'd have to try to find a place to live on only my salary. It's so expensive there! I'd probably end up in some tiny apartment way out in the suburbs and have to commute in every day."

Brandon said, "Prices here are crazy too, especially since the pandemic started. When I graduated and got my job, I wanted to get an apartment and start saving for a down payment on a house, but rent is astronomical! So Ryan and Aaron are letting me stay here so I can save up some more. Of course, you probably make a lot more than I do."

"Yeah, it would make sense for me to stay in Arizona from a cost perspective. Plus, I have you guys. And I'm glad I'm playing my sax again. So there's all that."

Ryan said, "And wait 'til you live through your first winter here. You'll never go back to snow and ice and freezing temperatures again."

Aaron said, "That's true. And you should experience a full year of living here before you decide for sure. As Ryan said, winters here are great. But you should probably wait until you live through an Arizona summer before you make your final decision."

"Yeah, but I've been out here to visit Seth's parents several times during the summer. It wasn't that bad."

Brandon said, "Especially if you have a pool!"

Ryan started thinking about Chris swimming with them in the pool.

Would that mean everyone would wear swimsuits? Or would Chris join them in swimming naked? That would be interesting – and potentially awkward.

Everyone finished dinner and helped clear the table. Chris stayed behind while Ryan washed the air fryer basket he had used to cook the sweet potato fries.

Chris asked, "So how are you doing?"

"Pretty good. How are *you* doing?"

"Okay, overall. Actually, considering that my 13-year relationship just crashed and burned in a fiery blaze, I'm feeling pretty upbeat."

"That's good. But let me give you a bit of advice I got from a friend at work named Eddie. He's the guy I stayed with the summer I was an intern here. He broke up with his partner a year or so before that. He said that when you break up, you ride a high for the first few days or weeks. You're getting support from your friends. You're excited about the possibilities for what might come next. It's like an adrenalin rush. But then after that, you crash. The novelty of being single again wears off and you realize what you've lost – especially when it comes to holidays or birthdays or reminders of things you used to do together. So be prepared for that."

"Thanks. But back to you. How are *you* doing? There were a couple of awkward moments at the table when everyone suddenly stopped talking. It felt like everyone was putting on an act now that I'm around."

"Let's step out onto the patio." After they settled into patio chairs, Ryan continued. "As you know, Aaron and I have some issues we're working through. We've been seeing a marriage counselor once a week, but I don't think it's helping. I guess I didn't realize how bad it was for Aaron while I was gone."

"There have been a lot of stories in the news about how the pandemic and the political environment have impacted people. I'm sorry it hit so close to home."

"Thanks. Hopefully it will work out. But we're not making much progress."

They stood up and hugged.

Chris said, "Thanks again for letting me be here. I'm always available if you want to talk."

"Thanks. I'm glad you're here too."

While You Were Away

Saturday, October 27, 2021

Dinner on Saturday evening was awkward. Nobody said much of anything. Ryan and Aaron's counseling session yesterday didn't go well, and they didn't want to talk about it in front of Brandon and Chris. Brandon and Chris knew better than to ask.

There were some stilted attempts at small talk, but there was obviously an elephant in the room. Ryan said very little.

Chris noticed Aaron and Brandon making frequent eye contact.

After dinner, Chris went back to his room to catch up on email and Facebook. Given the dynamic in the house, he spent a lot of time in his room entertaining himself online.

After about an hour, he got up and walked into the kitchen to get a can of Diet Coke. Aaron and Brandon were sitting on the couch in the family room watching the *Kids in the Hall* reboot. They were laughing and swigging beers. They seemed relaxed and very comfortable together.

As Chris returned to his room, he passed Ryan's office. On impulse, he stopped and knocked on the door.

"Come in."

Chris entered and closed the door behind him. Ryan was sitting in front of his computer. He was playing a CD with calm music. Whatever was on his mind was clearly weighing him down.

"How're ya doin'?"

Ryan turned away from his computer to face Chris. He didn't attempt to smile. "Hangin' in there."

"So... I know this may be none of my business, but there's a weird dynamic around here. I can't figure it out. Does it have anything to do with me being here?"

Ryan shook his head.

"'Cause if it does, I'll leave. I can stay at one of those extended-stay hotels for a few nights until I find an apartment. I don't want to cause any problems here."

"No, no... It doesn't have anything to do with you at all. It's just... Well, sit down."

Chris took a seat in Ryan's lounge chair. Ryan turned the music down a notch, then swiveled his desk chair to face him. "So... As you know, while I was in New Zealand, Aaron and I grew apart. And while Aaron and Brandon were cooped up here at home during the pandemic, they grew together. It seems like Aaron's more bonded with Brandon than he is with me. I've been hoping this counseling would set us back on the right path, but it doesn't seem to be working."

Chris really didn't want to say what he had to say, but he knew Ryan needed to hear it. It was the sort of thing he wished someone would have told him about Seth. He took a deep breath. "There's something you need to know. On Wednesday morning after you left for work, I heard Aaron and Brandon talking in the kitchen. I guess they thought I was still asleep or I couldn't hear what they were saying... I don't know. Anyway, they were saying stuff like, 'When are we going to tell him?' and, 'We were going to wait until after his birthday but now that's come and gone,' and then, 'I don't know how much longer I can go on like this.' So, they're hiding something from you. I couldn't figure out what they were referring to, but when it was time for Aaron to leave for work, they said 'I love you' to each other."

Ryan thought for a moment. "Yeah, I see how that could sound weird, but of course they love each other. They're brothers-in-law, and they're really good friends. I don't know if you've listened to any of their podcasts, but they have such a natural, comfortable rapport with each other. So yeah, they're close. And I'm really happy about that. But obviously, Aaron and I have grown apart, and we need to get close again, too."

"So you don't think..."

"What? That they've been screwing or something? No! Brandon's straight."

Chris paused to gather the courage for what he needed to say next. "Well, what do you think it is that they're trying to figure out when to tell you? Ryan... I just saw them sitting in the family room a few minutes ago, watching TV. They were sitting pretty close together on that big couch. The way they were laughing and the way they seemed so comfortable together... They were interacting the same way I would expect a couple to interact. I've noticed that ever since I moved in."

Ryan said nothing. What Chris said was sinking in. Ryan started wondering if he might be right.

Chris said, "See for yourself. Go into the kitchen like you're getting a soda and look at them."

For a moment, Ryan didn't move. He didn't want to see it. He didn't want to know. But he knew he couldn't ignore it and make it go away. He got up and slowly walked toward the door.

He walked into the kitchen and glanced at Aaron and Brandon sitting on the couch watching TV. Their shoulders were touching. They were laughing and joking about the funny stuff happening on screen. They seemed so comfortable together – like he and Aaron weren't.

Ryan opened the fridge and pulled out a soda. Then he walked into the family room. "What're you watching?"

Brandon turned his head toward Ryan and said, "*The Kids in the Hall.* It's hilarious!"

"So, uh... Can you pause it for a second?"

They exchanged nervous glances. Brandon reached for the remote and pressed Pause.

Ryan sat down in the side chair and angled his body toward Aaron and Brandon. "I'm glad you two are getting along so well together. I guess living together during a pandemic will do that."

Aaron said, "Yeah, I guess it was either that or end up being at each other's throats."

Brandon said, "Working on the podcast together really helped."

Ryan said, "Yeah, it's obvious that you two have developed quite a ... rapport."

For a few seconds, nobody said anything. Brandon reached for the remote to turn the show back on.

Ryan said, "Not so fast." Brandon settled back onto the couch. "Is there something you guys have been meaning to tell me?"

Aaron and Brandon looked dumbstruck. Neither said anything.

"I understand you were going to wait until after my birthday, but that was two weeks ago. So tell me now."

Aaron and Brandon looked at each other as if to ask which one would say something. Brandon took the lead. "Well, actually, yes. So, uh... I've never actually told you this before... I haven't told anyone, really, except Aaron... but... I know that up to this point, you've just kind of assumed I'm straight and... well... I don't like to use labels, but let's just say my interests are a little broader than that."

"So you're gay."

"Well, not necessarily. As I said, I don't like to use labels. I mean, I had girlfriends in high school, or at least girls who were friends. And yeah, I've had sex with women on numerous occasions."

"Yes, as I recall you were quite popular in high school, sexually speaking."

"Yeah. And actually, there was a guy in high school I messed around with a few times."

"So you're bi."

"I guess. But as I said, I'm not really into labels. I'm more interested in people for who they are, not so much for which set of genitalia they have."

"I see. How open-minded of you."

"Yeah, I guess that's a good way to put it. I try to be open-minded. I want to leave myself open to whatever possibilities may come along and not limit myself one way or the other."

Ryan stared at Aaron. Aaron stared at the coffee table, not wanting to make eye contact. Ryan waited to see what either of them would say next. They didn't say anything, so Ryan turned back to Brandon. "And since you were isolated here in this house for the last year and a half, the only 'possibility' that came along was Aaron."

Aaron squeezed Brandon's leg above his knee. "Yes. That's right. Brandon and I have grown very close over the past couple of years. He's been the emotional support I've needed to get through all this shit that's been going on. You have no idea how hard it's been, Ryan. He's the only reason I haven't gone totally insane. He was there for me..." He stopped himself before he said, "...when you weren't." Everyone felt it anyway.

"I see. I can only imagine how *hard* it's been." Ryan waited to see if either of them would say something. They didn't. "So, by chance, was this so-called emotional support delivered *in bed*?"

Aaron replied, "At first, it was just hugging, which I really needed. But then, yeah, it kinda moved on to other things."

Ryan sprang up from his chair. "JESUS FUCKING CHRIST! I CAN'T FUCKING BELIEVE THIS!" He turned to Brandon. "YOU FUCKED MY HUSBAND!"

Brandon stared at the coffee table.

"Look at me! YOU. FUCKED. MY. HUSBAND!"

Brandon nodded.

Ryan turned to Aaron. "And you cheated on me! WITH. MY. BROTHER!"

Aaron said, "I never meant for it to happen..."

"YOU BROTHER FUCKER! How long has this been going on?"

"Probably about a year."

Brandon said, "Yeah. Almost exactly a year."

Ryan said, "That would have been right around our anniversary."

Aaron said, "Yeah. After we got off our Zoom call, I had a breakdown. I was so upset that you weren't here and we had to celebrate our anniversary by talking to each other on a screen. And I had a really bad day at work and there was all this terrible shit going on in the news–"

Ryan interrupted. "And there was Brandon, ready to comfort you with a hug ... and a nice hot fuck. And on our anniversary, no less! God, how could this get any worse?"

Aaron said, "I'm really, really sorry, Ryan. I know it was wrong. I just–"

"BULL! SHIT! ... BULL! FUCKING! SHIT! You are *not* sorry. If you did it once, like you were drunk or something, but then you regretted it and never did it again, I could accept you saying you're sorry. But you guys have been doing this for a year! So no. You are *not* sorry. You're *not* fucking sorry. You're just sorry I found out. And you're sorry I came back home and interrupted your hot, torrid love affair."

Aaron said, "No, Ryan! I'm glad you're back home! It's what I've wanted all along. I wish you had never left."

"So this is my fault, huh? For going off on this work assignment. So that I could advance my career and earn more money so we could have a nicer life."

"Ryan, we didn't need more money. We had a nice life already. Everything was fine the way it was."

"That's not what you've been saying in counseling. Apparently, I have too much baggage from my past. Apparently, I'm not exciting enough. Apparently, Brandon's a lot more fun to be around."

"I didn't mean it that way."

"Well, if you didn't mean it that way, why did you say it?"

Aaron didn't have an answer for that, so he deflected. "The bottom line is, you put your career before our marriage. Your advancement was more important than me."

For a moment, no one said anything.

Then Brandon added, "Just like Dad."

That punch landed below the belt. Being compared to his estranged father stunned Ryan. He searched for a way to turn this confrontation back to his advantage. "Wait a minute. If you guys have been banging each other since our anniversary last year, that means last Thanksgiving when you suggested that you and I could have fun with other people while we were apart, you two had already been fucking for a month."

Neither of them said anything.

"So then you could say I gave you permission to fuck. And if I did it too, we'd be on equal footing. Is that it? God, I knew something was fishy when you brought that up, but never in my worst nightmares did I imagine you'd be fucking each other. And what if I had said no? Would you guys have kept fucking anyway?" Ryan paused. "I think we all know the answer."

Aaron and Brandon stared at the floor and remained silent as Ryan towered over them.

"Jesus Christ. I can't fucking believe it. I go away for two years, and I can't trust my husband and my brother not to fuck each other? How fucking sick is that? And you kept at it for a year! And if fucking each other wasn't bad enough, you fell in love. I mean, it would be bad enough if you were just getting off with each other, but NO! You're fucking in love. Now I know why you have so much trouble getting it up for me."

Aaron looked up and scowled at Ryan. "You didn't have to go there."

"Are you fucking serious? Neither did you."

Aaron and Brandon knew there was nothing they could say.

Ryan folded his arms across his chest and shook his head. "You disgust me. Both of you."

Brandon said, "I'm sorry. I guess I should move out."

"Why don't you take him with you? Then you two can live happily ever after without me in the way."

Ryan took a few steps toward the garage. Then he turned and glared at them. "I can't even. I can't. Fucking. Even." He stormed out the door and slammed it behind him. Aaron and Brandon heard the garage door open. Ryan's car started and the door closed again. They remained on the couch, unsure what to say or do next.

Finally, Aaron said, "Well, at least that's over with."

"That went a lot worse than I thought it would."

"Seriously? There's no way it could have gone well. There's no way that could have been anything but a disaster."

"Yeah, I guess you're right. At least we won't have to hide it anymore."

"Like that's supposed to make me feel better? I guess I should feel relieved, but I don't. I feel like shit."

"Yeah. So do I. I guess tomorrow we should go back to that apartment complex we looked at on Hayden and see if they have any vacancies."

Aaron nodded. They stood up. They hugged each other, but there was no joy in it.

Chris, still in Ryan's office, closed the door quietly.

He got out his phone and texted Ryan.

> I'm really sorry. Are you gonna be okay? Do you want to talk?

Three minutes later, Ryan texted back.

> I need some time to cool off. Maybe later.

Slush Fun

Saturday, October 27, 2021

Half an hour later, Ryan texted Chris.

> I've calmed down a little. We can talk if you still have time.

> Of course! Are you coming back?

> I'll swing by and pick you up in five minutes. Meet me out front.

> OK

Chris grabbed his wallet and keys and let himself out through the front door. He stood by the curb. Ryan drove up and stopped long enough for Chris to get in. Chris could see that Ryan had been crying. He put his hand on Ryan's thigh and squeezed it. "So where to?"

"I don't know."

"You know the area better than I do. Are there any gay bars around here?"

"There's one in downtown Scottsdale, but I don't want to go to a bar. I want to go someplace where we can talk in private."

Chris thought for a moment. "I know! They have Slush Fun out here, don't they? Is there one somewhere in this area?"

"Yeah, I think I know where one is. Let's ask Siri." Ryan picked up his phone and asked, "Siri, where is the nearest Slush Fun?"

Siri replied, "A slush fund is a fund or account used for miscellaneous income and expenses, particularly those which are corrupt or illegal."

"Siri, cancel!"

Chris chuckled.

Ryan tried again. "Siri, where is the nearest Slush Fun drive-in restaurant?"

"Here's what I found."

Ryan looked at the route and said, "Yeah, I was pretty sure that was the closest one." He set his phone down and started driving. "You know, I haven't been to a Slush Fun since the night we got caught kissing in that hidden parking lot."

"Too many bad memories, huh?"

"No, they were good memories, up until that moment. Maybe that's the reason. If I went there, I'd think of all the good times we had. It was always a you-and-me thing, and it wouldn't be the same without you."

"Awww... Thanks."

"I mean it."

Chris said, "I went to one in Northern Virginia a few times, but it's been years. And yeah, it wasn't the same."

"They had them in LA. But I remember one time, not long after I got there, I was having kind of a date with this guy–"

"*Kind* of a date?"

"We went out for coffee. It only lasted, like, fifteen minutes. I didn't know whether that counted as a date or not. Anyway, I mentioned Slush Fun and he looked at me like, 'You actually go to that place?' And my friend Ted was into healthy eating, so I knew he wouldn't go. So I never had anyone to go with."

"Besides, why go to Slush Fun when you can sip wine naked in a hot tub?"

Ryan smiled for the first time in hours. "There is that."

They pulled into Slush Fun and looked at the menu board. Ryan said, "So what chemistry-lab flavor are you going to get? Looks like they still have blue coconut, but I don't see mint chocolate banana or any of those other disgusting flavors you used to order."

"They have cranberry!"

"Gross. The only thing more gross than that would be cranberry mixed with blue coconut."

"That sounds awesome! I'll try that."

"Bleeecccchhhh...."

The disembodied voice on the squawk box asked, "May I take your order?"

Ryan said, "I'd like a large cherry-limeade slushie and my friend would like cranberry mixed with blue coconut."

The voice replied, "Bleeecccchhhh...."

Ryan and Chris howled.

The voice asked, "Would you like any food to go with that?"

Ryan turned to Chris. "You want anything?"

"Yeah, how about an order of chili-cheese tater tots, just for old-time's sake?"

Ryan said to the box, "And an order of chili-cheese tater tots."

Moments later, their food was delivered and they took the first sip of their slushies. Chris grimaced. "Oh my God! This is disgusting."

"See, I told you. And they're sooo sugary. Did we really enjoy these back when we were in high school?"

"And what's up with these tater tots? They're so greasy!"

Ryan said, "You sound like my mother. She always hated that we ate here."

"And this runny cheese shit is nasty!"

"I guess we shouldn't expect much from something that comes out of a pump dispenser."

They took a few more bites and slurps. Chris said, "They've sure gone downhill since we used to eat here."

"Maybe they're using cheaper ingredients to cut costs."

"Or maybe we just didn't care. Maybe our tastes have become more sophisticated as we've grown older."

Ryan sighed. "We were 17 back then. I just turned 32. God, that was almost half a lifetime ago. How did that happen?"

"I'm right behind you. My 32nd birthday is coming up in February." Chris paused. "I always had a thing for older men."

Ryan smiled at Chris and chuckled. Every little bit of humor helped.

A moment of silence passed while they nibbled on their tater tops and slurped their slushies.

Then Chris said, "Look at us. Over 30. Two failed relationships. Sitting here eating horrible junk food like we're teenagers. How did we get here?"

"Well, we got in my car, drove south on Hayden and–"

Chris playfully slapped Ryan's arm. "Silly. You know what I mean."

"I guess I've grown up but my sense of humor hasn't."

"Pretty soon, you'll be telling dad jokes."

"Hey, I like dad jokes. You should meet Aaron's dad. He tells the worst jokes ever. I love it! Aaron always rolls his eyes and groans, but secretly I think he loves them too." Ryan sighed. "I really like Aaron's parents. They're just plain folks, real salt of the earth. But they're so kind and generous and loving. I remember the first time I went to Ohio with Aaron for Christmas. I wasn't sure how that was going to go. When Aaron came out to them earlier that year, they didn't handle it well. They were hard-core religious, like my folks. Aaron didn't talk to them for two months. But they came around, and when I arrived for Christmas they treated me like I was part of the family. Brandon came with us and they welcomed him with open arms too. His mom even had stockings for us. She is so sweet! She's everything you want a mom to be. His dad's a real character. He loves to tease people. Like when he picked us up at the airport, he looked up at Brandon and me and said, 'How's the weather up there?' And then he asked Aaron, 'How do you kiss him? Do you have to stand on a stepstool?'"

Chris laughed. "He sounds like quite a character."

"Oh, he is. But in the nicest possible way. He's kind of crude and crusty on the outside, but he's really warm and kind on the inside. And they both love Aaron so much. And as soon as Brandon and I arrived, they loved us too. That was the nicest Christmas I ever had. There was so much love in that house. Everyone was so kind and..." Ryan took a moment to search for the right word. "Genuine. Authentic. It was so much different than my family, where everything was always so proper and emotionless. It's like we were all just playing our roles, going through the motions, acting like a family. I didn't realize it then because that was just how it was, you know?"

"I know what you mean. I could feel it whenever I went over to your place."

"Yeah. It was so much different at your house. I always felt so comfortable there. Your parents were so cool. And I could tell how much they loved each other. I remember how they would go on date nights, then come home and disappear into their bedroom. And they'd have their friends over for games that were sometimes kind of raunchy. My parents would never have done anything like that. But to your folks, it was no big deal. They laughed and had fun. They weren't all hung up about stuff like my parents."

"Yeah, I sure lucked out with my parents. Like when I came out to them, they were totally supportive."

"Yeah, I remember. And when my parents found out ... well, we know how that turned out. But anyway, after spending Christmas with the Bradburys, I could see how empty my family was. I mean, I know my parents loved me on one level, but..." Ryan left that thought hanging. He didn't want to finish that sentence. A tear ran down his cheek.

Chris reached over and held Ryan's hand. "Yeah, I remember meeting Aaron's parents at your wedding. They seemed like really nice people. His dad looked like he was so proud to be Aaron's best man. And that reading his mom gave was really touching. I could tell they were thrilled that you two were getting married."

Ryan sighed. "I wonder how they'll react when they learn what happened."

"Do they really need to know?"

"Well, assuming Aaron and Brandon continue being a couple, they'll have to tell them sooner or later. I'm sure his folks will wonder what led up to that."

"So, you don't think you and Aaron will be able to work things out?"

Ryan sighed. He turned his head away from Chris and stared out the car window as if the answer could be found somewhere in the restaurant's parking lot. Finally, he said, "I don't know. We've been seeing that counselor, but I think that's making it worse. It's bringing all of our problems out into the open and shining a spotlight on them. Like, let's focus on everything that's wrong with this relationship. I always thought our relationship was fine. At least it was before I went to New Zealand. I mean sure, there would be little things here and there, like with any couple. But I'd just let them go and move on. The good stuff always far outweighed the bad."

Ryan sniffled. He reached for the tissue box on the floor behind his seat. He pulled out a tissue and blotted his cheeks. "Now, in hindsight, I can see that everything was set into motion when I went to New Zealand. He didn't want me to go, but he relented when he saw how much I wanted it. It was supposed to help my career advancement, which would ultimately benefit both of us, you know? But he didn't care about that. He wanted us to be together."

"Well, you can't fault him for that."

"Yeah, I know. It made it look like I valued my career more than our marriage. So right off the bat, that caused resentment. But then, who knew COVID was going to come along? Since New Zealand had the good sense to isolate itself when it first started, we had almost no COVID there. It was something we read about in the rest of the world. I had no idea how much psychological damage it was causing people here, along with all the Black Lives Matter riots and the whole Trump thing. It was really rough for Aaron at his job because he couldn't work from home. He had to go in and be exposed to all those people. I didn't realize how bad it was. And it only made matters worse when I had to stay for another year. So that left Aaron and Brandon trapped at home together for almost two years, and... Well, basically, they bonded. And Aaron and I became un-bonded if that's a thing."

"And who even knew Brandon was gay?"

"I know, right? Or bi or pansexual or whatever. Anyway, you see how they interact. They're like two peas in a pod. In our counseling session yesterday, Aaron said I was too serious. I'm too jaded or damaged from what happened in the past. I can't let loose and just have fun. I guess Brandon's a lot more fun than I am."

Chris said, "In high school, you were shy and introverted. And I remember Brandon was always so outgoing and effusive. Almost hyper."

"Yeah. And so there you have it. He's more fun to be around than I am. More upbeat and light-hearted. I like to think I've moved on from everything that happened in the past. But apparently, I still carry a lot of that baggage with me. I guess I'm just damaged goods."

"Oh, stop! Don't talk like that! You are *not* damaged goods! Yeah, you've had some bad stuff happen to you. Yeah, you used to do porn. But you're still a good, decent person. And look at how successful you are now! After everything you've been through, you're the strongest person I know."

"Thanks."

"I mean it. But yeah, I know what you mean about feeling like you're damaged goods. In a lot of ways, our situations are similar. I prioritized my career over my relationship. Hell, I worked 50 or 60 hours a week, and even when I wasn't at work I'd always be thinking about it. I was pretty stupid not to see what was happening right under my nose. At first, I thought he started whoring around when he moved to Glendale and I stayed behind in Arlington. But then I learned he was fucking half of DC while I was so wrapped up in my work. I was never home. He could hook up with guys every night of the week if he wanted to. Hell, when I told our friends back east why we broke up, they said they thought we had an open relationship. It was that obvious! To everyone except me, of course."

"I hope he didn't give you anything."

"Oh, I got tested as soon as I found out. Thankfully, I'm negative. But the other thing is, even putting work aside, I wanted the relationship more than he did. I wanted us to be a permanent, monogamous couple. I guess he just wanted us to be roommates with benefits. But enough about me. Our relationship is officially over and done with. Back to you. If Brandon and I moved out and you and Aaron spent more time together, you could re-bond?"

"I doubt it. But it's not really about re-bonding. It's about who he loves more and who he'd rather be with. And, well, you see how they are. They're totally in love. Aaron went along with getting counseling, but I don't think he wants me back." Ryan sighed. "I've lost him, Chis. I've lost him."

Ryan stared straight ahead as if he could see Aaron disappearing into the horizon. A few tears ran down his cheek. He reached for another tissue and wiped the tears from his face.

They sat in silence. Chris tried to think of something to say that might help. He came up empty. There was probably nothing left to say. They wallowed in the hopelessness of their situations for a few moments longer.

Then Chris turned and looked at Ryan. Sensing this, Ryan turned and looked at Chris. Their eyes met.

Chris reached over and held Ryan's hand. "I love you."

"I love you too."

For a moment, they gazed at each other. They saw the sadness, pain, and brokenness reflected in each other's eyes. At the same time, they could still see a remnant of two 17-year-old boys – best friends feeling silly, horny, and in love.

They leaned into each other and kissed. They were quick kisses at first, but then they grabbed each other's shoulders, pulled themselves together, and opened their mouths.

Chris's kisses were just as passionate and delicious as Ryan remembered. For a few minutes, Ryan was transported back to high school. He remembered how kissing Chris felt so exciting and thrilling, especially since their feelings for each other were a special secret only they shared. For a few minutes, he forgot about the pain and disappointment of his failed marriage.

They stopped, knowing they couldn't progress farther since they were parked at a drive-in restaurant.

They sat in blissful silence for a moment. Then Ryan said, "Just think.

If I had been willing to kiss you in the car at Slush Fun back in Kansas, we probably wouldn't have gone to that deserted parking lot. We wouldn't have been caught by that cop, and my parents wouldn't have found out I was gay. Hell, if I had been willing to kiss you at Slush Fun, none of this would have happened and we could have been together all this time."

Chris thought about that. "Yeah, maybe. But we can't go back and change it. Besides, your parents probably would have found out sooner or later anyway."

"I suppose. Still, I wish we could have been together for the last 14 years."

"Me too. Think how much different everything would have been."

They finished their slushies, each trying to figure out the right words to move the conversation forward. Finally, Chris said, "Over the past 14 years, there was rarely a day when I didn't think about you. In my head, I knew I needed to move on. And I did, but... Well, I guess I've always had a special little place for you in here." He placed his left hand in front of his heart.

Ryan smiled. "Same here. That's why I never had much luck with dating. I'd meet a guy, and he'd be nice and everything, but something inside always said, 'He's no Chris.' I knew I'd never find anyone as good as you. Aaron came close. When he and I started getting serious, I thought maybe he'd be the one who would finally get me over you. In fact, he reminds me of you in some ways. That was part of his appeal. But I guess that didn't help, because it meant I'd always be reminded of you."

Ryan reached for Chris's hand and held it. They sat in silence. Chris glanced at Ryan, who was staring straight ahead, lost in thought. Chris allowed him a few minutes to think, then asked, "Whatcha thinkin'?"

Ryan turned to face Chris. "I'm thinking about our current situation. I'm thinking about the future. We both know we belong together. We're soulmates. We're joined at the heart. We've lost 14 years of our lives, and we can't do anything about that. But we can do something about the rest of our lives. This is our chance! This is our chance to finally have the life we want – together. And I have no intention of letting this chance pass me by."

Tears were streaming down Chris's face. Ryan said, "I love you, Chris Robertson. There's never really been anyone else. There will never be anyone else. It's only you." He paused. "So yeah, that's what I was thinking."

Chris threw his arm around Ryan's shoulder and kissed him. "I love you too. I want nothing more than to spend the rest of my life with you. I don't care where – here, or back in DC, or in New Zealand, or wherever. As long as I'm with you."

They hugged, as much as they could, sitting next to each other in a car.

Chris said, "Okay, so what do we do next?"

"Well, there's the inconvenient little fact that I'm still married. So I guess we need to cross that bridge first."

"How do you think you're going to handle that?"

"I think Aaron and I need to have a heart-to-heart talk. Actually, if I handle this right, this could be a win for all of us."

"Let's hope so."

Ryan said, "So, are we through here? Wanna head back home?"

"Sure. And I know what I want to do once we get there."

Ryan chuckled. "Yeah, me too, but we need to wait until tomorrow after I've talked to Aaron."

"Yeah, you're probably right."

"We've waited 14 years, we can wait another day."

Change

Sunday, October 24, 2021

On Sunday morning, Ryan woke up before Aaron. As he lay in bed, he replayed the conversation he had yesterday evening with Chris.

He looked at Aaron, sleeping on his left side, facing him. He looked adorable. Ryan still loved Aaron despite all the relationship problems they had been experiencing the past few weeks. Last night, he was confident of his decision that he belonged with Chris. At the same time, he was aware of the seriousness of the action he was about to take. He felt sad that his first marriage would end in divorce. It was hard not to take that as a personal failure. Ryan knew he needed to have a difficult conversation with Aaron, and it needed to happen today.

Ryan decided to go for a run. He quietly slipped out of bed and stepped into the master closet to put on his running gear. As he passed back through the bedroom, Aaron was still sound asleep.

As he ran, he generated more questions than answers.

Should I really divorce Aaron? Overall, we've had far fewer problems than many couples who stay together through thick and thin. Shouldn't we stay together and tough it out?

Is it right to leave somebody because somebody better came along? When you get married, aren't you promising your spouse you won't do that?

But then, shouldn't fucking my brother and falling in love with him be sufficient grounds for divorce? How much should I be expected to forgive? Can we work through this if we try hard enough? This would be easier if the person Aaron cheated with was somebody he could separate from and never see again.

Ryan ran five miles before it occurred to him to take a break. He found a grassy spot under a tree, sat down, and pulled out his water bottle. After he took a few drinks, he lay down on his back. He stared up at the leaves of the tree. It was a perfect sunny day. A light, refreshing breeze blew across his perspiring face and body. His body might be taking a break, but his mind

150

wasn't.

Here's another thing. Chris has been back in my life for only two months, and living with us for only a month. We're getting along great, and the magic we felt in high school is still there. But we've changed. I've certainly changed. We've had a lot of different experiences over the past 14 years. Do we really know each other as who we are today? Shouldn't we take time to find out?

And another thing. Chris only broke up with Seth a month ago, after being together for 13 years. Assuming I break up with Aaron, are we foolish to rush right into another relationship? Shouldn't we take time to heal?

Ryan stood up and started running back toward home. The more he hashed everything out in his mind, the more he knew that separating from Aaron was the right thing to do. Aaron belongs with Brandon, and he belongs with Chris. But they need to allow at least a year before they get married.

He rehearsed what he would say to Aaron. By the time he got home, he was ready.

***

As the day progressed, Ryan grew more comfortable with his decision.

At around 2:00, he retreated to his office. He sat quietly and tried to calm himself in preparation for the discussion he was about to have.

Then he left his office and went looking for Aaron. He and Brandon were in the family room watching TV. Ryan stood near the back of the room until a commercial came on, then he came forward.

Ryan said, "Hey, Aaron... could we talk for a moment when you get to a good stopping point?"

Aaron looked at Brandon. "Okay... I guess now's a good time." He stood up and followed Ryan into his office.

Once they were seated, Ryan said, "I've been thinking a lot about us and our situation."

"Yeah, me too."

"In fact, it's been about the only thing on my mind. So, let me ask you something. And be honest here. Do you think our counseling is helping?"

Aaron hesitated. "Well... not really."

"Me neither. It's like it's dredging up every little thing that's wrong with our relationship, rather than helping us work through our issues."

"Yeah, I'd say that's accurate."

"I admit, our marriage hasn't been perfect. No marriage is. We've had little problems here and there. But I think we've done a good job of dealing with things as they came up and then moving on. Wouldn't you agree?"

"Yeah."

"So I don't think what we need is to identify problems. I think the better question is, can we recapture the magic? It seems to me that – and I'm just being honest here – you're more attracted to Brandon than me. In terms of personalities, you two seem to be a better fit. You two connect in a way that you and I don't anymore. And I'm guessing you probably connect better in bed, too. If not, you wouldn't have done it so many times. And let's face it... since I've been home, it's obvious that the magic between us isn't there anymore."

Aaron squirmed in his chair. "Yeah, you're pretty much right about all of that."

"So is it even worth continuing to try?"

"I don't know... I feel really bad. I know what I did was wrong. I shouldn't have slept with him. I shouldn't have even kissed him the way we did that night it all began. But at the time, I felt lonely and sad and, well, angry. I know that doesn't excuse it or justify it. What I did was wrong. And I feel terrible about it."

"I understand why you felt sad, lonely, and angry. And that was my fault – for taking the assignment in the first place, then agreeing to extend it. But it happened, and we need to deal with it. But the fact remains that you two bonded. You became attracted to each other. You fell in love. Those feelings you developed for each other would probably have happened even if you didn't have sex."

"Yeah. But again, I let it happen."

Ryan said, "We've been together over five years and married for four. And yes, I realize we were having sex less frequently and it wasn't always as exciting as it was in the beginning. I guess it's only natural that the initial thrill would wear off after a while."

"I think it's that way with all couples. But I see what you're saying. Maybe my interest in Brandon was more about having fresh, exciting sex again. And who knows if the same thing will happen to us in five years?"

"I think another factor is that we got together pretty soon after you came out. I remember how much fun you had during Gay Pride weekend in

San Diego. Maybe, in hindsight, it was too soon for you to settle down with one guy."

"Yeah, maybe." Aaron thought for a moment. "But I don't want to be promiscuous all the time either. And you know, the reason I fucked around so much that weekend was that I was frustrated with you because we weren't having sex yet."

"So it's like you were having revenge sex in both cases."

"I guess. But San Diego was different. Those were just hook-ups. That's not the case with Brandon."

"Regardless, here we are now. What are we going to do? Is there any hope that we can rekindle the fire? Can we move past this and fall in love with each other again? Or is it hopeless at this point?"

Aaron said, "But I do love you. That's the thing. It's not like I hate you now, or even that I love you any less. And that means we shouldn't give up on our marriage so easily. I keep thinking that we owe it to ourselves to work through this. We shouldn't just quit when the going gets tough."

"Yeah, I know what you mean. Deciding to get a divorce would be a lot easier if we didn't love each other anymore. But I think it all boils down to this: No matter how much we try to revive our relationship and how hard we try to stay together, in the back of your mind would you still wish you could be with Brandon?"

Aaron stared at the floor, unable to answer. But Ryan wasn't going to say anything else until he did. Finally, Aaron said, "Yeah, probably."

"And now that Chris is back in the picture, it's the same with me." Ryan paused. Aaron didn't say anything. "Look at me." Aaron slowly raised his head and made eye contact. Ryan could see the pain, shame, and sadness in his eyes. Ryan scooted forward in his chair to be closer to Aaron. He reached out and held his hands. "I love you. And when you love someone, you want what's best for them. In our case, it's clear that you should be with Brandon instead of me. So I'm letting you go."

"But... but..."

"It's okay. I'm good with it. I want you to be happy, and clearly you'll be happier with him than with me."

"But what about you?"

"Well, I'll be honest with you. I have an opportunity now that I haven't had for 14 years. Chris and I talked last night. We want to see if we can pick up where we left off. We both realize that with him recently out of a 13-year relationship and assuming we end our marriage, it's the worst possible time to think about getting into another relationship. We know we need to allow ourselves time to heal. There are a lot of things we need to talk about before we move forward with getting married. We've both changed a lot since we were high school kids. We have to get to know each other as the people we are today."

"Kinda like how you and Brandon had to get to know each other again."

"Yeah. So who knows how that will turn out, but at least we want to try."

Aaron smiled. "I've always known that you still have a soft spot in your heart for Chris. You've never totally let him go. I've often wondered how I measured up next to Chris."

"I'm sorry. I tried my best to never make you feel that way."

"I know. Maybe it was just insecurity on my part, but anyway... I think in the long run, you'll be happier with Chris. I hope it works out for you."

"Thanks. But I want you to know, I've been happy with you. Very happy. I wouldn't trade the five years we've spent together for anything. You're a wonderful man and I'll always treasure everything we had – and have."

Aaron smiled. "You too. It's been wonderful. *You're* wonderful. I have absolutely no regrets."

Ryan stood up, so Aaron stood too. Ryan wrapped his arms around Aaron and said, "I love you."

"I love you too."

They looked into each other's eyes and kissed. They held each other for half a minute. The tension subsided quickly, and they both realized it still felt good to be in each other's arms.

After they separated, Aaron said, "So, I guess at some point I should move into Brandon's bedroom and let Chris move in with you."

"At some point. We can talk about that later."

"When should we tell Brandon and Chris?"

"Let's tell them at dinner tonight. Let's talk about this when all four of us are together."

Special People

Sunday, October 24, 2021

Ryan felt a tremendous sense of relief after the conversation with Aaron.

He considered what he would serve for Family Night dinner this evening. He had planned to grill hamburgers and serve them with salad and sweet potato fries. But then he thought, *We'll be having a heavy conversation at dinner. It's been awkward around here lately and I want that to change. What can I do to begin the healing process?*

Then he had an idea. He walked to the family room, where Brandon and Aaron had just finished watching TV. Brandon said, "We're gonna go see *The Eternals*. Wanna come?"

"Thanks, but I'll pass this time. I have some other stuff I want to do. What time will you guys be back?"

Aaron said, "Probably around 5:30 or 5:45."

"Text me if you're running late, okay?"

"Will do."

A few minutes after Aaron and Brandon left for the movie theater, Ryan got in his car and headed to Food World.

***

Aaron and Brandon returned at 5:50. A few minutes later, they and Chris converged in the kitchen. The kitchen table was not set. Ryan said, "Let's eat in the dining room this evening."

When they entered the dining room, they were surprised to find the table set with Ryan's good china and silverware. At each place was a small plate of chilled jumbo shrimp, a ramekin of cocktail sauce, and a chilled wine glass with a perfect pour of Chardonnay.

Aaron said, "Wow! Very fancy. This looks delicious!"

The guys didn't say much as they savored the shrimp and the wine.

Ryan asked, "How was the movie?"

Brandon said, "It was great."

Aaron said, "It took me a while to figure out the storyline, but once I got into it, I liked it."

Brandon said, "It continues the story of *The Avengers: Endgame*, so that made it easier to understand for me."

They finished their shrimp. Ryan stood up and cleared their plates. Aaron started to stand up, but Ryan said, "No, sit. I've got it."

Ryan carried their plates into the kitchen. He opened the oven and pulled out a platter of steaks he had grilled shortly before they arrived. He transferred them onto plates that already held sweet potato fries. He carried Aaron and Brandon's plates out first, then made a second trip for Chris and his. Then he picked up a wine bottle from the side table and said, "Shall we enjoy a nice Argentinian Malbec with the main course?"

The guys finished their remaining Chardonnay. Then Ryan swapped out their wine glasses and poured the Malbec into each new glass. Finally, he sat down.

Aaron, Brandon, and Chris exchanged glances, unsure what to make of all this. Finally, Brandon said, "This is all very nice, but... what's the occasion? Is this some holiday or birthday I don't know about?"

Ryan smiled. "Tonight it's not about a special occasion, it's about special people." He raised his glass and said, "Cheers! To my family, on Family Night."

Everyone clinked their glasses and took a sip.

Ryan continued. "I know it's been awkward and difficult around here for the past couple of months. I hope we can resolve this situation in a manner that's agreeable to everyone. But here's what's most important − to me, anyway. As I look around this table, I see the three people who matter the most to me. I love you guys more than anyone else on the planet. You're my family. You're everything to me. And I don't want to lose any of you. Brandon, we were separated for nine years, and I never want that to happen again. Chris, it's been 14 years for us. We've had occasional contact, but now we're finally back in each other's day-to-day lives. I never want to be separated from you again, either. And Aaron, in hindsight, I wish I hadn't taken that assignment. As much as I enjoyed New Zealand and it helped my career, I hated being separated from you. I never want that to happen again."

Ryan took a sip of his wine. "So anyway, I know we're working through some tough times, but regardless of what happens, you're my family. I love every one of you, and I hope we can always be part of each other's lives."

Ryan took a bite of his steak. The others thought about what Ryan said and contemplated what they should say in response. For a moment, no one said anything.

Ryan looked at Aaron. "Do you want to tell them or would you rather have me do it?"

"I will." He took a deep breath. "Okay, so Ryan and I had a heart-to-heart conversation earlier today. We agreed that our marriage counseling wasn't helping. And we agreed that Brandon and I are probably a better match as a couple. And the truth is, I feel a deeper connection with Brandon than with Ryan, and that's unlikely to change. So we both decided that the best thing for us to do is to end our marriage."

Ryan added, "And to be clear, I'm okay with it. I mean, nobody likes a break-up. I hoped our marriage would last for the rest of our lives, but it didn't turn out that way. It's sad to admit that your marriage failed. But given what's happened, this is for the best."

Aaron said, "And for the record, I'm really sorry this happened. I should have never allowed myself to fall for Brandon or acted on my feelings. But I did, and it happened, and I feel terrible about it. The last thing I wanted to do was hurt Ryan. But I did, and I'm sorry."

Ryan said, "And I have forgiven you and Brandon. As I said earlier, I love you both. I want us to remain close and be part of each other's lives. And to be honest, this works out well for me too. Now that Chris is here and he's single, we finally have the chance to continue the relationship we started back when we were in high school. At least we're going to try. We've changed a lot in 14 years. We have a lot to talk about. But I'm going to do everything I can to make it work."

Chris said, "Me too. I never thought I'd have this opportunity. Deep inside, I always hoped it would happen, but I didn't think it would." He turned to Ryan. "And you're right. We can't jump right into this. We need to get to know each other again and talk about our future. But I have no intention of letting you go."

Brandon said, "Wow. Just wow. Like Aaron, I feel really bad about what happened. Especially after everything you've done for me."

Ryan said, "It's okay. Really. I mean, yeah, I was furious about it when

I found out. But I realized that sometimes two people just connect. They don't plan to, it just happens. Even if you didn't act on it, the feelings would still have been there. But it makes me happy to know that the two of you will be happy, and it will work out well for me too. So it's all good."

With that out of the way, everyone felt more relaxed. Everyone took a few bites of their food. After a couple of minutes, Ryan said, "So what's everyone thinking? How are you feeling right now? Aaron, why don't you start?"

"I feel relieved. I'm glad we have this out in the open and we can talk honestly about it. I'm happy with the decision we've reached. As you said earlier, nobody wants their marriage to end in divorce. But I think we're handling this in the best possible way. It's not like we'll go our separate ways hating each other."

Brandon said, "I feel relieved too. But I have a lot of conflicting emotions. On the one hand, I'm happy because this means Aaron and I get to be together." He looked at Ryan. "But on the other hand, I feel terrible that your marriage ended because of me. You have every reason to hate me. I can't believe you're actually saying you love me and you still want me in your life. I mean, I'm glad, because I love you too and I hated living without you for nine years."

Chris said, "I'm sorry you guys have gone through all this, but as Aaron said, I think this ended in the best possible way. But here's something I'm feeling: included. Ryan, you said earlier that we are your family. Even though I've only been here two weeks, I already feel like I'm part of this family and it feels great. I mean, I have my parents and my brother back in Kansas. I'll always love them and they'll always be my biological family. Seth and I had an okay relationship, although it was better earlier. We had lots of friends, but they were more like good acquaintances. They weren't people I felt close enough with to consider family. Brandon, I always liked you when you were younger and I'd come to your house to see Ryan. And Aaron, since I met you when Seth and I visited and we started chatting on Facebook and getting to know each other, I've really grown to like you. And you guys have been so welcoming to me since I moved in. I know this house is kinda crowded with four people, but we're making it work."

Aaron said, "That brings up something I've been thinking about. Does this mean Brandon and I should start looking for someplace else to live?"

Ryan said, "I don't know. I've gotten used to having you all here.

Before any of you came along and I lived here by myself, this house seemed big and empty. There was furniture in every room, but it was only me. When I moved out of the house in LA and came here, I realized I had never lived alone before. I wasn't sure how I'd like it. In that house, it was nice having the other guys around. Once I got here, living alone was okay for a while, but there were plenty of times I wished there were other people around. So anyway, let's not decide on that right away, unless you two would prefer to live in your own place."

Aaron said, "But in any case, I should probably move out of the master bedroom and into Brandon's room and let Chris move into your room. I'm sure Chris is ready to be through with sleeping in a sleeping bag on an air mattress in the music room."

Chris nodded. Of course, he couldn't wait to sleep in the same bed with Ryan.

Aaron said, "Maybe if another house in this neighborhood goes on the market, we could buy it. Then we'd have our own place, but we'd be close enough to get together often."

Ryan said, "Possibly. I know you both have good jobs, but houses around here are pretty expensive."

Brandon lit up. "I know! We could have a house custom-built for us! It could have two master suites, one on each side of the house, and a couple of secondary bedrooms on each side for offices or a music room or whatever. Then there would be a family room, dining room, and kitchen in the middle we would all share. And, of course, a nice pool and stuff in the backyard. When you put all four of our salaries together, we could afford it!"

Ryan smiled. "That's a great idea, but I think we should wait and see how this new arrangement plays out. Let's not rush into it."

Aaron said, "And you know what else? We could have a double wedding! We could have it at the same place in Papago Park where Ryan and I got married. And we could be each other's best men!"

Ryan said, "Again, I think we're getting ahead of ourselves. It's way too soon for any of us to be talking about marriage."

Brandon said, "But we can dream, can't we? I think that would be wonderful."

Aaron said, "And besides, that would show everyone that all four of us want to stay close and be a family. Isn't that what you wanted?"

Ryan said, "Yeah, you're right. Sorry. I guess I shouldn't be a buzzkill."

For a few minutes, everyone enjoyed the rest of their dinner and made small talk. As they were finishing, Brandon said, "So what are we going to tell our friends? And how? And when?"

Ryan said, "Good question. I suppose you guys will want to broadcast it all over Facebook."

Aaron said, "Just tell Petunia. Everyone else will know within 24 hours."

Ryan laughed. "You got that right, only it would be more like two. Personally, I don't feel the need to tell everyone right away."

Aaron said, "Okay, but if we don't do it right away, then when? People in band are bound to notice a change in the dynamic among us. Then rumors will start spreading."

Chris said, "He's got a point. And with the holidays coming up, there will be parties and stuff. And what about Aaron's parents? And mine, for that matter?"

Aaron said, "That's a good point. We weren't planning to travel to Ohio this year because of COVID, but I still have to figure out how to explain this to my folks."

Ryan said, "I still think it's too early to tell our friends. I mean, Aaron and I are still married. And Chris and I are just starting to date."

Chris said, "Yeah, but we'll be sleeping together, starting tonight. And I sure hope it's more than just sleeping! But I agree with Aaron and Brandon. We need to tell people sooner rather than later or people will start spreading rumors. Who knows how people might distort things? Just tell everyone all at once and get it over with."

Brandon said, "As your resident Communications professional, I suggest we create a statement we can all agree with. Then the three of us can put it on our Facebook pages. Ryan, you can email it to people like your former housemates. That is, if you want to."

Ryan said, "Okay, okay. God, I never imagined I'd be issuing a press release announcing a change in my relationship status."

Brandon said, "I'll come up with something, then we can get together later and review it."

Since everyone had finished eating, they cleared the table and carried everything into the kitchen. Chris said, "I'll take care of loading the dishwasher and putting stuff away."

Brandon said, "I'll go out and clean the grill."

Aaron said, "Before you guys do that and we go our separate ways, I want to say thanks to Ryan for an absolutely incredible dinner, and for coming up with the idea of having a nice meal tonight."

Brandon, Chris, and Aaron clapped.

Aaron continued. "But more than that, Ryan, I want to thank you for being such a special man. You had every right to be angry with Brandon and me, but instead, you cooked us a nice dinner. Instead of hating us, you told us how much you love us and how important we are to you. And... well, anyway... I want to let you know how much I admire you, appreciate you, and love you."

Aaron stepped up to Ryan and hugged him. Chris said, "Group hug!" He and Brandon joined them, one on each side, and wrapped their arms around them.

***

After they finished cleaning up, Aaron began moving his clothes out of the master suite closet and into Brandon's room. Ryan said, "I know there's not going to be enough room in that closet, so you can spill over into the music room closet after Chris clears his stuff out." Chris moved his stuff, much of which was still in suitcases and boxes, into the master bedroom.

Brandon sat down at his computer to draft The Big Announcement.

After Aaron and Chris finished moving their stuff, Chris closed the bedroom door. He wrapped his arms around Ryan and began passionately kissing him. In between kisses, he pulled his shirt off over his head, then began removing Ryan's shirt.

Ryan said, "It's only 8:30. Can't you wait until bedtime?"

"I could, but I won't." Chris undid Ryan's belt buckle. "I've waited over 14 years for this, and I'm not going to wait anymore." He unzipped Ryan's pants, shoved his pants and underwear to the floor, and started stroking his cock to hardness. "I need you inside me. RIGHT. NOW!"

Ryan couldn't object. After all, he wanted it too. But he said, "I want you to go first. We never got to do that before."

"We can do everything you want. As much as you want. Whenever you want." Chris finished removing his pants and pulled Ryan onto the bed.

Episode 92

Saturday, October 30, 2021

On Saturday morning, Brandon and Aaron were preparing to record the next episode of their podcast. Aaron seemed nervous as they turned on the microphones, webcam, and lighting. This episode would be different from the 91 episodes that preceded it.

Brandon sensed Aaron's discomfort. "What's wrong?" He knew, but he wanted to get the discussion started.

"I can't believe we're going to do this."

"We don't have to if you're that uncomfortable."

Aaron paused. "No, we need to. Like you said, we need to be authentic with our listeners. It's just... well... this is rather personal stuff to put out there to the whole world. And we could get a lot of harsh judgment."

Brandon put his arm around Aaron's shoulder and kissed him. "I get it. But let's just do it. We'll see how it goes. If you don't like it, we can always do another take. And we have a couple of days before we release it. If we decide we don't want to, we can record something else."

Aaron tried to feel reassured. "Yeah, I guess. But you seem pretty upbeat."

"Yeah. In a way, I'm kinda looking forward to it."

After they finished setting everything up. Brandon said, "Are you ready?" Aaron nodded. Brandon gave him another kiss. "Let's do this." He clicked the button to start recording.

Brandon smiled into the camera and said, "Welcome to 'Brandon and Aaron Fix the World.' I'm Brandon Bauer."

"And I'm Aaron Bradbury. Each week, we'll look at what's happening in the world from a Millennial and Gen-Z perspective and discuss how we can make it better."

"This week's episode is going to be a bit different, wouldn't you say?"

"That's right. Today, instead of talking about the world out there, we're going to talk about the world in here. There's been a lot going on in our lives recently, and now we're ready to let you in on it. Brandon, why don't you start?"

"Yeah, okay. Well, uhh... So! If you've been listening to us for a while, you know that Aaron's the Millennial voice and I'm the Gen-Z voice. But also, Aaron represents the LGBTQ perspective. Up until now I haven't said where I'm coming from in that regard, so everyone probably assumes I'm straight. Well, for years I've shied away from using labels. Like I don't really need to identify one way or the other. I'm just me, you know? I want to be open to loving whoever I feel attracted to, on whatever level."

Aaron said, "It's like, why limit yourself? People are people. There are a lot of things that make people who they are besides their genitalia and who they're sexually attracted to."

"Exactly. And I know many people in our generation feel the same way. Anyway..." Brandon took a deep breath. "Over the past few years, I've been back in touch with my brother, who's gay. And I've gotten to know Aaron really well. I've seen how comfortable and natural they are together and met their friends, and I... Well, I've discovered that I'm attracted to men too. I mean, I still like women as friends and everything, but... over the past few years, I've gotten more in touch with myself, and I realize that guys are where it's at for me. Now I'm ready to wear that label."

Aaron smiled. "Well! Congratulations! Thank you for sharing that with our fam."

"Yeah. I mean, I wanna keep it 100 with you guys. We talk honestly about all kinds of stuff on this podcast, and I felt it was time to talk honestly about this."

"Well, on behalf of LGBTQ+ people everywhere, welcome to the fraternity!"

"Thanks. And now, you have some news to share too, right?"

"Right. Umm... Gee, where to start? Okay, so you know I'm married to Brandon's brother, Ryan. And he's great. He's wonderful. I love him to death. I fell in love with him soon after I first came out back in 2016. We got married in October 2017, so we just celebrated our fourth anniversary. Anyway... well... stuff happened. Back in 2019, Ryan accepted a business assignment in New Zealand that was supposed to last a year. But then the pandemic hit. Ryan's assignment kept getting extended and he ended up being there for two years. At the time, Brandon was in his senior year at ASU. When they closed the campus and shifted to remote classes, he came and lived here.

I mean, he visited a lot anyway, and he lived here between semesters. So living here full-time during the pandemic seemed like a no-brainer. So anyway, he and I have been cooped up in this house together for, like, the last year and a half. Obviously, we got to know each other really well. With Ryan gone, we became each other's support system during all the crazy shit that happened in 2020 and 2021. And, well, we ended up falling in love with each other."

Brandon cut in. "Obviously, neither of us expected this. Neither of us planned for it to happen. And for a long time, it was like, we have to resist this. We can't let this happen. I mean, he's married to my brother!"

"But it happened and we finally had to deal with it. So yeah... Brandon and I are now officially a couple. Now, I know what you're thinking. What about Ryan? Well, yeah, he was totally pissed off about it at first. I mean, who could blame him? He came back after two years to find out his brother and his husband had fallen in love with each other."

Brandon grinned. "Not to mention banging each other's brains out."

Aaron gave Brandon some side-eye. "But you just mentioned it anyway. But things have turned out well for him, too. He's now back together with his high school boyfriend after being separated for 14 years. I always knew Ryan and Chris were the perfect match for each other. I mean, Ryan and I love each other and we've had a wonderful relationship. But they really belong together. So now they have each other and we have each other, so it's all working out fine."

"And we're all living happily ever after."

Aaron said, "So there you have it. Like we said up front, this week it's about our world. I know many of you will have opinions about this, and that's fine. You're welcome to them. But things change. People change. Situations change. Stuff happens. And sometimes you just have to follow your heart and be honest about things the way they are."

Aaron smiled at Brandon, then looked into the camera. "Well, I guess that's it. Sorry this episode is so much shorter than the others, but that's all we have to say this week. So, thank you for joining us–"

Brandon cut in. "Actually, there is one more thing."

Aaron looked surprised. They hadn't planned to discuss anything else.

Brandon swiveled in his chair to face Aaron. "Aaron, I've adored you since the moment we met. I'll be forever grateful to you for reuniting me with my brother. Over the past five years, we've become best friends. You've supported my basketball career at ASU. We've supported each other through all the crazy bullshit of the past year and a half and come out stronger for it. You've been my partner in this podcast, and nothing would make me happier than if you would be my partner in life." Brandon dropped to one knee. At 6'7", he was still well-framed in the picture. "Aaron Michael Bradbury, will you marry me?"

During the prologue to The Big Question, Aaron could see it coming. Still, when the last four words came out of Brandon's mouth, it still seemed unbelievable. "Well... Yes! Yes! Yes, of course!"

They leaned into each other and kissed passionately. After about ten seconds, Aaron gently pushed Brandon away and whispered, "We're still rolling."

Brandon sat back down in his chair. He turned toward the camera wearing a sheepish grin.

Aaron said, "Thank you for joining us. Don't forget to hit that Subscribe button and share this with your friends."

"We'll be back next week with another edition of 'Brandon and Aaron Fix the World.' Until then, remember: Always be kind and be part of the solution. I'm Brandon Bauer."

"And I'm Aaron Bradbury. Later!"

Brandon reached forward and ended the recording. They stood up, wrapped their arms tightly around each other, and resumed their passionate kissing. Thirty seconds later, without saying a word, they let go of each other and hurried into their bedroom. They could shut everything down later.

Missionaries in an Awkward Position

Tuesday, November 23, 2021

On this particular Tuesday evening, two days before Thanksgiving, no one had any rehearsals or other activities scheduled, so all four men were home.

At around 7:30, the doorbell rang. Ryan was in the kitchen, so he headed toward the front door and called out to his housemates, "I'll get it."

Ryan looked through the peephole and saw a fish-eye view of two young men wearing white shirts, ties, and black pants. They wore black name tags on their chests and Ryan could see two bicycles in the driveway with helmets hanging from the handlebars.

Ryan was prepared to tell them, in no uncertain terms, that the residents of this household would not be interested in what they had to say and to please be on their way to their next conquest. Ryan opened the door and glanced at the young men. One was an adorable blond-haired, blue-eyed, clean-cut young man with an innocent smile. He was six feet tall, with a slender build that suggested he could be a runner or swimmer. The other young man was a few inches shorter and somewhat pudgy, with straight black hair. He attempted to smile, but he seemed nervous. The blond gave the impression that he was enthusiastically committed to his missionary work. The dark-haired one looked like he would rather be anyplace else and was on his mission only out of obligation.

On impulse, Ryan changed course. "Gentlemen! Welcome! Please come in!" Ryan pulled the door open wide and made a sweeping gesture toward the living room.

The young men seemed genuinely taken aback by this unusual display of hospitality. Even the people who allowed them into their homes and reluctantly listened to their pitch never welcomed them with this level of graciousness and enthusiasm.

Ryan glanced at their nametags and said, "Please wait here while I summon my loved ones."

The young men glanced at each other nervously and remained standing. They could hear Ryan down the hallway saying, "Please come join me in the living room. We have guests!"

In a moment, Ryan returned with three other men. The two missionaries exchanged confused glances.

Ryan turned toward his housemates and said, "Gentlemen, I'd like you to meet Elder Berry–" Aaron snickered. Ryan said, "Now, now, let's be polite to our guests."

Elder Matthew Berry, the dark-haired one, said, "I'm used to it. I get it at literally every house we visit."

Ryan continued, "And this is Elder–"

Chris interrupted him. "No, wait... let me guess. Elder Flower?" Brandon giggled.

Aaron guessed, "Elder Hostel?"

Brandon piped in with, "Elder Rado?"

Chris said, "Elder Housing?"

By now, Chris, Aaron, and Brandon were laughing out loud. Ryan was trying to maintain his composure, but he couldn't help grinning.

"Guys! Manners! Manners! Let's not be rude to our guests." He turned to the missionaries. "I'm so sorry. I can't take them anywhere."

Brandon added, "You can't leave us home either!" The others chuckled.

Despite the awkwardness of this encounter, the missionaries seemed somewhat amused.

Ryan said to his housemates, "None of you guessed correctly. This is Elder Larsen." He turned back to the missionaries and extended his hand. "My name is Ryan Robertson." Both young men took a step forward and shook his hand. "This is my husband, Aaron Bradbury. This is my brother, Brandon Bauer. And this is my best friend, Chris Robertson." Ryan decided that no further information about their relationship situation was necessary or appropriate.

Elder Jacob Larsen said, "Okay, wait a minute. You and he are married, but you have different last names. You and he are brothers, but you have different last names. And you and he are just friends, but you have the same last name."

"That's correct. It's complicated. More complicated than you can imagine. May I offer you a beverage? Let's see... we have a variety of cocktails and wines, coffee, sodas… no, wait. Your religion forbids you from having alcohol. So then I'm afraid we're left with either Coke, Diet Coke, Dr Pepper, or water. Will that suffice?"

Elders Berry and Larsen glanced at each other. Elder Larsen said, "Water will be fine. Thanks."

Ryan hurried into the kitchen. The other three men took turns shaking hands with the increasingly nervous missionaries. Then Aaron said, "Please sit down. Make yourselves comfortable."

Elder Berry asked, "So… do all four of you live here?" Everyone nodded. "And… I probably shouldn't even ask this, but are all of you gay?" Everyone nodded. "How does that even work?"

Aaron, Brandon, and Chris glanced at each other and silently agreed they should not disclose their relationship realignment.

Chris said, "It's complicated."

Aaron said, "Let's just say we all love each other very much, but in different ways."

Elder Larsen said, "My brain just exploded."

Ryan returned from the kitchen carrying a serving tray with six waters – in martini glasses. The others tried hard not to bust out laughing. Ryan served the guests first, then Brandon, Chris, and Aaron. Then he set the tray aside, sat down, and raised his glass. "Gentlemen, a toast! To the Church of Jesus Christ of Latter-Day Saints and its legions of devoted young missionaries!"

His three housemates said, "Here, here!" and clinked their glasses with those closest to them. The missionaries, now totally speechless, hesitantly raised their glasses and took a sip.

Ryan continued, "But enough ceremony. Let's get to why we are all gathered here this evening. Let's listen while these fine young gentlemen explain to us why four flaming, unrepentant homosexuals should join the Church of Jesus Christ of Latter-Day Saints. The same church that, in 2008, urged its followers to donate 38 million dollars to pass Prop 8 in California to deny us equal marriage rights. The same church that, in 2015, decreed that children who are being raised by same-sex couples cannot be baptized into the church unless they renounce their parents. Gentlemen, we're all ears. The floor is yours."

The missionaries looked terrified. They glanced at each other. Elder Larsen said, "Uh… I think maybe we should be going now." He grabbed his shoulder bag and stood up. Elder Berry couldn't move.

Chris said, "Seriously? You're not even going to try to save us from our sinful ways?" All four housemates feigned expressions of disappointment.

Elder Berry turned to Elder Larsen and said, "Can we stay? I'd like to ask these guys a few questions."

Elder Larsen seemed puzzled, but he sat back down in his chair.

Elder Berry said, "It's clear that we're not going to be able to lead you to join our church. But maybe we can talk for a little while and gain a better understanding of each other."

Ryan said, "Fair enough."

Elder Berry asked, "Okay, so first of all, are you guys happy?"

Aaron replied, "Yeah, overall. I mean, I get pissed off when I'm stuck in traffic. The COVID pandemic has been a real pain in the ass. We're working through some relationship issues, just like any other couple. But yeah, overall, I'm very satisfied with my life. I have a wonderful husband and two best friends whom I love very much. I have a good job, good friends, a lovely home, and two good bands I can play my trombone in. So yeah, life is good."

Chris said, "Well, I just went through a major break-up. That was painful. But straight couples have problems and break up too. But these guys have been a tremendous support system and, like Aaron, I love them a lot. I have a good career and the best family anyone could ask for – both my biological family and my chosen family. So, I'm very happy and very fortunate."

Ryan said, "If you're asking whether we are happy about being gay, I don't think that's the right question to ask. Whether you're happy or unhappy doesn't depend on whether you're gay or straight. Being gay has brought a lot of challenges I wouldn't have had if I were straight, but they've made me a stronger person. I'm happy that I can be openly gay and I have these people in my life whom I love and who love me for exactly who I am. Would I be happier if I was straight? I don't know. I have no way of knowing. But I don't think so. I'm really happy with who I am. And being honest with myself and others about who I am is a big part of being happy. You can choose how happy you're going to be, and being straight or gay doesn't really enter into it."

Brandon said, "I read once where someone said 'Happiness is being able to live your life the way you want to.' That pretty well sums it up for me."

Elder Berry said, "Okay, so… I know I probably shouldn't ask this, but… Do you guys go to church? Or did you? How do you reconcile being gay with God?"

Ryan said, "First of all, let's dispense with this 'I shouldn't ask you' stuff. You may ask us anything you want. Let's be open and honest here. And we may want to ask you some stuff. Anyway, let me start by telling you some of my story.

"My father – and Brandon's – was the head pastor at this huge church in Prairie Village, Kansas. That's just outside of Kansas City, across the state line. They were really right-wing and conservative, like the LDS church. Anyway, when my father found out I was gay, first he sent me to this bogus so-called therapist who tried to tell me that I could pray the gay away."

Elder Larsen said, "Well, you can."

"No, you can't. That's all bullshit. God created me exactly the way I am, just like he created you exactly the way you are. Anyway, when that didn't work, they were going to send me to some gay conversion therapy place where they torture kids to try to make them straight. Fortunately, I found out about it in the nick of time and managed to escape. I ran away to Los Angeles. I had to go undercover until I turned 18 so they wouldn't find me and force me to go back home. That's why I changed my name and I no longer have the same last name as my brother. Even after that, I didn't want them to find me and try to get me to go back home and live in those conditions.

"Anyway, that tore me away from my brother. Brandon and I finally found each other and were reunited about five years ago."

Brandon said, "You have no idea how painful that was. He's eight years older than me. At the time, I was nine and he was 17. I looked up to him so much. He was my hero. He still is. He wasn't just my big brother, he was almost like a father to me. Dad was so wrapped up in his church that he never had time for Ryan and me. But Ryan always had time for me."

Ryan continued. "And then there's Chris. Chris and I were best friends for three years during high school. Then when we figured out we were gay, we kinda transitioned from friends into boyfriends. It was wonderful. But then, when I had to run away that meant I had to leave him behind, too."

Chris said, "I was devastated. We had plans to go to college and spend our lives together. Then when he suddenly disappeared, all that got ripped away. At first, I didn't even know what happened to him or why. I wondered if he had killed himself."

Ryan said, "So now maybe you can understand why I have no use for organized religions, especially the ones that are so anti-gay."

Elder Larsen said, "See? This illustrates how homosexuality destroys families. If you follow God, learn about his teachings, and pray for forgiveness for your sins, you can live a holier life the way God intended. And you wouldn't have suffered through all that pain and separation."

Chris said, "Homosexuality doesn't destroy families. Bigotry and intolerance destroy families. Adhering to religious dogma that tells you to judge other people and try to force them to live the way you think they should live destroys families. Rejecting your kids for being who they are destroys families. Look at my family. My parents stopped going to church a long time ago. When I came out to them and my brother, they were full of love, support, and acceptance. My family became stronger after I opened up and was honest with them about who I am."

Aaron added, "When my parents found out I was gay, they threw all that religious crap at me. We didn't speak for two months. But then one Sunday, they were sitting in church listening to their pastor preach all this hatred toward gays and they thought, 'Wait a minute. You're not going to talk about our son like that.' And they gave it all up, and we reconciled, and we've been really close since then."

Elder Larsen said, "Okay, well I can kind of see how your parents' religious beliefs would go against your homosexual lifestyle. But what if you had been more open to accepting the Lord and his teachings, and leaving the homosexual lifestyle?"

Chris replied, "First of all, it's not a 'lifestyle,' as you call it. It's part of who we are. Being attracted to men is as natural to me as being attracted to women is to you – or at least I assume."

Aaron said, "We have a life, not just a lifestyle. Although you could say that *our* lives *have* style!"

Ryan said, "And remember, I've been through that gay conversion therapy crap. Not only does it not work, it's psychologically harmful."

Elder Larsen said, "But even if you feel some attraction to men, you can still marry a woman and have children and live as God wants you to live."

Ryan said, "Yeah, well let me tell you more about that. I dated an LDS guy in college. He told me he wasn't really into the church anymore. He said he was only LDS because that's what his parents were. He was a 'Jack Mormon' as he called it. Anyway, we dated for about a year. Then in my senior year, I got a job offer to work here in Scottsdale. I asked them if I could work at their office in Lehi, Utah so he and I could continue to live together after he graduated. Then he told me he didn't want me to move to Utah to be with him.

No! He was going to go back in the closet and marry his high school girlfriend and have kids, just to please everyone in his family. And nobody would ever know how much he loved to get it up the ass."

Elder Larsen winced, then replied, "Well, again, he chose to live as God intends for us to live."

Aaron said, "He's living a huge lie. He's being fundamentally dishonest. There's nothing in the Ten Commandments or the Gospels about being gay, but there's a commandment that says 'Thou shall not bear false witness against thy neighbor.' In other words, thou shall not lie."

Chris asked, "Would you want to marry a woman if, in her heart, she really wished she could be with a woman instead of you?"

Ryan said, "And let me tell you how it ended up with that guy, who chose to go back in the closet and get married and have kids. A few years ago, Aaron, Brandon, and I were flying home from visiting Aaron's parents in Ohio, and we had a layover in Dallas. And who would you guess also had a layover in Dallas? That's right – Mister Closeted LDS Guy and his lovely wife and two adorable little kids. And when Aaron went to use the restroom, who do you suppose was in there cruising for sex? That's right – Mister Closeted LDS Guy. He even tried to cruise Aaron. Anyway, he hooked up with some other guy and gave him a blowjob in a toilet stall. Then I went in to take a leak. While I was there he got busted by airport security. And to top it all off, I ended up being the one to explain to his wife why her husband was being led away in handcuffs – because he was secretly a big ol' homo who got caught giving head in the restroom. So tell me, is that the way God intended for him to live?"

Elder Larsen said, "Even if he had those thoughts, he shouldn't have acted on them."

Brandon said, "No, he shouldn't have. But wouldn't it have been so much better for everyone concerned if he lived his life honestly?"

Elder Berry had been sitting silently throughout this entire discussion with a distressed look on his face. Finally, he spoke. "You have no idea how much pressure the church puts on people to conform to their teachings. Being gay isn't an option. You could get disowned by your family, or at least it causes a lot of problems."

Aaron asked, "Can't you just leave? Other churches welcome LGBTQ people. My parents joined one, and they like it so much better."

"You can, and sometimes people do. They call it taking your name off the rolls, and it's really serious. It means you'll have eternal separation from

God. It brings dishonor upon the whole family. So not only are you leaving the church, you're going to be separated from your family – not just now, but for eternity."

Everyone was trying to decide whether Elder Berry had just told them something. He sat hunched over, with his forearms resting on his thighs, hands clasped between his knees. He stared at the floor and said, almost inaudibly, "And I'm scared that's what's going to happen to me."

Silence fell over the room. Ryan walked over and knelt in front of Elder Berry. He placed his hands around Elder Berry's clasped hands. Elder Berry looked up and they made eye contact. Ryan said, "You're gonna be okay. There will be some difficult moments. You'll lose some people, but you'll gain so much more. There are lots of wonderful people out there who will love you for who you are – both gay and straight. There will be people who can help you along the way – including us."

A couple of tears ran down Elder Berry's cheeks. Aaron went to fetch a box of tissues.

Ryan continued. "When I needed to leave home, the manager at the grocery store where I worked was there for me. He helped me decide where to go and how to get there. He had friends in LA whom he called, and they offered to let me stay with them. When I got to LA, there was an organization called the Los Angeles LGBT Youth Project to help me. And I found a good place to live with a group of gay guys who became like brothers to me. There were supportive faculty members at my high school. So what I'm saying is, there are people out there who will help you.

"You have to be true to yourself. People will be attracted to you if you're authentic and honest. You seem like a really nice young man. People will like you for exactly who you are. Those that don't – just let them go and keep looking for the good ones."

Elder Larsen asked, "Can't he just not tell anybody?"

"Well, that's his choice. And that's what I tried to do in high school. I thought, well, nobody needs to know but me and Chris. Why should I have to come out to anyone? Well, first of all, that wasn't fair to Chris. It's like we were each other's dirty little secret. But also, it's stressful to always worry about someone finding out. You have to watch everything you say or do, all the time."

Ryan turned back to Elder Berry. "But it all comes down to this: You shouldn't live your life for other people. They have their own lives to live. You need to live your life for yourself. You should live the way it will make you happy and satisfied. You can't do that if you pretend you're someone else and keep your true self bottled up inside. Now, you don't have to run out and tell everyone right away. You get to decide who you want to tell when you feel the time is right. But people may find out anyway, even if you don't want them to. That's what happened to me when my dad found out. So, you have to be prepared to deal with that."

Ryan turned to Elder Larsen. "It's up to him who he tells, and when. It's not up to you. So don't you tell the church or his family. Understand?"

Elder Larsen said, "Yes, sir."

"Good. What he needs from you right now is support."

Elder Larsen nodded.

Ryan asked Elder Berry, "What questions do you have for us? What concerns do you have?"

Elder Berry grabbed another tissue and blotted a few tears from the corners of his eyes. "What's going to happen if my parents find out, and they kick me out?"

Ryan looked around the room at Aaron, Brandon, and Chris. They knew what he was about to say, and they nodded.

"I'm going to give you my phone number. If that happens and you need a place to stay, call me. I'm serious. You are *not* going to live a day on the street if we have anything to do with it. And you can call anytime you have questions or need advice."

Elder Berry said, "Thanks. And one other thing. I don't want to continue on my mission. But if I quit early, they'll want to know why. But if I keep going, I'll feel like such a hypocrite. I already do."

"Well... I don't know what to tell you on that one. Ultimately, that's a decision you have to make for yourself."

Chris said, "I read somewhere that 30% of all missionaries leave their missions early. They leave for a variety of reasons, not necessarily because they're gay. It's very stressful."

Elder Larsen said, "Yeah, tell me about it."

Elder Berry looked overwhelmed. There was so much he needed to process and so much more he needed to talk about, but this was enough for one day. "Okay. Well, I think we should probably go now."

Everyone stood up. Ryan asked, "May I give you a hug?"

Elder Berry tentatively held his arms open, and Ryan stepped forward and hugged him. Ryan said, "Trust me. Everything will work out fine for you in the long run. And never apologize for who you are. You're beautiful and you're exactly the way God made you to be."

Elder Berry formed a weak smile. "Thanks. I really needed that."

Aaron, Brandon, and Chris each hugged him. Then, to everyone's surprise, Elder Larsen stepped up and hugged his companion. He whispered, "I've got your back."

The missionaries turned to go. Then Aaron said, "What are you guys doing for Thanksgiving?"

They looked at each other and shrugged. Elder Larsen said, "Oh, we'll probably just get some sliced turkey and some green beans and mashed potatoes from the store and eat at our apartment."

"Why don't you come here and celebrate Thanksgiving with us?"

The look on their faces said yes, but Elder Larsen said, "Well, we don't want to impose…"

Ryan said, "No, seriously. We'd love to have you. And no ties and name tags. Just wear something comfortable. We don't have to talk about religion or being gay or any of that stuff unless you want to. We can just relax and enjoy eating way too much food. Are you in?"

They looked at each other. Elder Berry asked, "Can we? I'd really like that."

Elder Larsen said, "Sure. What time? And can we bring anything?"

Aaron said, "How about 4:30? We'll eat around five. And no need to bring anything but yourselves. We've already bought everything, and we'll have plenty."

Ryan wrote his number on a piece of paper and handed it to Elder Berry. "Here's my number. Call anytime. Really."

Brandon walked to the front door and opened it for the missionaries. Everyone said a round of goodbyes. Then Ryan said, "Oh, and one other thing. I'm sorry I was rude to you guys when you first arrived. That was way out of line."

Elder Berry said, "That's okay. It forced me to deal with some things I needed to deal with."

Elder Larsen said, "Some of the things you said the church had done really opened my eyes. I had no idea."

Ryan said, "Okay. Well, you guys get home safely, and we'll see you Thursday at around 4:30."

Let Us Give Thanks

Thursday, November 25, 2021

Elders Larsen and Berry arrived a few minutes before 4:30. They wore polo shirts and jeans. Brandon greeted them at the door and welcomed them in.

They smiled when they caught a whiff of the delicious food being prepared in the kitchen. Elder Larsen said, "You have no idea how good a home-cooked meal smells right now."

Brandon led them back to the kitchen/family room. "You're in for a treat. My brother is an awesome cook."

When the missionaries entered the room, everyone stopped what they were doing. Ryan said, "Welcome, Elder Berry," and hugged him. Then he said, "Welcome, Elder Larsen," and offered his hand for a handshake.

Elder Larsen opened his arms. "It's cool. I like hugs too. And please... call me Jake. I'm off-duty today."

Elder Berry said, "Same here. Just call me Matt."

With that out of the way, everyone hugged everyone else.

Aaron said, "Guys, there are nibbles on the coffee table in the family room. May I offer you guys anything to drink?" The missionaries noticed that the four housemates all had cocktails in their hands.

Matt really wanted to try one, but he knew he shouldn't. "The other night you said you had Diet Coke. May I have that?"

Aaron said, "Sure."

Jake said, "I'll stick with water."

Chris said, "I thought you guys weren't supposed to have caffeinated drinks. I mean, I don't care, but..."

Matt replied, "They changed that a few years ago. My family still doesn't drink soda, but I did when I was out with my friends in high school."

Aaron handed them their drinks, then led them over to the family room side of the great room. He motioned for them to have a seat on the couch. Chris followed them in. "Where are you from?"

Jake said, "I'm from Ogden, Utah, north of Salt Lake City."

Matt said, "I'm from Inkom, Idaho. It's a small town with less than 1,000 people, southeast of Pocatello."

Chris said, "I'll bet Phoenix is a big contrast to Inkom."

Matt said, "Oh, yeah. It's like I'm in a different world. But we're still limited by how far we can ride on our bikes."

"How did you like living in a small town?"

"Growing up, I didn't think much about it. I mean, it's what I grew up with and I didn't have much else to compare it to. Like, that was my reality. Pocatello is only 15 minutes away, so we went there pretty often."

Chris asked, "Do you think you'll keep living there after your mission?"

"I sure hope not. I mean, my family's there. And if I go to Idaho State, that's in Pocatello. I don't know whether I'll live on campus or commute. But now that I'm coming to terms with being gay, I can see that Inkom is no place for a gay person to live. Everyone knows everyone else's business. I've only been here for three months, but I think I'd like living in a big city better."

Aaron said, "Trust me, you will. I grew up in Troy, Ohio, which has about 25,000 people. It was an okay place to grow up, but I wouldn't want to live there now – especially not as a gay person. I want to live someplace where they have a gay community and there are things like a gay band. I went to Ohio State, and I really liked Columbus. But I love it out here, mostly because it doesn't get cold and snow in the winter."

"Yeah, there's that, too."

Chris asked, "What about you, Jake? What do you plan to do after your mission ends?"

"Mine ends in February, so I'm almost done. I'm going to go to Utah State. It's up in Logan, which is an hour north of Ogden. I'll miss the start of the spring semester, so I'll start the summer semester on May 9. Having a few months to re-acclimate to regular life will be nice. Maybe I'll get a job and pick up some extra cash."

Aaron asked Matt, "Do you have any brothers or sisters?"

"Yeah. I'm the oldest of four boys. My brother Mark is a year younger than me. Then there's a five-year gap, then my younger brothers, Luke and John, are a year apart."

Ryan, who could hear their conversation from the kitchen, said, "Wait a minute. Your parents named their four sons Matthew, Mark, Luke, and

John?"

"Yep. That's right."

Aaron said, "I guess we shouldn't be surprised. What about you, Jake?"

"I'm the middle kid of three – also all boys. Joseph, Jacob, and Jeremiah. We're each two years apart."

Chris said, "Just think. If you were a twin, they could have named your brother Esau."

While Aaron and Chris engaged Matt and Jake in conversation, Ryan and Brandon set the serving dishes in a row on the kitchen island. Then Ryan announced, "Okay, we're ready to eat!" As everyone approached the food line, Ryan said to Jake and Matt, "Since you're our guests, why don't you go first? Will it bother you if we have wine?"

Jake said, "No, not at all. This is your home."

"It's a nice Pinot Grigio. It pairs well with turkey. I'd offer you some, but I know–"

Matt said, "Actually, I'd like a glass if you don't mind."

Jake looked surprised but said nothing.

Once everyone had served themselves and sat down, Ryan raised his glass and said, "A toast – to family, to new friends, and to all we have to be thankful for!"

Ryan, Chris, Aaron, and Brandon started clinking their glasses with those they were sitting closest to. Matt and Jake were unaccustomed to such rituals, but Matt picked up his wine glass, Jake picked up his water glass, and they followed suit.

Everyone took a sip and set their glasses down. The four housemates picked up their knives and forks.

Jake said, "Umm... May I say grace?"

Everyone paused. Ryan said, "Well... okay."

Jake extended his hands to his sides. Matt, to his left, took Jake's hand and extended his left hand to Ryan. The others put their silverware down and joined in holding hands and bowing their heads.

"Our Heavenly Father, please bless this food we are about to share, that it might nourish and strengthen our bodies. Bless those who prepared it, those who served it, and those who have worked to make today a special occasion. For all of this, we give you thanks. Amen."

Everyone else muttered, "Amen." They opened their eyes, dropped their hands, and returned their attention to the feast before them.

Brandon said, "That brings back memories. When Ryan and I were growing up, our father said grace before every meal – even in restaurants."

Jake said, "So you guys don't say prayers anymore?"

Ryan said, "Nope. Honestly, I'm over the whole organized religion thing. I know you guys are into it, and that's fine. You do what's right for you. But everything my father did to me – in the name of Jesus Christ, of course – left a bitter taste in my mouth. I've come to believe that all organized religions are man-made institutions. As such, they're imperfect. Personally, I don't believe there's some deity up there who cares whether we gather in fancy buildings once a week and sing songs and recite pre-written prayers. I believe the higher power, in whatever form, is much more interested in how we live our lives outside the church buildings; how we treat each other, the animals, and the environment. And sadly, as a species, we're failing big time. But I'm much happier now. I'm living a more authentic life without church being part of it. But that's just me. I certainly won't tell anybody that I'm right and they're wrong. I'm probably just as wrong as everyone else."

Chris added, "The fact that so many churches still believe homosexuality is a sin is enough reason for me to stay away. God created me the way I am, and I'm just as good as anyone else."

Everyone silently agreed that enough had been said about religion. Jake realized he and Matt weren't going to convince any of these guys to join their church. But they were nice, they were being kind to them, and they were fascinating in their own way.

Matt had remained silent since they sat down at the table, but now he was ready to talk. "Guys, first of all, this meal is fantastic. Brandon was right. Ryan, you're a terrific cook. Everything is delicious."

Jake said, "It sure is. It was very kind of you to invite us to come today. Sometimes LDS families in the area invite us to their house for dinner, and we're always grateful, but this is on a whole different level!"

Ryan smiled. "Thank you. And it's our pleasure. I'm sorry if I came on a little heavy a minute ago. It's a sore subject for me."

Jake said, "I understand."

Everyone sensed that Matt had more he wanted to say, so nobody said anything. Matt sensed that the others were giving him space. He took another sip of his wine. It was having the desired effect of calming him and soothing his anxieties. "I've been thinking a lot over the past couple of days. I'm going to quit my mission. I think I'm going to quit the church too."

Everyone glanced at Jake. He didn't look shocked. They had probably talked about it already.

Aaron said, "What are you going to tell your family?"

"I'm going to tell them I'm suffering from too much anxiety. It's preventing me from doing an effective job as a missionary. That's actually true. I'm not going to tell them I'm gay right away. In fact, I don't know when, or even if, I'll tell them. I guess I'll have to do it sooner or later."

Chris said, "You're right. You don't have to tell them right away, especially if you still need to rely on them for support."

Jake said, "They'll probably have a hard enough time dealing with you quitting your mission. Maybe you should at least wait until they've gotten over that."

"Assuming they do."

Brandon asked, "Do you really think that's going to be a problem?"

Jake said, "For many families, it is. There's a lot of stigma attached to not going on a mission or quitting once you're on it. Some girls won't date a guy who didn't complete his mission." He paused, then turned to Matt. "I guess that doesn't apply in your case, but still – yeah, his family might react badly. Some people think that brings disgrace upon the parents."

Matt said, "I'm not going to tell them I'm leaving the church right away, either. I hope I can convince them to let me live on campus rather than staying at home."

Chris said, "Yeah, it'll be easier if you can live somewhere else during college."

"Yeah, like I'm ready to start living my own life, without being under their watchful eye. Still, I'm really scared about how they'll react."

Aaron said, "I hear you. Coming out to your parents is one of the hardest things most gay people ever do."

Ryan said, "And you have the added layers of quitting your mission and leaving the church."

Matt said, "Yeah. Even if they get over me quitting my mission, they'll probably still freak when they find out I'm gay."

Aaron said, "Even if they freak out at first, they'll probably come around. My parents did."

"I don't know... My parents are, like, totally bought in. I don't think it's very likely that they'll change."

For a few minutes, everyone focused on eating. Then Ryan announced, "There's plenty more on the counter. Feel free to get up and help yourselves to seconds. And save a little room – there's pumpkin cheesecake for dessert." He got up and asked, "Would anyone like more wine? Don't be bashful – I have another bottle in the fridge."

Everyone nodded. Jake asked, "May I have a glass?"

Ryan smiled. He disappeared into the kitchen to get the second bottle and a glass for Jake. He returned and filled everyone's glass.

As Jake took his first sip of wine, Aaron said, "Good lord, we've corrupted you guys so quickly!" He turned toward Jake. "Next thing you know, you'll be coming out too!"

Jake chuckled. "No, I don't think so. I still like girls. But I'll tell you, these past couple of days have really changed how I think about these things. I mean, I never knew any gay people. I always thought people could quit being gay if they wanted to. And it's something that was never talked about, except to say it's a sin and it's not what God wants for us. I've never thought about how the church's teachings affect gay people until now. But now I see how much pain it causes people and how harmful it is, especially if people really are born that way. Until two days ago, I had no idea what Matt's been going through. And I guess in a way I was part of it. But I want him to be happy. And like you said, he should be able to live his life the way he wants, being who he really is. And you guys have shown me that gay people can be loving and caring and good, like anyone else."

Matt said, "Thanks for being so cool about it. I had no idea what you'd do if you found out. I felt like I had to watch everything I said and did all the time so you wouldn't figure it out."

Jake said, "So basically, you've been nervous around me all the time."

Matt nodded.

Jake put his hand on Matt's shoulder. "No wonder you're always so quiet. I've always felt like there was some kind of barrier between us, but I couldn't figure out what it was. I'm really sorry, man. I had no idea. I hope I didn't say or do anything wrong."

Matt said, "It's okay. You didn't. And it's not just you. This is how I have to be around everybody, all the time."

Ryan said, "Yeah. That's what it was like for me in high school until I got outed. And at first, being outed was awful. But after that, I decided to be honest about who I am with everyone I meet. If they're fine with it, great. If they're not, that's their problem. Let me tell you, being openly gay isn't always easy, but it's a hell of a lot easier than being closeted."

Jake said, "Well, now that I know and we have that out of the way, I hope we can be more comfortable around each other." Matt smiled.

Chris said, "Jake, it's great that you're so supportive of Matt. Now that you're aware of the struggles gay people face, what are you going to do about it?"

"I don't know. I've been thinking. Since I'm so close to the end of my mission, I'm going to finish it. But after that, I'm not sure whether I'll stay in the church or not. Aside from the gay thing, I've been thinking about what Ryan said earlier about all religions being man-made institutions. Maybe there really isn't a deity up there who wants us to do all the stuff churches say we have to do. Over the next few weeks, I'm going to be questioning a lot of things."

The conversation moved on to other topics. After dessert and more talk around the dinner table, Matt and Jake felt it was time to go.

Ryan said to Matt, "You have my number. Please stay in touch. Let me know how it goes. And don't hesitate to call if you need anything."

"Thanks. I really appreciate it."

Jake asked, "May I use the bathroom before we head out?"

Brandon pointed toward the bedroom hallway. "It's the first door on your left."

As soon as Jake had closed and locked the door, Matt asked, "So, I know Ryan and Aaron are a couple, but are you guys single?"

The situation suddenly turned awkward. The four housemates exchanged nervous glances, knowing where this question might lead.

Ryan said, "Okay, so remember when you guys first got here on Tuesday and asked about our last names, and I said it was complicated?" Matt nodded. "Well, it is." Ryan gave Matt a brief, high-level explanation of everything that led to the realignment of the couples.

As Jake returned from the bathroom, he heard Ryan saying, "I love Aaron and I truly want him to be happy. And I could see that he was happier with Brandon than with me, so I let him go. I guess the bottom line is, I love all these guys so much, so I needed to forgive them and accept things the way they are."

Chris said, "We all love each other, in different ways. We've been through a lot of disruption and turmoil these past few weeks, and it's taken an emotional toll on all of us. But at the end of the day, we all love each other. We're a family, and we're stronger than ever."

Everyone was so focused on this discussion that nobody noticed Jake had returned from the bathroom. When they saw the confused look on his face, Matt said, "I'll fill you in later."

As they headed for the door, Chris pulled Matt aside. He put his hand on Matt's shoulder and spoke softly. "I know you can't wait to find out what it's like to be with another guy, but I think you need to deal with the issues at hand first. Don't worry, you'll find someone special. You'll know when the time is right. It'll all work out." Matt nodded. Chris leaned in close to Matt's ear and whispered, "And try to keep your hands off Jake!" Matt chuckled.

The four housemates took turns hugging Matt and Jake. After more goodbyes, Matt and Jake rode away on their bicycles.

The guys returned to the kitchen, put the leftovers away, and loaded the dirty dishes, silverware, and glasses in the dishwasher. Brandon said, "So, how much do you wanna bet they get it on with each other tonight?"

Aaron added, "If they haven't already."

Ryan stopped scooping the leftover mashed potatoes into a container. "Seriously? Jake's straight."

Brandon said, "Oh, please! Did you see how quickly he went from, 'We need to accept the Lord's teachings and leave the homosexual lifestyle,' to telling Matt, 'I've got your back?' He's got his back, all right – his backside."

Aaron said, "And you know Matt wants it."

Ryan shook his head. "You guys are pervs."

Chris said, "Just because a guy's cute, doesn't mean he's gay."

Brandon said, "Yeah, but come on. They're young, they're constantly horny, and they're not allowed to have any contact with women. Hell, they're not even supposed to beat off. And they're with another guy 24/7. Shit's bound to happen. Even if Jake's straight, a blowjob is a blowjob."

Aaron said, "Besides… From what I've heard, a lot of straight guys fantasize about doing anal with women. I bet a lot of them would fuck a guy in the ass if that was all that was available."

Brandon said, "There are a lot of guys who will do stuff with another guy if they're horny enough." He grinned. "Trust me on that."

Aaron said, "It didn't take much for him to drink a glass of wine. I bet it won't take much for him to throw his legs up in the air."

Ryan said, "Well, it sounds like you two have some new JO fantasies. Anyway, I think it's highly unlikely. But that's totally between them and we'll never know." The tone of Ryan's voice signaled that this discussion was over.

After they finished cleaning up, they migrated into the family room to relax. Everyone was thinking back on everything that had taken place. Finally, Aaron said, "Well, I hope it goes well for Matt."

Chris said, "Yeah, but something tells me it won't."

Ryan said, "Me too. And that sucks. I can see the same thing happening to him that happened to me." He sighed. "Why does it have to be this way? What's it going to take for churches and parents to lighten up and accept their gay kids for who they are?"

Of course, nobody had an answer for that. Ryan said, "I told him to call me if anything happens. I think I'll text him now and then to check in on him."

Help!

Thursday, December 9, 2021

After Desert Pride rehearsal, Ryan, Chris, Aaron, and Brandon gathered in the parking lot to chat with several of their band friends. They still weren't comfortable going to a bar, even though the pandemic was loosening its grip.

Chris asked the group, "How do you think rehearsal went?"

Kent said, "There were some rough spots here and there, but I think we're in good shape for the concert on Sunday."

Ryan said, "Me too. A lot of times, a shitty dress rehearsal means a great concert."

Aaron asked, "I wonder why that is?"

Rob said, "It's a wake-up call. People will practice more between now and Sunday. And people will focus more. If the rehearsal had gone well tonight, people might be more complacent on Sunday."

Kent said, "Yeah, I've seen it happen that way many times."

Ryan could feel his phone vibrating in his pocket. He pulled it out and looked at the Caller ID. It was Matt. He touched Answer. "This is Ryan. Hello?"

"Hey Ryan, it's Matt. Thank God you answered." Matt was speaking softly, just above a whisper. Ryan could barely hear him.

"Why? What's up?" Ryan walked around to the other side of his car where it would be quieter.

"It happened. My parents found out I'm gay. They're totally freaking out. They're making me go to this therapist who says he can make me straight. I had my first visit with him earlier today and, oh my God! It was awful! He started asking me all kinds of questions about–"

Ryan tried to interrupt him. "Matt? Matt?"

Finally, Matt stopped talking and took a breath.

Ryan said, "My parents did the same shit to me. It's totally bogus, and it will only get worse."

"Yeah. There's no way I'm going to keep seeing him."

"Have you told your parents that?"

"Yeah. But Dad says as long as I'm living under his roof, I have to do what he says. He said either I keep going to this guy until I turn straight or he'll kick me out."

"Okay, so how can I help?"

"I need to get out of here. I really want to come back to Scottsdale, or at least somewhere in Phoenix. But I'm not sure how I'll get there or where I'll stay or anything else. But I can't stay here."

"Can't you just book a flight and come here? I'll send you some money by Zelle or Venmo if you need it."

"I have the money I saved up for my mission. But how would I get to the airport in Pocatello? My parents aren't going to drive me there."

"Call an Uber or Lyft. You have them up there, don't you?"

"I don't know. I've never used them."

"Hmmm... Okay, I need some time to think about this and explore our options. Can I call you back in about an hour?"

"Yeah. My parents should be in bed by then, but I'll put the phone on vibrate. I'll stay up until I hear from you."

"Okay, cool. Oh, and... Do you have a credit card?"

"No, but I have a debit card."

"Okay. Well, I'll call you in about an hour. Maybe an hour and a half."

"Thanks, Ryan. I really, really appreciate it."

"You're welcome. Don't worry, we'll get you out of there somehow. Bye!"

"Bye."

Ryan slid his phone into his pocket and walked back to the group. "Matt's folks found out he's gay, and the shit hit the fan."

Rob said, "Who's Matt?"

"A Mormon missionary. He and his companion came to our house just before Thanksgiving. Long story short, after he saw that we were gay, he came out to us. Last week, he quit his mission and went back home."

Chris asked, "How did they find out he's gay?"

"I don't know. We didn't get into that."

Petunia said, "I don't envy him. A lot of Mormons don't look kindly upon quitting your mission or being gay. He's got both going against him."

"Yeah. They're making him see some bogus shrink who says he can convert him, like my dad did to me."

Aaron said, "So what are you going to do?"

Ryan said, "Well, obviously, he wants to get out of there. He said he wants to come back here, but I don't know what he's going to do once he gets here. We can put him up for a little while, but that's not a permanent solution. I want to help him out, but I don't want five people living in our house long-term."

For a moment, everyone pondered the situation. Then Petunia spoke up. "He can live with me."

Kent said, "Are you serious?"

"Of course I'm serious. I wouldn't have said it if I wasn't serious. Look, I used to be a Mormon. That is, until my parents found out I was gay and kicked me out. I know exactly what he's going through."

Justin said, "I didn't know were a Mormon."

"That's because I don't talk about it. That's buried in the past. But I have a guest bedroom no one ever sleeps in. He can stay there."

Ryan said, "That's really kind of you. Now I need to figure out how he's going to get out of there and get down here."

Aaron said, "Can't he just get on a plane and fly down here?"

"Yeah. But this just happened. He's panicking and not thinking clearly yet."

Chris said, "Maybe he could take a bus like you did."

"Maybe. I don't even know if Greyhound serves Pocatello. And he has to get from Inkom to Pocatello somehow. Anyway, I need to think about this some more and research his options." Ryan turned to Chris, Aaron, and Brandon. "Guys, sorry to cut this short, but I need to get back home."

They circulated among their friends, hugging them and saying goodbye. Then they piled into Ryan's car and began the drive home.

Aaron said, "Do you think it's a good idea to let him stay with Petunia?"

"Why not? Do you think he'd try to take advantage of him or something?"

"No, it's just... Well, let's just say he's not one of my favorite people. Especially after a couple of the things he did to me."

"Like that time he practically outed you to your parents?"

"Yeah. And the time he loaned me his copy of *The Boys of Breckenridge* to tell me you used to do porn."

Chris spoke up. "Yeah, but weren't you better off because he did those things? Remember, he's the one who told me Seth had been whoring around on me."

Aaron thought for a moment. "Yeah, I guess. But do you think Matt will want to live with someone who's so ... out there?"

Ryan said, "You mean effeminate and flamboyant? He's going to meet all kinds of gay people soon enough. I don't care about that. I'm more concerned that he's safe. And since Petunia has been through the same thing Matt's going through, that's a big plus."

"Yeah, I guess."

They arrived home. Ryan headed straight for his office and fired up his computer.

A half-hour later, Chris opened the door to Ryan's office and leaned his head in. "How's it going?"

Ryan was focused on his computer with a perplexed look on his face. "Geez. Pocatello really *is* a small town in the middle of nowhere. There's only one flight in and out every day. It goes to Salt Lake City. The flight in arrives at 11:46 p.m., and the flight out leaves at 6:30 a.m."

Chris walked in, closed the door behind him, and knelt next to Ryan's chair. "Seriously? There aren't even flights to Denver or Boise?"

"Nope. Only Delta goes there, and Salt Lake City is their hub. So if he flies from Pocatello to Salt Lake City to Phoenix, it'll cost around $500. I looked into Greyhound, and the ride from Pocatello to Phoenix costs around $135. But it takes 28 hours and three transfers."

"Well, he's not pressed for time."

"True."

Chris said, "But what about COVID? I mean, we're driving to Prairie Village for Christmas because we think it's still too risky to fly. And a bus would be even worse. They don't have filtered air circulation like they do on planes. He'd be sitting in an enclosed space with others for 28 hours. And I'll bet a lot of them won't be wearing masks."

Ryan sighed. "Yeah, that's a good point. We don't want him coming here a few days before Christmas and giving everyone else COVID."

"Can't we ask him to stay there until after Christmas? He'll get to spend one last Christmas with his family."

"He seemed pretty desperate to get out now. Besides, that would be one awkward Christmas. And even if he waits until after Christmas, the

COVID risks are still the same.”

For a moment, they stared at each other. Neither of them could think of anything else.

Chris suddenly lit up. “Wait! I have an idea. He could rent a car.”

“Hmmm... Assuming he can get one. I wonder how much it would cost. And he’d probably have to spend at least one night in a motel. And then there’s food and gas.”

“It would be less than an airplane flight, for sure. But he’d be safe from COVID.”

Ryan opened Orbitz and searched for prices for Pocatello to Scottsdale on December 18. “They start at $72 a day for a subcompact or an economy car. And they have some available.” He scrolled down some more. “Wow. You can get a midsize for $75 or a full size for $76. Still... that’s a lot higher than it was in 2019 when I rented a car in Washington for that training class.”

Chris said, “Well, it’s not 2019 anymore. The rental car companies sold off most of their fleets in 2020 because nobody was renting cars and they needed the cash. Prices went through the roof. You couldn’t even get a car in a lot of places. I read where people were renting U-Hauls in Hawaii because there weren’t any cars available.”

“I guess it is what it is. Still, that’s doable. He’ll probably have to rent it for two days and stay in a motel somewhere. I wonder how far it is.” Ryan opened another window and launched Google Maps. “It’s only about 12 hours. I thought it would take longer than that.”

Chris said, “Maybe he could drive it in one day. It would be a hell of a long drive, though.”

“Let’s call him and find out.” Ryan picked up his phone and called.

After one ring, Matt answered. “Hey, Ryan.”

“Hey, Matt. Is this a good time to talk?”

“Yeah, my parents and my little brothers are in bed. I still need to keep quiet, though.”

“Okay. Chris is here with me, so let me put you on speaker.”

Chris said, “Hi, Matt.”

“Hi, Chris.”

Ryan said, “So we looked up how much it would cost for you to come here by airplane or by bus. But both of those put you at risk of catching COVID. We’re not flying to visit our families for Christmas because of COVID.”

"I'll wear a mask the whole time."

"That would help, but there will probably be plenty of other people around you who won't. But then Chris came up with the idea of you driving here in a rental car. You have a driver's license, right?"

"Yeah."

"It's a 12-hour drive. You could try to drive it all in one day or break it up and stay in a motel somewhere."

"How much would that cost?"

"Well, the car rental itself is around $75 a day. Of course, there will be taxes, so that will bring it to around $90. Plus you should probably opt for their insurance. I don't know whether your parents' auto insurance policy would cover this, so you'd better take it. And then there's gas... It's 817 miles, so if the car gets 25 miles to the gallon, that would work out to... hmmm... 33 gallons at around $3 a gallon... about 100 bucks. And you'll stop a couple of times for meals. So let's see... probably around $250 if you did it all in one day. If you split it into two days, there would be another day of car rental and a night in a motel, so add around $200 or so."

Matt thought for a moment. "I can try to do it all in one day."

"Good. Renting a car will be a lot safer. And you can operate on your own timeline."

Chris said, "But here's another thing. He doesn't have a credit card."

Ryan typed in a couple of searches. "You can rent a car with a debit card. They might put a hold on a larger amount, but it will work."

Matt asked, "So where would I get the rental car?"

"At the airport in Pocatello. I checked, and both Uber and Lyft serve Inkom. They'll pick you up wherever you tell them and take you to the airport for about $20."

"Cool. How do you set that up?"

"It's an app you put on your phone. You have to link it to a payment method, like your bank account, a credit or debit card, or Venmo."

"Okay, but I can't just have them come to my house and pick me up."

"Why not? You're over 18. Your parents can't stop you. Besides, won't your dad be at work? And what about your mom?"

"Yeah, they'll be gone. He works in Pocatello. She works at our local grocery store. She got a job there when my youngest brother started school so they could save money for our missions."

"Okay, then they won't be there to stop you."

Chris asked, "But why sneak out on them? Can't you sit down with them and have a conversation about it? Tell them you're an adult now and you want to be out on your own, and can't we deal with this like grownups? You'd be leaving on better terms. And maybe they'll drive you to the airport."

"I don't know..."

"At least try. If they're willing to be reasonable, great. If they're not, you can just leave."

"When would we do that? They've already gone to bed, and tomorrow morning Dad will be in a hurry to get to work. I was hoping to leave tomorrow."

"Maybe talk to them tomorrow night and leave Saturday?"

"Yeah, but if it doesn't go well, it will be harder to sneak out on Saturday. They'll be home."

Ryan said, "Remember, you're an adult. They can't stop you. Now, do you have any suitcases?"

"Yeah, I have the one took on my mission."

"Okay, good. Fill it with as much as you can. One bit of good advice I got when I had to leave home is to take the stuff that's most meaningful to you. You know, stuff that can't be replaced, like mementos, pictures, awards you got at school, or souvenirs from trips. Take as many clothes as you can, but you can buy clothes once you get here. Do you get what I'm saying?"

Chris said, "Why is he limited to a suitcase if he's renting a car?"

Ryan said, "That's true. Once you have the car, you can stop back at your house and load it up."

Matt said, "True, but I don't have that much."

"Okay. Do you have a Social Security card or a passport?"

"Yes and no."

"Make sure you take your Social Security card. Also, if you have your final report cards from each year of school, take them. You may need that to get into college. Any other records or important stuff like that, you should take."

"Okay, but I think my parents have that stuff."

"Do you know where they keep it, and can you get to it if they're both out of the house?"

"Yeah, I think so."

"Okay. So let's talk about money. You said you had some money you had saved up for your mission."

"Yeah, a little over $2,000."

"Is it in your account or a joint account with your parents?"

"It's mine. They kept the money they saved from my mom working, but I have the money I made from my summer jobs."

"Okay, what bank is it with?"

"The Ireland Bank."

"What? Your money is in a bank in Ireland?"

"No, that's just the name of it. It's the only bank with an office in Inkom."

"I've never heard of it."

"I think they're only in Idaho."

"Okay, then you should probably go there tomorrow morning and close your account. Take some of it in cash and ask them to write you a cashier's check for the rest."

"Won't I need to use my debit card to pay for the rental car and the Uber?"

Chris asked, "Can you close it online or over the phone?"

"I don't know."

Ryan said, "I guess you need to go into your bank tomorrow morning and ask if you can close your account remotely and if so, how."

"Okay."

"So it looks like we're all set."

"So... Uh... Where will I stay once I get there?"

Ryan and Chris glanced at each other and nodded. "You can stay here, at least for a few days. Another guy we know has offered to let you stay with him. We'll have you meet him once you get here. We also need to think about what you're going to do once you're here, like get a job or go to college or whatever. Where you live might depend on that."

"Okay, we can deal with that when I get there."

Chris added, "You'll have plenty of time to think about that while you're driving for 12 hours."

Matt said, "Wow... I can't believe I'm actually doing this."

Ryan said, "Yeah, well, don't do it unless you're really sure. If you need to take a couple of days to think about it, do it. It won't matter in the long run."

"I'm really sure. Well, I guess I should let you go. I want to talk to Mark a little bit and maybe start packing my suitcase."

"Cool. Call me if you need anything. And let me know when you expect to arrive."

"Okay. And thanks! Thanks a lot!"

"You're welcome. Good night."

"Bye."

Matt Arrives

Sunday, December 12, 2021

At 1:15 a.m., Matt turned his rental car into the driveway and shut it off. Ryan heard the car door slam and said, "He's here!"

Ryan, Chris, Aaron, and Brandon had been waiting up for him. They helped him carry his possessions into the music room where he'd be staying temporarily. There was still some space in the closet from when Chris had stayed there. The sleeping bag and air mattress Chris used were out and ready for Matt.

Chris asked, "How was your drive?"

"Long. Very long. Sorry I got here so late. I stopped a couple of times for meals and gas, and at several rest areas to pee."

Aaron said, "No problem. You got here safely. That's all that matters."

Ryan asked, "How did it go with your parents?"

"Ehhh... not terrible, but they weren't happy. They didn't try to stop me, though."

"Well, I can tell you're exhausted. Why don't we let you get some sleep and we can talk about it tomorrow? Speaking of which, Desert Pride, the band we all play in, has a concert tomorrow. We have to be there from 10:00 to 12:00 for the dress rehearsal. The concert isn't until 3:00. We get a two-hour break for lunch, so we can come back home, eat lunch, and take you with us when we go back for the concert – that is, if you want to go. You don't have to."

Aaron added, "If you want to sleep all day, that's fine."

Matt said, "No, I want to go. But I need to return my rental car by 10:00 a.m. or I'll get charged for another day."

Everyone stared at each other as they pondered the logistics of how this would work. Matt could easily make it to the rental car center near the airport by 10:00, but nobody would be available to drive him home.

Brandon said, "I guess we could go return it now. They're probably open 24 hours a day."

Chris said, "Even if they're not, there's probably a box where you can drop off the keys."

Aaron said, "Yeah, but he's exhausted. I'd hate to have him drive another 20 miles and fall asleep."

Ryan said, "How about this? One of us can drive the rental car to the airport tomorrow morning on the way to rehearsal. I'll follow with the rest of us and pick up that person, then we ride the rest of the way to the rehearsal together."

Brandon asked, "Really? Doesn't Matt have to be the one who returns the car?"

"Nope. They never check who's driving when you return a car."

Chris said, "Well, okay then. Sounds like a plan." He turned to Matt. "Get some rest and we'll see you when we come home for lunch."

Matt handed Ryan his keys and said, "Sounds good. Thanks guys! You don't know how much I appreciate this."

They all hugged Matt, then everyone retreated to their bedrooms to get some sleep.

***

When Ryan, Chris, Aaron, and Brandon left at 9:00 a.m. to drop off Matt's car and go to the dress rehearsal, he was still sound asleep. When they returned for lunch, he was up, dressed, and ready to go.

After lunch, the four band members went to their bedrooms to change into their tuxes. When they came out, Matt asked, "Do I look okay? Or should I put on a suit or something?"

Brandon said, "No, you look fine. The audience will be dressed pretty casually."

Aaron said, "Yeah. I wish we didn't have to wear tuxes. It's a bit much, in my opinion."

Ryan said, "We should probably get going. With five people, we should take two cars."

***

After the concert, the band members went to the lobby to meet and greet their friends. Matt found Ryan and Chris and tagged along. They introduced Matt to their friends.

At one point, Petunia sashayed up to them and exclaimed, "Well! Is this our newly liberated missionary?"

Matt was taken aback. *How does this swishy, effeminate person know about me?*

Ryan said, "You could say that. Matt, this is Petunia. Petunia, this is Matt."

Matt looked even more perplexed. *Is this person's name really Petunia?*

Ryan saw Matt's puzzled look. "His name is actually Stephen, but everyone calls him Petunia."

"That's right, dear. And I'm *always* in full bloom!" Petunia extended his hand to Matt, palm down and limp at the wrist. Matt shook it cautiously, and Petunia curtsied. "Honey, about the LDS thing? Been there, done that, paid the therapy bills. Trust me, it wasn't pretty. I'm always available to talk if you want to."

"Uh... Thanks." Matt forced a smile as he tried to visualize Petunia showing up at someone's door wearing a white shirt, black pants, a tie, and a name tag.

"Well, I have more adoring fans to greet, so I'll be on my way. Ta-ta!" Petunia spun around with a flourish and headed for a nearby group.

Ryan whispered, "We'll talk more later."

For the next 15 minutes, Ryan and Chris greeted their friends and acquaintances, usually with hugs. They introduced Matt to their bandmates. Everyone seemed so friendly and affectionate toward one another. It was a happy scene. Matt realized he had never been part of a large gathering of gay people before. He marveled at this new world he was being introduced to and that he was now a part of.

Matt rode with Ryan and Chris on the way home. Chris asked, "How did you like the concert?"

"It was awesome! I had no idea what to expect, but you guys were really good!"

"Have you ever played a musical instrument?"

"Not really. When band started in 5th grade I tried playing the clarinet, but I never really got into it. I like music, though."

Ryan said, "So, about Petunia. He's quite a character, isn't he?"

"That's one way to put it."

"Yeah. A little goes a long way with him. He's actually a nice guy. You get used to the campiness after a while. And yes, he used to be LDS. His parents kicked him out when they found out he was gay. We just learned that on Thursday night. We were talking with some friends after rehearsal when you called. So I told the other guys what was going on. Petunia offered to let you stay with him. I told him you'd stay with us for a few days until you decided what you're going to do. Then we'll see where it makes sense for you to live. Of course, you should meet him again and get to know him better before you decide whether you want to live with him."

Chris said, "He lives in Phoenix, a couple miles north of downtown. That area is the closest thing we have to a gayborhood here. It's more centrally located and not too far from the light rail."

Ryan added, "It's near where the concert was held."

Matt said, "Yeah, okay. To be honest, I was hoping I could stay with you guys. I don't have much stuff, so I wouldn't take up much space."

Chris said, "Actually, Aaron and Brandon are moving into their own apartment after the first of the year, so there will be more room after that."

Ryan said, "But that will depend on whether you decide to go to college or get a job or whatever – and if so, where. We can talk about all that later."

They arrived home. As they walked into the house, Ryan said, "I'll start fixing dinner as soon as I change out of my tux. I'm just going to keep it simple and make spaghetti and meatballs. So we'll probably be eating in 15 or 20 minutes."

***

Once the food was served and they were seated, they talked about how they felt the concert went. Ryan, Chris, Aaron, and Brandon caught each other up on their jobs. Ryan explained how his Sunday family night dinner tradition got started. Then Aaron turned to Matt. "Tell us more about your trip."

"It went pretty smooth."

Brandon asked, "What was the scenery like?"

"The first five hours driving south on I-15 was pretty boring. There are some mountains and hills, but it's all brown. It was a little more interesting around Salt Lake City. At least I could see some buildings and there were more signs and exits. But then, southern Utah got boring again."

Ryan said, "Yeah, I remember riding the bus through southern Utah on my way to LA. Lots of nothing for miles and miles."

"By the time I got to Arizona, it was dark. It looked like it might be interesting, and at least there were more mountains and stuff."

Aaron said, "Yeah. The drive on I-17 between here and Flagstaff is pretty nice."

Ryan asked, "So, did you think about what you want to do now that you're here?"

"Well, I want to go to college, that's for sure. But I don't think $2,000 will get me very far. I have no idea how much ASU costs, but I'm sure it's a lot more than that. I'll probably need to get a job first and save some money."

Brandon said, "It's like $30,000 a year for out-of-state students. Of course, I got a basketball scholarship, so it didn't cost me much."

Matt let out a huge sigh. "Crap. I have no idea how I'm ever going to afford that."

Brandon said, "There's a lot of financial aid available, and there are work-study programs. I read somewhere that 87% of the students get financial aid of some sort."

Chris said, "Plus, that's for out-of-state tuition. Once you've lived here for a year, you'll qualify for in-state."

Matt said, "So I guess that means I should work for a year, then apply next year."

Ryan said, "Or, there's this. Scottsdale Community College is only a few miles away. A lot of kids go there for two years, get an Associate's degree, and then transfer to ASU for their junior and senior years. That would be much cheaper."

Matt thought about that for a moment. "Yeah, that could work." He hesitated for a moment. *I might as well put this out there and see what they say.* "Especially if I could stay here with you guys."

Ryan and Chris exchanged glances. Chris nodded. Ryan said, "Well, Chris and I have talked about that. As we mentioned on the way home, Aaron and Brandon are moving out after the first of the year. You can move into their room. Rent would be $500 a month, plus you'd be responsible for your own food."

Aaron said, "You could get a job at the Food World where I work. They're always hiring."

Brandon said, "I worked there during the summers while I was in college. It's pretty decent. They paid, like, $10 an hour."

Aaron said, "It's more than that now. During the pandemic, a lot of people quit. So they had to pay more to get people to work there. I think it's around $12 now."

Brandon said, "And the hours are pretty flexible. If you tell them when your classes are, they'll work around that."

Matt asked, "How far is it?"

Chris said, "It's less than a mile. You could walk."

Ryan said, "Yeah, but once you start at Scottsdale Community College, you'll need some form of transportation. It's close enough to ride a bike but too far to walk. I'll ask our neighbors if anyone has a bike we can borrow."

Aaron said, "If not, maybe you can find something on Craigslist."

Ryan said, "Sometime this week, I'll take you to SCC and you can visit their admissions office. Then we can stop at Food World and you can fill out an application."

Aaron added, "Come see me in the pharmacy, and I'll introduce you to the store manager."

Matt smiled. "Thanks, guys. I don't know what I'd do without you. Well, I guess I do. I'd probably still be in Idaho, seeing some quack about turning straight."

Ryan thought, *Or you'd be on a bus heading for LA and end up at the LGBT Youth Project.*

With that topic finished, everyone ate silently for a few minutes. Ryan got up and refilled people's wine glasses.

Matt brought up another topic that was on his mind. "So, uh... What are you guys doing for Christmas?"

It dawned on the others that Christmas was less than two weeks away, and Matt would be spending Christmas without his family.

Chris said, "Well, COVID has altered our Christmas plans. None of us want to fly, so Ryan and I are driving to Prairie Village, Kansas to spend Christmas with my folks."

Ryan added, "It's two days each way, and I imagine our driving experience will be much like yours."

Aaron said, "Brandon and I are staying here. It's too far to drive to Ohio to see my folks, and I couldn't get that much time off anyway. So we'll be here. We'll figure out something to do."

Matt looked relieved. Still, he knew Christmas would be different this year.

Across the Heartland

Friday, December 24, 2021

At 7:01 a.m., the sunrise sent light peeking around the edges of the curtains in Ryan and Chris's motel room in Tucumcari, New Mexico.

Ryan woke up first. He was spooning Chris from behind with his right arm draped across his waist. They had been sleeping together for two months, but Ryan still savored waking up each morning and seeing Chris beside him. The queen-size bed in the cheap roadside motel was a poor substitute for their comfortable California King at home, but at least Chris was in it. And they were about to spend their first Christmas together.

Their naked bodies resting against each other stirred feelings in Ryan. Seconds later, his growing erection was pressing against the underside of Chris's crotch. Ryan wiggled his body forward a couple of inches until his chest and stomach pressed firmly against Chris's back.

Chris stirred. He slowly opened his eyes and saw the cheap curtains with the light streaming in around the edges. It took him a few seconds to remember where he was and why he was there. As he awakened, he became acutely aware of Ryan's skin against his back and his hardness pressing against his butt crack.

Ryan leaned forward and kissed the side of Chris's neck. "Good morning!"

Chris turned his head to the right enough to meet Ryan's lips for a light kiss. "I can tell *you're* having a good morning."

"I know how we can make it even better."

"What time is it?"

"A little after seven. C'mon, we have time. If we get on the road by eight, we should still arrive at your parents' house by six."

"Seven. We'll lose an hour when we cross into Central time."

"And your point...?"

"Oh, all right. But let me get up for a second. I need to piss like a racehorse." He pulled the covers aside and climbed out of bed. He glanced

204

down at Ryan. "Speaking of racehorses..."

"I'll be waiting right here. Oh, and bring one of the hand towels, please."

When Chris emerged from the bathroom three minutes later, Ryan had turned toward the bathroom. He was propped up on his right elbow and gazing seductively at Chris. A bottle of lube was waiting on the bedside table.

Chris smiled. During the last few years of his relationship with Seth, their sex life had slowed to a crawl. He was thrilled to have someone show so much desire for him. And he was thrilled that it was Ryan. It was fun to act like horny teenagers again. He knew he should enjoy it for however long it lasted. If they arrived at his parents' house a little later than planned ... oh well.

***

As they snuggled afterward, Ryan said, "Remember the time we stayed at that cheap motel in Wichita when we went to the state track meet?"

"I'll never forget that night. God, I wanted you so badly."

"Yeah, I'm sorry I was too scared to do it. Anyway, I guess we made up for it now."

Chris chuckled. "And remember how we were so tired we slept through the wake-up call? And you set the alarm for 6:30 p.m. instead of 6:30 a.m.?"

"Yeah. Coach Riley finally called the room at 7:15. We had to throw our clothes on and rush downstairs so the team could leave on time."

"Ah, the good old days."

"Yeah, kinda. It was a mixed bag for me. But anyway, let's take our showers and get out of here."

***

After driving three hours northeast on US 54, they were now in the Oklahoma panhandle. The CD they were listening to ended, so Chris ejected it and put it back in its case. "Man, this has to be the most boring drive ever. Straight, flat, and not a thing to see."

"I know, right? I'm glad I brought plenty of big band CDs along."

"Yeah, they do keep the energy up. But let's take a little break, okay?"

"Sure. Hey, it's almost noon. I'm getting hungry. What do we have up ahead?"

Chris opened the map app on his phone. He snickered. "Get this! The next town is Hooker, Oklahoma!"

Ryan chuckled. "Not exactly where I'd want to eat out. What do they have there?"

"Not much. We might be better off to wait until we get to Liberal, Kansas. It's only twenty miles further."

"Liberal, Kansas. Isn't that an oxymoron?"

"Probably. Oh, and there's a town east of here called Beaver."

"I wonder what their high school mascot is."

"I dunno... do you think it's actually a beaver?"

"It could be worse. It could be a crab."

"The Beaver Crabs. Ewww..."

"The beaver should be the mascot for Hooker."

When they entered Hooker, they passed a small building labeled the Hooker Chamber of Commerce. Outside, a portable roadside sign read, 'Get your Hooker T-Shirts here.'

Chris took a picture of it on his phone.

Ryan asked, "You took a picture of *that*?"

"It's the most interesting thing we've seen all day. I'm posting it to my Instagram." Chris typed for a moment, then said, "I captioned it, 'Hooker, I'm in you.'"

Ryan laughed. "Good thing we aren't passing through Beaver."

Twenty minutes later, they reached Liberal. Ryan said, "I'm seeing lots of motels and gas stations, but not much in the way of restaurants. Don't they eat out here?"

"I know. I'm surprised all these little motels still exist."

"Maybe they charge by the hour."

"I would have expected that back in Hooker."

"This part of the country seems like it's still stuck in the 50s or 60s. It's like they're frozen in time."

Chris scrolled ahead on the map. "Hey, there's a Pizza Palace ahead on the right."

"Is it an actual restaurant, not just a delivery and pick-up place?"

"Yep. What do you think?"

"Sold." Ryan turned into the restaurant and parked. "I didn't know Pizza Palace still had sit-down restaurants."

"Well, like you said, they seem to be frozen in time."

***

At 4:30, they were driving through Wichita. Chris said, "Hey, I wonder if that motel we stayed at when we were here for the state championship meet is still there?"

"Probably."

"You know what? I think it would be cool to go back there and spend the night. Maybe we could get the same room! Do you remember what it was?"

"Room 253, I believe. But seriously? You want to spend Christmas Eve in a cheap motel? That means we wouldn't arrive at your parents' house until 10 or 11 on Christmas morning."

"Yeah, I guess you're right. But maybe we could do it on our way home."

"Why? Is sex in cheap motels a turn-on for you?"

"It's not that. It's because that's the first night we spent together."

Ryan glanced at the clock on the dashboard. "So anyway, it's 4:30 now. Do you want to stop and get dinner here or power through to your parents' house? We still have three hours to go."

"I think they're expecting us for dinner. We should probably keep going."

"Maybe you should call and tell them our ETA is 7:30."

"Okay."

"Maybe we could get a snack when we stop and get gas. Would you mind driving the rest of the way? I'm starting to fade."

"Yeah, okay."

***

At 7:30, Chris turned into the driveway and parked. They climbed out of the car and headed toward the front door. Chris's mother Kathleen was waiting and opened the door for them to enter.

She gave Ryan a kiss and a big hug. "Oh, honey, it's so nice to see you again!" She kissed him again. "I've been so concerned about you all these years."

"Uh... Mom? It's me, Chris. You know, your son. I'm here too."

She released Ryan and turned to hug Chris. "I know, honey. But it's been over 14 years since I last saw Bryan. Oh, I mean Ryan." She held Chris and kissed him. "You know I'm always happy to see you."

Chris's father Tom approached and Ryan offered him a handshake. Tom wrapped his arms around Ryan. "We don't shake hands in this house, we hug. Welcome back!"

"Thanks, Mr. Robertson. It's great to be back."

"And call me Tom. We're all adults now."

"And call me Kathleen. I'll bet you boys are hungry."

Chris said, "Starving!"

"Well, come into the kitchen and I'll get the food on the table. We've been keeping it warm for you."

***

At 11:00, Chris and Ryan were still talking with Tom and Kathleen. Ryan had been nodding off for the past half-hour. Finally, he said, "I'm sorry, but after two long days of driving, I'm exhausted. I need to get some sleep."

Everyone stood up and hugged. Kathleen said, "You boys can sleep in as long as you like. Tyler and his wife and kids are coming over at around 12:30 or 1:00. We'll eat lunch when they get here and then open our presents. We'll have Christmas dinner at around 5:00."

Chris said, "Sounds good."

Tom said, "It's nice to have you home, son. And Ryan, it's nice to have you here, too. We're really happy for the two of you."

Ryan said, "Back in high school, this was my home away from home. It's great to be back."

Everyone hugged again, and Chris and Ryan climbed the familiar stairs to Chris's bedroom.

After they had settled into bed, Chris said, "And here we are. Remember the last time we were in this bed?"

"I'll never forget that night. I've replayed it in my head so many times."

"Me too. I guess it's true that you never forget your first time."

"And now, I can stay all night. I don't have to get back home by midnight."

Chris snuggled up closer. "So, whaddya say we stage a reenactment?"

"Tonight? Honey, I'm exhausted."

Chris sighed.

Ryan said, "I promise we can make love in your childhood bed while we're here. Just not tonight, okay?" He turned toward Chris, leaned in, and gave him a long kiss. "Good night. I love you."

"I love you too."

Ryan felt something pressing against the side of his waist. He reached down. "Well, somebody's not tired."

Chris kissed Ryan's cheek and whispered, "Stuff your stocking, mister?"

"Oh, geez..." He let out a dramatic sigh. "What am I going to do with you?"

"Well, you could keep me forever." Chris paused. "Wanna know what I'm going to do with you?"

"As if I couldn't guess." Ryan realized Chris was not going to take no for an answer. He rolled onto his left side, with his back toward Chris. He backed up to Chris until only a few inches separated them. "Just don't expect me to flip-flop tonight."

Fifteen minutes later, they kissed and said good night again. Chris whispered in Ryan's ear, "Just think... in the middle of the night some man might show up with a great big package just for me! He'll enter my chimney and whisper, 'Santa's *coming!*'"

"Go to sleep."

Three seconds later, Ryan did just that.

Christmas in Prairie Village

Saturday, December 25, 2021

Chris woke up at 7:45. Ryan was still sound asleep beside him. Chris thought about all those times in high school when he fantasized about spending the night with Ryan in this bed. Not surprisingly, that put him in the mood again.

He let Ryan sleep until 8:00, then he gave him a gentle kiss on his lips. Ryan stirred. He slowly opened his eyes and took in his surroundings.

Chris draped his arm across Ryan's body and snuggled in close. "Merry Christmas!"

Ryan yawned. "Merry Christmas. What time is it?"

"Eight o'clock."

"Geez, I could sleep for three more hours."

"Well, you stay here and rest a little longer. I'll go take my shower and get dressed. But don't stay in bed too late. It's Christmas!"

Ryan lay in bed for another half-hour. He dozed a couple of times, but he realized he wasn't going to get any more quality sleep. He got up, showered, got dressed, and went downstairs.

Tom and Kathleen were already up. Kathleen opened the oven and pulled out a bowl of scrambled eggs and a plate with some bacon strips wrapped in paper. There was a plate of cinnamon rolls with icing in the center of the table.

Chris had been waiting for Ryan, so they ate breakfast together. Tom and Kathleen sat down too, although they had already eaten.

Chris asked, "Why are Tyler, Chloe, and the kids not coming until 1:00?"

Kathleen replied, "I think Chloe wanted to take the kids to church for the Christmas morning service."

"Oh, so they're going to church now?"

Tom said, "Tyler isn't. As you know, we haven't been church-goers for years. But Chloe started going again after the kids were born. She says she wants to introduce the kids to religion. They can decide whether they want to continue when they get older."

Ryan said, "Gotta get 'em indoctrinated early."

Nobody said anything, but they all agreed.

Kathleen asked Ryan, "Is this the first time you've been back to Prairie Village since you left home?"

"Yep. For many years, I told myself I would never set foot in Kansas again. But now that my mother's dead and my father doesn't live here anymore, there's no reason to avoid it now. And of course, you live here, which is a great reason to return."

Kathleen said, "I'm so sorry about your mother. That must have been rough on you."

"Actually, since I was out of touch with my family for so long, I didn't find out about it until a couple of years later. But yeah, the whole thing about how she suffered from depression for many years and then died was so sad."

"And it's too bad you'll never get to see her again."

"True, but... Well, I don't know whether you believe in this sort of thing, but there's a guy in our band, Desert Pride, who's a medium. One time he told me that my mother's spirit often shows up at rehearsals and stands behind me, listening to me play. I booked a reading with him and my mother came through. We were able to talk about a lot of things, so we're at peace with each other now. So while I'll never see her again in this life, it's comforting to know she's there."

Chris said, "Tell them about her at your wedding."

"Oh, yeah. Paul, the medium, was one of the guests at my wedding with Aaron. He said she walked up the aisle as if she was the flower girl, and stood up there with us during the ceremony."

Kathleen said, "That's really sweet."

Tom said, "So what about your dad? I haven't heard anything about him since he got caught in that sex-and-drugs orgy and his congregation booted him out." He paused. "But if you'd rather not talk about him, that's fine."

"No, that's okay. He's living in Mesa now. He moved out there when Brandon started at ASU. And speaking of my wedding, he showed up. He stayed in his car in the parking lot and watched it from there. I had no idea he'd be there, but he found out about it from someone's Facebook post. Anyway, when I found out he was there, I totally lost it. I almost ruined the wedding. But Aaron calmed me down, and then everything went on like it was supposed to."

Chris said, "Yeah, I remember that. You guys were having some big argument off to the side right after the ceremony when you were supposed to be signing your marriage license. Most of the other people had no idea what was going on and we were all like, 'Oh shit, what's happening?'"

"I admit, that wasn't one of my better moments. Anyway, he and I met a couple of weeks later and we cleared the air about some things. He asked me to forgive him, and I did. But I still don't like him and I don't want him to be part of my life in any significant way. Brandon still has contact with him, so I know I'll cross paths with him once in a while. But I can't just pretend that nothing ever happened."

Tom said, "I can see how it would be difficult to maintain a normal relationship with him after everything that happened."

Kathleen added, "And it's probably awkward for Brandon to be caught in the middle."

Ryan said, "Yeah, he shouldn't have to pick sides. I have no right to tell him who he can or can't associate with. He's a lot closer with me than he is with his father, but they're in touch and they see each other every so often. Brandon doesn't usually talk about it in front of me, which is fine."

Having exhausted that topic, they moved on to other things. After fourteen years, there was a lot of catching up to do. The time flew by and the next thing they knew, Tyler and his family arrived.

Tom, Kathleen, and Chris hugged Tyler, Chloe, and their kids. Then Tyler turned to Ryan and said, "Dude! Long time no see!" He gave Ryan a big hug. "I'm so happy you and Chris finally get to be together! This is my wife, Chloe. Chloe, this is Ryan. He and Chris were best friends in high school. And more!"

Chloe stepped forward and extended her hand. "Yes, I've heard all about you."

Ryan wondered how much Chloe had heard, and what. He shook her hand. "Pleased to meet you." He couldn't tell whether Chloe was pleased to meet him.

Chloe said, "And this is our daughter Whitney and our son Austin."

Ryan did everything he could to stifle an outburst of laughter. He wasn't very successful. Everyone glanced at Ryan with curiosity, wondering what was so funny.

Chloe turned to the kids and said, "And this is Uncle Chris's friend

Ryan."

Friend, Ryan thought. *Okay, so that's how this is going to go.* He decided to let Chris and Tyler deal with that – if at all.

At 6'6", Ryan towered over the kids. He dropped to his knees so he could address them on a more even level. "Hi, Whitney! Hi, Austin!" He smiled broadly as he shook their hands. "Are you all excited for Christmas?"

The kids lit up. They both said, "Yeah!"

"What did Santa bring you?"

Whitney said, "I got a Barbie Dreamtopia Color Change Mermaid and a Bluey Family Home Playset!"

Ryan said, "Wow! I didn't know Barbie came as a mermaid now."

"Yeah! Her tail changes color and everything!"

"And how about you, Austin?"

"I got Hot Wheels Massive Loop Mayhem and a Star Wars Lego set!"

"Cool! I had Hot Wheels and Legos when I was your age. They were loads of fun. I'm glad they still make them."

"Do you still have yours?"

"No, I gave them to my younger brother. Anyway, I think some of those presents under the tree have your names on them."

Austin became even more excited. "Can we open them now?"

Chloe said, "After we eat. It's time for lunch now."

Kathleen said, "Since there's eight of us, we're going to eat at the dining room table. We're having sandwiches. That should tide us over until our big dinner at 5:00. So come into the kitchen first to get your food, then carry it into the dining room."

Everyone filed into the kitchen. Ryan held back to let the others go first. After everyone else had passed, Tyler said, "The kids really seem to like you."

"They're adorable! And Austin reminds me of Brandon when he was nine."

"Oh, yeah. I remember you played with him a lot. No wonder you're good with kids."

Ryan lowered his voice to a whisper so only Tyler would hear him. "So... Whitney... Austin... Seems like Darnell made quite an impression on you. Or *in* you, as the case may be."

Tyler glared at Ryan. "Dude..."

Ryan put his hand on Tyler's shoulder. "Don't worry, the Vegas Rule applies."

Tyler looked Ryan straight in the eye. "Not a word. Ever."

Ryan nodded. "Not even to Chris."

Tyler smiled, relieved. He glanced down. "Chris is a lucky man."

"So am I."

Ryan wondered who among his former housemates at UCLA had shared this bit of personal information with Tyler. They knew Tyler since he had classes with Ted and had visited the house to study with him. He attended some of their wild parties. Tyler was probably still friends with them on Facebook. Maybe Tyler had seen some of his videos. Ryan realized his private parts weren't very private. At this point, it hardly mattered.

They started toward the kitchen. Ryan thought of something and put his hand on Tyler's shoulder. Tyler stopped and turned to face Ryan. Still whispering, Ryan said, "Hey, I've got a favor to ask. Later, right after all the presents have been opened, have your phone ready to record some video."

"Okay... Of what?"

"You'll see. C'mon, let's go eat."

Kathleen had laid out an assembly line of bread, a variety of lunchmeats, lettuce leaves, sliced tomatoes, and condiments. She also put out peanut butter and jelly, which the kids went for. There was a big bag of potato chips and everyone took a handful for their plate.

Tyler, Chloe, Whitney, and Austin sat on one side of the table and Tom, Kathleen, Chris, and Ryan sat on the other. Ryan sat across from Whitney and Austin.

"What grade are you in, Whitney?"

"Fifth."

And how about you, Austin?"

"Third."

"What school do you go to?"

Whitney answered, "The Young Disciples Christian Academy."

"Here in Prairie Village?"

"No, in Ashland Ridge, where we live."

"Oh, okay. I went to Young Disciples here in Prairie Village when I was in elementary school." *And I hated it.*

Chloe, who had been listening to the conversation, chimed in. "They have nine locations throughout the Kansas City metro area. I want our children to get a good *Christian* education."

Chloe's emphasis on the word Christian was not lost on Ryan. "Yeah, my parents felt the same way." He glanced at Tyler, sitting at the far end of the table beyond Chloe. Tyler rolled his eyes.

After everyone finished lunch, they gathered in the family room to open presents. Of course, most of the attention was focused on Whitney and Austin, but the grownups exchanged small gifts too.

When all the gifts had been opened, photos had been taken, and the excitement died down, Kathleen started gathering up the piles of discarded wrapping paper and ribbons. Ryan said, "Wait. I have one more."

She sat back down and everyone turned their attention towards Ryan.

Chris was sitting next to Ryan on the couch. Ryan reached over to the lower shelf on the end table next to him, where he had placed a small gift-wrapped box out of view. He handed the box to Chris. Chris looked at the box with curiosity. Ryan said, "Well, open it."

Chris pulled the bow off the top and slid his thumb under the ribbon to loosen and remove it. He picked at the tape at the end of the neatly wrapped box until he could undo the paper folds. All eyes were on Chris. Everyone wished he would just rip the paper off instead of trying to be so neat about it.

Ryan looked over at Tyler. When Tyler sensed Ryan's glance, Ryan nodded. Tyler reached into his pocket and pulled out his phone.

Chris opened the box and pulled out a small jewelry box. He stared at the box in disbelief, unable to speak or move.

Ryan slid off the couch, turned, and knelt in front of Chris. "I've waited 14 years to ask you this question. Until a couple of months ago, I didn't think this day would ever come. But it has, and I don't want to let another day go by without you by my side. Chris Robertson, will you marry me?"

Chris opened the box and gazed at the beautiful ring it contained. Tears started streaming down his face. Emotions poured over him. Then he realized he needed to answer. "Oh my God! Yes! Yes! Oh my God, yes!"

Tom, Kathleen, Whitney, and Austin clapped and whooped with joy. Tyler did his best to hold the phone steady as he hollered out, "Way to go, dude!"

Chris leaned forward, placed his hand behind Ryan's head, and pulled it toward him. They exchanged a few passionate kisses. They pulled back, their faces still a few inches apart.

Ryan said, "I love you."

"I love you too."

Kathleen, in particular, was overcome with joy. "My baby's getting married!"

Tom said, "Well, put it on!"

Ryan reached into the box and removed the ring. Tyler got up from his seat and moved within a couple of feet of Chris and Ryan to capture this moment close-up.

Chris said, "Which hand?"

Kathleen answered, "The left hand, just like the wedding ring."

Chris held out his left hand, and Ryan placed the ring on the end of his finger. He paused for dramatic effect, then slowly slid the ring down Chris's finger.

Chris held it up for all to see. "Oh my God, I never expected to get an engagement ring! I mean, I'm a guy, you know? But... Oh my God, it's beautiful!" He turned to Ryan. "You didn't have to do this."

"Yeah, but I wanted to. And I got a matching one for me." He reached over to the lower shelf of the end table and retrieved another small jewelry box. He handed it to Chris and held his left hand out. Chris opened the box and slid the ring onto Ryan's finger.

Kathleen said, "Hold on, let me get my phone. I want some pictures of this!"

After everyone had taken pictures and hugged each other, Tom asked, "So have you guys talked about when and where you're going to get married?"

Ryan replied, "Not yet. I wanted this to be a surprise. I know, it's only been two months since we got back together, but I think it's obvious we both want to be with each other for the rest of our lives."

Chris said, "Yeah, like there was no way I was going to say no to him."

"We'll probably talk about it on our way home. It's a long drive, so we'll have plenty of time. But I'm thinking maybe sometime in the fall." He turned toward Chris. "What about you?"

"Yeah, that sounds about right. We wouldn't want to rush into it, would we?"

"And it will probably be in Scottsdale. And of course, you'll all be invited. Sorry, I know that means there will be travel expenses."

Kathleen said, "Oh, honey, that's no problem. I know your friends are there. It makes more sense for us to travel there."

Tyler said, "We wouldn't miss it!"

Ryan said, "And I want to say one more thing. They say that when you marry someone, you also marry their family. Well, I couldn't be any luckier. One of the reasons Chris is such a wonderful man is that he comes from a wonderful family. I always enjoyed coming here when we were kids. You always made me feel welcome and special. And the same is true now."

Tom said, "You are special, and you'll always be welcome. I think I speak for everyone when I say we're thrilled to have you as part of our family."

In all the excitement, nobody noticed that Chloe had been sitting in her chair silently. She wasn't nearly as thrilled.

***

Later that afternoon, people broke off into smaller groups to fill the time before dinner. Tom and Tyler were watching a football game in the den. Chloe was in the kitchen helping Kathleen prepare Christmas dinner. The kids were restless, so Chris and Ryan offered to play a game with them.

They looked in the closet where Tom and Kathleen kept their games. Most games were geared toward adults since Tom and Kathleen frequently had friends over for game nights.

Ryan spotted The Big Black Deck and smiled. When he and Chris were 17, playing that game led to their first time together in Chris's bedroom. Chris noticed Ryan looking at the box and nudged him with his elbow. They winked at each other.

Whitney pointed at a game and exclaimed, "How about this one? My friend Samantha has that!"

Chris pulled the box off the shelf. The game was called 'Farty Marty: The Gut-busting Game That's a Blast.' The drawing on the box depicted a corpulent man eating a hot dog, with ketchup and mustard stains on his sizeable belly.

Ryan looked at the box and said, "It says it's for ages 4 and up."

Chris added, "Or moderately intoxicated adults."

Ryan grinned. "Okay, let's try it out."

Chris carried the game to an open spot in the middle of the family room and the four of them sat on the floor. Ryan said, "Whitney, since you've played this before, why don't you tell us how it's played."

"Okay! So each player gets five food cards and two Belly Buster Soda cards." Whitney dealt the food cards while she talked. "When it's your turn you put one of your food cards on Marty's tray. Then you have to pump

Marty's head up and down the number of times it says on the card. Someone else can play one of their Belly Buster Soda cards if they want to. That means you have to pump three more times. After Marty gets pumped up a certain number of times, he blasts. If he blasts during your turn, you have to draw two more food cards."

Chris asked, "What's the object of the game?"

"To get rid of all your cards. The first person to get rid of their cards wins."

Ryan said, "Okay, then, let's get started."

Whitney said, "The youngest person goes first. Austin, play one of your food cards."

Austin played a card with a drawing of corn on the cob and the number 2. He pumped Marty's head twice. Nothing happened. He turned to Ryan, who was sitting to his left. "Your turn!"

Ryan decided to play his highest-value card to get things going. He played a card with a bowl of beans and the number 6. Whitney threw one of her Belly Buster Soda cards on top of his card and said, "Three more!"

Ryan started pumping Marty's head. After the seventh pump, Marty blasted a noisy, blubbering fart sound. Whitney and Austin squealed with delight, while Chris and Ryan chuckled. When the laughter subsided, Whitney said, "Okay, now you have to take two cards!" Ryan drew two cards from the draw pile.

Whitney went next. "I'm going to feed Marty a watermelon." She pumped Marty once. Nothing happened.

Chris played a card with a plate of French fries and the number 4. Ryan threw a soda card down. Chris pumped Marty's head seven times, and he farted after the fifth pump.

The kids squealed again. The joy they were experiencing while playing this juvenile, tasteless game made Ryan smile.

The next time it was Ryan's turn, Marty farted again. More helpless, giddy laughter ensued. The kids were laughing harder and louder each time. Chris and Ryan were getting caught up in the silliness and laughing more too.

Suddenly, Ryan remembered the time Ricky, one of his housemates in LA, farted at the dinner table. He busted out laughing. That set the kids off on another round of silly laughter. Chris gave Ryan a look that said, 'What's so funny?' Ryan mouthed the word 'Later' and Chris got the message.

In the kitchen, Chloe turned to Kathleen and said, "What in the world are they up to?" Without waiting for an answer, she walked into the family room and demanded, "What is going on here?"

Austin stopped laughing long enough to look up at his mom. "Uncle Ryan made Marty fart!"

Whitney giggled some more. She pumped Marty's head until he farted again. "See?"

Chloe's mouth dropped open. "That is *disgusting*! Where did you find that?"

Whitney replied, "In Grandma and Grandpa's closet."

Chloe shook her head in disbelief. "Put that away this instant! Then we'll see if they have something more tasteful and appropriate for children." She glared at Chris and Ryan as if they had shirked their duty as responsible adults for allowing this debauchery to take place.

Austin cried out, "Awww, Mom! We were having fun making Marty fart."

"I don't care. And another thing. We don't use that word in our family. We say 'pass gas' or 'break wind,' if we say anything at all."

Chris stood up. "Seriously? Fart is a bad word? Come on, lighten up."

"I am quite serious. I am raising my children to be polite, decent people who don't say crude words, make crude noises, and play crude games." Chloe knelt down and hurriedly crammed Marty and the cards back into the box.

Chris said, "Well, alrighty then. From now on, we shall not refer to flatulence as farts, ass gas, bottom burps, fluffer-doodles, air biscuits, or barking spiders, and we shall only refer to them by their proper name, poots."

Whitney and Austin knew this would be the worst possible moment to laugh, but they couldn't help it. They turned their faces away and quietly giggled. Tom and Tyler had stepped away from their football game to see what was happening, and they laughed. Kathleen, who had come in from the kitchen, chuckled.

Chloe stood up, box in hand, fuming. She glared at Chris and muttered, "It's a good thing you'll never have children."

"Yeah, but we're gonna keep trying."

The other grown-ups in the room smirked. Tyler laughed out loud and high-fived Tom. Chloe realized nobody in the room shared her objection to the game and they were, in fact, laughing at her. She turned to Austin and said, "And Mr. Ryan is *not* your uncle."

Whitney said, "But they're going to get married. After that, he will be."

"We'll talk about that later." Chloe stormed back into the kitchen. She shoved the game into Kathleen's hands as she passed.

Everyone glanced at the others in the room, unsure what to say or do to diffuse this awkward situation.

Tyler realized Chloe was his wife, so it fell on him to do something. He rolled his eyes and headed into the kitchen. He kicked aside the doorstop that kept the door propped open and closed it behind him.

"Way to ruin Christmas, Miss Righteous."

"Oh, is that it? *I'm* ruining Christmas? I wasn't the one who was playing that tasteless, vulgar game with our children, teaching them it's perfectly acceptable to laugh at the sounds people make when they pass gas. It was your brother and his new ... whatever."

"Fiancé. They are engaged to be married, so the proper word is fiancé. Or at least partner."

"Oh. Sorry I'm not politically correct enough."

"It's not political correctness. It's basic decency and respect."

"Oh, so they're laughing at flatulence and I'm the one who's being indecent. And if Chris and Ryan had any basic decency and respect, they'd be more discreet about what they do. And they would *not* flaunt their lifestyle choices in our faces *and* in front of our children."

"What are you talking about? They're not 'flaunting their lifestyle' any more than you and I do when we hold hands or kiss."

"Yes, but that's normal. And did you see the way they were smashing face after that whole marriage proposal stunt? Yes, I'd say that was flaunting it in our faces."

"Yeah, well, so what if it was? It was a beautiful moment. It was two people in love. I have no problem with our children seeing that. It's not like they were fucking."

"And that's another thing. They don't need to talk about what they do in bed in front of our children."

"What the hell are you talking about? They never did that."

"Not in so many words. But that remark about 'We're going to keep trying?' Everybody knew what he was referring to."

"I'm sure that went over the kids' heads."

"I guess we'll find out when they start asking questions about everything they were exposed to today. And I'm certainly not looking forward to explaining to my children how two men sodomize each other in bed."

"What??? There's no need to tell them anything about that. They're way too young for that sort of information."

"My point exactly."

"I will handle whatever questions come up. Besides, how do you know what two men do in bed?"

"How do *you*?"

They exchanged icy stares.

"I would imagine they do pretty much the same things you and I do – or *used* to do." Tyler paused to make sure that jab landed. "But that's not the point. They love each other and they want to spend the rest of their lives together. That's the point. And I'm happy for them. Overjoyed, in fact. And the kids are happy for them. It's too bad you're not."

"I'm entitled to how I feel. And I'm entitled to my religious beliefs."

"Yes, you are. But as Ryan said earlier, when you marry someone, you marry their family. You knew I had a gay brother soon after we met. Back then, you didn't seem to have any problem with it. But since you started going to church, you've become a lot more unkind and intolerant. And up to this point, I've remained silent about you taking the kids to church. But if this is how you're going to be and how you want them to turn out, we need to talk more about that. And not here. Another time."

"After what they saw today, they absolutely need to keep going to church. I don't want them to think two men getting married is normal. Good lord, Austin was already calling him Uncle Ryan."

"By next Christmas, he will be. He will officially be part of the family – every bit as much as you are. As far as I'm concerned, given their history together, he is now. The kids already like Ryan. They can plainly see that Chris and Ryan love each other. That's beautiful and there's absolutely nothing wrong with that. They understand what love is. Ryan is going to be part of our family and part of our lives from now on. Our kids are going to grow up with two gay uncles. I'm totally fine with that. And you need to be fine with it, too."

"I'll do my best." The sarcasm dripped from her voice.

"You'd better. Gay people face enough hostility in the world. They should be able to relax and feel loved and accepted when they're home with their family."

Chloe realized this argument had run its course – for now. There would be more to talk about later.

Tyler said, "Okay. We need to return to the family and let Mom get back to fixing dinner. But I need more Suzie Sunshine out of you and less Debbie Downer. Or Rachel Righteous."

"Stop talking down to me like I'm a little girl."

"Stop acting like one."

Tyler and Chloe emerged from the kitchen with fake smiles pasted on their faces. Everyone else had gathered in the den to watch the football game, although it was clearly of more interest to some than to others. Mostly, they wanted to distance themselves from the kitchen.

Chloe said to Kathleen, "I'm sorry we held up dinner."

Kathleen said, "That's okay. Would you please help me finish?"

***

Twenty minutes later, everyone was seated around the dining room table. Kathleen had spread an elegant red and white tablecloth across the table, and the table was now adorned with two long red candles with small clusters of fake greenery wrapped around the candle holders. Each place was set with good china and stainless steel silverware.

Everyone sat in the same seats they had occupied at lunch. Kathleen said, "Help yourself to whatever's in front of you and then pass to the right."

Chris said, "Everything looks fantastic, Mom! Thanks!"

Chloe said, "Ummm... May we take a moment to give thanks?"

Everyone stopped and set down whatever they were holding.

Chloe extended her hands to Whitney on her left and Tyler on her right. Everyone else took the hands of those they were sitting next to. For Tom, Kathleen, Chris, and Ryan, this was not a ritual they were accustomed to.

Chloe said, "Let us pray. Dear Lord, we have gathered to celebrate the birth of your son, our Lord and Savior Jesus Christ. We give thanks for the bounty that has been lovingly set before us. As we share the love and joy this day brings by giving gifts to each other, may we never forget the gift You gave us over two thousand years ago when You sent Your son to live among us. May we never forget the ultimate gift our Savior gave us when He died on the cross for our sins. Now bless this food for the nourishment of our bodies. In Jesus' name, we pray. Amen."

Everyone else muttered, "Amen," released each other's hands, and resumed passing the food.

After everyone had taken a few bites, Ryan asked Whitney, "What activities are you involved in at school?"

"I'm in the band and Girl Scouts."

"Oh, cool! What instrument do you play?"

"Clarinet."

"Oh, I like the clarinet. They make such a beautiful sound."

Chloe said, "They make a lot of squeaks and squawks, too."

Chris tried to smooth over that remark by saying to Whitney, "Don't worry, they'll go away. When I was learning to play the alto sax, my mouthpiece used to squeak all the time. You just have to keep practicing."

Whitney asked, "Do you still play your sax, Uncle Chris?"

"Yes, I do! I stopped playing it for many years. But a few months ago, I picked it up again, and now I play in two bands with Ryan."

Austin asked, "What do you play, Unc— I mean Mr. Ryan?"

"I play the trumpet. And like Uncle Chris, I stopped playing for a while, but now I'm back at it. Playing music is something you can enjoy your entire life."

Tom said, "When Chris and Ryan were in high school, we used to go hear their concerts. They were so good!"

Kathleen said, "That's right. Ryan used to come over and they'd practice together in Chris's room. I loved listening to them play."

Ryan looked at Austin, who was sitting directly across from him. "Do you play an instrument?"

Austin shook his head. Whitney said, "He's still in third grade. They don't start band until you're in fifth grade."

Ryan asked, "Is there an instrument you'd like to play when you get to fifth grade?"

Austin lit up. "I wanna play the trumpet!"

Chloe said, "Oh! I didn't think you were interested in music." She shifted her attention to the rest of the table. "I tried to get him to take piano lessons, but he wouldn't hear of it."

Austin said, "Piano lessons are for girls!"

Some of the adults chuckled. Ryan said, "You know, my mother forced me to take piano lessons when I was in third and fourth grade. I hated it back then. I thought they were for girls, too. But you know what? When I started learning the trumpet in fifth grade, I was really glad I had those piano lessons. Learning the piano taught me how to read music and count rhythms and lots of other things. That made it a lot easier for me to learn the trumpet. It's like I had a head start on all the other kids."

Austin looked excited. "Really?"

"Really!"

Chris added, "I wish I had taken piano lessons."

Chloe turned toward Austin and said, "Think about it. We can talk later, and if you're still interested, we can see about getting you lessons."

Austin looked across the table at Chris and Ryan. "I wish you guys lived here. How come you live so far away?"

Chris said, "Well, that's where our jobs are. And other than the fact that we don't get to see you very often, we like living in Scottsdale. It's warm and sunny and really beautiful. And you know what? We have a swimming pool at our house."

Austin lit up. "Really?"

Ryan smiled. "Really!"

Austin turned to his parents and said, "Can we go visit Uncle Chris and Uncle Ryan sometime? I wanna swim in their pool."

Tyler cut in before Chloe had a chance to answer. "Maybe we can go there on vacation this summer. You know what else is in Arizona? The Grand Canyon! We could all go and see that too."

Whitney and Austin were giddy with excitement.

Chloe said, "Don't forget, you'll also have Bible Camp this summer. I don't know if we'll be able to squeeze in a trip to Arizona. It's pretty far away."

Austin said, "Pleeeeze, Mom?"

"We'll see. It's a long way off."

Kathleen sensed it was time to change the subject. "Ryan, tell us more about the bands you and Chris are in."

Ryan and Chris talked about the holiday concert they had just played and the jazz concerts they played in the Bird's Nest, a jazz club in downtown Phoenix. They conveniently neglected to mention that these were LGBTQ+ bands.

The rest of the dinner went off without incident. Soon after they cleared the table, Tyler, Chloe, Whitney, and Austin said their goodbyes and headed home to Kansas City.

***

On the way home, Whitney asked, "When is Uncle Chris and Mr. Ryan's wedding?"

Tyler replied, "They haven't set a date yet. I think it's going to be sometime in the fall."

"Can we go? Please?"

Chloe answered, "I don't think so, dear. Weddings are for grown-ups."

Whitney said, "Samantha got to go to her uncle's wedding."

"Well, we'll have to see who gets invited. We can't go if we're not invited. Besides, if it's this fall, you'll be in school. It's a long way to drive and flying on an airplane costs a lot of money."

Austin said, "I don't care! I wanna go! I'll start saving up my allowance." Tyler smiled.

Chloe loosened her seatbelt and pivoted to face her children in the back seat. "So... we need to talk about what you saw this afternoon. Now, as you know, the Bible says a marriage is between a man and a woman. That's what God wants for us. That way, mommies and daddies can have children and give them a good home and keep the human race going. Now, once in a while, a man might go astray and feel like he loves another man–"

Whitney interrupted, "Mom, Uncle Chris and Mr. Ryan are gay. We know what gay is. You don't have to explain it to us. It's when two men or two women love each other. Duh...!"

Austin said, "I like Mr. Ryan! I'm glad he and Uncle Chris are going to get married!"

Chloe said, "Well, yes, Mr. Ryan seems like a nice man. But as I said, God teaches us that a real marriage is between a man and a woman. What they want to have is... I don't know... kind of like a pretend marriage."

Whitney said, "That's not true! Two men or two women can get married now! They made it legal several years ago. Anyway, if Uncle Chris and Mr. Ryan love each other, they should be able to get married. I want them to be happy together!"

Tyler was grinning as he drove the car. "Out of the mouths of babes."

Whitney said, "Daaad...! We're not babies!"

Tyler chuckled. "I said babes, not babies. It's an expression. It means sometimes kids will speak the truth when nobody else will."

Chloe turned around and faced forward. She said nothing for the rest of the drive home.

Christmas in Scottsdale

Saturday, December 25, 2021

When Matt woke up on Christmas morning, he was understandably depressed. It was his first Christmas away from home. He would have spent Christmas away from home if he had remained a missionary, but this was different. He had been rejected by his parents. He was out on his own.

He emerged from his bedroom and headed toward the kitchen. He didn't know whether Aaron or Brandon would be up and fixing breakfast. If not, he'd find something to nibble on in the fridge.

He glanced at the Christmas tree as he passed through the family room. He stopped dead in his tracks.

In front of the Christmas tree was a brand-new bicycle with a huge rainbow-colored bow on the seat.

He couldn't believe his eyes. He had only lived here a week, and these guys were doing him a big enough favor by giving him a place to live. He had no reason to expect that they'd give him a Christmas present, and certainly not one as expensive as a bicycle. His momentary elation subsided as he convinced himself that the bike was probably a present for one of the others.

Still, he wandered over to get a better look at it. He saw a card on the seat, tucked under the edge of the bow. The card had his name on it.

He stared at the card and the bicycle in disbelief. He wasn't sure whether he should open it now or wait until Aaron and Brandon were up. But then, he heard a door open. Moments later, Aaron appeared in the family room. "Merry Christmas!"

"Oh my God! I can't believe you guys did this!"

Aaron smiled. "Open the card!"

Matt pulled the card off the seat and worked his finger under the envelope flap. He pulled out the card. It was signed by all four of them.

"Aaron, I... I... I don't even know what to say. Thank you!"

Aaron smiled and hugged Matt. "Do you like it?"

"I love it!"

"We figured you'd need it to ride to Scottsdale Community College and back. According to Google Maps, it should only take about 15 minutes."

"Still... you shouldn't have. I was planning to look for a cheap used bike on Craigslist or something."

"We wanted to do something a little special for you so you'd have a nice Christmas."

Brandon entered the family room and smiled when he saw Matt standing next to his new bike. "Merry Christmas!"

"Thank you! Thank you! Thank you!" Matt walked up to Brandon and hugged him. "You guys are the greatest!" He paused. "But now I feel bad because I didn't get you guys anything."

Aaron said, "You've been here less than two weeks. Until now, you didn't have transportation to go shopping. So don't worry about it. We weren't expecting anything."

Brandon said, "C'mon, let's get some breakfast. Then after that, you can take it out for a ride."

***

Since Ryan and Chris were spending Christmas in Prairie Village, Brandon invited his father to spend Christmas Day at their house.

Brad arrived at 1:00, after attending a Christmas morning service at a church near his apartment in Mesa. Brandon welcomed him at the door. "Merry Christmas!"

Brad stepped inside and they hugged. "Merry Christmas to you too! Thanks for inviting me. I spent last Christmas by myself and, well, it was rather depressing."

"No problem. We're hanging out in the family room."

Brad scanned the living room as he followed Brandon, then scoped out the family room and kitchen when they arrived. "Hello, Aaron."

"Hello, Rev. Bauer." He stepped forward and offered his hand to shake.

Brad shook it and said, "Please, call me Brad. We're all adults, and I'm not actively pastoring these days." He glanced out the sliding glass door and noticed the patio and pool. "Good heavens! This is quite a place you have here."

Aaron said, "Thanks. Ryan already had this place when we met."

"Speaking of Ryan, where is he?"

Brandon and Aaron exchanged nervous glances. Brandon said, "He's spending Christmas with Chris's family in Prairie Village."

Brad thought, *Okay, so that's why they invited me over. They probably wouldn't have if Ryan was here.* "Who's Chris?"

"You know, his best friend from high school."

Brad looked down. "Oh yeah, right. I remember him." *The guy Ryan was kissing in the car when they got caught by the policeman. The guy I accused of recruiting Ryan and turning him gay. The guy I told Ryan he could never see again. Ryan probably still hates me for all that.* "So they're back in touch."

Aaron glanced at Brandon. "You could say that."

Brad said, "I'm surprised he's not spending Christmas with you guys. You're his husband and his brother, after all."

Brandon took a deep breath. "Well... Some things have changed around here. Have a seat." He gestured toward the seating area of the family room. "Can I get you a cocktail or a glass of wine or something?"

Brad sat down on one of the side chairs. "Bourbon on the rocks, if you have it."

Brandon nodded and turned to Aaron. "How about you?"

"A Long Island."

Aaron sat down on the couch while Brandon walked over to the wet bar and mixed their drinks. Brad looked bewildered. Aaron looked nervous. Nobody spoke.

Brandon served their drinks and sat down on the couch next to Aaron. He took a sip of his Long Island, then set it down on a coaster. "Okay. So, as I said, things have changed. Long story short, while Ryan was away in New Zealand, Aaron and I were trapped in this house together during the pandemic. And uh... we kinda fell in love with each other. Well, not kinda. We did."

Brad was stunned. "So you're..." He couldn't bring himself to say it.

"Yes. I'm gay too. For a long time, I thought I was more like bi or fluid or whatever..."

"But you dated girls in high school."

"Yeah, mostly because I didn't want you to find out. Especially after what happened to Ryan."

Brad was too stunned to speak. *Not after what *I* did to Ryan. Now I really feel like shit.*

Brandon continued. "Plus, I thought maybe if I found the right girl, I could be straight for her. Kinda like with you and Mom."

So Ryan told him. I guess I couldn't expect him not to. But still...

Brad shot an angry glance at Aaron. He felt like saying, 'How could you? How could you cheat on Ryan – with his brother?' Instead, he said, "So what about Ryan? How is he handling this?"

"Well, it actually worked out well for Ryan, too. You see, Chris was with this guy for thirteen years. They lived in Arlington, Virginia until a few months ago when they moved out here. Chris found out his partner was cheating on him and they broke up. Chris came to live with us. It was supposed to be temporary until he figured out what he wanted to do next. But when Ryan found out about us, there was Chris. So they're finally together again."

Aaron said, "Ryan and I love each other very much. But I always knew his heart belonged to Chris. I knew he chose me because he couldn't have Chris. Now, after all these years, they can finally be together."

Brandon said, "He was really good about it. He had every right to hate Aaron and me for what we did. He could have kicked us out. But since this meant he could finally have Chris, it was kinda like we did him a favor."

Aaron said, "It was a win all the way around. Now everyone is coupled with who they really want to be with, and we all love each other. We get along great."

Brandon scooted closer to Aaron and put his arm around him. "We're a family."

"Ryan and I will get divorced after the first of the year. Then, probably later in the year, they'll get married and so will we."

"We've only talked about it. We haven't made any definite plans."

Brandon and Aaron stopped talking to give Brad a chance to respond.

After a moment, Brad said, "Well, that's quite a story. I've never heard anything like it. But I guess if you're all happy..."

Brandon said, "We are. We're very, very happy." He kissed Aaron on the cheek. "And so are they."

"Well, all right then."

Aaron said, "Brandon and I have found an apartment. It's not too far from here. Our lease starts on January 1, so we're going to move in next weekend."

Brandon said, "We talked about the four of us staying here, but it's been kinda crowded. We all agreed it might be nice for each couple to have their own space."

Aaron stood up. "So now that we have that out of the way, we have someone else we'd like you to meet. Let me go get him."

Aaron walked down the hallway to the music room where Matt was staying. They decided he should stay in his room until they told Brad about their new arrangement. Aaron knocked on the door.

Matt called out, "Come in!"

Aaron pushed the door open. "Okay, we've had our talk with Brandon's father. Would you like to come out and join us?"

Matt followed Aaron back to the family room.

Brandon said, "Matt, this is my father, Brad. Dad, this is Matt. Matt moved in about a week ago. He'll be living here for the next year or two."

Brad looked bewildered. "So there's five of you living here now."

Brandon said, "Temporarily, until next Saturday when we move into our apartment. And Ryan and Chris will be gone until late Thursday."

Brad turned to Matt. "Okay, so how did you end up here?"

"Well, it's kind of a long story. But the short version is, I'm LDS. Or at least I was. I was on my mission and one day my companion and I stopped here. When I figured out these guys were gay, I came out to them. I decided I didn't want to continue my mission, so I quit and went back home to Idaho. My parents were upset enough that I quit my mission, but when they found out I'm gay they totally freaked out. They made me go into therapy because they thought it would make me straight. When I said no, they told me to move out. I called Ryan, 'cause he said I could call him if I needed help, and he told me I could come and live here."

Brad sighed. "Well, that sounds familiar, doesn't it, Brandon?"

Brandon nodded. "Yeah. Ryan already gave him that background."

Brad sighed. *Yet another person who knows the dirt from my past.*

Aaron said, "Let me go check on the ham. Hopefully, dinner should be ready in 15 minutes or so." He turned toward the kitchen.

Brandon and Brad stood up. Brad said, "What can I do to help?"

Brandon said, "We're good for now. Why don't you come over and sit on one of the stools? Do you want another bourbon?" As an afterthought, he added, "We're going to be serving wine with the meal."

"Well, then I'd better hold off. I don't want to get drunk on Christmas." *Although I sure could use another one.*

Aaron poured some mixed nuts into a bowl and set it on the kitchen island near Brad. "Would you like a soda or water?"

"If you have something diet, that would be great. Otherwise, water is fine."

Aaron reached into the fridge and pulled out a can of Diet Coke. He opened a cupboard and retrieved a glass. Brad said, "Don't bother. I don't mind drinking it from the can."

Aaron put the glass back and peeked into the oven. "Lookin' good. It should be ready soon. He set about preparing to serve the side dishes.

The mood in the room seemed awkward. Brad was still processing everything he had just learned. There were things he could say, but he knew he had no room to talk about morality after everything he had done. Aaron and Brandon were trying to gauge his reaction, not that it mattered much.

Brandon said, "So, what's the latest on your book?"

Brad perked up. "Well, as you know, my book was picked up by a publisher back in July. It's an indie publisher that specializes in books for progressive Christians. It will be released in April, but I have some advance copies now. It looks great! They did a nice job on the cover."

Brandon said, "Oh, cool. I'd like to read it sometime – that is, if you don't mind."

"Well, I can't stop you. After it comes out, you can order it from Amazon like anyone else. But I'll warn you. Some things might be unpleasant to read since I talk about what happened with Ryan – well, he's Bryan in the book – and all the things I did wrong. You'll probably find that it hits pretty close to home."

"Is there stuff in there I don't already know?"

"Probably not. But still..."

"I think I can handle it."

"Well, in that case, I have a few in my car. I'll go out and give you one."

Brad left and returned a minute later with a copy of his book. "Do you have a pen?" Brandon handed him one. He wrote a message on the front page, signed his name, and handed it to Brandon.

"Thanks!" Brandon glanced at the front and back cover, then handed the book to Aaron.

Aaron said, "Congratulations on getting it published. I'm sure it wasn't easy." He glanced at the table of contents, then started thumbing through the book.

"No, it wasn't. And I know it won't sell nearly as many copies as my past books. It's a smaller publisher, so they don't have much of a marketing budget and they don't have as big a reach into bookstores. A lot of Christian bookstores probably won't carry it anyway. But I wanted to tell my story. If it helps some people, I'll be happy about that. So we'll see what happens."

Matt asked, "What's your book about?"

"Basically, it's about my journey from being a widely-known self-righteous Christian evangelist with a right-wing agenda to a more humble, loving servant of the Lord who believes in kindness and acceptance for all people, including sexual minorities. We're all God's children. It's not up to any of us to judge others, but rather to seek to be more understanding and compassionate toward those who are different from us and love them for who they are."

"Sounds nice. I hope a lot of people read it."

"To be fair, a lot of the book isn't nice. I built my empire by preaching messages of intolerance and homophobia that were not Godly or Christ-like at all. My whole life, I struggled with same-sex attraction. I married a wonderful woman because I thought that was what God expected me to do. I hoped that would fix everything, but it didn't. We had two beautiful boys whom I completely ignored. I was so caught up in expanding my ministry that I neglected my responsibilities as a husband and father. Ultimately, I was outed in the most humiliating way. My world crashed down around me. I lost everything I worked for my entire life. But I knew I deserved it. It forced me to face the truth about myself. They say that your greatest personal growth occurs when you're face-down in the mud. That was me. I had to pick myself up and recreate myself truthfully and authentically. After years of lying, I had to put the truth out there. The whole process of writing the book was both painful and cathartic. But I knew I had to write it. I want to reach parents of gay kids who are having a difficult time reconciling their faith with their desire to love their children. I hope to convince parents that their religious beliefs against same-sex love are wrong and that their gay children are just as beautiful and worthy as their other children. My goal is to keep families together and make the world a safer place for gay kids."

"Wow. Sounds exactly like what my parents need to read. But I know they never will."

Brad thought for a moment. "Matt, what are your parents' names and what's their address?"

"Why?"

"I'd like to send them one of my advance copies, along with a personal note from me."

"Well, you can if you want, but don't get your hopes up. They're, like, totally bought in. They'll probably throw it in the trash. Or burn it in the fireplace."

"I'll leave that in their hands. But it's worth a try."

Brad reached for the pen he had used to sign Brandon's book and handed it to Matt. Brandon handed Matt a piece of paper.

Matt wrote his parents' names and address on it and gave it to Brad. "Thanks."

Aaron was carrying food into the dining room. "Dinner's ready!"

The four of them sat down at the table and Brad said grace. They enjoyed their food and kept the conversation focused on pleasant topics, like Matt starting college at Scottsdale Community College, Aaron and Brandon's initial plans for their wedding, and Brad's upcoming book promotion activities.

Brandon said, "We could have you as a guest on our podcast!"

"Do you think that would do any good?"

"We have over 32,000 subscribers."

Brad lit up. "Really? That's amazing!"

Aaron said, "Yeah, it has succeeded beyond our wildest dreams."

"Do you think your audience would be interested? I mean, I don't really know who your audience is."

"Mostly young, progressive people. But they like stuff that's unique and different, and a bit controversial. The whole mission of our podcast is to inspire people to bring about change and fix what's wrong with the world. That's exactly what you're trying to do."

Brandon said, "When we announced that I'm gay and we're a couple, it was our most listened-to episode. So yeah, they'll eat this up. Especially since you're my father, not just some guy."

Brad said, "You mean you talk about your personal business on your podcast, where anyone in the world could hear it?"

"Heck yeah! Why not? People like that kind of stuff. It lets them know more about who we are. It makes us seem genuine and authentic, not a couple of showbiz personalities. They feel more connected to us."

"Well, okay. Let's do it! I'd be delighted to be a guest on your show."

Aaron said, "We'll set up a date to record it a couple of weeks before your book comes out, and then we'll release the episode when your book is released."

A few moments later Brad said, "I have a favor to ask. And it's perfectly okay for you to say no. But..." He paused. "I would be honored if I could officiate your wedding."

Aaron and Brandon looked at each other, trying to gauge each other's reaction.

Brandon said, "Well... We'll talk about it. We'll give it serious consideration."

Brad said, "That's fine. That's all I ask. If you'd prefer to have someone else, that's perfectly fine."

They finished dinner. Everyone pitched in to clear the table and put away leftovers.

Aaron glanced at the time on the microwave control panel. "It's almost 3:00. We're going to have a Zoom call with Ryan and Chris in a few minutes."

Matt said, "I want to call my brother Mark. Hopefully, he can get away from the rest of the family for a few minutes."

Brad said, "I suppose I should stay out of your way. Could I watch television somewhere?"

"Sure." Aaron picked up the remote, turned the TV on, and handed it to Brad. "Make yourself at home. We won't be too long."

Aaron and Brandon left the family room, walked into the office, and closed the door. "Do you think we should invite him in long enough to say hi to Ryan and Chris?"

"I thought about that. I'm sure Dad would like that, but I don't think Ryan would."

"We've got to get them past this impasse somehow."

"That would be nice, but it's really up to them. Or, more accurately, Ryan."

Aaron knew Brandon was right. He turned the computer on and they settled into their desk chairs. A few minutes later, they were connected and smiling at Ryan and Chris.

After a round of Merry Christmases, Brandon asked, "So how is Prairie Village?"

Ryan said, "Cold and dreary, just like I remember it. Not much has changed."

"How are Chris's parents?"

Chris said, "They're fine, just a little bit older. My brother Tyler and his wife and two kids are here, too."

Aaron said, "Sounds like a full house."

Chris said, "Yeah. The kids are really cute. I wish I could see them more often. They're growing up so fast."

Ryan asked, "So, what are you guys doing today?"

Brandon said, "Matt's here, and we invited Dad to come over. We finished dinner a little while ago."

Ryan frowned.

Brandon said, "Hey, you weren't going to be here, so I thought, why not?"

Chris asked, "How's he doing?"

"Pretty good, all things considered. He's happy to be here. Last year, he spent Christmas by himself."

Aaron said, "He's excited because he found a publisher for his book. It will be out in April, but he gave us an advance copy." He held the book up.

Ryan said, "So are you guys actually going to read it?"

Aaron nodded and Brandon said, "Yes. And we're going to interview him on our podcast."

Chris knew this conversation needed to move in a different direction. He turned to Ryan and said, "Tell them who we'll be visiting while we're here."

Ryan stopped frowning and said, "Tomorrow we're going to visit Russ Simonton and his husband Frank. Russ was my manager at Price Cutter, where I worked right before I left home. He's the one who helped me escape from there and get to LA. Anyway, we're going to have dinner with them at Burger Betty's. It's this really cool place where they took me for dinner the day I left home."

Aaron said, "That'll be nice. I'm sure you'll enjoy catching up."

Chris said, "And before that, we're going to meet up for a drink with a couple of friends from high school."

Ryan said, "Remember Officer Crockett, the police officer in that clip from the local TV program you showed me?"

Aaron said, "The guy who went undercover and busted your dad at that orgy?"

"That's the one. And our other friend Trevor is the manager of the hotel where it happened. So yeah, we're gonna hang with them for a little while before dinner."

Chris added, "And while we're here, we're gonna hit up some used record stores in Kansas City like we did in high school."

Aaron rolled his eyes. "Just what you need – more CDs."

Ryan chuckled. "It's more for old time's sake than anything else."

"Uh-huh. Tell me that when you come home with fifty CDs."

They all laughed. Then Ryan turned to Chris and said, "Don't you have some other news to share?"

Chris lit up. "As a matter of fact... Look what I got for Christmas!" He extended his hand toward the laptop camera so they could see a close-up view of his engagement ring.

Aaron and Brandon clapped. Brandon said, "Congratulations!"

Aaron said, "So you proposed on Christmas Day! Hmmm... Something about that seems familiar."

Ryan laughed. "I realize it's not quite the same as proposing in front of 32,000 of your closest friends, but it was the best I could do. Besides, it produced the desired result last time. How could he say no in front of his family?"

Chris said, "Like I'd ever say no to you."

Aaron said, "So, did you get the desired result this time?"

Chris showed them the ring again. "Well, duh..."

"No, I meant did you get a great reaction from his family?"

Ryan said, "Mostly. His sister-in-law was a little weird about it."

Chris looked puzzled. "She was?"

"Didn't you notice?"

"I guess not. I was so wrapped up in you asking me to marry you."

"Oh, well. Maybe I misread her. We can talk about it later. Anyway, we should probably get back to your family."

Aaron said, "And we should get back to Matt and Brad. Oh! And Matt was totally blown away by the bike. He said to tell you thank you very much."

Ryan said, "I'm glad we did that for him. Tell him we said Merry Christmas."

Brandon said, "We will. And..."

For a moment, no one said anything.

Then Ryan said, "And tell Brad I said Merry Christmas."

Aaron perked up. He got up and hurried out to the family room. "Hey,

Brad, would you please come in here for a moment?"

Brad looked puzzled, but he got up and followed Aaron into the office. Aaron motioned for Brad to sit down in his chair.

Brad looked at Ryan and Chris, and they looked back.

Aaron said, "Why don't you tell him yourself?"

After a brief, awkward moment, Ryan said, "Merry Christmas, Brad."

"Hello Ryan, and hello Chris. Merry Christmas to you too."

No one knew what to say next. Chris wasn't sure whether he should tell Brad they were engaged. He decided to let Ryan handle that. So he said, "Congratulations on your new book."

"Thanks. I gave a copy to Brandon and Aaron." Then Brad remembered they were about to move into their own apartment. "I can leave a copy for you if you like."

Ryan wasn't the least bit interested, but he didn't want to be rude and say that.

Chris said, "That would be nice of you. Thanks!"

Ryan let it go. "Well, we were about to sign off. Chris's family will be having dinner soon."

Everyone said goodbye and they ended the call.

Ryan turned to Chris and said, "I can't believe Aaron ambushed me like that."

"Ambushed?"

"Okay, maybe that's a little over the top."

"Ya think? Let it go, honey. Let it go."

A thought occurred to Ryan and he laughed.

Chris asked, "What's so funny?"

"I think I'll divorce him for doing that."

Chris was stunned, but then he remembered that Ryan and Aaron were getting a divorce after the first of the year anyway.

Ryan asked, "Know any good attorneys?"

"Yeah, but... I understand his fees are pretty stiff."

"I'm sure we can work out a payment plan. You know, spread the payments out over, I dunno, forty or fifty years."

They both laughed. Chris leaned over and kissed Ryan. "I love you."

"I love you too." Ryan paused. "Just don't go collecting from your other client."

It took Chris a second to realize that Ryan was referring to Aaron.

"Well then, I guess I'll have to charge you double."

Ryan smiled. "Deal!"

***

While Aaron and Brandon were on their Zoom call, Matt grabbed his phone and stepped onto the back patio. He texted his brother Mark,

> Merry Christmas. I miss you.

A few minutes passed. Matt didn't expect to get a response right away, since Mark was probably involved with their family. But then a reply came in,

> Merry Christmas! Can I call you now?

> Sure!

A few seconds later, Matt's phone rang. He tapped the Accept button as fast as he could. "Hey, Mark! Merry Christmas!"

"Hey! Merry Christmas! How ya doin'?"

"Okay, I guess. It's kinda weird. Part of me wishes I was back home with the family. But part of me is glad I'm not. It's hard to describe. But I wish I was with you."

"Yeah, me too. What's the weather like there?"

"It's perfect. That's one thing I love about living here. It doesn't get cold in the winter and it never snows."

"Nice. It's cold and dreary here. It's, like, 25 degrees."

"I sure don't miss that. Where are you?"

"In my room. As long as I keep my voice down, I should be able to talk for a few minutes. So what's your day been like?"

"As good as possible, I guess. I'm just thankful I have a place to live. Two of the guys who live here, Ryan and Chris, went to Kansas to visit Chris's family. The other two stayed here. They're inside having a Zoom call with each other right now. And their dad came over. He's in there watching TV now. I'm out on the back patio."

"So wait a minute. How many people live there?"

"Five, counting me. It's kind of complicated. The guy who owns the place is Ryan. Then there's his husband Aaron, his brother Brandon, and his best friend Chris. So anyway, Ryan went to New Zealand for a couple of years on a work assignment. While he was gone, the pandemic hit. Brandon, who was going to Arizona State, moved in when they shut down the campus. So it was him and Aaron living here together for two years. So anyway, I guess they started messing around, and next thing you know they fell in love with each other."

"No shit?"

"No shit."

"Man, that's totally fucked up."

"I know, right? So anyway, not too long after Ryan got back, his friend Chris broke up with his partner. That meant they were both single, so now they're in love."

"Okay, mind blown. You totally lost me."

"The bottom line is, now Ryan and Chris are a couple, and Aaron and Brandon are a couple."

"Sounds like a big cuppa what-the-fuck. What's it like living there?"

"Well, it's only been two weeks, but so far it's been great. They're all really nice, and they're being so kind to me. And get this! They gave me a bike for Christmas!"

"What...? Seriously?"

"It's a nice one, too. I'll need a bike when I start going to Scottsdale Community College in January. It's like a 15-minute bike ride away."

"Nice. So... Okay, I know I probably shouldn't ask this, but... You're living with four gay guys. Have any of them tried to... you know..."

"Have sex with me? No! No way, man. It's not like that at all. They'd never do anything like that. They're two couples. They're only interested in each other."

"So, have you done it with a guy yet?"

"No. I wish I could have done it with my mission companion, but I knew he was straight. He was, like, totally hot. Anyway, I can't wait to find out what it feels like. It's making me insane."

"I know what you mean, man. I can't wait, either. I mean, with a woman."

"So, back to today. How has your day been?"

"Weird. And not in a good way. It's like everyone's avoiding the issue. Mom and Dad are trying to act like nothing's wrong. Like they don't want to spoil Christmas for Luke, John, and me. But it's already spoiled. And Luke and John know they're not supposed to ask questions, especially when other people are around. Like at church this morning, people asked about you. Everyone knows you quit your mission, so Mom and Dad are already embarrassed about that. And they don't want to tell them you left home, 'cause then they'd ask why. So it's really awkward. The only thing Dad has said to us is that if you were still on your mission you wouldn't be here either, so you'd be gone either way. But it's not the same thing, and everyone knows it."

"And next year, you'll be on your mission, so Luke and John will have to get used to that too."

"No, I won't."

"Huh?"

"I'm not going on a mission. And I'm probably going to leave the church."

"Seriously? Mom and Dad are gonna shit."

"I don't care. I never really wanted to do it anyway, but we're kinda forced to, y'know?"

"Tell me about it."

"And after what they did to you, and after learning more about what the church teaches about being gay... Hell no. I don't want any part of it."

"So what are you going to do?"

"Tell them, I guess. Mom's already trying to get me to fill out the application. They want me to go right after I get out of high school, so I've got to apply now."

"When are you going to tell them?"

"I guess I'm gonna hafta do it in the next couple of days. I didn't want to do it before Christmas."

"So you know they're gonna freak out. How are you going to handle it?"

"I don't know. I doubt that they'll kick me out, but they'll make my life hell for the next six months. Like it isn't hell already."

"I'm sorry, man. I don't envy you at all."

"Thanks." Mark paused. "Man, I wish I could come live with you. Sounds like you've got it made."

"Dude, I just got kicked out by my parents and I'm spending Christmas without my family. I have to work a job at a grocery store to earn enough money to live on and I have to ride to a community college on a bike. I wouldn't say I've got it made."

"Yeah, but at least you got out of your mission and you have a nice place to live."

"I do like Scottsdale. As soon as I got here at the start of my mission, I thought, damn! This is how some people live? This is so different from Inkom, it's like night and day. And when I went home after I quit my mission, I looked around and thought, God, I never want to live in a small town again."

"Yeah, me too. But I guess I'll have to stick it out for another six months."

"Maybe after you graduate, you can live here too. If we both worked, we could get an apartment. I'm planning to get my Associate's degree at SCC, then transfer to ASU starting my junior year. By then, I'll be able to get in-state tuition. You could do the same thing."

"That sounds great, but... what if you find a boyfriend? You're not gonna want to have your straight brother around."

"Dude... You're my best friend. You're willing to quit the church because of me."

"What the church says about being gay is bullshit. I'm on your side, bro. And I can't wait to get outta here!"

"Thanks, man."

"Well, I should probably go. I don't want them to start wondering where I am."

"Okay, well take care. I hope Mom and Dad don't freak out too bad."

"You know they will."

"Let me know how it goes."

"I will. Later, bro."

"Later."

Old Friends

Sunday, December 26, 2021

At 4:30, Ryan and Chris pulled into the parking lot of the Helton Grande Inn and Suites in Kansas City. They entered the lobby, turned right, and walked into the hotel bar.

They spotted Trevor Zimmerman and Rocket Crockett seated at a four-top table near the center of the room. Rocket saw them first and sprang up out of his seat. "Dudes!"

When Ryan and Chris reached the table, Rocket flung his arms around Ryan and gave him a huge bear hug. Then he gave Chris a nice long hug. Trevor gave each of them a more typical bro-hug.

Rocket said, "Awww, man, it's so great to see you guys!"

Trevor said, "What do you want to drink? Anything you want... it's on the house."

Rocket grinned. "It helps to know the manager."

Ryan and Chris glanced at each other. They knew they'd be drinking when they had dinner with Russ and Frank later. Ryan said, "Maybe just a glass of wine. What do you have?"

Trever replied, "Oh, the usual stuff. Our house wines are your basic Chardonnay and Cabernet Sauvignon. We also have sangria, if you're into that."

Chris smiled. "The sangria sounds good."

Trevor asked, "Red or white?"

"Red."

Ryan said, "Make that two."

Rocket and Trevor already had beers in front of them, but Rocket said, "I tried sangria once a few years ago. It was pretty good! Can you bring me one?"

Trevor said, "Sure, I'll have them bring a pitcher over." He walked up to the bar, placed their order with the bartender, and returned to their table.

When they were all seated, Chris said, "Welcome to the 14-year reunion of the Prairie Village High School all-star 4x440 relay team!"

Trevor said, "God! Has it really been 14 years?"

Rocket said, "Yeah, man. Hey! There's a high school half a mile away. We oughta go over to their track and run a relay one more time!"

Trevor said, "Uh... no. I haven't run for at least ten years. I'm so outta shape, I'd probably drop dead from a heart attack."

Rocket said, "Yeah, I hear ya. I still go to the gym and work out but I don't run anymore. I've put on 20 pounds. How about you guys?"

Ryan said, "I still run two or three times a week. There's a running trail a few blocks from my house. It goes on for miles in either direction. And the weather's always nice, except in the middle of summer. You have to get up really early if you wanna go running then."

Chris said, "Since we've gotten back together, I've run with him a few times. I'm still trying to get back into it. But man, he can still run like he used to!"

"Well, not quite. I don't think I could win any track meets today. But I guess I do okay."

Rocket said, "Yeah, my days of doing 11-second sprints are long gone."

The waiter delivered a large pitcher of red sangria, four glasses, and a generous bowl of pub mix to the table. Trevor poured the sangria and the guys clinked their glasses.

Chris said, "You know, on Christmas Eve when we were driving here, we passed through Wichita. It brought back all those memories of the state championship track meet."

Ryan said, "Including some I wish I could forget. Like dropping the baton and ruining the race for us. Man, we would have taken first for sure if I hadn't done that."

Rocket said, "Awww, man, don't worry about it. Like Coach Riley said, stuff happens in sports and you just have to put it behind you and move on. Like when I was playing football at TCU. One year we went undefeated the whole season, and then we went to the Rose Bowl and won. But Auburn was ranked number one and we were ranked number two, so we didn't get the national championship. And then the next year, we went undefeated during the regular season but then we lost the Fiesta Bowl. So we came that close to the national championship twice but we didn't make it."

Ryan said, "But at least you got to play college football on a championship-worthy team. And I'm sure you were one of the reasons the team was so good. It must have been a great experience."

"Oh, it was! And I wouldn't have been able to attend college without that scholarship."

Ryan said, "Chris wanted to drive past that motel where we stayed. But it was already a long enough drive and we wanted to get to his parents' house as soon as we could."

Chris said, "Maybe on the way back. And we could stop by the stadium."

Ryan said, "They're just buildings, anyway. We'll always remember what happened there, whether or not we see the actual buildings."

Rocket said, "Man, that motel was skanky! It was, what, 31 bucks a night? I bet I know what went on in there most of the time."

Chris said, "Yeah, it was nothing like this place. Man, this looks pretty swank! Looks like you got yourself a good gig, man."

Trevor said, "Yeah, it's a nice property, especially for this area. But I know a lot of stuff goes on in these rooms, too."

Rocket said, "Yeah, like big gay orgies."

Chris said, "Oh, that's right! This was the scene of the crime!"

Trevor said, "I can take you back and show you the room if you want."

Ryan said, "That's a hard no. I'll pass."

Rocket grinned. "So let's talk about that motel for a second. I remember how you guys overslept and you were so tired the next day. So tell me – and be honest. Were you guys banging each other all night long?"

Chris and Ryan exchanged cautious glances.

Rocket said, "C'mon. We're all friends."

Ryan said, "Actually, no. It was true that we both couldn't get to sleep until 3:00 in the morning and we were exhausted the next day. And I admit, that's why I didn't do as well as I should have at the meet. But no, we weren't screwing. I wish we had! But that was the night we finally admitted to each other that we were gay."

Chris added, "And in love."

Rocket said, "What??? You mean you didn't know you were both gay? Hell, even I knew that!"

Ryan said, "Well, in hindsight, we both knew. But we didn't know how to bring it up. We were both scared to be the first to say it to the other one. And remember, I was the preacher's kid, right?" Ryan glanced at Rocket, who had teased him by calling him 'PK' in high school.

"Yeah, I'm sorry I always called you PK."

"Don't worry about it. Anyway, I knew there was no way I could come out. I mean, what if my dad found out? Of course, he did – and we all know what happened. I was even scared to tell Chris. I was pretty sure he was, but what if he wasn't? What if I had been wrong? That could have ruined our friendship."

Chris said, "There was no question in my mind – I was gay and I was totally in love with him. But I knew he wasn't ready to deal with it. I was afraid that if I brought it up, it would scare him away."

"And it probably would have. I was deep in denial at that point."

Rocket said, "Man. I had no idea it was so hard for you."

Ryan said, "Anyway, that night, we were in a room with a queen-sized bed."

Chris added, "Appropriate, right?"

Ryan continued, "Remember, we were all supposed to be in rooms with two beds. But anyway, that night we watched Brokeback Mountain on HBO."

Trevor said, "That was the movie about the gay cowboys, right?"

Chris said, "Yeah. And so we were sitting there on the bed in our underwear and we were both thinking, *I wonder what he thinks about all this?*"

Ryan jumped in, "And we had drank a whole 2-liter bottle of Dr Pepper, so we were both pumped up on caffeine. So when we tried to go to sleep, it was like, we're in this strange bed, and there's Chris right next to me. I wondered if I should do something, or should I wait for him to do something, or what. And as much as I wanted it, I was scared to death. I mean, if I did something, that would mean I couldn't deny the fact that I was gay any longer."

Rocket and Trevor were staring at them with rapt attention.

Chris said, "So finally, I could tell he was still awake, so I asked him why he was having trouble falling asleep. And he said all this stuff about the caffeine and the strange bed and thinking about the track meet the next day. Finally I said, 'Or maybe we're both waiting for something to happen.'"

Ryan said, "So there it was, finally out in the open. Anyway, we hugged and kissed a lot – it was pretty hot, actually – but we didn't do anything else."

Rocket asked, "Why not?"

"Because I was too scared. In hindsight, I really wish we had."

Rocket said, "No shit? Man, I figured you guys were boning each other all the time."

Ryan said, "Seriously? You guys knew?"

Trevor said, "Oh, hell yeah. Everyone could see you guys were a couple from a mile away. Nobody had any real problem with it."

Rocket said, "Well, there was one time when I heard a couple of guys making some lame-ass jokes about it in the locker room. I went over and told them to shut the fuck up. I said, 'If you mess with them, you mess with me. Understand?' And they shut up after that."

Chris said, "Really? Wow. Thanks, man!"

"Seriously, I didn't have any problem with you guys at all. Hell, I figured at least you were getting some. Which was more than I could say for me and most of the other guys on the team."

Ryan said, "Speaking of that, let's talk about another night in a hotel. So, Rocket... That night you were at the orgy. There must have been stuff going on all around you."

"You can say that again."

"There must have been stuff going on all around you." The others groaned. "So... Did you get any? Maybe a little handie or a BJ?"

It was all Chris and Trevor could do not to burst out laughing. Rocket was caught off-guard and a bit taken aback.

Ryan said, "C'mon. Like you said earlier, we're all friends. You can tell us. With all that sex going on, are you sure you didn't dip your toe in the water, so to speak?"

Chris said, "As they say, when in Rome, do as the Romans do."

Trevor added, "I'll bet there were some roamin' fingers that night."

Ryan said, "After all, you wouldn't want to *blow* your cover by not doing anything, would you?"

Rocket wasn't about to mention that he got hard when he saw Ryan in the porno they were showing. "No way man. One guy wanted to give me a hand job, but I said no. I left right after that."

Ryan said, "I'm surprised. You're open-minded. You're comfortable around naked guys. I bet you're kind of curious about what gay guys do. That would have been your chance to satisfy your curiosity. You know, take a walk on the wild side. I figured you'd be down for that."

Trevor added, "Besides, if you close your eyes, it all feels the same."

Rocket turned to his buddy. "And how would *you* know?" He turned back to Ryan and Chris. "You know I don't have any issue with guys having sex. But there's a big difference between being okay with it and actually doing it."

Ryan said, "Fair enough. I was just teasing you. But if you had experimented a little, we wouldn't think any less of you."

Chris said, "I read somewhere that they did this study in the 40s. Even back then, they found that 37% of all men have at least one sexual experience with another man sometime between adolescence and old age."

Rocket's eyes popped open. "Seriously?"

Ryan said, "Ah, yes... The Kinsey Report. I believe they also found that if a guy was still unmarried by the time he reached 35, that percentage went up to 50."

Rocket said, "No shit?"

Chris said, "No shit. Look it up on the internet. So you guys are, what? 31 or 32? Hmmm." He grinned at Rocket and Trevor.

Ryan said, "Well, anyway... Enough teasing. We have some big news!"

Ryan draped his arm across Chris's shoulder and gazed at him fondly. It took Chris a moment, but then he said, "Oh, yeah!" He held his hand out and showed Rocket and Trevor his engagement ring. Ryan held his hand out next to Chris's so they could see his matching ring.

Rocket said, "Wow, man! You guys are engaged?"

Ryan and Chris grinned and nodded.

Trevor said, "Congratulations! Man, you guys don't waste any time, do you? It's been, what ... two months?"

Ryan said, "Yeah. But in a way, it's been 14½ years. We went on about our lives and had other relationships, but we always knew in our hearts we were meant for each other."

Chris said, "Not a day went by when I didn't think about him. Anyway, he popped the question yesterday at my parents' house right after we opened our presents. I was totally shocked, but I mean, come on! There's no way I was going to say no to him."

Rocket stood up. "Guys, I'm so happy for you!" He walked around to their side of the table with his arms open. Chris and Ryan stood up and let Rocket hug them.

Trevor hurried over to the bar and said something to the bartender.

When they sat back down, Rocket said, "So, have you guys picked a date yet?"

Ryan said, "No, but probably sometime in the fall."

Chris grinned. "We wouldn't want to rush into it, would we?"

Trevor asked, "Have you thought about where you're going to have it?"

Chris said, "In Scottsdale. Or somewhere in the Phoenix area."

Trevor said, "No, I mean, are you going to do it in a park, like you did last time, or in a wedding venue, or something else?"

Ryan and Chris looked at each other. Ryan said, "We haven't gotten that far yet. We'll probably talk about it on our way home. It's an 18-hour drive that'll take two days."

Trevor said, "Well, if you decide to have it at a resort, I can probably get you a really sweet deal at the Helton Grande in Paradise Valley."

Chris said, "Seriously?"

"Yeah. Every year, they send their highest-performing managers to one of their luxury properties for a week. There are some meetings and training, but there's a lot of partying and sightseeing too. They totally wine and dine us. One year, I got to go to our resort in Paradise Valley. It's amazing! It's totally over the top. I got to know the manager there and we've stayed in touch. So yeah, I could contact him and ask him to give you a great rate. And he can give you a discount on the rooms for your out-of-town guests. It would have to be during one of their less busy times. They're booked solid every winter with conferences and holiday parties and people there on vacation. And during spring training in March? Forget it. But September or October should be fine. They're less busy then."

Ryan said, "Man, that's really nice of you! We'll give it some serious thought."

"Let me touch base with him, then I'll send you his contact info."

The bartender arrived at their table carrying a tray with four chilled champagne flutes and a bottle of champagne submerged in an ice bucket. He set the tray down on the edge of the table and proceeded to tear the foil off the top of the bottle and pop the cork. Then he poured champagne into each of the four glasses.

Ryan and Chris exchanged glances. They had already consumed plenty of sangria. But there was no way they could politely refuse.

Trevor picked up his glass. "A toast!" Rocket, Chris, and Ryan raised their glasses. "To the happiest, most perfectly matched couple on earth!"

They all clinked glasses and took a few sips. Trevor had ordered a good bottle.

Rocket said, "So, uh... I know this is kind of pushy, but... Could we be invited? We watched your last wedding on the livestream, and that was nice but it wasn't the same as being there. And this time, since I know both of the grooms..."

Chris and Ryan glanced at each other and nodded.

Chris said, "Yeah! Of course!"

Rocket said, "Cool! And I'd like to see Scottsdale, too. You keep talking about how nice it is. And who knows, someday I might get tired of KC and decide to move someplace else."

Trevor said, "Man, I reached that point several years ago. I keep thinking about getting a transfer to one of our other properties that's someplace nice. But my dad's been having some health issues over the past few years, so I need to stay close to home for the time being."

Ryan said, "I'm sorry to hear that. What's going on? ... That is, if you want to share."

Trevor sighed. "Oh, part of it's just getting older. He's 68. I was kind of a 'late in life' kid for them. And he's never taken care of himself. He's overweight, diabetic, high blood pressure, and all that. He's already had two hip replacements. He had a mild heart attack last summer."

Chris frowned. "I'm sorry to hear that. How's your mom?"

"She's doing okay physically, but all this is bringing her down. She has to drive him everywhere for appointments and take care of him while he's recuperating. Like this wasn't exactly the retirement she was hoping for. Dad retired a couple of years ago, and he just sits around the house and gets on her nerves."

Ryan said, "What about you, Rocket?"

"I haven't talked to either of my parents in years. I have no desire to. I check in on my brother once in a while, but he's kind of a sad case. I'd rather not talk about it."

"No problem. I understand."

Chris glanced at his watch. "Shit. We need to get going."

Ryan checked his watch and said, "Yeah. Guys, I'm sorry, but we've got to run. We're having dinner with the guy who was my manager at Price Cutter when I worked there. He helped me a lot when all the shit went down with my parents."

Everyone stood up. Trevor said, "That's okay. We knew you had dinner plans. But it was great to see you."

Rocket said, "Yeah. It was nice to chat on Skype, but it's nothing like seeing you in person."

Ryan said, "Now that Chris and I are a couple, we'll be coming here to visit his parents once or twice a year. We'll always make time to get together with you guys."

Chris said, "And we'll see you when you come out for the wedding!"

Ryan added, "And any other time you want to come and visit, just let us know."

Rocket said, "I will, man. Count on that."

Chris turned to Trevor and said, "And thanks for the libations. That was really nice of you."

"No problem. Being the manager has its privileges."

They hugged and said goodbye.

As they walked across the parking lot to their car, Ryan texted Russ to let him know they'd be 15 or 20 minutes late.

***

Traffic was light since it was Sunday evening, the day after Christmas. Chris and Ryan drove the 15 miles to Russ and Frank's home in record time. They climbed the front steps and before they could ring the doorbell, the front door swung open. Russ grinned and held his arms open wide.

Ryan rushed up and hugged him. Then he stepped aside and hugged Frank while Russ hugged Chris. He remembered Chris from a few days before Christmas in 2008, when Chris came to Price Cutter to ask him if he knew of Ryan's whereabouts. That inquiry led to Ryan and Chris getting back in touch.

After Russ released Chris, he said, "Chris, this is my husband Frank." Frank and Chris shook hands.

Ryan gazed at Russ and Frank. That summer when Russ was Ryan's manager at Price Cutter, he was in his early 40s. Ryan only met Frank once, but he guessed they were about the same age. Now, 14½ years later, they were in the upper 50s. They had both put on weight and their thinning hair was now mostly gray.

The house was almost the same as Ryan remembered it, but something was missing. Then it hit him. "So I guess Ralph and Herbie are gone now."

Russ sighed. "Yeah... We had to put Ralph to sleep back in, what? 2018? 2019?" He glanced at Frank.

"I'm pretty sure it was 2018."

"Anyway, before the pandemic. He was 15. He was going blind and deaf and he started having seizures. So we had to put him down. Herbie died in his sleep a few weeks later."

Frank said, "He was getting pretty old too, but we think he died of a broken heart. He wasn't the same after Ralph died. The two of them were so close."

Ryan said, "Awww... I'm really sorry."

Russ said, "Thanks. But you know, it happens. Fifteen years is a long time for larger breeds."

"Have you thought about getting new dogs?"

"We've talked about it. If we do, we'll adopt middle-aged dogs. Neither of us has the energy for puppies."

Frank glanced at his watch. "Well, let's get going. I don't know about you guys, but I'm gettin' pretty hungry."

Ryan said, "Sorry we got here late."

Russ said, "No problem. We can all go in my car." He led them through the kitchen and into the garage. They climbed into his aging Toyota Camry – the same car Russ owned in 2007 when he took Ryan to the bus station for his journey to Los Angeles.

Burger Betty's was only a few miles away. During the drive, Ryan took in the surroundings and tried to remember what was the same and what had changed over the past 14 years. When they drove past the World War I Museum and Park, Chris said, "There's the park where they had the Gay Pride Festival! Remember that?"

"How could I ever forget? You drove us past it on purpose, then you said, 'Hey, let's go check it out!' like it was a spur-of-the-moment thing."

"Well, yeah, but if I had suggested that we go there in advance, you wouldn't have gone."

"Yeah, probably not. And when we arrived, there were those protesters at the entrance."

"I remember. That really shook you up. But anyway, I had a great time and you... well, not so much. In hindsight, I was sorry I took you there."

"Yeah, I admit I didn't deal with it very well. It was too much gay for me at the time. I wasn't ready to come out yet."

Chris put his hand on Ryan's leg. "We were so innocent and naïve back then."

"*That's* certainly changed. But after I moved to LA, I went to their Gay Pride a few times. Then a few years ago, Aaron and I and a couple of others went to San Diego's. Talk about too much gay! Compared to LA and San Diego, KC's Pride Festival was tiny."

"Yeah, but at the time, we were shocked that there were so many other gay people."

Russ said, "KC's festival has gotten larger over the years, but I'm sure it's still small next to LA's. We went to LA's when we lived there. I'm with you – it was too much gay."

They arrived at Burger Betty's and parked. After they had ordered and their festive cocktails were delivered, Frank said, "A few minutes ago when we were talking about LA, that brought back some memories."

Ryan asked, "Do you miss living there?"

Frank replied, "Kinda. For one thing, there was so much more to do there. The society was much more accepting of gays. And the weather was certainly nicer. But on the other hand, I got tired of the freeways and the pollution and all that."

Russ added, "And it's certainly a lot cheaper to live here."

Frank said, "The main reason we moved here was to look after my parents, who were getting older. And that was the right thing to do at the time. And I guess it did us some good to get out of LA and settle down a bit."

Chris asked, "How are your parents now?"

"Oh, they've passed away. But we don't want to disrupt our careers at this point, so we'll stay here. At least until we retire – which is coming up in only a few years."

Russ said, "I'm a regional training manager for Price Cutter now, so I'm making pretty good money. I'll be eligible for retirement in two years, but I'll probably stay for the health benefits – at least until we're both 65 and on Medicare."

Their food was delivered by a perky young man who looked about 20, with purple streaks in his hair, a nose ring, and several tattoos. "Can I get you guys anything else?"

Everyone looked at the fabulously presented, nutritionally disastrous entrees that awaited them. There were already condiments on the table. Russ said, "No, I think we're okay for now." The young man smiled and scurried off. Everyone dug in.

Ryan asked, "What do you think you'll do after you retire? Stay here or move someplace else."

Frank said, "Probably move someplace else. Not back to LA. We'd never be able to afford it. We've been thinking about Palm Springs. A lot of gay people retire there. And it's close enough to LA that we can go once in a while, like for a concert or something."

Russ said, "It's pretty expensive too, but not as bad as LA."

Ryan said, "You should check out Phoenix! I really like it. It's almost the same weather as Palm Springs, but a lot cheaper. And there's a lot going on. We have theatre and concerts and nice restaurants, too. Trust me, I've lived in LA, and I'll take Phoenix any day!"

Chris said, "You should come out and visit us sometime! We'd love to show you around."

Ryan said, "You can check out Phoenix when you come for our wedding!"

Russ and Frank looked confused.

Chris held out his hand and showed them his ring. "See what I got for Christmas?"

Russ and Frank fawned over the ring. Russ said, "Congratulations!"

Ryan said, "Thanks! We haven't picked the exact date or place yet, but it will probably be sometime in the fall. And I'd love it if you guys could be there."

Russ smiled and said, "We'll give it serious consideration. And it will be nice to check out Phoenix. We've driven through on I-10 a couple of times, but that doesn't really count."

Frank turned to Russ with mock indignation. "You never gave me an engagement ring."

Russ waved him off dismissively. "We couldn't even get legally married back then. Hell, I'm just grateful we could finally get married here in 2015. Besides, would you have worn it?"

"Probably not. I've never been into jewelry. Even in LA, we had to be kind of discrete about our relationship sometimes. Especially at work. But I proudly wear this wedding ring now." He held out his hand.

Ryan said, "I remember the day I ran away from home. You guys took me here for dinner. At the time, this was a total revelation. I had no idea there could be a fabulous gay restaurant, complete with drag shows, in a conservative place like Kansas City."

Frank said, "KC's not so bad. It's the rest of the state."

Ryan continued. "Then you took me back to your house and we watched *Priscilla, Queen of the Desert* until it was time to take me to the bus station. Russ, I'll never be able to thank you enough for everything you did for me that day. And both of you guys – you were so nice to me. And I remember seeing what a happy couple you were. You were the first gay couple I ever saw in real life. I remember thinking, 'That's what I want. I just want to settle down with a nice guy and a comfortable little house with a couple of dogs and live happily ever after.' And of course, I wanted that guy to be Chris. But that day, I wasn't sure if I'd ever see him again."

Russ said, "Yeah. I remember how you debated whether or not you should call Chris and say goodbye. You really wanted to, but we agreed it would be better not to since we couldn't have anyone find out where you were going. You weren't 18 yet."

"In hindsight, I wish I had called."

Chris reached over and held Ryan's hand. "I wish you had, too. But we can't go back and change it." He looked across the table to Russ and Frank. "But we've already worked through all that. I'm just glad I have him now."

Russ said, "So are we. I could tell how much he loved you back then, and it's certainly obvious now."

Chris turned to Ryan and grinned. "So... Does that mean we're going to get a couple of dogs?"

"We'll talk about it. Our lives are pretty busy, especially now that we have a wedding to plan. Dogs are a big commitment. Maybe someday."

Russ said, "We really miss Ralph and Herbie. But we're okay with not having dogs at this time."

They finished their meal and drove back to Russ and Frank's house.

Ryan said, "We'd better get back to Chris's parents. But it's been wonderful to see you again and catch up."

Russ's eyes grew moist. "It's been great to see you again, Ryan. You were an excellent employee and I knew you were an above-average kid. It's wonderful to see the man you have become." He kissed Ryan on the cheek and gave him a warm hug. Then he hugged Chris and said, "I'm so happy that you two are finally together."

Chris said, "Me too! And thanks for putting me back in touch with him when I came into the store back in 2008."

"Wow. That was so long ago."

Ryan and Chris hugged Frank. Ryan said, "I'm serious about you guys coming out for our wedding. And any other time you want to come. It would be great if you moved to Phoenix after you retire."

Frank smiled. "We'll give it serious consideration."

With that, they parted.

The Future

Wednesday, December 29, 2021

On Wednesday morning, after a delicious breakfast served by Kathleen and tearful hugs and goodbyes, Ryan and Chris began their two-day drive back to Scottsdale.

They drove several miles west on 75th Street until they reached I-35. While they waited at the light to turn left onto the freeway, Ryan said, "You know what's just up ahead? That Slush Fun where we used to go all the time."

"Yeah, that's right. Looks like it's still there. Want me to drive past?"

"No, go ahead and turn onto the freeway. But wow – so many memories. We had so much fun there. We'd hang out, tell jokes, and talk about all kinds of things. But then... there was the time right after we came out to each other and we wanted to make out. So we went to that parking lot a couple of blocks behind it and started kissing. That's when we got busted by that cop."

Chris put his hand on Ryan's leg. He fervently hoped their day wouldn't start with Ryan getting depressed about everything that happened after that.

Ryan knew he shouldn't go there either. "You know, coming back to Prairie Village after all these years was better than I thought it would be. I hardly thought about my old house or the church. It was great to spend so much time with your parents. Back in high school, I came over to your house a lot. But it was always for a couple of hours and it was mostly with you. I really got to know your family a lot better on this trip."

"Plus, we're all adults now. That made things kind of different."

"Yeah. Anyway, you have the greatest parents! I'm really glad they're going to be my in-laws."

"They've always liked you. After I came out to them, they said they hoped you and I would be together forever."

"And finally, now we can."

"When the shit hit the fan with your parents, they said that if you wanted to come live in our house, you could. But, of course, now I understand why you had to get away."

"Still, the fact that they were willing to do that says a lot."

A few minutes later, they passed the exit for Route 169. Ryan said, "And right over there is our old stomping ground, the Great Mall of the Great Plains."

"Not anymore."

"Huh?"

"They tore it down five years ago."

Ryan sighed. "I guess I'm not surprised. Even back then, we could see how it was declining."

"You said we should call it The Mediocre Mall instead of the Great Mall, remember?"

Ryan chuckled. "Yeah. Still, we had fun there. I'll never forget that day we went into Book Galaxy and you put those books with the provocative titles on the front display tables."

Chris laughed. "Oh, God! I haven't thought about that in years! Let's see, there was *Validate Your Vagina* and *The Gay Men's Guide to Anal Health*. What were some of the others?"

Ryan laughed. "I think one was *Gay Sex 101*. Oh, and *The Tao of the Female Orgasm*. I remember I was so shocked that you did that. Like everyone who walked past the bookstore and looked in would see them."

"You have to admit, it was funny."

"Yeah, it was. And remember that time we were at Slush Fun and we made up names for people that would fit their occupations."

"Yeah." Chris smiled as he recalled some of the names. But then, that was the night they got busted by the cop. Better to let that go. "We sure had some good times."

Ryan thought a moment. "You know, that was one of the things that made me like you. You knew how to have fun. I always felt good when I was with you. You made me laugh. You were always happy and funny and cheerful. That really attracted me to you."

"You mean it wasn't because I was so irresistibly cute and sexy?"

"Well, it certainly wasn't because you're modest." They both laughed. "Of course, you were irresistibly cute and sexy. You still are. But back then, I was so conflicted. On the one hand, I was scared to admit that I was gay, because, you know, my parents. On the other hand, I jerked off fantasizing about you constantly."

Chris said, "On the other hand – literally!" They both laughed.

"We never laughed in my house. My folks were so uptight with their religion. There was so much stuff that was off-limits."

"Yeah... I remember you could never see any movies rated higher than G."

"And not even any Disney movies. 'Cause, you know, they supported the gays. But yeah... So much humor is based on topics that were off-limits at my house. That's one reason it was such a culture shock when I got to LA. In that house, nothing was off-limits. Those guys said stuff around the dinner table I couldn't believe. And they picked up on that right away. Looking back, I'll bet they purposely said shocking shit just to draw me out of my shell. They were always cracking jokes and teasing each other. It was great. And it was all done with love – nobody got offended by anything."

For a couple of minutes, neither of them said anything.

Then Ryan said, "You know, that's something I miss. I never laugh anymore. When we were in high school, we could joke around and not be too serious about stuff. We didn't have to worry about being PC. And yeah, some of it was immature, but so what? But now that we're adults, we've got to be all mature and responsible and shit. That's one thing that came out in my counseling sessions with Aaron. He said I was too serious. I didn't know how to kick back and relax. And I guess he found that with Brandon. He said Brandon made him laugh. *He* knew how to have a good time."

Chris said, "I remember back in high school, you were pretty quiet and shy. But whenever I went to your house, Brandon was always such a hyper bundle of energy. He was always smiling and upbeat."

"Yeah, I was an introvert and he was definitely an extrovert. He still is."

"I had to work hard to pull you out of your shell. But it was totally worth it. I loved what I found inside."

Ryan reached over and held Chris's hand. "Thanks. I always felt comfortable with you."

They held hands for a moment. Then Chris said, "I guess I haven't been much fun to be around these past few months. What with leaving my career in Washington and moving to Arizona, then finding out my partner was the Whore of Babylon, and breaking up... It's been the most difficult time of my life. Well, that and when you disappeared."

"Yeah, you haven't had much to laugh about over the past several months. Neither have I."

"But you know what? That's a choice we can make. We can change that. We can decide that we're going to have fun and laugh more. Let's go out to some comedy clubs! Watch some funny movies and TV shows! Have some friends over and play funny games!"

"Right! Besides, now that we're together again and we have the rest of our lives to spend together, why shouldn't we be happy? Why shouldn't we laugh? The tough times have passed, and I see nothing but good days ahead."

"Yeah, but you know there will always be difficult times. But maybe the secret is to laugh even when times are tough. You can always find humor in something if you look for it. They say laughter is the best medicine – whoever 'they' are."

Ryan chuckled. "You know, I've always wondered about that. Who are these 'They' people we always refer to? 'They' say this and 'They' say that. What is it, like a secret committee that meets somewhere and gets to choose which sayings we're supposed to live our lives by? How do I get on that committee?"

Chris laughed. "I know, right? And people say, 'They repainted the street lines' or 'They need to pick up the litter in the park.' It's like there's a network of stealth workers who wear uniforms with THEY printed on the back in big block letters, and 'They' show up in the middle of the night when nobody is around and take care of all that stuff."

"I wonder if they're the same 'They' people who decide which expressions we're supposed to live by. Maybe that's their reward for doing all the thankless shit work behind the scenes."

They both laughed. Chris said, "See? We can find stuff to laugh at if we try."

"You know? I think your parents have figured that out. They're always so laid back and relaxed. They never get uptight about things. They have friends over and play games like The Big Black Deck and that fart game we were playing with the kids. And they go out on date nights and see movies and stuff. I'll bet they see funny movies and romcoms and stuff like that, not movies where there's a lot of shooting and killing."

"Yeah, you're right. They could be serious when they needed to deal with something important, but most of the time they kept it pretty light. And Tyler was always cracking jokes and teasing me about stuff and trying to be funny."

Ryan said, "Speaking of Tyler, what was the deal with Chloe? God, she got so bent out of shape when we were playing that fart game with Whitney and Austin."

"I don't know. She didn't used to be that way. Back in college, they'd go out drinking and partying all the time. The first few times I met her, I really liked her. And she didn't seem to have any problem with me being gay. But all that changed when they had kids. It's like she thought she had to be responsible and watch everything they said around the kids. And Tyler was like, whatever. Let them learn about life the way it is. They'll turn out fine."

"And they *are* turning out fine. They're adorable and so precocious! I can tell they're taking after Tyler in that regard."

"Yeah, and it pisses Chloe off to no end. And when she decided to start going to church again, Tyler wanted no part of that."

"So that's probably why she got so bent out of shape when I proposed to you in front of Whitney and Austin."

"Exactly. But that reminds me. How come you cracked up when you were introduced to the kids?"

Ryan paused. He knew he needed to proceed carefully here. "Okay, so you know how he knew the guys I lived with in LA? Well, one of them, Darnell, was a drag queen. He had a wonderful voice, and he sang his songs for real. He didn't just lip-synch. Anyway, his idol was Whitney Houston, and his drag persona was Whitney Austin."

"What??? So you think he named his kids Whitney and Austin because of that guy?"

"Yep. He said so. He and I talked about it for a moment."

"I wonder if Chloe knows."

"I seriously doubt it."

Chris took a moment to process this new information. "So... Wow... That's kind of mind-blowing that a drag queen would make such an impression on Tyler that he'd name his kids after her."

"Remember, he hung out at the house a lot. He was going to live there his senior year until he lost his scholarship."

"Tyler's always been cool around gay people. When I came out to the family, he told me he supported me 100%. That is, after he said I was so obviously gay I might as well have been wearing a gold lamé gown, high heels, and a pink feather boa. Who knows? Maybe he picked up that imagery from Whitney Austin. But still... It seems odd that he'd be so smitten with her that he'd name his kids after her."

"Well, either Whitney or Darnell. Or both."

"What do you mean?"

Ryan suddenly recalled telling Tyler, 'Don't worry, the Vegas Rule applies.' He thought, *Shit. Why did I even say that? How can I get out of this now?*

After a moment of awkward silence, Ryan said, "So... remember when we were having drinks with Rocket and Trevor, and you quoted that statistic that 37% of all men had experimented with another man?"

"Yeah, but what's that got to do with .... Oh."

"You didn't hear that from me."

They rode for a few minutes in silence. Chris recalled a conversation he and Tyler had in his room later in the evening after Chris came out to his family.

> *Tyler asked, "So, have you and Bryan done it yet?"*
>
> *"Sorry to disappoint you, but I'm not telling you about my sex life."*
>
> *"Awww... I was hoping to learn more about what guys do together."*
>
> *"If you want to find out what guys do together, go find one and do it with him."*

Apparently, he had.

The more Chris replayed bits of that conversation, the more the pieces fell into place. Finally, he asked, "Are you sure? How did you find out?"

"Well, remember how I said that my housemates would sit around the dinner table and talk about all kinds of stuff? One time, that came up."

"So did Darnell say he fucked him?"

Ryan felt terrible because he had broken his promise to Tyler. But Chris was his fiancé, the love of his life, and he needed to be honest with him. "All three of them did."

"WHAT....??? Oh... My... God."

"I know, right? I couldn't believe it either."

"My brother ... my supposedly straight brother who now has a wife and kids ... has taken it in the ass."

"Multiple times. And he probably fucked guys in the ass too. I don't know. They didn't get into that level of detail."

"Mind. Blown."

"Maybe he's bi. Or maybe he was just horny and drunk at a wild party. And let me tell you, they had some wild parties. At any rate, let's just say he's in that 37%. We don't really know where he is on the Kinsey Scale, and that's his business. I'm certainly not going to ask him."

"Yeah, me neither."

"Especially 'cause you're not supposed to even know. Seriously, you can't ever let on that we talked about this."

"I get it." Chris paused. "I wonder if Chloe knows."

"I can't imagine he'd tell her."

"Maybe she suspects. Sometimes women have intuitions about things like this. If he has some level of interest in guys, she may have noticed. Maybe that's why she's so uptight about us."

"Maybe. But again, we'll probably never know. I'm sure as hell not going to ask her about it. It's none of our business."

Chris asked, "So, are we going to invite them to our wedding?"

"How could we not? I mean, he's your brother! We can't invite only him and not invite his wife and kids."

"Yeah, you're right. I just don't want her making a scene or bringing her negative energy to it."

"Maybe Tyler will come by himself. But we have to leave it up to them."

"So, let's talk about who we're going to invite. My parents, of course. And we've already invited Rocket and Trevor, and Russ and Frank. How big a wedding do we want to have?"

"I don't know. I guess I'd rather not start by picking some arbitrary number and trying to stick to that. I'd rather approach it by listing the people we want to be there. Then we'll see how many that is and cut back if we need to. But what about you? What are your thoughts about whether to have a small, medium, or large wedding?"

Christ thought about that for a minute. "Hmmm... I guess I don't want it to be too large. But I don't want it to be just, like, four people at our house. So, somewhere in the middle. Your wedding to Aaron seemed like about the right number of people."

"Yeah, I thought so too. I wouldn't want our wedding to be too much larger than that. For one thing, there's the cost. Weddings are expensive.

Assuming we're going to feed people a nice meal and have an open bar, we're looking at easily $100 per person. And it's not even the money so much. I mean, you and I can afford a nice wedding. But we also want to spend some time with everyone who comes. After all, we're inviting them because they're special. If we have a large wedding and people are only a small part of a crowd of 150 or 200 people and they never get to spend a moment with us, they won't feel very special."

"Yeah, I see what you mean. Anyway, I can't imagine inviting 150 or 200 people. I'm thinking 30 or 40. Fifty, tops."

Ryan said, "Well, if we invite 50 tops, we'll have to invite 50 bottoms." Chris snickered. Ryan continued, "You'll be surprised how quickly the list will grow. But anyway, back to who we'll invite. Aaron and Brandon, of course. And Rob and Eddie. Maybe a few of my gay friends at work. And I'd like to invite Ted, Ricky, Darnell, and his husband. They might not come because they're so far away – especially Ted in Australia – but I'd like to invite them and let them decide."

"What about people in Desert Pride and Desert Jazz Connection?"

"I'd like to invite some of them – the ones we hang out with more. I don't think we need to invite everyone. What about you? Do you want to invite any of your friends from high school, college, or DC?"

"I've been thinking about that. I'm friends on Facebook with some of our high school friends and a few from the marching band in college – but we're not that close. And my friends from DC... You know, I'm disappointed that none of them told me about Seth cheating on me. They knew, but they didn't say anything. And in the four months since I've lived in Arizona, most of them haven't kept in touch much. So maybe only four or six of them that were my closest friends. And as you said about your housemates, they live far away so they may or may not come."

Ryan said, "Well, let's continue this discussion when we're home and we can write all this down. Moving on, what do you think about Trevor's offer to get us a discount at the Helton Grande Resort in Paradise Valley? I've never been there, but I've driven past it, and it looks really swank. It's right in the middle of the nicest part of Paradise Valley. It probably has spectacular views."

"I think we should at least look at it. If it's as nice as you say, it will probably cost a small fortune even with a discount. But you know, I'd be happy having it at that park where you and Aaron got married. That was nice. It felt comfortable. One thing about having a wedding in a big, expensive resort is that it may seem too formal. I don't want people to feel like they have to get all dressed up. I don't want it to be stuffy."

"Yeah, I know what you mean. I feel the same way. But it's up to us to determine how we want people to dress. We can let them know in the invitation. But here's another thing. I like that park where Aaron and I got married, but I kinda want ours to be different. I don't want people thinking, 'This is just like Ryan and Aaron's wedding, only with Chris instead of Aaron.' I don't want it to seem like you're Aaron II. If we want to have our wedding in a park we should pick a different one."

"I hadn't thought about that, but I see your point. So do you want to have Rob officiate, or would you rather pick someone else?"

"That's a good question. If we follow the same logic as we did with the park, then we should have a different officiant. But I can't think of anyone else offhand, and Rob did a great job. And I consider him a close friend. What do you think?"

"Yeah, I thought he did a great job too. I'd be okay with having him do it. What about the reception? Would we have it at that same Brazilian place?"

"Well, if we have the wedding at the resort, the reception would be there. But even if we don't, I'd like to find a reception hall or something. At my last wedding, we only had dinner. This time, I'd like to have dancing too."

"So we'll need to hire a DJ. Do you know anyone?"

Ryan thought for a moment. A smile crossed his face and he became excited. "You know what? Wouldn't it be totally dope if we had Desert Jazz Connection there playing live music? They could play Glenn Miller and Tommy Dorsey and stuff from the swing era and people could dance to it!"

"I guess... But wouldn't that mean we'd have to spend the whole reception playing in the band?"

"No, of course not. We could get subs. But we could play, like, the first three or four numbers. Maybe do songs where we have solos. God, the more I think about this, the more I love it! We'd have live jazz and get to play at our own reception!"

"Well, okay, but... Do you really think people will dance to it? Most of our guests will be same-sex couples. They're not used to ballroom dancing. All they know is disco and club music."

"Or country line-dancing, but I don't want to have that."

"Exactly."

"Okay, maybe you're right. Maybe we could have the band do just one set, like for a half-hour or forty minutes. Then we could have a DJ for the rest of the evening. That way, our friends in the band can enjoy the rest of the reception too."

Chris thought about it some more. "I admit, the idea does have some appeal. We can talk about it more later."

For the next few minutes, Ryan drove down the highway with a big smile on his face. Then he said, "And! ... AND! ... How about this? If Darnell comes, he could sing a few songs as Whitney Austin!"

"Do you really think he'd do that? That means he'll have to bring his outfit and make-up and all that stuff."

"Oh, he'd totally do it. Plus... He'd get to sing in front of a live band! He always had to sing to tracks. He would eat it up!"

"But where would we get the arrangements?"

"He probably still has the arrangements from when he had the tracks recorded. If not, Colin can probably find something. I could probably transcribe the arrangements from the recordings if I had to."

"Sounds like a lot of work, on top of planning a wedding and doing your regular job."

"I don't care! It would be totally worth it!"

"Well, start by talking to Darnell and see if he'll do it. Then we can take it from there."

"Oh my God! This is going to be totally awesome! We are going to have the greatest wedding ever!"

Chris loved seeing Ryan so excited. He didn't want to burst his bubble, but he was still trying to picture how all this would work. "So is this guy really that good?"

"Oh my God, yes! When we were in college, he'd perform in P-town for like eight weeks every summer. Oh, by the way, I want us to go to P-town sometime. And he'd perform on gay cruises in front of, like, 2,000 guys. And he used to sing at Gay Pride Festivals all over the country. I mean, he's really big. Or he was, anyway. Now that his nursing career has taken off, he doesn't have much time for that. He only performs locally for benefits and stuff. That's another reason I think he'd do it. He doesn't get to perform much anymore."

"Well, okay. Do you have any videos of him performing?"

"Check out his YouTube channel! He's got dozens of videos on there.

Some he had professionally recorded and edited. Others are videos people took at his gigs."

Chris reached for his phone and launched YouTube.

Ryan said, "Just search for Whitney Austin. They'll come right up. See if you can find one called 'I Can Cook Too.' That one has a big band track."

"Here it is." Chris watched the video. "Okay, I have to admit, that was pretty awesome."

"I know, right? Now, pick one where she's singing 'The Greatest Love of All.' That was always her finale. She totally owns it."

Chris scrolled through the listings. "There's several..."

"Pick one she did live, not the professionally produced one, so you can see what she's like in person."

"Here's one from the San Diego Gay Pride Day in 2016."

"2016... Oh my God, I was at that one! That was the year Aaron, Kent, Justin, and I went. Play that one!"

Chris started playing the video. Ryan had to keep his eyes on the road, so he could only listen. The video began with Whitney introducing the song to the audience.

"Folks, I'm so glad I had the opportunity to come to San Diego and be part of your special celebration. Nobody does Pride like San Diego!" The crowd cheered. "Thank you, thank you. You've been a fabulous audience. Now, I would like to dedicate my last song to someone very special to me who's sitting in the audience right now. I met him when he was still a teenager. He had just arrived in Los Angeles all by himself, having just been forced to leave home because his parents couldn't handle the fact that he was gay. So there he was, on his own, alone in the big city. And by God's grace, he came to live with us. And I watched him grow from a scared, clueless high school kid into a beautiful, strong, successful, proud man. I watched him endure bullying and humiliation and become stronger and better for it. And now... Oh my God, I still can't believe he's here today. So this goes out, with all my love, to Ryan Robertson!"

Chris paused the video. "Are you shittin' me? She gave you a shout-out in front of the whole crowd?"

"I had no idea whoever uploaded that included it on the video. I figured they'd start with her singing. But yeah... And Ricky was there that day too. I hadn't seen either of those guys in four years. We got together backstage and caught up with each other. It was great! Anyway, play the rest of the video."

After Chris watched the video, he said, "Well, now I see why you're so into Whitney Austin."

"It's not just that. It's Darnell. He's very special to me. We lived together for four and a half years until his dad died and he had to move back to Atlanta to take care of his mom. He was my brother. He gave me so much love, support, and guidance. He's one of the strongest, most decent people I've ever met in my life. I really looked up to him. He made a big difference in my life. So yeah, it would mean a lot to me if he could sing at our reception."

"Okay, I totally get it now. Ask him and see if he'll come."

Ryan reached over and held Chris's hand. "Thanks. That means a lot to me."

"Hey, we're getting close to Wichita. Wanna stop for lunch somewhere?"

"Yeah, we probably should. It'll be slim pickings after that. And we'll get gas."

"Well, that depends on where we eat."

Ryan groaned loudly.

"Hey, we're supposed to be laughing at things and having fun, remember?"

Ryan smiled. "Yeah, you're right. What are you in the mood for?"

"An eight-ounce bacon-wrapped filet mignon, accompanied by mashed sweet potatoes, a steamed vegetable medley, and warm dinner rolls with garlic butter. And hot chocolate lava cake and a scoop of French vanilla ice cream for dessert."

Ryan rolled his eyes. "In Wichita. Right. I suppose we could find that Western Corral place where we ate dinner after the track meet."

"Blech." Chris pulled up the map app on his phone. "Let me see what there is at the exits coming up. ... Well, it looks like we have our choice of hamburgers, fried chicken, or tacos."

"Blech. Whatever. How about burgers?"

"There's a Here's The Beef at the second exit."

"Where is Slush Fun when you need it?"

"I'm sure there's one somewhere in Wichita."

"No, Here's The Beef will do."

***

While they were eating, Ryan's phone buzzed. He picked it up and looked at the caller ID.

"It's Aaron." He pressed the button to accept the call. "Hey, Aaron, what's up?"

"Hi, Ryan. Where are you now? Do you have a moment to talk?"

"We're eating lunch at a hamburger place in Wichita. Yeah, I can talk."

"How was the rest of your visit?"

"Really nice. Wonderful, actually. It was great to see Chris's parents and brother again. And we caught up with a few others I used to know when I was in high school. How about you?"

"Pretty good. So anyway, here's why I called. While we were on our Zoom call on Christmas Day, Matt called his brother Mark up in Inkom. Mark decided he isn't going on his mission and he's leaving the church, because of what happened to Matt."

"I'll bet that'll go over well with his parents."

"Exactly. So he told them the day after Christmas and yeah, the shit pretty much hit the fan. So now they're giving him all kinds of crap and he wants to get outta there."

"I can't blame him. I couldn't imagine living in a tiny little town like that anyway."

Aaron paused. "He wants to know if he can come live here."

"WHAT?"

"He wants to come live here. Matt says he and Mark can stay in the same room. They've shared a bedroom all their life."

"Yeah, but in the same bed?"

"I don't know. Anyway, they're willing to do that now."

Ryan thought about it for a moment. He remembered what it was like when he needed to leave home and he had no place to go. "How old is he?"

Aaron asked Matt, then replied, "He turned 18 on December 5th."

Ryan thought, *At least we won't be harboring a minor runaway, which is illegal.* He looked across the table at Chris, who was trying to make sense of what he was hearing from only half of the conversation. "I need to think about it and talk it over with Chris. Can I call you back later this afternoon?"

"Sure."

"Okay, well, talk to you soon. Say hi to Brandon and Matt for me."

"And say hi to Chris. Love you."

"Love you too."

"Bye."

Ryan set the phone down. "Long story short, Matt's brother Mark told his folks he's not going on a mission and he's leaving the church. They lost their shit, and now he wants to come live with us. He would stay in Matt's room."

Thoughts swirled in Chris's head. He had no idea what to say.

Ryan said, "We can talk about it more on the drive home. You want a refill?" Chris nodded. Ryan stood up and grabbed both of their cups. "Oh, and Aaron says hi."

***

Once they were on the road again, they listened to a couple of Ryan's CDs as they drove across the bleak, featureless plain on the straight highway. Neither of them said much. When the second CD ended, Chris ejected it and reached for the CD box in the back seat. "What do you want next?"

"Let's talk for a little while."

Chris put the CD in its case, put it back in the box, and put the box on the back seat.

Ryan asked, "So, what are your thoughts?"

"Well... This wasn't what I signed up for. I was looking forward to Aaron and Brandon moving out. I mean, I like them and everything, and it was nice to have the energy of all that activity going on. It really helped me move on from Seth. It gave me new things to put into my life to replace everything that was taken away. But I was looking forward to living only with you. You know, to get settled into our life together without having other people around. But now we have Matt living with us, and if we say yes to Mark, we'll have two. But then, I guess two won't be much more inconvenient than one."

Ryan had things he wanted to say – especially about calling Matt and Mark an inconvenience. But he decided to let Chris finish before he chimed in with his opinions.

Chris continued. "On the other hand, I really want to help them. Matt's a nice guy, and I'm sure Mark is too. And it's not lost on me that they're now facing a similar situation to what you faced when your parents found out."

Ryan smiled and nodded. Chris was getting it.

Chris said, "So I guess what it comes down to is this. We have a room available. These two guys have been forced to leave a bad situation at home and need a place to stay. We'd be doing a good thing to help young people in need, and it would be kind of selfish of us to say no. But on the other hand, I'm thinking about how it will impact our day-to-day lives. Like, it would be nice to be able to get in the pool or the hot tub naked with you. And if one of us wakes up in the middle of the night thirsty, we shouldn't walk into the kitchen naked. We'd have to put something on. And another thing... Mark's still in high school and Matt's just starting college. In some ways, we'd be their de facto parents. So would we be responsible for cooking their meals and doing other stuff parents do?"

"All good questions. I've been wondering those same things. I thought back to what it was like for me to live in Hal's house and how he handled those things. We would need to set some ground rules, like always cleaning up after yourself, emptying the trash when it's full, and so on. We need to make it clear that this is our home and they're temporary residents. We're not their parents. They're both 18 now, even though Mark is still in high school. They're adults now, and they need to start taking full responsibility for their lives. In Hal's house, everyone bought their own food and cooked their own meals, except for condiments and stuff. He cooked dinner for everyone on Sunday night, but other than that, we were on our own. For most of us, that usually meant frozen entrees or eating out.

"As for things like being naked in the pool and hot tub, again, this is our home. Like if it's some Saturday afternoon and we all want to get in the pool, we should wear suits. But if they're gone, there's no reason we shouldn't go naked. If one of them comes home and they don't want to see us naked, they shouldn't look out the window. And if it's after dark and we want to get in the hot tub, we should. It's our home. If they see us in the hot tub, they can stay inside and use it some other time. Most high school and college kids aren't that interested in hot tubs anyway, and that's not something they should feel entitled to."

Chris said, "Okay, I guess that addresses most of my concerns. But when you lived in Hal's house, how much time did he spend dealing with the guys who lived there?"

"Not much at all, aside from cooking dinner for us on Sunday night. And that was something he wanted to do. He took great joy from it. He was there anytime I wanted to talk about something, but that wasn't too often. Otherwise, we pretty much kept to ourselves. Our schedules were full of things like going to classes, studying, and working. A lot of times, I barely saw the other guys, except in the kitchen if we happened to be eating at the same time. Once they get settled into school they'll make friends. And they'll have to study and work their jobs. So I don't think they'll be in our way too much."

"Okay, then, I guess I'm good with it."

"I'm sure things will come up, and we'll sit them down and talk about it. But they're adults now, so we should treat them like adults and expect adult behavior from them. That's the main reason I'm charging Matt $500 a month rent. Now that he's out on his own, he's not entitled to a free ride. He needs to learn that life costs money and he needs to provide for himself. It's not like I need the money."

"Are you going to charge Mark $500 too?"

"I was thinking about that. They'll be in the same room. I was thinking I'd just charge $600 for the two of them. They can work out how to split it between themselves. Mark will probably have to get a part-time job, too."

"That sounds fair."

"If it doesn't work out, we can help them find an apartment or someplace else to live. I'm sure they'll realize how important it is to behave and not cause any problems."

"Yeah, you're probably right. I just didn't expect that we'd be starting our relationship by opening the Robertson Home for Wayward Mormon Boys."

Ryan chuckled. "Me neither. But as we know, life sometimes throws unexpected things at us. Hey, how far is the next town? We need gas and I need to take a wizz."

Chris checked his phone. "Minneola, in about ten miles. It looks like there's two gas stations there and not much else."

"It'll have to do."

After they had filled up and relieved themselves, Ryan said, "You want to drive the next stretch?" Chris nodded and Ryan handed him the keys.

Once they were on the road, he called Aaron. "Hey. Go ahead and tell

Matt that Mark can stay with us. How's he going to get here, and when?"

"How about if I let you talk to Matt?" Aaron handed the phone to Matt.

Ryan said, "Hey, Matt. How's everything?"

"Well, aside from being kicked out of my house and rejected by my family, and now having my brother essentially kicked out too, everything's great!"

"I guess that was an insensitive question. Sorry."

"That's okay. I know I'm going to be better off here. And hey, thanks for the bike! That was, like, totally awesome! I really appreciate it. You didn't have to do that."

"Good, I'm glad you like it. I guess we're going to have to find another one, too."

"Oh! So does that mean it's okay for Mark to come live here too?"

"Yeah. Chris and I talked, and we're okay with it. Is he going to fly, take the bus, or rent a car like you did?"

"Rent a car."

"So when do you think he'll get there?"

"Well, if he leaves first thing in the morning and drives it all in one day, he'll be here late tomorrow night."

"Okay, good. We'll be home tomorrow night too. He can sleep on a couch or something. Then after Aaron and Brandon move out this weekend, you guys can move into their room."

"Oh, God, thank you, thank you, thank you! You guys are awesome. You are literally saving our lives."

"I know. I've been there myself. Anyway, I'll see you tomorrow evening. Can I talk to Aaron again?"

"Yeah, sure. Bye! And thanks!"

"Bye, and you're welcome."

Matt handed the phone back to Aaron.

Ryan asked, "How's the packing going?"

"Pretty well. We should be ready by Sunday."

"And now, you'll have two strong young bucks to help you move."

"It was really nice of you to let Mark come and stay here."

"Yes, I know."

Aaron chuckled. "You're a wonderful man, Ryan. Even though things happened the way they did, I'll always admire and respect you." He paused. "And love you."

"I love you too. Well, I'll let you get back to packing. See you tomorrow night."

Big Plans for 2022

Sunday, January 2, 2022

Sunday was usually reserved for Ryan's traditional family night dinner. But today Ryan, Chris, Matt, and Mark helped Aaron and Brandon move into their new apartment. Aaron and Brandon took everyone to Kahuna's Tiki Paradise in downtown Scottsdale to thank them.

Eventually, the conversation turned to each person sharing their hopes and plans for the new year. For Matt and Mark, that consisted of settling into their new home, starting classes at their new schools, and acclimating to living on their own.

Aaron and Brandon were excited about setting up their new apartment, but they were already looking forward to house hunting and planning their wedding.

Ryan let everyone else go first. Then he said, "I did a lot of thinking during our drive back from Kansas. The whole thing with Matt's parents kicking him out made me remember what I went through in 2007. I thought about the Los Angeles LGBT Youth Project. Even back then, I remember thinking, 'Where do kids from all over the country go? Surely, they don't all go to places like LA, San Francisco, and New York. A lot of them don't have older gay people they can turn to for help, like I had with my boss Russ Simonton, or Matt had with us. They have no idea where to go or what resources are available.

"The more I thought about it, the more I thought there ought to be some kind of national network to connect gay kids who have to leave home with places they can go. There should be information on the web and a toll-free number to call like the suicide hotlines have."

Brandon said, "That sounds great, but how many places like the LGBT Youth Project are there? I bet there are only a few in the largest cities. They probably don't have anywhere near enough capacity to handle kids from all over the country. Didn't you say the place in LA couldn't always accommodate all the kids who needed a place to stay?"

Ryan nodded. "They had some housing available, kinda like dorm rooms. I think it would be great if there were places like that in cities all across the country."

Aaron said, "Yeah, but where are we going to come up with the funding for that sort of thing? That would cost a fortune."

Brandon said, "Maybe some famous people would get on board with it."

Chris said, "Well, don't forget that I spent the last fourteen years working for Senator Snelling in DC. I have connections all over Congress. We might be able to get funding for this project included in a spending bill. And I know the heads of all the national LGBT organizations. Some of them might be able to provide funding for this, too. They're pros at fundraising and they have huge lists."

Ryan said, "That's fantastic. And they could increase the visibility of this project. Funding is important, of course, but we have to be able to reach the kids who need it. Most of them have no connection to the gay world yet."

Matt said, "I sure wouldn't have known where to look."

Aaron said, "This needs to be as visible as the Trevor Project is for kids who are contemplating suicide."

Brandon said, "We can interview you on our podcast. We've got 32,000 followers now."

Ryan said, "That's great. Thanks! But here's another thing. We need to look beyond setting up big operations like the LGBT Youth Project. We can't expect all the kids to travel to magnet cities like LA. We need a huge network of people all over the country who have an extra bedroom and would be willing to let a runaway kid stay with them for a while. Like us."

Chris said, "I don't know. That opens up all kinds of issues. Like how can we be sure that some pervert isn't going to sign up and then sexually abuse the kids who go live there?"

Ryan sighed. "Yeah. We'd need to have a vetting process. We'd need to set up some guidelines for both the hosts and the kids. And here's another thing. If the kid is under 18, it's illegal for someone who's not a relative or a legal guardian to house them. Believe it or not, it's not illegal for a minor to run away from home, but it *is* illegal to house a runaway. Hal took that risk when he let me move in three months before I turned 18. We'd have to work with the Child Protective Service agencies in the various cities and have the kids go through their system."

Aaron said, "Maybe if people who were willing to be hosts got approved to be foster parents, then the CPS agencies could match the gay kids with the people who are willing to house them."

Brandon said, "I could see that happening in blue states and blue cities, but not in red states."

Matt said, "I couldn't see anything like that happening in Idaho. But think about this. If a kid's going to run away, they don't want to stay where they are. They'll want to go someplace that's more accepting."

Ryan said, "Yeah, but we've gotta start somewhere. Even if we get a network that covers only half of the country, that's better than what we have now. But anyway, that's my idea. I want to at least look into it and see what I can do. So that's my goal for the new year."

Chris said, "That's pretty ambitious. But I'm here to support you all the way. You have an attorney at your beck and call whenever you need one. And I'm happy to work my connections in Washington."

Brandon said, "And you have your friendly neighborhood Communications professional available to help get the word out. You need to come up with a name for it, like the Trevor Project or Emily's List. Something with somebody's name will resonate with people better than some official-sounding organization."

Ryan thought for a moment. "I know! The Hal Morris Project."

Aaron said, "How will people know who Hal Morris is – or was?"

Brandon said, "It doesn't matter. Who's Trevor? Who's Emily? People don't know, but it gives a personal identity to the effort. I like it."

Ryan said, "Hal was a huge supporter of the Los Angeles LGBT Youth Project. He served on their board, donated his legal services, and gave them tons of money over the years. He'd be doing that today if he were still alive. I see this as a way to carry on his work. This can be his legacy."

The Divorce

Monday, January 24, 2022

On Monday morning at 11:00 a.m., Ryan, Aaron, and Chris entered the courtroom of Judge Katherine Hardesty in the municipal court building in downtown Scottsdale.

When their case was called they approached the bench. Chris, now licensed to practice law in Arizona, handed the completed paperwork to the judge. He had no experience in marriage and family law, but it would hardly matter in this case since the divorce wasn't contentious. It was a mere formality.

The judge skimmed the forms. Then she raised her eyes, looked at the three men over the top of her reading glasses, and asked, "Which one of you is Ryan Robertson?"

Ryan answered, "I am, your honor."

She looked at Aaron, "So you must be Aaron Bradbury."

"That's correct, your honor."

"Do you not have counsel? The court can provide a public attorney if you need one."

Chris said, "That won't be necessary, your honor. I am representing both of them."

The judge raised her eyebrows but said nothing. She skimmed the paperwork again.

"On what grounds are you seeking divorce?"

Ryan and Aaron looked at each other and shrugged.

Judge Hardesty was not amused. "Divorce is a serious matter. You shouldn't just waltz into my courtroom on a lark and request a divorce because you feel like it today. And while Arizona is a no-fault divorce state, establishing the grounds for divorce will assist me in arriving at an equitable settlement." She turned her gaze toward Chris. "Surely, as an attorney, you must know this."

Chris stepped in close to Ryan and Aaron and they whispered a few things among themselves. Chris turned toward the judge and said, "Adultery."

"And who committed adultery against whom?"

Ryan and Aaron glanced at each other. Aaron said, "Well, we both did."

Ryan added. "It's okay. We've forgiven each other."

By now, Judge Hardesty was thoroughly confused. She asked Chris, "Have Mr. Robertson and Mr. Bradbury reached an agreement regarding their requests for a settlement?"

"Yes, your honor."

Aaron said, "We have it all worked out. I'll keep what I brought into the marriage and he'll keep what was his. He already owned the house."

Judge Hardesty asked, "What joint assets did you acquire during your marriage?"

Ryan said, "Not much. When we moved in together, we both had a household's worth of furniture. It was hard to figure out where to put it all. So we didn't buy much else. We had a joint bank account for household expenses. But we've divided that 50-50 and closed it already."

Judge Hardesty glanced at the paperwork for a few more seconds, then looked up again. "I must say, this is highly unusual. You two appear to get along better than most couples who stay in their marriages. Why are you seeking a divorce?"

Aaron said, "Well... We both found someone else who is an even better match."

Ryan said, "We still love each other very much. We'll always be family. But we want the best for each other. And for both of us, that's someone else."

Judge Hardesty shook her head. "I still don't get it. But clearly, this is what you both want, so who am I to stand in your way? Divorce granted."

Ryan and Aaron hugged each other. Chris turned to the judge and said, "Thank you, your honor."

The three of them turned to leave. They walked side-by-side down the center aisle toward the door in the rear of the courtroom, with Ryan in the center, Chris to his left, and Aaron to his right. About halfway down the aisle, Ryan draped his arms across their shoulders.

As they walked across the parking lot to their cars, Ryan said, "How about lunch at Kahuna's Tiki Paradise? It's only a few blocks away."

Aaron said, "Hey, I'm always down for Kahuna's."

Chris said, "As long as we don't stay too long. They're expecting me back at the office at one."

Once seated inside, Aaron said, "I didn't think about this until now, but this is where we came on our first date."

Ryan said, "Yeah, you're right. I don't think I considered it a date then, but in hindsight, I guess it was."

"Yeah, me neither, but I definitely came away knowing that I liked you and wanted to get together with you some more."

"Me too. I really enjoyed meeting you. I thought we had a lot in common. And I remember thinking that you might be the one."

Chris said, "Okay, this is getting weird. So this is where you came for your first date, and now we're in the same place celebrating your divorce."

Aaron said, "And I was represented by the attorney who's going to marry the guy I got divorced from, and I'm totally cool with that."

Chris shook his head. "If this was a sitcom, nobody would believe it."

Ryan said, "Well, what would you prefer? That we be angry and sad and hate each other for the rest of our lives?"

"Good point."

Ryan's phone vibrated. It was Matt. The food hadn't arrived yet, so he said, "Hang on a sec." He got up from the table, and as he walked toward the front door, he pressed the button to accept the call. "Hey, Matt."

"Hi, Ryan. Sorry to bother you. Is this a good time?"

"Yeah. We got through with the divorce quickly, so we're having lunch. The food hasn't arrived yet, so I have a few minutes. What's up?"

"Well, my Mom just called. She and Dad are coming here this weekend, the 29th and 30th."

"Do you think they'll try to talk you and Mark into going back to Idaho?"

"Oh, for sure. But there's no way we're going back. But maybe we can at least talk things out. They're also going to get together with your dad."

"Why would they want to do that? How do they even know him?"

"He sent them a copy of his new book, along with a personal note. He said they could contact him if they wanted to ask questions. So they're going to meet him on Saturday. Maybe it's a good thing. But they also want to come to the house so they can see where we're living and meet you guys."

"Do they need a place to stay?"

"No, they're getting a hotel room."

"Well, invite them over for brunch on Sunday. What time do they have to be back at the airport?"

"Their flight goes out at 2:13, so they'll need to be at the airport by noon, so they have enough time to return their rental car."

"Okay, then tell them 10:00." Ryan looked inside. The waiter was delivering their food. "So how do you feel about this?"

"I don't know. I guess it all depends on how things go this weekend. But they're talking to me differently now than they did when they found out I was gay and kicked me out. I think they're figuring out how to deal with it."

"Let's hope so. Anyway, I need to go now. We can talk more about it sometime this week."

"Okay, bye. And thanks!"

"No problem. Bye!"

Ryan walked back inside, sat down at their table, and told Chris and Aaron what happened.

Aaron said, "It looks like your dad's book helped them change their mind."

"Yeah, maybe. I guess we'll find out."

You really should read it, Ryan. It's pretty powerful."

Ryan's expression clearly communicated that he had no interest in doing that.

The Visit

Sunday, January 30, 2022

By 9:45, everything was in place. The dining room table was set with six place settings. Ryan had baked quiche and cinnamon rolls and Chris had fried a pound of bacon. They put the food in the oven to keep it warm.

The only thing left to do was wait. Ryan, Chris, Matt, and Mark sat in the family room, consumed with nervous energy. Ryan glanced at the bar. As much as a nice cocktail might have relaxed him and the others, now was not the time. And of course, no alcohol would be offered during brunch. "I hope your parents don't flip out when they see the bar." He glanced at his watch. "Maybe there's enough time to put the bottles away."

Matt said, "No, leave it. I'm not going to hide anything from them."

Precisely at 10:00 a.m., the doorbell rang. They rose from their seats and headed into the living room. Ryan opened the door. "Mr. and Mrs. Berry? Please come in." When they stepped inside, Ryan closed the door and extended his hand. "I'm Ryan Robertson." They shook his hand, then turned toward their sons.

Mrs. Berry ran up to Matt and hugged him. "Oh, honey, I'm so glad to see you!" She hugged Mark next and said, "I'm glad to see you too."

Mr. Berry seemed uncomfortable, perhaps about hugging his sons in front of homosexuals. He was at a loss for what to say or do. Ryan wondered what their custom was for greeting each other at home. "This is my fiancé, Chris Robertson." Chris stepped forward and offered his hand to Mr. Berry, then to Mrs. Berry. They shook it politely.

Mrs. Berry seemed puzzled. "You're both named Robertson...?"

Ryan was about to say, 'It's complicated,' but Chris spoke first. "It's a common last name."

Ryan said, "I know you must be curious about your sons' accommodations, so let me give you a quick tour. Follow me, please." Ryan led them down the hallway and showed them the music room, his and Chris's office, and the bedroom Matt and Mark were sharing.

Mark could tell his parents were taken aback when they saw one queen-sized bed in the room. "We don't mind sharing a bed."

Matt added, "Nothing's going to happen."

Ryan pointed out the entrance to the master suite but didn't take them inside. He led them back down the hallway and into the great room which held the kitchen and the family room. Mr. Berry remained silent and Mrs. Berry occasionally muttered, "Uh-huh" or "That's nice." Nobody said anything about the bar.

Ryan led them through the sliding glass door out to the back patio. They were clearly in awe of the swimming pool, hot tub, barbecue island, and beautiful landscaping. It wasn't lost on anyone that this upscale home in a very nice part of town was a far cry from their modest house in Inkom. The parents realized that trying to convince Matt and Mark to return home would be a hard sell.

They went back inside and Ryan led them to the dining room. "Mr. and Mrs. Berry, why don't you sit on that side? Mark, you can sit next to them and Matt, you sit across from Mark. Before you sit down, would you please help us serve the food?"

Moments later, the four men carried the food in from the kitchen. Once everyone had been served and started eating, Mrs. Berry said, "This is all delicious. Thank you for having us over. This is quite a place you have here."

Ryan smiled. "Thank you. It's our pleasure. It's nice to meet the parents of these two fine young men."

Mr. Berry, who had said very little up to this point, asked, "So, what made you decide to get into the business of renting rooms to teenage boys?"

Neither Chris nor Ryan cared for the insinuation behind that remark. Ryan said, "They may still be teenagers, but they're both over 18. They're adult men now."

Chris said, "Ryan and I are a monogamous couple. We have no interest in your sons – or anyone else, for that matter."

Ryan said, "To answer your question, we didn't plan on it. But we'd rather see them safe and with a roof over their head than homeless on the street."

Before they could respond, Ryan said, "Let me tell you my story. Rev. Bauer, whom you met yesterday, is my biological father."

Mr. Berry said, "I thought you said your name was Robertson. And the son Rev. Bauer talked about in his book was named Bryan."

"That's right. I changed my name the day after I turned 18. Anyway, I haven't read his book so I don't know what's in it, but here's what happened. Chris and I were best friends in high school." He smiled at Chris. "We still are. But the summer after my junior year, my parents found out I was gay. By that time, Chris was my boyfriend. Being gay was totally unacceptable to my parents – especially my dad. So first they sent me to this bogus 'counselor' who claimed he could turn people straight. He believed we could just pray the gay away – which is nonsense. After three sessions, I told my parents I wasn't going to continue seeing him and they needed to accept me for who I am. Well, my dad and this quack plotted to send me away to some secret gay conversion therapy camp in Alabama. Thankfully, I found out about it the day before they were going to kidnap me and force me to go there. I decided if I didn't want to get sent there, my only choice was to run away from home – which I did. I ended up in Los Angeles. Luckily, I met an attorney named Hal who lived near UCLA and rented rooms to gay college students. I was about to start my senior year of high school, but he rented a room to me anyway. That's where I lived for the next five years. Hal and the other three guys became my new family. If I hadn't lucked out and met Hal, I could easily have ended up living on the street. As it was, I had a safe and loving place to stay so I could work, finish high school, attend college, and get my degree. Now, fast forward to one evening this past November. Your son and his missionary companion called on us. There was another couple here at the time. We didn't hide the fact that we're gay and before the visit was over, Matt came out to us."

Matt took over the narrative. "I had never met any gay people up to that point – at least none that I was aware of. I've been attracted to guys for as long as I can remember, but I knew I couldn't say anything to anyone. I knew I had to keep it a secret. You have no idea how hard that was and how miserable I was inside. But that night, for the first time, I saw gay men who were happy and successful. They lived in this nice home and they had good jobs and other people like them to share their lives with. And in that moment, I knew there was hope for me. I knew there was some way forward. I saw that it was possible to be gay and still have a good life. So I came out to them. And they were so supportive! They invited me and my companion, Jake, here for Thanksgiving and we talked some more. And that's when I knew I couldn't continue as a missionary. More importantly, I knew I couldn't continue hiding and pretending to be someone I'm not."

Ryan said, "I told him he could call if he ever needed help. So when he came out to you and it didn't go well, he called. We told him he could stay here – at least until he got on his feet and decided what to do next. After what Hal did for me, I knew I had to. There's no way I couldn't. So I'm paying it forward, you might say." Ryan paused. The Berrys remained silent. "So how does that compare with what's in my father's book?"

Mrs. Berry replied, "Well, he didn't go into all the details about what happened to you in Los Angeles. But the part about them sending you to counseling and you running away from home lines up."

Ryan asked, "What did he say in the book about my mother?"

Mr. Berry replied, "He said she fell into a downward spiral of drinking and taking anti-depressants. She eventually died. It was so tragic."

"Yes, it certainly was. Did he accept any of the blame for that? Because sending me away to the gay conversion therapy camp was his idea. She felt like she had no choice but to go along. According to my brother, Mom was never the same after I left. And who can blame her? She lost one of her two sons to her husband's stubborn intolerance while knowing that he was secretly gay." He turned to Mrs. Berry. "How would you feel if Matt was taken away from you and you knew you would probably never see him again?"

"I'd feel terrible! I've been miserable ever since Matt left home. That's why we came here, to try to work things out."

"Right. And she's not the only one who was hurt by that separation. The difference is, they never reached out. According to my brother, Dad wouldn't hear of it. My running away was all my fault, not his. He had this glorious vision of becoming a nationally-known author and televangelist. Having a gay son was completely incompatible with that. It was easier for him to pretend I ran away on my own. People could pity him and my mom because they lost their son. Then he could go on as if I no longer existed. But the bottom line is, thanks to him I'll never be able to see my mother again."

Chris said, "I have a few things I want to say. So yeah, Ryan and I were boyfriends. He was the greatest guy I had ever met. He still is to this day. We loved each other so much. We had plans to go to college and spend the rest of our lives together. Then suddenly, he disappeared. Just ... gone. Not a word. This man that I loved so much, my dreams, my future ... all ripped away. You have no idea how painful that was. Now, after 14 years we're finally able to be together. But that's 14 years we lost. Fourteen years we'll never get back."

Ryan said, "And besides that, there was my brother. I had to leave him behind, too. He's eight years younger than me, but we were really close, like Matt and Mark. Suddenly, we got ripped away from each other, too. We were reunited nine years later when he came here to go to ASU. Those nine years, when he grew from a third-grader to a college freshman, were years we didn't get to be part of each other's lives. That's nine years we'll never get back. So, the bottom line is, we aren't about to stand by and see Matt homeless. We intend to offer him the same security and support Hal offered me. And we're happy to have Mark here too so he and his brother won't be separated."

Mr. Berry said, "Well, what about them being separated from us?"

Matt jumped in. "Dad, you're the one who said I couldn't stay there if I'm gay."

Mark added, "And you flipped out when I said I wasn't going to be a missionary and I was going to leave the church. As I said back then, I don't want to be part of any church that rejects its own members because of who they love and teaches parents that they should do the same. I'm not havin' it. I want to be with my brother, so at least he has one family member who accepts him. We can support each other. I'll finish high school, then I plan to work while he goes to college. Then after he graduates and gets a job, he can support me while I go to college."

By this time, everyone had finished their meal. Ryan said, "Perhaps the four of you would like to talk privately. Why don't you go into the living room? Chris and I will clear the table, then we'll go to our office for a while."

Once the Berrys were seated in the living room, Mrs. Berry looked at Matt and asked, "Honey, are you happy?"

Matt thought about it. "With all the changes that have taken place, there have been times when I've been happy and times when I've broken down and cried. It's like I'm on some kind of emotional roller coaster. Coming out was the hardest thing I've ever done. But now that I've done it, I feel better about myself. At least I know I'm being honest with myself about who I am. And after being around Ryan and Chris, and Ryan's brother Brandon and his partner Aaron, I can see there's hope that I can live a normal life and have friends. It's like I'm not alone in the world anymore. There are other people like me. So I feel good about all that. But then I thought, what if I never see you guys again? And even if I do, it probably won't ever be the same. And what about Luke and John? I don't want to get cut off from them like Ryan was with Brandon."

Mrs. Berry said, "We don't want that either, honey. But do you think you'll enjoy living here?"

"You mean in this house or in Scottsdale?"

"Both."

"I like living here. I mean, look at this place. But the most important thing is, Ryan and Chris are really nice. And they're being very good to us."

Mr. Berry said, "What about Scottsdale? I can't get over how big this city is."

"I like Scottsdale, and Arizona in general. When I first arrived here on my mission, I was kind of overwhelmed. But it's so beautiful and modern. There's lots of stuff to see and do. It's so much different from Inkom. I mean, face it. Our town is tiny. There's never anything going on. Even Pocatello isn't very big. While I was growing up I thought, 'Well, this is how it is.' But when I got out and experienced more of the world, I realized there's so much more out there. After about a week on my mission, I realized I liked living here."

Mrs. Berry asked, "What about the schools? Where are you going to go to college?"

"Scottsdale Community College. It's about four miles away. Classes started two weeks ago, and I like it so far. I'll go there for two years and get my Associate's degree, then transfer to Arizona State for my junior and senior years."

Mark said, "My high school is less than two miles away. I love it. It's huge! They have all kinds of sports teams and activities. It's a totally different vibe. I'm still trying to make friends and fit in, but I like it."

Matt added, "And the Food World where we work is less than a mile away."

Mr. Berry asked, "How do you get around? Do you walk or do Ryan or Chris drive you?"

Matt replied, "I ride my bike. Ryan, Chris, Aaron, and Brandon pitched in and gave me a bike for Christmas. I was going to buy a used one on Craigslist, but they surprised me."

Mark said, "One of their friends has a bike they're not using, so they're loaning it to me for the time being."

Mrs. Berry asked, "And how do you like living here?"

Mark replied, "It's only been a month, but I really like it so far."

Mr. Berry leaned toward Mark and lowered his voice, although everyone could still hear him. "So, uh... Do you feel safe here? Are you going to be okay being the only... you know..."

"Straight guy here? Yeah, totally. I mean, seriously? C'mon, man. Nobody's gonna put any moves on me."

"Well, okay, but... I guess what I meant is... Are you worried that living here might, you know... affect you sooner or later?"

"You mean am I going to turn gay? Are you kidding me? Dad, It doesn't work that way. You're either born that way or you're not. I mean, look at Matt. He didn't have any gay people around him his entire life, yet he's gay. But I'm not. I'm, like, totally straight. I'm not going to turn gay just because I live in a house with other gay people."

For a moment, no one said anything.

Finally, Mr. Berry said, "Your mother and I would prefer that you come back home and live with us in Idaho. We know you're over 18 now, so we can't force you. And we know you would have moved out on your own sooner or later anyway. But can't you live someplace nearby, like Pocatello or Idaho Falls? Somewhere closer to the family so we could see each other more often?"

Matt sighed. "No, Dad. Sorry. I really want to live in a larger city. For one thing, there's a gay community here. Up in Idaho... Well, I'm sure there are other gay people, but... I know I'm going to be happier here."

Mark added, "Me too. Honestly, no offense, but... I don't want to live in a small town anymore. I've only been here a month, but I can tell this is where I belong."

Mrs. Berry sighed. "Well, okay. But will you at least come home and see us every so often? And can we talk on the phone every week or two? Like your father said, we realize you're grown up now and you would have moved out on your own anyway. But we don't want to be separated from you. We still want you in our lives. We don't want to make the same mistake Rev. Bauer made and cut you off completely. We love you."

Matt said, "I love you too. And I don't want to be cut off either. This past Christmas was really hard. But you have to accept that I'm gay. This is who I am. I'm not going to change. And I don't want to go back in the closet. I don't want this to be something we don't talk about like we're pretending it doesn't exist. You have to accept that I'm gay."

Mr. Berry said, "We're trying. It may take us a while. It goes against everything the church has taught us our entire lives. We can't change overnight. But we're trying."

Mrs. Berry said, "Rev. Bauer said that coming out is a process. It probably took years for you to come to terms with being gay. Well, it's the same for us. Coming out as the parents of a gay child is a process, too. It will take some time for us to come to terms with it."

Matt said, "That's okay, as long as you're trying."

Mr. Berry said, "There's one other thing we're concerned about. That is how you boys are going to support yourself and go to school at the same time. Are these guys charging you to live here?"

Matt said, "Yeah. $600 a month for the two of us. But we're both working in a grocery store, so we can afford it. And my tuition at Scottsdale Community College is only around $2,000 a year."

"Okay, but what happens in two years when you transfer to ASU? Your tuition is going to be a lot more then."

Matt said, "By then, I'll qualify for in-state tuition. And I'll probably be able to get some financial aid."

Mark said, "And remember, after I graduate from high school I'm going to work to put him through college, then he's going to pay for me after he graduates and gets a real job."

Mrs. Berry said, "But honey, are you sure you want to wait three years before you begin your college education?"

"Well, if we went on our missions, we'd be delaying college for two years."

Matt said, "Speaking of that, you know how you saved $12,000 for each of us to pay for our missions? It sure would be a big help if we had that money to pay for college. I can pay for my tuition at SCC for the first two years, but that money will certainly help pay for ASU."

Mark said, "Yeah. If we spent that money on our missions, how would we have paid for college after that?"

Mr. and Mrs. Berry looked at each other. Their expressions signaled agreement. Mr. Berry turned to his sons and said, "Well, okay. I guess that seems reasonable."

Mrs. Berry added, "Just make sure you spend it on college – not fancy cars or anything like that."

Matt said, "Seriously? You think we'd do that?"

"Well, no, but... Never mind, I shouldn't have said that. I know you are responsible young men."

For a moment, no one said anything. Everyone felt they had discussed everything they needed to discuss. They were mostly satisfied with how it turned out.

Mrs. Berry broke the silence. "Well, it seems as if you boys are pretty well set. You have a nice place to live, you're going to school, you have jobs to support yourselves, and you seem to be happy here."

Mr. Berry said, "And as much as we'd like to have you back home, perhaps this is where you need to be now."

Mrs. Berry said, "But stay in touch, please? We'll always love you and care about you. We want you in our lives."

Matt stood up, and the others followed. "Thanks, Mom. Thanks, Dad. That really means a lot to me." He hugged them both.

Mark said, "Me too. And we'll call you at least once a week."

Mr. Berry glanced at his watch. "Well, I guess we'd better get going. We have to return the rental car full of gas and get to the airport."

Mrs. Berry said, "Would you please get Ryan and Chris? We should say thanks and goodbye to them."

Matt hurried down the hall and summoned Ryan and Chris. When they arrived in the living room, Mrs. Berry said, "Thank you for the lovely meal. It was delicious. And thank you for caring about our boys."

Ryan said, "You're welcome. They're wonderful young men, and we enjoy having them here."

Mr. Berry said, "Now, we're counting on you to keep an eye on them. Don't let them get into any mischief."

Everyone knew he was kidding. Chris replied, "Yes, sir. We'll take real good care of them. And please feel welcome to visit whenever you'd like to see them."

Ryan and Chris shook hands with the Berrys and they hugged their sons again. Then they left.

Ryan asked, "So how did it go?"

Matt said, "Really well. A lot better than I expected."

"Good. Why don't you tell us all about it at dinner tonight? Aaron and Brandon will want to hear all about it, too."

***

Even though Aaron and Brandon now lived on their own, they usually returned to the house on Sunday evenings to continue the Family Night dinner tradition.

After Ryan, Chris, Aaron, and Brandon had updated everyone on their weeks, Ryan said, "So, Matt and Mark, tell us about the visit with your parents."

Matt said, "Well, I guess the biggest thing is, they're willing to accept that I'm gay. They said it will take a while for them to get completely comfortable with it, but they're trying."

Mark said, "That's a huge turnaround from where they were only a month ago. I mean, seriously... I almost didn't recognize my own parents."

"And of course, they tried to talk us into going back to Idaho, but there's no way. And I think they came to see that."

"My dad said a few stupid things, like asking us if we feel safe around you – like you're going to molest him or try to convert me. But we set him straight on that – so to speak."

"I could tell my mom really likes you. And after we cleared up Dad's misconceptions, he seemed to be okay with it too. In the end, he said that, although they'd prefer that we went back to Idaho, he can see that we're in good hands here."

"And that we'd rather be here. I could tell they were totally blown away by this place. They didn't say anything, but I could see it on their faces. They were a little weirded out that we're sleeping in the same bed, but I said I'm cool with it."

"And it's not just this house. It's Scottsdale and the whole area. Oh, and the other thing? They had saved up $12,000 for each of us to go on our missions, and they agreed to let us use that money to help pay for tuition at ASU once we go there."

Chris said, "Wow! That's really great! Sounds like you got everything you wanted."

Matt said, "Yeah. But even more than the money, I wanted Mom and Dad to accept me for who I am. I don't want our family to break up over this. And I got that."

Mark added, "It will take them a while. But they're trying."

Brandon said, "They met with my dad too, right?"

Mark said, "Yeah, they had dinner with him on Saturday. They had a bunch of questions about how to reconcile being gay with what it says in the Bible and what their church says and all that. And they talked about his story and how your family was torn apart. They didn't want that for our family."

Chris said, "Ryan and I told them our sides of the story and how that impacted us. He told them about being separated from Brandon and I talked about how we lost 14 years we should have been able to spend together."

Matt said, "Anyway, between your dad's book, their talk with him, and your stories, they got a pretty clear picture of what would happen to our family if they didn't accept me."

Ryan had remained silent during this discussion. Finally, he said, "So I guess Brad and his book made a big impression on your parents."

Mark said, "He saved our family."

Brandon said, "You haven't read it yet, have you?" Ryan shook his head. "You really should. It's powerful. It's going to help a lot of families after it's published."

Aaron said, "Your idea of forming a network to help runaway kids find housing is wonderful, Ryan. But wouldn't it be even better if they never had to run away in the first place?"

Ryan said, "Yeah. the best possible outcome for my project would be that someday it's no longer needed. But we're a long way from that."

Aaron said, "True. But Brandon's right. You really should read his book."

Ryan sighed. "Okay, okay. I will."

Common Causes

Sunday, February 6, 2022

The next week, Ryan invited Brad to join them for Family Night. He arrived at a quarter to six. Brandon met him at the door and welcomed him in.

Brad approached Mark and shook his hand. "It's a pleasure to meet you, Mark. Thank you for standing with your brother and supporting him."

"Of course. He's not just my brother, he's my best friend. I couldn't give two shits that he's gay. Oh... sorry."

"No problem. I understand your visit with your parents last Sunday went well."

Matt said, "Way better than I expected. Thanks for meeting with them. I think that turned them around."

"Well, I wish I could meet with every parent who reads my book. But if my book is successful, that won't be physically possible."

Brandon said, "You could do Zoom meetings."

"True. But if sales go well, there wouldn't be enough hours in the day." Brad paused. "I guess that's a good problem to have, though."

"You could do webinars! Or YouTube videos! I'd be willing to help you. After all, I've been pretty successful at that."

Ryan announced, "Okay, dinner's ready. We're having chili and jalapeno cornbread. Everybody serve yourself in the kitchen, then we'll eat in the dining room."

Ryan and Chris had been busy in the kitchen up to this point, but now it was time to face Brad. Even though Ryan had invited him to attend, he still wasn't thrilled that this visit was taking place. This would be the first time he and Brad had seen each other in over five years. Their last meeting was three weeks after Ryan and Aaron's wedding when Ryan aired his grievances and Brad asked for forgiveness. Chris wasn't looking forward to seeing him again either, since Brad had been the cause of his 14-year separation from Ryan. But they both realized that Brad had changed and maybe it was time for healing to begin.

Brad entered the kitchen. He smiled with joy as he approached Ryan. When he was a couple of steps away, he opened his arms for a hug and said, "Hello, son!"

Ryan extended his hand. "Good evening, Brad. Thanks for coming." Brad shook his hand.

Brad turned to Chris. "Chris, it's nice to see you again after all these years."

Chris shook his hand but said nothing.

Once seated at the table, people engaged in small talk and shared what happened during the past week. Once those topics were exhausted, there was a brief lull in the conversation.

Ryan said, "Brad, I read your book. I gotta say, you really laid everything out there."

"Well, yes. I felt I had to. For one thing, it was cathartic. At the same time, it was the most humbling, soul-baring experience I've ever been through. Sometimes when I got to a particularly painful part I'd ask myself, 'Does this really need to go in there?' I lost count of how many times I'd delete something and then retype it. But ultimately, I decided that it all had to be included – even the most destructive, depraved things. I wanted people to understand just how insidious these hateful, homophobic beliefs are, and how they ruin people's lives – both for those who are hiding their homosexual feelings and those who are oppressing others. I wanted people to get a clear picture of all the damage it does.

"Even to this day, I'm filled with shame and regret for all those years I stood up on that stage at the church and preached those hateful, misguided sermons. And hosted those awful Rescued Through Love conferences. I shudder to think how much damage I did and how many lives I messed up with all that talk. So the whole reason I wrote that book – and what I've dedicated my life to now – is to try to undo that damage. I want to save families from going through what we went through, and what thousands of other families have gone through. I want gay kids and their parents to know that God loves them too. He created them just the way they are, and they're beautiful and worth loving just like everyone else."

Mark said, "It sure helped our family."

"I don't know whether I'll reach dozens or hundreds or even thousands of families, but it'll be worth it even if it's only a few. Anyway, it's what I needed to do to redeem myself." Brad turned to Ryan. "Brandon tells me you have a new project you're launching."

"That's right. Ever since I arrived in LA, met Hal, and learned about the Los Angeles LGBT Youth Project, I've been acutely aware of the homelessness many LGBTQ youth face. The Youth Project has an impressive operation they've built over many years, with dormitories, programs to help the kids, and many other resources. LA seems to be a popular place for kids to go, but even what the Youth Project has is not enough to meet the demand. And what about the kids who end up someplace else? In most of the country, there's nothing. I want to change that. I want to create a network where kids can get linked to people who will take them in and provide them with the acceptance and support they need. I'm calling it the Hal Morris Project, after the guy who took me in."

Brad said, "That's a pretty ambitious goal."

"Yeah, but somebody's gotta do something. Like you said earlier, even if it only reaches a few people, at least they'll be better off. My mentor at work is the head of the Public Affairs and Government Relations division. They choose which charities the Technovations Foundation gives money to. Since one of their focus areas is youth at risk, he's working on getting funding from the company. And our IT division will set up the website and the resource database."

Chris said, "From my eight years of working in Washington, I have connections with the national LGBTQ organizations. They can help publicize it. I have connections with some senators and representatives who may be able to secure government funding. I've just started contacting them."

Brad said, "You know, I see some synergy between our two endeavors. On the surface, it looks like we have separate goals. I'm trying to prevent kids from being rejected by their families, while you're trying to help those who have been kicked out. But we're trying to reach the same population – that is, families with gay kids who are having trouble accepting them."

Aaron said, "Your message is aimed more at the parents, and Ryan's is aimed more at the kids, but the situation is the same."

Brandon said, "In some ways, they're working against each other. I mean, if Dad's book reaches a lot of people, there will be fewer runaway kids."

Ryan said, "I'm perfectly okay with that. I hope someday there will be no need for the Hal Morris Project. But that day is a long way off, so until then..."

Matt said, "And in our case, even though we've reconciled with our parents, we're better off here anyway."

Ryan looked at Matt and Mark and thought about how his father helped reunite their family.

Brad said, "My publicist is arranging a book signing tour and lining up some media appearances. I'd be happy to mention the Hal Morris Project wherever I go. As I said, we're trying to reach the same audience."

Ryan smiled for the first time since Brad arrived. "Really? You'd do that for me?"

"Yes, I would. I believe the Hal Morris Project is sorely needed. And I'm realistic enough to know that my book isn't going to convince everyone."

Chris turned to Ryan. "As the HMP gets off the ground, a lot of people will hear about it. The national organizations have a wide reach. I can see you getting a lot of media attention. You could mention his book wherever you go."

Brandon added, "And you should put a link to it on your website."

The mood in the room had lightened considerably.

A new idea occurred to Brad, and his face lit up. "My publicist is trying to get me on the Shelly Show."

Aaron's eyes popped open. "You mean THE Shelly Show – one of the highest-rated daytime talk shows on television?"

Brad smiled. "The one and only. She's a lesbian, so she's all about LGBT causes. That would be a huge win if I get on. But I was thinking... What if we have you on too? Her audience is mostly women, many of whom are mothers. Since they're huge fans of Shelly, they're likely to be supportive of gay people. You could reach a huge audience of people who might be willing to take in a homeless LGBT youth."

Aaron said, "And besides... In your book, you talk about how you failed your kids and what happened with Ryan. That's a perfect lead-in to talk about the need for homes for runaway LGBT kids."

Brandon said, "And when the audience sees you together supporting each other's efforts after everything that happened – man, that's huge! That is television gold! When word gets out, everyone's going to watch it."

Ryan said, "Yeah, that would be huge. But do you think they'll go for it?"

Brad said, "My publicist is talking with her producers now. I'll let her know, and she can suggest it to them. We should know in a week or two."

Ryan asked, "When would this happen?"

"Oh, probably in two or three months – maybe longer. They get a lot of requests from people to be on her show and they book guests pretty far in advance. But if we could get on her show in April, that would be close to the book's release date."

Chris said, "That means we need to move fast to get the HMP up and running by the time you go on her show."

Brad asked Ryan, "So would you be willing to go on the Shelly Show with me if they agree to it?"

Ryan's mood brightened as he dreamed about the possibilities. "Sure, Dad. I realize it's kind of a long shot and I don't want to get my hopes up too much, but yeah. If that happened, it would be awesome!"

Brandon said, "Even if Shelly doesn't work out, there are other shows you could go on."

Brad was stunned. "You just called me Dad. Not Brad... Dad."

"That's right, Dad." Ryan got up from his chair and walked over to where Brad was sitting. "That time when we met five years ago, after you showed up at our wedding, I said 'I forgive you.' And I did on one level. That didn't mean I liked you or wanted to have you back in my life again. And I admit I've been pretty stubborn about dealing with you. After all, what you did totally altered the course of my life in all the wrong ways, and there's no way I can ever forget that. But you're a different man today. You've turned your life around. Honestly, it's pretty amazing. You're going to help a lot of people with what you're doing. Your book saved the Berry family, so imagine what it's going to do when it's published and you start going on these shows. So yeah. I'm proud of you, Dad."

Brad stood up. Tears ran down his cheeks. They hugged and held each other for at least ten seconds. Brad whispered in Ryan's ear. "I love you, son."

"I love you too, Dad."

Everyone else couldn't believe what they were witnessing. For a moment, nobody said or did anything. Then Aaron started clapping and everyone else joined in.

***

Later in the evening, after Brad, Aaron, and Brandon had gone home and Matt and Mark were doing their homework, Ryan and Chris sat in the office and caught up with email and the news.

Chris said, "I still can't believe what happened at dinner."

"Yeah, me neither. I mean, never in a million years did I think I'd be on the Shelly Show. I realize it's only a possibility at this point, and maybe a slim one, but I'm still excited about it."

"I don't mean only that. I mean what happened with you and your father."

"Yeah, that's pretty mind-blowing too. But I feel good about it. You and Aaron always said I needed to forgive him, let go of what happened, and move on. In hindsight, you were right. I wish I had done it sooner."

"But you've done it, and that's what counts."

A moment later, Chris said, "I just thought of something else. You know how you avoid going out to gay bars and pride festivals and stuff because you don't want people to recognize you from when you were a porn star?"

"Yeah..."

"Well, if you go on national TV, some people are bound to recognize you."

"Shit." Ryan thought about that some more. "I wonder how that could fuck things up. Back then, a few people said, 'I hope you have no plans to run for public office.' This would be kinda similar." His exuberant mood deflated quickly.

Chris said, "Do you really think that will make any difference? Besides, the primary audience for the Shelly Show is women."

"Yeah, but some gay guys watch it too. Maybe you should do it. You could be the face of the project, not me."

"No. That wouldn't be right. I'd love to go on national TV, but this is your baby. You deserve this. Besides, you're naturally photogenic and articulate. And the presentation skills training you got as part of the LDP will help too."

"I guess." Ryan still wasn't sold. "Let me think about it. But I want the story to be about the project and the kids, not my past."

Why don't you ask Brandon whether he thinks it would be an issue? And if so, ask him what he thinks you should do about it."

For a few minutes, neither of them said anything. Then Ryan said, "I've made up my mind. I'm going to do it. I've always said I want to focus on the present and the future and not dwell on the past. I can't hold back because I'm afraid people will find out I used to do porn. I'll deal with that if it comes up. But I have to do it for the kids."

Chris smiled, stood up, and walked over to Ryan's chair. Ryan stood up and Chris hugged him. "I'm so proud of you. This is going to be so successful – because of you."

"Thanks, honey. I appreciate your support."

"I'm with you all the way. I'll work every connection I have and do everything I can to make this succeed."

"Thanks."

The Shelly Show

Thursday, April 14, 2022

At 10:45 a.m., Ryan turned their rental car into the Warner Bros Studios parking garage, across Olive Avenue from the studio's Gate 2, and parked.

The entrance to the studio complex was surprisingly nondescript. From the street, the studios appeared as a row of windowless three-story buildings built up to the sidewalk. Nothing about the buildings would suggest what went on inside were it not for the colorful 25-foot-tall signs spaced at even intervals along the wall, advertising some of the TV shows currently being produced by the studio.

Ryan and Brad wore nice suits and sported fresh haircuts. Chris would be in the audience, so he wore a nice dress shirt and pants. As they stood waiting to cross the street, Ryan realized the significance of this moment. He was about to enter one of the country's most famous studios. He was about to appear on national television on a highly-rated daytime talk show, hosted by a major celebrity.

Ryan pulled his phone out of his pocket and handed it to his father. "Dad, take a picture of us with the entrance in the background."

Brad took a few steps back from the street and framed a shot with Ryan and Chris in the foreground and the building with the small sign announcing 'Gate 2' in the background.

"Thanks. Let me get one of you."

They traded places and Ryan took a similar picture of his father. Then he joined his father and Chris took a few pictures of them. They attempted a selfie with all three.

Ryan turned to Chris and said, "I think at this point you're supposed to go to the studio visitors' entrance in the garage and join the other people who are here to be in the audience."

Chris nodded. "I'm so happy for you! I know you guys will do great."

Chris and Ryan hugged and gave each other a quick kiss. Then Chris walked back into the garage to the elevators.

Ryan and Brad crossed Olive Avenue to the Gate 2 entrance. After passing through the security checkpoint, they proceeded to Studio 1, the first building on the left. They stopped at the Vaccination Verification checkpoint and showed their vaccination cards and negative test results from two days before. Then a production assistant met them at the front desk and led them to makeup. A makeup artist applied a light dusting of powder to their faces to prevent glare. She applied a little more makeup to Brad to mask the wrinkles that had become more pronounced over the past few years.

The makeup artist led them to the green room, where they would wait. Brad sat down on one of the couches. Ryan was too excited to sit, so he wandered around the room, looking at the framed posters and photos that adorned the walls.

After twenty minutes, a woman entered the green room and said, "Brad Bauer and Ryan Robertson?" Brad stood and Ryan took a few steps toward her. "I'm Morgan Farrell, the assistant producer." They shook hands. "Please come with me." She led them into her small office. She went over a variety of pointers to ensure their interview went smoothly. "Don't look at the camera, look at Shelly. Only look out at the audience when Shelly does, which is usually during applause. Sit upright near the edge of your seat and don't slouch, but try to look relaxed and natural. Don't interrupt Shelly or talk over each other. Keep your answers brief and concise, and don't go off on tangents. Let her guide the interview. If you stumble over your words or forget what you're about to say, that's okay. Just pause a few seconds and start over. They can edit that out. Any questions so far?"

Brad replied, "None for me. I've done dozens of TV appearances for my previous books."

Ryan said, "Nope. It all makes sense."

"Okay, so we'll bring on Rev. Bauer first. Shelly will ask you to summarize your book and tell why you wrote it. Again, be as concise as possible. You can't tell your whole story, so just hit a few high points. Then she'll dive into your transformation from being a conservative pastor of a large mega-church to where you are now. She's going to ask some pointed questions. Don't shy away from them, be willing to confront the topic directly."

"I went through all that hand-wringing and self-condemnation as I was writing the book. I can talk openly about it now."

"That's good. Shelly will lead the conversation to the separation from your son, and that's when we'll bring Ryan on. Ryan, she'll ask you to talk about what happened to you, all in about 15 or 20 seconds." Morgan smiled, knowing that was a tall order. "Then she'll ask you about your new organization and why you started it. We'll end with what people can do to support you, like signing up to offer housing to displaced youth and donating. She will mention your group's URL and we'll display it on the screen. Then Shelly will thank you for being on the show and wrap up the interview. Got it?"

Ryan said, "Got it. I hope I can remember it all."

Morgan said, "I know, it's a lot to absorb. The most important things are to look natural, stay focused on Shelly, let her guide the interview, and keep your answers as brief as possible. She's a pro. You'll feel at ease in her presence."

Ryan said, "Okay. Thank you for all your help. And thanks for having us on the show! I'm nervous, but I'm really excited."

"I'm sure you'll do fine. It will be over before you know it. Don't stress over it and try to enjoy the experience. And remember to smile!"

She stood up and led them back to the green room. "Someone will come get you a few minutes before you go on." Morgan hurried out the door.

Brad turned to Ryan and said, "Do you know the 'sit on your suit tail' trick?"

"No..."

"When you sit down, grab your suit tail with the hand that's away from the camera. Sit on it. If you don't, then when your butt hits the seat, it will push the back of your collar up higher on your neck. That will look bad on camera. You want your suit collar to stay down like it is when you're standing." Ryan nodded. "Let's try it now."

Ryan tried sitting down on the couch while he held his suit tail.

"Yeah, that's it." Brad paused. "How are you doing?"

"I don't know. Until now, I've been excited, but it's been positive energy. Now, the longer I wait and the more times I run over what I'm going to say in my head, the more nervous I get."

"You've probably rehearsed what you're going to say enough. You don't want to sound like you're rattling off a speech you've memorized word for word. You want it to sound spontaneous and conversational."

"Yeah, you're right. It's like in band, if you rehearse the music too much, the performance doesn't go as well. You peak too soon."

Brad reached for the remote on the table in front of the couch and unmuted the sound on the TV. A comedian was on stage warming up the audience before Shelly came on. That helped relax Ryan.

A sound technician arrived with a pair of Lavalier mics. He attached one to Ryan's lapel, then stuffed the transmitter and the tiny cable into Ryan's interior breast pocket. He did the same for Brad. "Don't worry, you're muted. I'll bring your sound up when you go onstage."

At 12:30, Shelly walked on stage and chatted with the audience for a few minutes. Then she left the stage. They started taping, the theme music began, and Shelly made her entrance. The crowd applauded enthusiastically. After a brief comedy monologue, she entertained the audience by showing images of funny text messages that had been bumbled by auto-correct. Ryan became absorbed in what was happening onstage and forgot his nervousness.

At 12:45, Morgan entered the room. "Okay! It's time to go on." Brad and Ryan followed her to the stage door. She put her fingers to her lips, opened the door, and led them to a dimly lit area just off-camera and out of the audience's view. Ryan caught a glimpse of Shelly and his excitement level soared. He straightened his tie and tugged at his lapels, being careful not to disturb the mic.

A moment later, Shelly said, "Folks, our guest today was formerly a nationally known evangelical preacher with seven best-selling books to his credit. Then one day, he got caught in a scandal that ruined his career and his life. Now, he's back with a compelling new book. Please help me welcome Rev. Brad Bauer!"

Morgan motioned for Brad to enter. He squared his shoulders and stood tall, as he had done every time he walked onstage at the Eternal Savior Christian Church. He walked quickly and confidently onto the stage and enthusiastically shook hands with Shelly. The audience applauded politely. As she stepped back to her chair, Shelly motioned for Brad to sit in the guest chair. He surreptitiously grabbed his suit tail and sat on the edge of his seat with perfect posture, angled toward Shelly.

Shelly wasted no time getting down to business. "Rev. Bauer, until 2016 you were the pastor of the largest church in Kansas. You had seven best-selling Christian books and you were well on your way to becoming a nationally known televangelist. What happened?"

"Well, as you alluded to in your introduction, I was caught in a most compromising position. I literally got caught with my pants down."

"To be more specific, you got caught at a drug-fueled gay orgy. Am I right?"

"That's correct."

Ryan heard some tittering among the crowd, but nobody shouted anything.

Shelly continued. "And would I also be correct that in your church, you preached negativity toward LGBT people?"

"Among many other things, yes."

"And yet, you were gay yourself."

"That's right. Getting caught at that orgy changed everything. I was fired from my church, my books were dropped from my publisher's catalog, and my reputation was ruined. I lost everything – not only my career but also my family. But I needed something that terrible to happen for me to realize what a hypocrite I had become. I realized that everything I believed, and everything I had been preaching, was wrong."

Shelly picked up a copy of his book and held it for the camera. "So you wrote this book, *To Hell and Back*. Why did you feel it was necessary to describe your ordeal in such vivid detail?"

"After so many years of telling lies, I had to tell the truth. And the truth is that gay, lesbian, bisexual, and transgender people, are God's children just like everyone else. God created them that way, and they're beautiful just the way they are." The audience applauded briefly. "But I also needed to call out all the misguided, intolerant pastors who continue to tell lies and spread hate in the name of the Lord. It's wrong, and it ruins lives. It tears families apart. I hope that after reading about what I did to my family, other families with LGBT children won't make the same mistake with their kids."

The audience applauded. Brad was winning them over.

Shelly said, "Tell us, briefly, what happened to your family."

"At the time I found out my older son is gay, I had just signed a contract for my first three books. Attendance at my church had reached an all-time high, and thousands watched our services online. Everything was going great. But there was no way I could let it be known that I had a gay son – not with everything I was preaching and writing about. And I totally bought into all that gay conversion therapy crap, so I tried to force him into it. And that led him to run away from home.

"What I'm going to say next will sound absolutely horrible – because it is. But at the time, my son running away from home was a relief. It removed my problem. I felt like I had dodged a bullet. I was so wrapped up in myself and trying to save souls and glorify the Lord, that I was willing to sacrifice my own son to accomplish that.

"But it wasn't only my son who suffered from my misguided beliefs. My marriage crumbled. My wife entered a long spiral of depression, taking pills and drinking to try to deal with her deep despair. One of her anti-depressants finally led her to commit suicide. My younger son suffered, first by losing his older brother and then by losing his mother. And that was all caused by me and my homophobia and my misguided beliefs."

Shelly asked, "So after causing all this harm to your family and yourself, what are you doing to redeem yourself?"

"It wasn't only my family I harmed. I also harmed countless other families through my preaching and my books. I shudder to think how many families rejected or harmed their gay children because of me. So I'm devoting my life to undoing that damage. My book was the first step. Thankfully, it's selling well. But I don't rejoice in that for the money. I look at my book sales in terms of how many families I'm helping."

Shelly turned toward the camera. "We need to take a break. We'll return for more with Rev. Brad Bauer and a special surprise. Don't go anywhere!"

Even though the commercial break would last several minutes, the taping resumed promptly.

Shelly said, "Welcome back. We're talking with Rev. Brad Bauer, author of the new book, *To Hell and Back*." She held the book up for the camera as she spoke, then set it on the table. "Rev. Bauer, tell us more about your older son who ran away. Have you been able to reconcile with him?"

"That's been a long, hard journey. Understandably, for years he wanted nothing to do with me. Now, thankfully, we have reconciled."

Shelly smiled and turned to the audience. "Rev. Bauer's son Ryan is with us today. Let's bring him out and hear from him!"

The director signaled for Ryan to walk on. Ryan smiled and walked briskly across the stage. The audience welcomed him with a warm round of applause. Shelly and Brad stood, and Ryan shook Shelly's hand. Brad moved to the second guest chair so Ryan could sit next to Shelly. They all sat down and the applause abated. Ryan remembered to grab his coat tail.

Shelly said, "Welcome, Ryan. Thanks for being here."

"Thanks for having us on."

"In the few minutes we have left, please tell us briefly what happened to you after you left home."

"I came here to Los Angeles. I chose LA for a few reasons. First, because I hoped to go to UCLA. Second, the city was large enough that I hoped I wouldn't be found and sent back to Kansas. Third, the manager of the grocery store in Kansas where I worked used to live here and he had friends who were willing to let me stay with them for a couple of weeks."

"Then what happened?"

"Fortunately, here in LA, there's an organization called the Los Angeles LGBT Youth Project. They have a lot of resources for runaway LGBT youth, including some beds where they can stay. I went there because they had attorneys who could help me change my name and get emancipated from my parents. The attorney they assigned to me was Hal Morris. Hal owned a house near UCLA where he rented rooms to gay college students. Thankfully, at that moment, he had a room available. Long story short, I lived there until I graduated from UCLA and got a job in Scottsdale, Arizona, where I live today. But Hal was more than just a landlord. He was like a father to me, and the other guys became my brothers. So I had a support system. I had people who loved me for who I was. I totally lucked out. I could have easily ended up homeless, as so many kids do. Sadly, Hal died shortly before I graduated. He was a huge supporter of the Los Angeles LGBT Youth Project. He volunteered and donated. I donate to them too, but I've been looking for a way to do more. Most gay kids who have to leave home don't end up in a place that has a large organization to help them. They don't know where to go. They end up homeless and endangered. Often, they turn to unsafe, unhealthy, and illegal activities to earn money to survive. I want to create a national network to connect runaway kids with people who will take them in, give them a safe place to stay, and give them love and guidance. So I created the Hal Morris Project. Now I need to raise awareness of the Project so that runaway gay kids will know where to turn. I'm so thankful to you, Shelly, for having me on your show. This will raise a lot of awareness."

Shelly said, "That's a remarkable undertaking." She turned toward a camera. "Folks, the URL is Hal Morris Project dot org. It's on your screen now. I urge you to go there and learn how you can help. Maybe you can open your home to an LGBT youth who needs shelter and support. And you can donate."

She turned back to Ryan. "I understand you and your father didn't speak for many years. How are things now?"

"That's right. For years, I kept a low profile so my parents wouldn't find me. I changed my name. I wanted no contact with him whatsoever. Sadly, that meant I had no contact with my mother or brother either. Thankfully, about five and a half years ago, I was reunited with my younger brother, Brandon, when he came to Arizona to play basketball at Arizona State. That was around the same time my dad got caught at that orgy. After he lost his job at his church, he came out to Arizona since that's where Brandon was. Inevitably, we met, and he asked me to forgive him. I did on one level, but I still didn't want to have him in my life. But now that he is focused on helping families stay together and accept their LGBT kids, he has earned my respect. I'm proud of him for the work he's doing."

The audience burst into applause.

Brad turned to Ryan and said, "I'm proud of you too, son. I'm proud of the man you have become, despite everything I did to harm you. And I'm proud of the work you're doing. In fact, I have decided to donate 25% of the proceeds from my book to the Hal Morris Project."

That left Ryan speechless. The audience applauded and cheered. Ryan stood up and gestured for Brad to stand. Ryan gave him a big hug on national TV. The audience continued to cheer.

When the commotion subsided, Shelly said, "I have a surprise for you too. As you know, The Shelly Foundation supports several wonderful organizations, such as the American Animal Welfare Association and the National Domestic Violence Prevention League. We are pleased to add the Hal Morris Project to the list of worthy causes we support." The audience cheered. "And to help you build this important and much-needed organization, we are making an initial donation of $500,000!"

Ryan could hardly believe his eyes and ears. The stage manager walked on stage with an oversized cardboard check for $500,000 made payable to The Hal Morris Project. Shelly presented it to him and they shook hands and smiled for the audience and the cameras. "Wow, Shelly... Thank you! Thank you so much!"

The commotion died down and everyone took their seats. Shelly turned to the audience and said, "On that happy note, thank you so much for tuning in today and–"

Ryan spoke. "Shelly? Sorry to interrupt, but could I say one more thing?"

She knew they were out of time and some of this segment would probably have to be edited, but she didn't want to appear ungracious on television. "Okay..."

"I didn't get to mention this earlier, but when I ran away from home, that also meant leaving my boyfriend Chris. We loved each other so much, and we planned to spend our lives together. We were apart for over 14 years, but we're reunited now and we plan to get married this fall." The audience reacted with a smattering of applause. He turned to Brad. "Dad, we would be honored if you would officiate our wedding."

The audience exploded. Everyone leaped to their feet, clapped, and cheered. Shelly reached for a tissue and blotted the tears from her eyes. She grinned. This was ratings gold.

Finally, Brad said, "Why, yes, of course!"

They stood, and Ryan hugged his father again.

Shelly turned to the camera and said, "We're out of time. Thank you for joining us, and remember to say 'Thank you,' 'I'm sorry,' and 'I love you' as often as you can. See you tomorrow!"

The theme music played, the audience continued clapping, and Shelly, Ryan, and Brad, microphones now muted, engaged in a moment of conversation for visual effect. Ryan motioned for Chris to come on stage to meet Shelly.

Just like that, it was over. Ryan and Brad were led offstage and the sound tech removed their microphones. Chris was permitted to stay with them. Ryan and Brad were led back to the makeup room, where the makeup artist removed their makeup. Someone led them to the studio entrance. They retraced their short journey through Gate 2 and across the street to the parking garage.

They drove Brad to the Burbank Airport in plenty of time for his short flight back to Phoenix. Ryan and Chris returned to their hotel and changed into casual clothes. They would stay in Los Angeles through the weekend to visit Universal Studios and Disneyland.

One Good Deed

Tuesday, September 20, 2022

Rocket Crockett was driving his squad car north on Arrowhead Trafficway in the northern part of Kansas City. Until now, it had been a slow day with few calls. The afternoon rush hour was just getting started.

He spotted a car pulled off to the side of the road with its hood open. He turned on his flashers, slowed down, and pulled onto the right shoulder behind the stranded car. He spotted a woman standing on the side, accompanied by a boy who appeared to be 7 or 8 years old. The woman held a cell phone to her ear.

"Good afternoon, ma'am, what seems to be the problem?" Before he finished asking the question, he noticed the right front tire was flat. "Oh, I see."

She lowered her phone and said, "I'm on hold with my insurance company's Roadside Assistance." She sighed. "I've been waiting for 15 minutes now."

"I'd be happy to change your tire for you."

"Would you, please? I'd be so grateful." She pushed the button to hang up her call and slid her phone back into her purse.

Rocket lifted the thin board that formed the floor of her trunk. He pulled the temporary donut spare and the scissor jack from the trunk and carried them to the side of the car.

The little boy was full of energy and excitement. "Can I help?"

Rocket smiled. The kid was cute, with his straight blond hair and friendly smile. He was wearing a soccer uniform. "No, but I'll tell you what. If you stand right there and stay a couple of feet away, I'll teach you how to change a tire."

"Okay!"

Rocket held out his hand. "What's your name?"

"Caleb!" Caleb enthusiastically shook Rocket's hand.

"I'm Officer Crockett."

Caleb's mother stepped up. "I'm Catie Stanford. Thanks for coming to our rescue."

"My pleasure." Rocket smiled at Catie. She seemed nice. She was pretty, too, in a girl-next-door kind of way.

He knelt beside the car. He positioned the scissor jack behind the front wheel well and started cranking the car up, explaining each step to Caleb. Caleb was brimming with curiosity and excitement as he took it all in. He asked a lot of questions.

After Rocket finished changing the tire, he stood up. "Okay, you're all set. Those donut spares are only rated for about 30 miles, so I suggest you get that taken care of right away. Also, if I may, I recommend buying a full-sized spare. You can probably find a wheel for this car at a junkyard or a used parts store, or else the tire store can sell you one. I don't know why they put donut spares in cars – they're almost worthless."

"Thank you so much, Officer Crockett. I'm so grateful you came along. Who knows how long we would have waited for Roadside Assistance? Now we can still make it to Caleb's soccer match." She reached into her purse and pulled out her wallet.

"Oh, no, ma'am, I can't accept gratuities. It's against department rules and I wouldn't do it anyway. I'm happy to help. It's part of my job."

Catie slid her wallet back into her purse.

Caleb was still giddy with excitement over their adventure. "When I grow up, I wanna be a policeman!"

Rocket smiled at Caleb. "Really? I bet you'd make a fine police officer."

A sad expression crossed Catie's face. "His father was a police officer. He was killed two years ago in a traffic accident. He was on his way home from work one night and got hit head-on by a drunk wrong-way driver."

Rocket frowned. "I'm so sorry to hear that, ma'am."

"Anyway, I wish there was some way I could thank you. Could I invite you over for dinner some evening?"

Rocket hesitated while he debated whether this would be allowable. The department regulations specifically stated that officers could not accept money. They didn't say anything about food. He was about to decline, but he saw the hopeful expression on Catie's face.

Caleb was smiling at him with admiration. "Please?"

Rocket said, "Okay, I suppose I could do that. My days off are Thursdays and Fridays."

"How about this Friday, then? Five o'clock?"

"Sounds good."

She opened her purse and frantically searched through its contents. "Darn it. I don't have anything to write my address down on."

Rocket was about to retrieve the notepad from his car, but then he said, "No problem. Why don't you text it to me?"

She pulled out her phone and he gave her his number. Then he smiled and turned to go.

Catie said, "Thanks again, Officer Crockett."

Caleb echoed his mother. "Thanks, Officer Crockett!"

Rocket turned and waved, then climbed back into his squad car. As he was pulling away, he thought, *What just happened? I just got invited to dinner by a woman!*

A Home-Cooked Meal

Friday, September 23, 2022

As Friday approached, Rocket grew more and more excited. He still wasn't sure whether this dinner qualified as a date, but he was looking forward to it. If nothing else, it would be a pleasant break from his routine. It was a chance to enjoy a nice home-cooked meal he didn't have to fix himself.

Friday afternoon, he went shopping for a nice shirt to wear. Nothing too fancy, but something nicer than the years-old collection of casual shirts in his closet. Then he wondered, *Should I bring anything? Maybe a bottle of wine? No, if this isn't a date that would seem too forward. Besides, I don't even know if she drinks. And I want to bring something Caleb can have too.*

He reached for his phone and texted Catie.

> Can I bring anything?
> Maybe dessert?

A few minutes later, she replied.

> Dessert would be great.
> Thanks!

> What's Caleb's favorite
> dessert?

> He loves cheesecake.
> Any kind.

Rocket replied with a thumbs-up emoji. On his way home, he swung by Price Cutter and picked up a pre-cut cheesecake with four flavors.

***

Rocket arrived at Catie's home promptly at 5:00. It was a modest, two-bedroom bungalow in a safe but lower-end neighborhood. *As a single mom trying to raise a kid, this is probably all she can afford. But then, look at me. I still live in an apartment.*

Catie opened the door wearing a nervous smile and Rocket stepped in. He handed her the cheesecake. Caleb came running up. "Hi, Officer Crockett!"

"Hey there, Caleb!" He held out his fist and Caleb fist-bumped him.

Catie lowered the cheesecake so Caleb could see. "Look what Officer Crockett brought!"

"Cheesecake! YAY! Thanks, Officer Crockett!"

Rocket said, "Since I'm off-duty, you don't have to call me Officer Crockett. You can call me Clay, okay?"

Catie would have preferred to have Caleb call him Mr. Crockett, but she let it pass. "I made lasagna. Is that okay?"

"I love lasagna! I haven't had it in years. I usually cook for myself, so I keep it pretty simple."

They sat down at the table and started eating. Rocket asked Caleb, "How did your soccer match on Tuesday go?"

"Great! We won, 4 to 2. I scored a goal!"

"Congratulations!" Rocket held his hand up and Caleb gave him a high-five. "When I was in high school and college, I played football."

"Really?"

"Yeah. I was a running back. I ran on our high school's track team too. I used to be able to run fast, so they called me Rocket Crockett."

"Wow! That's a cool name!"

"I liked it. Some of my friends from high school still call me Rocket."

Catie said, "Wait a minute. *You're* Rocket Crockett? You went to Prairie Village, right?"

"That's right."

"I went to Overland Park North. Our team was usually good, but you guys beat us every year. I remember the announcer saying your name whenever you ran a big play or scored a touchdown."

Rocket smiled. "I'm surprised you remember that. That was what, like 14 or 15 years ago?"

"You have to admit, it's a memorable name. I played in the marching band, so I was at all the games."

"What did you play?"

"Clarinet."

"Two of my buddies from the track team were in the marching band.

I never got to see them 'cause the football team was in the locker room during halftime. I heard they were pretty good, though."

"Yeah, Prairie Village always had a good band. What college did you go to?"

"TCU. I got a scholarship to play football. We had a couple of undefeated regular seasons while I was there."

Probably because *you were there*, Catie thought.

Rocket continued. "I was hoping I could play pro football after that, but I didn't get drafted. I majored in Law Enforcement and Criminal Justice, so that's how I ended up being a police officer."

Caleb was fascinated by all this. "Will you teach me how to play football?"

Rocket smiled. "Well, it's a pretty rough game. But they have flag football for younger kids. You shouldn't start playing tackle football until you get to high school. Maybe we can start with me teaching you how to throw and catch a football." He glanced at Catie. "But I think your mother should have the final say about that."

Caleb looked up at his mother with his sweet 'Can I, Mom? Please?' smile. She said, "We'll talk about it. You already have a lot on your plate."

"Not anymore! See?" It was true – Caleb had made fast work of his lasagna.

Rocket chuckled at Caleb's attempt at humor. Catie smiled. "Very clever."

Rocket asked Catie, "What do you do?"

"I'm an elementary school teacher. I teach fifth grade. It works out well because I can bring him to and from school with me. On days when he has soccer practice or something, I can stay and grade papers."

Rocket asked Caleb about what he was learning in school. That kept the conversation going for another ten minutes. Catie served the cheesecake, and Caleb talked about what was happening in his Cub Scout pack.

They finished and got up from the table. Caleb dutifully carried his plate, glass, and silverware to the sink, rinsed them off, and put them in the dishwasher. Catie said, "Okay, it's time to do your homework."

"Awww... Can't I stay out here with you and Clay?"

"No, honey, you know homework comes right after dinner. And we want to have a little time for grown-up talk."

"Oh... All right." He looked up at Rocket and said, "But don't go without saying goodbye!"

"Oh, I won't. Now, do as your mother says. The sooner you get started, the sooner you'll get finished."

Caleb scampered off to his room. Catie and Rocket sat down in the living room. They spoke softly so Caleb wouldn't be distracted from his homework.

Rocket said, "He's really something. And I mean that in the best possible way."

"Yeah, he is. It was hard on him to lose his dad at six. Of course, it hasn't been easy for me either. But kids can be so resilient. And his Uncle Mark helps out a lot. He has two kids, but he often takes Caleb along when they do something, and he fills in as his dad for things like Cub Scouts. So we get by."

"That's great that you and he have a support system. My dad wasn't a very attentive father, so I felt alone most of the time."

"Caleb certainly likes you."

"Well, maybe it's because I'm a policeman like his dad was."

"I think it's because you're nice to him and you've taken an interest in him."

"Oh... Well... Thanks."

"And thanks for deferring to me about the football thing. I have nothing against him learning to play football when he gets to the right age, but... I don't even think he understands what football is. He may have seen a game or two on TV, but I don't think he's ever been to a game. I think he was only interested in football because he likes you."

"Maybe I could see about getting tickets to a Chiefs game. The three of us could go and I could explain how it's played."

"Oh, Clay, that's sweet of you, but wouldn't that be expensive? Honestly, he'd be just as happy going to a high school game on a Friday night. It would be all the same to him. Let's wait to see if he gets into football before you spend a lot of money on a Chiefs game. Or you could come over and watch a game on television with him."

Rocket knew she was right. He'd be willing to spend the money on them, but Catie was correct that it wasn't practical. "Okay, let's go to a game next Friday night! And I'll take us out to eat somewhere. What's your favorite place? And what's his?"

"We both like Bateman's Barbeque, and that sounds like a fun idea."

"Bateman's it is."

"And you know what? I think it would be fun to go to either Prairie Village or Overland Park North. It would be like a homecoming, at least for one of us."

Rocket pulled out his phone and searched for the Overland Park North High School football schedule. He lit up. "You know what? By amazing coincidence, Overland Park North is playing Prairie Village on Friday, October 7th – two weeks from now!"

"Let's do it! Of course, that means we'll be rooting for different teams."

Rocket chuckled. "Nah... That doesn't make any difference now. I'll even sit on your side of the field."

"Which team is the home team?"

"Prairie Village."

"I want to sit on the home team side. The marching bands always play to the home stands."

"Cool. And I'll finally get to see a halftime show!"

"Well, then it's settled. High school football on Friday, October 7th."

"And Bateman's Barbecue."

There was a brief pause as they both wondered what to say next. Rocket wanted to see Catie and Caleb sooner than two weeks from now. "So... When is Caleb's next soccer match?"

"Let me see..." Catie got up and walked over to the wall calendar in the kitchen. "Next Thursday at 4:00. They play over at Oak Park."

"I should be able to make it. That's my day off."

"He'd be thrilled to see you there." Catie paused. "And so would I."

Rocket smiled. There was another lull in the conversation. Rocket sensed that this was enough for a first date, if that's even what this was. "Catie, that dinner was delicious! Thanks for inviting me over."

"You're welcome. And thanks for rescuing me the other day."

Rocket stood up. "May I say goodbye to Caleb before I go?"

Catie stood up and led Rocket to Caleb's bedroom. She knocked on the door. "Mr. Crockett is leaving now."

Caleb opened his door and smiled up at Rocket. "Bye!"

Rocket squatted so he could face Caleb on his level. He held out his fist for a fist bump. "You take good care of your mother now, you hear?"

"Are you going to come back again sometime?"

"Well, I guess that's up to your mother." Rocket decided to keep his appearance at Caleb's next soccer game a surprise. "Good night!"

"Good night!"

Rocket stood up. He and Catie turned toward the door. Caleb started to follow, but Catie motioned for him to go back to his bedroom.

When they reached the front door, Rocket turned to face Catie. *Okay, what do I do now? A handshake seems too businesslike. It's probably too soon to go in for a hug or a kiss.* Catie looked like the moment was awkward for her too. Rocket smiled nervously. "Thanks again for the delicious dinner. I enjoyed this evening."

"You're welcome. I did too."

Rocket lowered his voice to almost a whisper. "I'll see you Thursday afternoon at Caleb's soccer match."

Catie smiled. "That will be nice."

"And don't tell Caleb. I want to surprise him."

They smiled at each other again. Rocket turned and walked out the door. As he walked to his car, he wondered whether he should turn and look back. As he pressed his key fob to unlock the door, he turned. She was still standing in the doorway. He waved and she waved back. Then she closed the door.

Happy Hour

Friday, October 14, 2022

Trevor Zimmerman invited Rocket to join him for happy hour on Friday afternoon.

Rocket had plenty of news to share since they last saw each other a month ago. He offered to meet Trevor at one of the local bars. But as usual, Trevor preferred to meet in his hotel bar where, as general manager, he could comp their drinks.

They sat in a booth at the far end of the room with beers and a bowl of popcorn. Rocket said, "What's wrong, man? It's happy hour and you don't look happy."

"I'm not. Things aren't looking good for Dad. We're moving him into hospice care this weekend."

"Oh, man... I'm really sorry. That totally sucks."

"Tell me about it. And it's not like we didn't see it coming. He had another heart attack earlier this year and had to have a triple bypass. Then in July, he found out he had colon cancer. It was pretty bad, and the cancer was spreading to other parts of his body. So yeah, he's been going downhill fast."

"Man, I am so sorry. That must be really hard on you."

"Thanks. But it's so much worse for Mom. Honestly, it will be a relief when it's over. I know that sounds harsh, but he's suffering and so is Mom. It's not going to get any better. He has no quality of life anymore."

Trevor took a long swig of his beer and finished the glass. He waved, caught the bartender's attention, and held up two fingers. The bartender nodded. "Anyway, that means I'm going to have to back out of going to Ryan and Chris's wedding next weekend."

"Aw, c'mon, man! Can't you get away for three days? Taking a break will do you good."

"Yeah, it probably would. And believe me, I'd much rather be there. I'm sorry I'm going to miss it. But he could go any time, and I need to spend as much time as possible with him before he goes. And Mom will need the support when the time comes."

"Yeah, I guess you're right. But, man, that sucks."

"No shit. I'll call them tomorrow and let them know. You'll have to represent for both of us. Take lots of pictures!"

"I will."

"And just think... You'll have that nice hotel room all to yourself. So if you meet some nice babe at the pool or something, you can take her back to your room!"

Rocket thought about Catie. They hadn't made any commitments. They hadn't even done it yet. But still... "Nah, man. That ain't gonna happen."

Trevor grinned. "Well, it's a gay wedding. There will be lots of guys there. You could pick up some hot stud and take him back to your room."

Rocket half-heartedly lifted his middle finger. "Blow me, dude. On second thought, no. You'd enjoy it too much."

Trevor laughed. "Relax, man. I was just teasing you." *Mostly.* Trevor recalled the time five years ago when he and Rocket watched the livestream of Ryan's wedding to Aaron, and how Rocket got strangely emotional. Trevor couldn't pass up this moment to tease his buddy. "Besides, I know you have your secret man crush on Ryan, but he's taken now."

"Dude... What the hell are you talking about? Yes, I like him. That doesn't mean I wanna fuck him."

Trevor glanced around the room. Thankfully, no one was sitting close enough to have heard that.

"Besides..." Rocket smiled. "There's this woman I've been seeing lately."

"What? No way, man!"

"Way!"

"Seriously?"

"Dude, why are you acting so surprised that I have a girlfriend?"

"Well, you gotta admit, you've never lasted more than one or two dates. And even that's been, what? Ten years? Ever since college?"

"Well, okay, you've got a point. But what about you? I don't see you dating any women."

"We've had this talk. I'm married to my job. And I have to take care of my parents. But this is about you. So, tell me about her! How did you meet her?"

"Well, her name's Catie." Rocket told Trevor about how he changed her flat tire and she invited him over for dinner to thank him. "And she has this super cute little boy named Caleb."

"Wait a minute. She's not married, is she?"

"No, douchenozzle. I wouldn't do that. Her husband was a police officer, but he got killed in a car crash a couple of years ago."

"Oh, wow, I'm sorry. So anyway, what does she look like? Is she hot?" Trevor cupped his hands under his chest. "Does she have a nice personality?"

"Seriously, dude? No wonder you're still single."

"C'mon, man. I know you've always been a big-boobs kind of guy."

"She's cute, in a girl-next-door kind of way. And she's really sweet." He pulled his phone out of his pocket and scrolled through his photos. "Here, let me show you her picture."

"Not bad."

"Yeah, but what's important is, she's nice. She's really down-to-earth. And, I don't know... I feel comfortable around her. It's like I always used to get nervous around women, and I'd never know what to say. But with her, we just click. It seems natural, like I can just be myself and she likes that." He scrolled through a few more pictures. "And here... this is Caleb."

"He *is* a cute kid."

"And he's smart and full of energy and very well-behaved. And..." Rocket paused. "He likes me. He really looks up to me. He always gets so excited when I come around."

"So just think, if this works out, you'll be both a husband and a father."

"That's right. And I'd be fine with that."

Trevor took a moment to process all this new information. "You know... no offense, but I never really thought of you as a father."

"What do you mean? I'd be a damn good father."

"C'mon, I didn't mean it that way..."

"Nah, I hear what you're sayin'. You're right. I've never thought much about it. Like, maybe sometime in the future I'll get married and have kids. But now, suddenly, here it is. And I think if it gets that far, I'm gonna love being his father."

"Well, at least you won't have to change his diapers and all that shit."

"Yeah, there's that. But... Isn't that redundant?"

It took Trevor a second, but then he chuckled. "Yeah, I guess so."

There was another question Trevor had to ask. "So..." He lowered his voice. "Have you been gettin' it?"

Rocket scowled. "None o' yer fuckin' business, dude!"

Trevor laughed. "That means no."

"Oh, for Christ's sake. I'm not in this just to get laid. I'm sure we'll get there when the time is right."

"Seriously? Dude... you've changed."

At that moment, Rocket realized he had. "Yeah. It's called growing up. Maybe you should try it."

Trevor brushed that off. "You must really like her."

"I do. Actually..." Rocket paused. "I think I love her. And Caleb."

"I'm happy for you. I hope I get to meet her sometime."

"Yeah, maybe. If you behave."

That took Trevor aback. Then Rocket broke into a grin. "I'm just fuckin' with you, man. It works both ways."

So Far, So Good

Saturday, October 15, 2022

Rocket's surprise appearance at Caleb's soccer game the week after their first dinner was a huge hit. He showed up moments before the game started, and Caleb ran up and hugged him. Caleb played enthusiastically and scored two goals.

After the game, Rocket followed Catie and Caleb to their home for dinner. When they arrived at the house, Rocket gave Caleb a present – a brand-new football. Catie fixed pizza for dinner. While it baked, Rocket gave Caleb his first lesson in throwing and catching a football in their backyard.

On Friday, October 7, the three of them went to the high school football game as planned and had a great time. Caleb was confused by some of the rules and asked a lot of questions, but Rocket answered them patiently. By the end of the game he mostly understood, and it was clear that he enjoyed it.

On this particular weekend, Caleb had a camping trip with his Cub Scout pack. Uncle Mark accompanied him. That meant Rocket and Catie could enjoy an evening to themselves. Rocket suggested dinner at Maggini's Italian Ristorante, a local chain with several locations around the Kansas City metro area.

The conversation flowed easily. At one point, the conversation turned to Caleb. Catie said, "You know what he said to me the other day? This was so cute! He said, 'Mommy? Are you and Mr. Crockett going to get married?'"

Rocket immediately tensed up. *Whoa...! Marriage? I mean, she's nice and everything, but isn't this rushing it a bit?* He tried to remain calm. "So, uh... What did you say?"

"I said, 'Well, honey, it's way too soon for that. Marriage is a major commitment. You're promising that you're going to spend the rest of your life with someone. So you need to spend a lot of time with them to make sure they're the right one.'"

Rocket smiled and convinced himself he could breathe normally again.

Catie continued. "I told him his father and I dated for two years before we got married. Then after we got married, we waited two years before we had him. He seemed to understand."

"He's a super nice kid. He's so well-mannered and he seems pretty smart."

"Yes, he is. He gets straight As in school."

"You and Michael have done a really good job with him."

"Thanks. Michael was a great father. I'm doing my best to carry on without him. Caleb is doing well, and Uncle Mark spends time with him whenever he can. But I can tell he wishes he had a father again."

Rocket wasn't sure what he should say here. He took a stab at it. "Yeah, I can see how he would."

"Remember the first time you came over? When you said goodbye to him you said, 'You take care of your mother now, you hear?' Well, he really does. He takes on plenty of chores around the house – more than I would normally expect of an eight-year-old. Like, he always empties the waste baskets and takes the trash and the recycling out to the curb without having to be reminded. And..." Catie suddenly got more serious. "Shortly after Michael was killed, I was sitting at the kitchen table crying, and he came up and put his arms around me. And he said, 'Don't worry, Mom. We'll make it. We're a team.'"

Rocket could see that Catie's eyes were moist. She didn't cry but she looked like she could at any moment. For that matter, so could he. He searched for what he could possibly say. "Wow. That was really sweet. He's a special little guy, that's for sure."

"Thanks. It means a lot to me that you two get along so well." She took the last sip of wine from her glass. Rocket reached for the bottle and divided the rest between their two glasses. Catie took a deep breath and continued. "Dating has been challenging, being a single mom. I've met some guys who seem nice at first, but sooner or later I figure out that they view Caleb as extra baggage. I can tell they're debating whether it's worth it to get a kid as part of the package. But my primary obligation has to be to Caleb – at least until he goes off to college, assuming he does. If that means I'm single for the next ten years, then so be it. It would be wonderful to have a partner and for Caleb to have a father again, but it has to be the right guy. Finding the right father for Caleb is just as important as finding the right husband for me."

"Yeah, I totally get it. That must be challenging for you. And you know, not everyone wants to date a policeman. It's a dangerous job and sometimes the hours aren't great. And some people have a stigma against police officers, for whatever reason."

"Yeah, I'm sure some women think, 'I don't want to get a visit one day from someone telling me my husband was killed in the line of duty. Been there, done that."

"But seriously, who couldn't love Caleb? He's nice, he's smart, he's well-behaved... and when he looks up at me with that cute smile and those big blue eyes... I just melt, you know? Anyway, to be honest, I've always been kind of uncomfortable about dating. Like, what if I say or do the wrong thing? I always figured the right woman would come along at some point and we'd get married and have kids – someday. But, you know... it doesn't have to be my biological kid. I don't get all hung up about 'oh, he has to be from my gene pool' or any of that. Like, I'd be totally open to adopting if it turned out that she or I couldn't have kids. They're just little human beings who need to be loved and cared for. Heck, my biological father didn't do that. I would have much rather had a father who wasn't my biological dad but who loved and cared for me."

Now it was Catie who felt at a loss for how to respond.

They finished the last few bites of their dinners and the last sips of their wine. The server stopped at their table and asked, "Would you like to see our dessert menu?"

Catie said, "Oh, I don't know... I'm kinda full."

Rocket could tell she really wanted dessert. And he wanted to prolong their date a few minutes more. "They have amazing cannoli here. I'll split one with you!"

Catie smiled. "Okay!"

Rocket turned to the server and said, "We'll split a cannolo."

"Let me get these out of your way." She gathered up their place settings. "I'll be right back with your cannolo."

Sharing the cannolo brought their date back to a lighter, more comfortable place. Catie asked, "Are you free next weekend? Caleb wants to see *Pinocchio* and I thought maybe we could all see it together."

"I'd love to, but I'm going to be out of town next weekend. A couple of friends from high school are getting married in Scottsdale, Arizona, and I've been invited." For whatever reason, he decided not to mention that it was a same-sex wedding.

"Oh, how nice. What are their names?"

"Ryan and Chris."

"Okay, no problem. I'll take him myself. There's another movie coming out later this month called *My Policeman*. It's set in Brighton, England in the 1950s. A policeman marries a school teacher. Maybe you and I could go see that."

"A policeman and a teacher – what a coincidence! Sure, that sounds like fun. Is it something Caleb might be interested in?"

"Well... It's rated R. You see, the policeman is secretly gay, and that was illegal in Great Britain back then." Catie paused for a moment. "Unless you'd rather not see a movie that involves gay people."

Rocket laughed. "Oh, I don't have any problem with that. In fact, the wedding I'm going to next weekend is a gay wedding."

"Oh, cool! I assumed Chris was a woman. So these guys were friends of yours in high school?"

"Yeah, they were on the track team with me. They weren't officially out back then, but I could tell there was something special going on between them. I think everyone else knew."

Catie looked at Rocket with renewed appreciation. "Really! You know, I have to be honest. With you being a policeman and a former football player, I wasn't sure whether you'd be cool with the gay thing or not. I remember Michael telling me that some of the other police officers were pretty homophobic."

"Yeah, I guess that's true. There are a couple of gay guys in my precinct. I mean, they're not a couple, just... there are two of them. One of them is married to another guy. They think they have to keep it on the down-low at work, but I told them I'm cool with it. I think most of the other guys are too. But I really liked Ryan and Chris, so when I figured out they were gay it was no big deal. In fact, one time I heard one of the guys in the locker room tell a fag joke and I shut that down right away."

"I'm really happy to hear that, Clay. You know, I haven't mentioned this to you yet because I didn't know how you'd react, but my best friend is gay. His name is Patrick. We've known each other since high school. In fact..." Catie stopped herself. *Should I really tell him this? Oh heck, why not? We've come this far and he'll probably find out sooner or later.* She leaned in and whispered, "He's the one I gave up my virginity for."

Rocket almost cracked up. "Really? I mean, did you know at the time?"

"That he was gay? No. I mean, I could tell there was something different about him. It's like I could relate to him better than most other guys. We seemed to have more in common. But you know, in high school everyone expects you to be straight and date the opposite sex. Especially in Overland Park, Kansas."

"Oh, I get that."

"Anyway, he was going through that phase where he thought if he found the right woman..."

Rocket finished her sentence. "...and he hoped the right woman would be you. Well, he made a good choice."

"Thanks, but... At the time, I was shocked. I thought, 'What? Did I turn him gay? Did he get so turned off by being with me that he'd rather have a man?' But then I realized that was crazy. He is the way he is, and he was trying to be someone he was not. So he and I are still best friends to this day. He and Caleb really like each other too, but of course Patrick isn't in the running to be his father. But I want Caleb to have a good gay role model in case he turns out gay."

"That's totally cool. I can't wait to meet Patrick."

"I've been telling him about you. And he's like, 'What? A policeman and a former football player?' So he'll be happy to know that you're so cool with gay people. He'll probably want to hear all about the wedding."

"Cool. Maybe we can all get together after I get back."

"He and I get together once or twice a month. We love to hang out at Burger Betty's down in the gayborhood. Do you know where that is?"

"I've passed it many times but I've never gone in."

"Oh, it's fabulous. I mean, it's not healthy eating, but they have great cocktails. And some nights there are drag shows. It's a lot of fun."

The server brought the check and Rocket paid for dinner.

Neither of them said much during the drive back to Catie's house. Rocket was processing everything they had talked about this evening, and he assumed Catie was too.

Rocket parked his car in her driveway. He got out, assuming they'd step inside for a good night kiss. As soon as they were inside, Catie turned to Rocket and smiled. "I really enjoyed this evening. The dinner was good, but the company was even better."

"Yeah, me too. You know, I really feel comfortable with you."

"I feel like I got to know you a lot better. And I like what I see."

Rocket couldn't believe that a woman was actually saying these things to him. And he could tell she meant it. He smiled, leaned down, and kissed her. It was a light kiss, but he hoped he could go in for some more serious kissing if she signaled that she wanted it.

Catie looked up at Rocket with sweetness in her eyes. "Since Caleb is gone... Will you stay?"

Rocket wanted to pump his fist in the air and yell, 'Yessssss!' Thankfully, he contained his enthusiasm. "I'd love to, but uh... I should probably make a quick trip to the drugstore first."

"That's okay. I have a few." She wrapped her arms around Rocket and held him. "It means a lot that you were going to use a condom without being asked. A lot of guys aren't like that."

The Reception

Saturday, October 22, 2022

As the guests made their way from the outdoor terrace where the wedding was held to the ballroom for the reception, they encountered a line forming in the hallway. As they would soon discover, Ryan and Chris were standing in front of a colorful backdrop. Each guest or pair of guests was invited to stand with Ryan and Chris for a photo. The photographer hustled the guests through quickly, so each photo took about 15 seconds. Ryan and Chris planned to include a copy of each guest's picture with their thank-you note.

When the guests entered the ballroom, they discovered that the big band jazz they heard in the hallway was being performed by a live band. Since both grooms were members of Desert Jazz Connection, the other members cleared their calendars so they could perform for their bandmates. Subs had been recruited to cover Ryan and Chris's parts.

A server greeted the guests with a tray of yellow cocktails garnished with a strawberry and a pineapple wedge. "This is a Tiki-Tini. It was created especially for this occasion by Ryan." The glasses were etched with Ryan and Chris's names and the date – a souvenir for the guests to take home.

Other servers circulated among the guests offering trays of colorful, perfectly-presented hors d'oeuvres.

Brad stood just beyond Ryan and Chris to greet the guests and perhaps accept compliments for the ceremony he had performed. Soon, Tom and Kathleen approached. Brad took a deep breath and compulsively wiggled the knot of his tie to make sure it was perfectly centered. *Might as well get this over with*, he thought. He took a few steps toward Tom and Kathleen. They looked as uncomfortable as Brad felt.

Kathleen spoke first. "That was a beautiful ceremony, Rev. Bauer. And you have a lovely speaking voice."

"Well, thank you. The guys wrote most of it. I just gave them some suggestions here and there. Anyway... I would like to apologize for how I treated you when you visited our house when we first found out about Ryan and Chris. I realize now that I was quite obnoxious and rude. And wrong. I was wrong about everything. I'm so sorry for ... well, for being such a pompous ass. And for all the pain I caused for your son."

Tom extended his hand, which Brad shook. "That's very decent of you to say that. Apology accepted."

Kathleen added, "According to Chris, you've completely changed. And you're doing a lot of good work to help gay kids and their families."

"Yes, well, I'm trying. That's my goal, anyway. And I'm working hard at becoming a better person."

Kathleen said, "I can see that. And I'm thrilled that you and Ryan are on speaking terms again."

Brad smiled. "No one is more thrilled than me. And I'm thrilled to have Chris as a son-in-law. He's a fine young man. And I'll be forever sorry that my actions kept them apart all these years. I'll carry that burden for the rest of my life."

Tom said, "Well, the boys have forgiven you and we have too. Onward!"

Tom and Kathleen smiled and moved on.

A few minutes later, it was Rocket's turn to be photographed with the grooms. After that, he headed quickly for the entrance to the ballroom, hoping not to make eye contact with Brad.

No such luck. Brad approached Rocket and said, "You look familiar. I'm trying to figure out where we might have met."

Rocket was not about to tell Brad that he was the undercover officer who infiltrated the orgy where he was arrested. Nor that he appeared on TV to refute Brad's false accusation that the police had arrested someone else who had his name and picture on a fake ID. "Um... I went to high school with Ryan and Chris."

"Oh. Okay. Well, glad you could come."

Rocket hurried into the ballroom.

The guests mingled and enjoyed Tiki-Tinis and hors d'oeuvres for half an hour. Then the band stopped playing and Colin, the band leader, invited the guests to take their seats. He started playing a CD containing a mix of softer jazz tunes curated by Ryan. The band members left the stage and walked to two round tables designated for them. As they sat down, servers offered them Tiki-Tinis.

The guests from Prairie Village and Kansas City were seated at the same table: Tom and Kathleen, Tyler and Chloe, Russ and Frank, and Rocket. Trevor would have been the eighth guest had he not canceled.

Ryan's former housemates Ted, Ricky, Darnell, and Darnell's husband Raythan sat at another table, along with Kevin and Chase from San Diego. Kent and Justin completed this table since they met Ted on a gay cruise and stayed at Kevin and Chase's home during San Diego Gay Pride weekend a few years ago.

Rob and Eddie, Ryan's mentor Bob Fordham and his wife and son, and several other colleagues from Technovations made up another table of eight, and other local friends, mostly from Desert Pride, filled two more tables.

After dinner, the fun began. The grooms surreptitiously left the ballroom and walked to a side room down the hall where the musicians had warmed up and left their cases. The members of Desert Jazz Connection returned to the bandstand, but the subs remained seated at their table. To everyone's surprise, Ryan and Chris entered the ballroom carrying their instruments. They took their places on the bandstand and Desert Jazz Connection performed a mini-concert for the attendees. Two tunes were selected to feature the grooms: Chris on alto sax and Ryan on trumpet.

After Chris's feature, Rocket leaned over to Tom and Kathleen and said, "Damn! I knew Chris and Ryan played in the bands at school, but I had no idea they were this good!"

Kathleen smiled and said, "Oh yes. Ryan and Chris used to get together at our house and practice. They had CDs that had only piano, bass, and drums playing so they could practice improvising solos."

Tom added, "They'd spend hours doing that. And they knew where every used record store in Kansas City was. Sometimes they'd drive into the city on a Saturday and come back loaded with CDs."

Rocket said, "I wish I had listened to the bands more when we were in high school. I was on the football team, so I never saw the marching band. We were always in the locker room at halftime."

Kathleen said, "Chris was in the marching band at the University of Maryland, too. But he stopped playing after he graduated. We have Ryan to thank for convincing him to play his sax again."

Tom added, "He's every bit as good now as he was back then."

After Ryan's feature, Colin announced, "And now, ladies and gentlemen, we have a special treat!"

The guests exchanged glances, wondering what could be more special than two grooms playing at their own wedding reception.

"Our next performer is truly a world-renowned talent. She's performed many summers in Provincetown, on gay cruises, and on Gay Pride stages across the US and Canada. Please put your hands together for the one! The only! MISS! ... WHITNEY! ... AUSTIN!!!"

The band launched into a brisk, upbeat instrumental number. The doors to the hallway opened, and Darnell, fabulously dressed as his alter-ego, confidently entered, waving at the crowd and blowing kisses on the way to the bandstand. The gays in the crowd who knew who she was whooped and applauded vigorously. The others applauded politely and wondered who this elegant yet over-the-top Black diva was, and why some of the guests were making such a big deal about her.

When Whitney arrived at the bandstand, Colin cut off the band. Whitney pulled the wireless mic out of its stand and said, "How lovely that you have a band here just for me."

The crowd chuckled.

Whitney handed a stack of paper to Colin with a theatrical flourish. "I just happen to have some lead sheets with me."

Colin smiled and passed the papers out to a few band members. It was all a joke – the band had received her arrangements in advance and had been practicing them for weeks.

Chloe was stunned. She turned to Tyler and asked, "Who is this ... person?"

"It's Whitney Austin, dear. Wait 'til you hear her sing!"

"I don't care about that. How do you know him?"

"Her. You refer to a drag queen as 'her' when she's in costume."

"It's a man dressed up as a woman. It's a him. Answer my question."

"Shhh... Let's not talk during the performance."

Chloe didn't care, but she looked around the table and noticed others scowling at her, wishing she would shut up. She leaned into Tyler and whispered loudly, "We need to talk." She stood and grabbed his wrist, pulled him out of his chair, and dragged him out the door into the hallway.

"Okay, so answer my question now. How do you know him?"

"I knew the guy performing as Whitney Austin when I went to UCLA. He and two other guys sitting at that table were my friends."

"They look like they're probably homosexuals."

"Well, duh! This is a gay wedding. Most of the guests are gay."

"So you were hanging around with homosexuals while you were in college?"

"Sometimes. The red-headed one and I had some classes together. Sometimes we got together to study. He and the other guys lived in a house a few blocks off campus, so I got to know the rest of them. They're really nice guys."

"Maybe they are, but let's get to the point." Chloe became even more angry. "You named our children after a Black homosexual drag queen!"

"Not necessarily. Whitney and Austin are common names. They're nice names. You said so yourself when I suggested them. You agreed to name them that."

"Yeah, but why did you pick them? It's a bit much to believe it's just a coincidence."

"Whatever. Like I said, I thought they were cool names. So what now? Are you going to insist that we have their names legally changed?"

"No, but..."

"Well then, what difference does it make?"

Chloe decided to give up on this point. "Okay, so you knew those guys in college. How did they end up here?"

"They're friends of Ryan's. He lived in the same house with them when he went to UCLA. Now can we go back in? I want to see Whitney's performance."

Chloe rolled her eyes. "Oh, all right."

They quietly reentered the ballroom and returned to their seats. Whitney did two more numbers. Then the subs returned to the bandstand, and Whitney and the band performed a slow, romantic number for Ryan and Chris's first dance.

The musicians took a break while the grooms cut the cake. The three-layer cake was lavishly decorated, with a cake topper of a male couple perched on the top layer. After the servers cut slices and distributed them to the guests, people were free to move about the room and socialize. Many, including Tyler, returned to the open bar for another Tiki-Tini.

When Tyler returned to the table with his drink, Chloe gave him a disapproving look. "Isn't that, like, your third or fourth drink?"

"Yeah."

"Well, you'd better make that your last one. I don't want you getting drunk and making a fool of yourself."

"Jesus Christ, take a chill pill. It's a special occasion! We don't have to drive anywhere. The kids aren't here. I wanna have some fun for a change."

"*For a change?* Oh, is that it? Is being a husband and a father not enough fun for you?"

"Oh, come on. You know what I mean. But let's get real. Since the kids came along, we don't go out as much as we used to."

"It's called being adults and responsible parents. We're not in college anymore. I have no interest in getting stupid drunk or seeing you that way."

"We can cut loose for one night. Maybe you ought to get another drink. It might lighten you up a bit."

"Sorry I'm such a downer. No, wait. Not sorry."

"Well, I'm going to get up and mingle. You can come with me, or mingle on your own, or sit there like a wet blanket. Your choice."

Chloe fumed. Tyler got up and wandered through the crowd. He finished his drink and ordered another.

Ted, Ricky, Darnell, and Raythan were standing near the bar. Ted, Ricky, and Darnell were catching up with each other's lives, recalling their fun times in college, and commenting about how nice the wedding was. Raythan didn't have much to add, but he enjoyed meeting Darnell's college buddies and listening to their stories.

At one point, Ted said, "Hey, you see that guy sitting alone over at that far table?"

Ricky said, "The hunky one with the dark hair?"

"Yeah. Do any of you know who he is? He's been looking at me all night."

Darnell winked at Ted. "Honey, who can blame him?"

Raythan said, "He's sitting at the same table as Chris's family. Why don't you ask him?"

Ted said, "I think I might."

Ricky said, "And if you're not interested in him, you can send him my way."

Darnell smiled at Ricky. "You haven't changed, have you?"

"Why should I? A hard man is good to find."

Ted scanned the reception hall. He spotted Chris and Ryan on the dance floor. He made his way through the crowd, and then asked Chris, "Hey, can I talk to you for a second?"

Chris glanced at Ryan, who nodded. "Sure."

Ted and Chris took a few steps off the dance floor. Ted asked, "You see that guy sitting over there at the table your parents were at?" Chris nodded. "Do you know who he is?"

"Yeah. He went to high school with Ryan and me. We were on the track team together. He was also a big star on the football team. He's a cop now."

"Oh, okay."

"Funny story. You know how Ryan's dad got busted in a big gay sex-and-drugs orgy?" Ted nodded. "Well, he's the cop they sent undercover to investigate what was going on."

Ted cracked up. "Are you serious?"

"I know, right? I couldn't believe it either. I mean, he had all that macho jock bullshit going on back when we were in high school. He used to tease Ryan about being a preacher's kid." Chris paused, but then he remembered Ryan and Ted's history. "And about his cock. He couldn't take his eyes off it in the shower room."

"So is he gay?"

"I don't think so. They probably picked him to go to the orgy undercover because he's good-looking and well-built. And you have to admit, he is."

"Yeah, I can see how he'd be some guys' type, especially if they have a thing for men in uniforms."

"Or out of them."

Ted and Chris both chuckled.

Ted said, "Okay, well I'll let you get back to dancing." He turned to go, but then he turned back. "Hey. I want you to know something."

Chris looked curious.

"Ryan used to talk about you all the time. Like what a great guy you were and how much he missed you. He resigned himself to believe that you and he would never get a chance to be together. But I could tell, deep inside, he would always be sad about that. Anyway, I'm so glad things worked out and you can finally be together. You guys are perfect for each other. I know Ryan really well. He's the greatest guy in the world."

Chris said, "Oh, I know he is."

"I'm really happy for you."

Chris hugged Ted. "Thanks. That means a lot. He's always spoken highly of you too. He's lucky to have you as a friend."

Ted smiled. "You know, Ryan has visited me in each place I've lived. I hope both of you will visit me in the future. You're welcome anytime."

"Thanks! I'd love that. And anytime you're in the US, I want you to come visit us. You're always welcome. And thanks for coming. It means a lot that you came all the way from Australia for this."

"I wouldn't have missed it for the world."

They hugged again. Chris gave Ted a light kiss. Then Ted returned to Ricky, Darnell, and Raythan. Chris scanned the room for Ryan. He saw him sitting at a table talking to Rocket. He spotted a few of his band friends dancing in a group and joined them.

Ryan said, "Hey man, I'm really glad you could come."

Rocket replied, "Me too. It was a beautiful wedding. Just beautiful. Trevor is sorry he couldn't be here. He's going to be really sorry after I tell him all about it."

"I understand. I hope things with his dad turn out okay."

"Yeah, well, it's not looking good. It's only a matter of time."

"Tell him I'm sorry. I'll call him sometime soon. Anyway, I hope it's not too awkward being around all these gay people."

"No, that doesn't bother me. It was awkward running into your father, though."

"Oh, shit! I didn't even think about that. I'm sorry! I should have warned you ahead of time."

"It's okay. That wouldn't have stopped me from coming. Hey, it was great to hear you play your trumpet! Man, you kicked ass!"

"Thanks. I didn't play for the first few years after I graduated, but Aaron talked me into joining the band after I met him."

"Cool. I can see why you like living in Scottsdale. Man, it's really beautiful."

"Well, this is Paradise Valley. My part of town isn't quite as nice as this, but yeah, I love it. It sure beats the hell out of Kansas. Especially in winter."

"I hear ya. I came here twice when I played football at TCU – once for the Fiesta Bowl and once for the Buffalo Wild Wings Bowl. I couldn't believe how nice it was! And it was so great that it wasn't freezing in December."

"Well, maybe you should move out here. What's keeping you in Kansas City?"

Rocket smiled. "Well, there is one thing. Two, actually."

Ryan eagerly waited for what Rocket would say next.

"You're never gonna believe this, man, but I've met someone."

"Seriously?"

"Uhhh... You didn't have to sound *that* surprised."

"Sorry, I didn't mean it like that."

"Oh, I know. I was just fuckin' with ya. Nobody's more surprised than me."

"That's awesome, man!"

"Her name is Catie. I was on patrol one day and saw this car pulled off to the side of the road with a flat tire. So I stopped to see if I could help. And it was Catie, and she had her son with her. His name is Caleb. He's eight years old and he's just adorable! Anyway, when I finished changing her tire, Catie invited me to dinner. Normally I wouldn't, but something told me to say yes. So that was just over a month ago, and we've been seeing each other ever since."

"That's great, man. Sometimes you meet your special someone when you least expect it. I hope it works out."

"Yeah, me too. I've never felt like this before. Her husband was killed in an auto accident a couple of years ago, so she's been raising Caleb by herself. She says he needs to have a father figure. And I can tell she's kinda lonely and she needs someone to love. So yeah. We all get along great, and I'm pretty sure I'm in love with her. But aside from that, they need me." Rocket paused and lowered his voice. "No one's ever needed me before."

Ryan reached over and placed his hand on Rocket's knee. "It sounds like maybe you need them too."

"Yeah, I think you're right."

"So do you think you'll enjoy being a father? I mean, that comes with the package."

"Oh, hell, yeah. You should see how Caleb looks up at me with that smile and those big blue eyes. Like I'm his hero."

"Maybe you are. And maybe you're Catie's hero, too."

Rocket smiled. "Yeah. Who would've thought?"

"Hopefully, I'll get to meet them next time we visit Chris's parents."

"You bet! Anyway, you guys had a beautiful wedding. It was perfect. I kept thinking about how, if Catie and I get married, I hope our wedding will be as nice as yours."

"Awww... Thanks. At first, I was opposed to having my dad officiate. But now I'm glad I did. Anyway, I need to circulate some more. But let me offer you a bit of unsolicited advice."

"Okay..."

"Don't marry someone because they're the only one who's come along. And give it time. Sooner or later, the initial euphoria will wear off. Then if you realize you still want and need each other, you know you've got something. Don't just marry someone you can live with. Marry someone you can't live without."

Rocket let that sink in. "Yeah. That's good advice, man. Thanks."

Ryan stood up, so Rocket stood too.

There was one more thing Rocket wanted to say. "Hey, Ryan. I'm really happy for you and Chris. When we were in high school, I could tell you two belonged together."

"Really? Was it that obvious?"

"To me it was. Anyway... There's something else." Rocket took a deep breath. "I wish we could have been better friends. I know it was my fault because I was such an asshole back then. But anyway, I've always liked you and admired you. And I'm glad we're back in touch and everything worked out for you."

Ryan gave Rocket a nice hug. "It's all good. We're friends now. And I'm happy about that. So let's stay in touch. We can get together whenever we go to Kansas."

Rocket sat back down. Ryan turned to go, but he realized Rocket would be sitting there alone. Ryan grabbed Rocket's hand and pulled him up out of his chair. "Come on!"

"What? Where are we going?"

"Out on the dance floor." Ryan led him to an open spot next to where Chris was dancing with several of their friends.

"But... I don't know how to dance."

"You don't have to know how. There's no right or wrong way. Just move back and forth with the music."

Chris turned to Rocket and grinned. "Feel the beat down to your feet!"

Rocket awkwardly started moving back and forth.

Ryan said, "There you go. See? It's not rocket science."

Rocket and Chris laughed. Within a few minutes, Rocket shed his inhibitions about dancing with gay guys and was having a great time.

While Ryan and Rocket were talking, Ted returned to his former housemates. "He went to high school with Ryan and Chris. He's a cop now."

Darnell glanced at Rocket. "Well, he certainly is an *arresting* officer."

A devilish grin appeared on Ricky's face. "I wonder if he brought his handcuffs."

Ted continued. "And get this! He was the undercover cop who busted Ryan's father at that orgy." That left everyone speechless.

Raythan said, "Wait a minute. The same guy who officiated the wedding?"

"The very same. So yes, they're both here in the same room."

Darnell let out a theatrical gasp. "Awk ... ward!"

Ricky said, "So he *is* gay."

Ted replied, "Chris said he's not. But then, he's been staring at me all night."

Tyler strolled up to them, oblivious that he might be interrupting a conversation. "Dudes!"

Darnell exclaimed, "Well if it isn't Tyler Robertson! Long time no see!"

Tyler hugged Darnell, Ted, and Ricky. Chloe, who was staring at him from across the room, noticed that he held each of them a second or two longer than most guys do for a simple 'hello' hug.

Darnell said, "This is my husband, Raythan. Raythan, this is Tyler. In addition to being Chris's brother, he was a frequent visitor to our house in LA."

Tyler and Raythan shook hands. Tyler said, "Whitney killed tonight! Man, I'm so glad I got to see you perform again!"

"Why, thank you. It was an honor to be a part of this auspicious event."

Ted said, "I understand you're married now. Is that your wife over there?"

"Yeah."

"Do you have any kids?"

"Two. A boy and a girl. Here, let me show you their pictures." Tyler pulled his phone out of his pocket. After a few taps and swipes, Tyler turned his phone around and slowly waved it past each of them.

Darnell said, "Oh, they're adorable! What are their names?"

Tyler paused. There was no way he could avoid answering this simple question. "Uh... my son's name is Austin and my daughter's is Whitney."

For a long moment, nobody said anything. Even Darnell, who was always ready with the perfect response, whether it be a witty retort, a comforting remark, or the gracious acceptance of a compliment, was speechless.

Finally, Tyler said, "I've always liked those names."

After more awkward silence, Ted asked, "So what are you up to these days?"

Tyler said, "I work for an accounting firm in Kansas City. How about you guys?"

The others, in turn, updated Tyler on where they lived and their current jobs.

Then Darnell said, "Let's see... You were at UCLA until, what? 2007?"

Tyler nodded. "Yeah, it's hard to believe that was 15 years ago. But man, I'll never forget some of those parties you guys had at your house. We had so much fun."

Ricky smirked. "Yeah. Sooooo much fun."

The innuendo wasn't lost on any of them except Raythan, who didn't meet Darnell until years later. He had heard the stories about the shenanigans during those wild parties. And that sometimes those parties ended up with people naked in the pool and hot tub. But he did not know that Tyler had 'experimented' with all three of them.

Darnell glanced over at Chloe, sitting alone at her table stewing. "So much has changed since then."

Ted and Ricky got the reference.

Tyler said, "Yeah, it's too bad I couldn't have moved in with you guys for my senior year. But, oh well. I guess if I hadn't moved back to Kansas and gone to UK for my senior year, I wouldn't have met Chloe."

Ted said, "And there wouldn't have been a place for Ryan to live when he arrived in LA. So it all worked out for the best."

There was a lull in the conversation. There seemed to be a consensus among the three former housemates that they were through catching up with Tyler.

Darnell took Raythan's hand and said, "I don't know about you, but I'm ready to do some more dancing." Raythan nodded, and they headed over to the dance floor.

Ricky said, "And I need to go take a leak." He excused himself and headed for the door to the hallway.

Ted said, "I'm starting to fade. I'm still jet-lagged from my flight from Australia. I'm gonna talk to Ryan and Chris for a few minutes, then call it a night."

He found Ryan out on the floor dancing with Rocket, Chris, and several others. He motioned for Ryan to step aside for a moment. "Hey, man. Congratulation! That was a beautiful wedding. Everything was perfect."

"Thanks. And it wouldn't have been perfect without you here."

"I'm so glad I could hear you play your trumpet and see Darnell perform again. It was great to meet Chris. And you're right – he's everything you said he was. You guys are perfect together."

They hugged and held each other for at least ten seconds.

Ryan said, "I know Chris is the man I'm supposed to spend the rest of my life with, but after him, you're the best friend I've ever had. I'll never forget all the nights we spent in the hot tub talking and drinking wine. And when we did it for the first time on my 21st birthday. And how you gave me all your furniture when you went to London and I moved here. I still have it in my house. It always reminds me of you."

Ted smiled. "And I love how you always visited me in each city I've lived in. I told Chris this earlier, but I don't want you to stop coming now that you're married. I want you both to visit me whenever you want. And I want to get to know Chris better."

"Same goes for you! You're always welcome in our house. You need to come and visit your furniture."

They both laughed.

Ted said, "Oh, hey, I almost forgot. Look at this." He pulled out his phone and skimmed through the pictures he had taken. "Look at this one. I took it while you and Chris were exchanging rings. It looks like there's a ball of light right behind you."

Ryan took a look. "Wow. That *is* weird. It's kinda bluish. It's like you can see through it, but there's definitely something there." They looked at each other and shrugged. Then Ryan's face lit up. "Or some*one*. Come with me."

Ryan led Ted through the crowd to one of the band tables where a flute player in the band was seated. "Hey, Paul. Would you mind taking a look at something?" Paul stood up. "Oh, and by the way, this is Ted. Ted and I lived together when I went to UCLA. We've remained friends ever since."

Paul and Ted shook hands. Ryan said to Ted, "Paul is a medium. He did a reading for me once, and my mother came through. So did Hal."

"Oh, wow! How was Hal?"

"Fine. In fact, the message he had for me inspired me to start the Hal Morris Project for gay kids who have to leave home. Anyway, show Paul that picture you took."

Ted showed his phone to Paul. Paul smiled. "Yep. That's your mother. She was there during the service. She moved back and forth between you and Brandon. She was here at the reception, too, while you were playing your trumpet. She's gone now."

Ryan thought for a moment. "How did she feel about Dad being here?"

"She didn't seem to mind. Remember, she's moved on from everything that happened in her last lifetime. She's not carrying a grudge. Oh, and by the way, Hal was here too. A while ago, he was standing near that table over there." Paul pointed to Ted, Ricky, Darnell, and Raythan's table.

Ted said, "We used to live in his house. He was like a father to us."

Ryan said, "He probably enjoyed seeing us together again."

Paul nodded.

Ryan said, "Thanks, Paul. I feel good knowing Mom was here."

Ted asked Paul, "Do you do readings by phone or Zoom?"

"Yeah. I did a lot of those during the pandemic."

"Do you have a card?"

"No, sorry, I didn't think to bring any."

Ryan said, "I'll send you his contact info. Anyway, thanks, Paul!"

"You're welcome. And thanks for inviting me."

Ted turned to Ryan and said, "I'm going to call it a night. I'm still jet-lagged from my flight."

"Thanks so much for coming." They hugged again. Ryan whispered in Ted's ear, "I love you."

Ted whispered, "I love you."

They kissed and released each other.

Ted said, "Let me say goodbye to Chris."

They motioned for Chris to come over, and he and Ted hugged. Ted whispered, "I'm counting on you to take good care of him."

Chris chuckled. "That's a given."

They released each other. Then Ted said, "You guys must promise you'll come see me."

Ryan said, "We're talking about going to New Zealand for our honeymoon, so we could probably swing by Sydney while we're in the same hemisphere."

"Or I could fly over there for a day or two."

"We'll work it out."

Ryan and Chris hugged Ted again, then he left.

When Ricky emerged from the men's restroom, Chloe was heading toward the women's. Chloe froze in her tracks. They locked eyes. Chloe said, "Ummm..."

Ricky stopped. "Yes...?"

Chloe faked a nervous smile and extended her hand. "My name's Chloe. I'm Tyler's wife."

Ricky shook her hand gently. "I'm Ricky."

"I saw my husband talking with you and your friends. How do you know him?"

"We all went to UCLA at the same time."

"I see." She paused. "It looked like he knew you guys quite well."

"Yes. Three of us lived in a house together. Tyler and one of the other guys were in some of the same classes, so they'd get together to study. So yeah, he came to the house a few times." Ricky didn't mention that Tyler attended many of their parties and almost moved in for his senior year.

Chloe took a few seconds to absorb that information. "So... would I be correct to assume that you're all homosexuals?"

Ricky laughed. "What gave it away?"

"Sorry... I suppose that wasn't very PC or whatever."

Ricky desperately wanted this conversation to end, so he resumed his journey toward the ballroom. As he passed Chloe, she touched his arm and he stopped. "One more thing. Is there anything I need to know about my husband?"

Ricky studied the look on Chloe's face while he contemplated what he should say.

"Nope. Not a thing."

Ricky walked briskly into the ballroom. As he walked, he replayed their conversation. He was satisfied with his response. She didn't *need* to know. He hoped Chloe wouldn't pin him down for more information.

After Chloe finished in the restroom, she walked back into the ballroom and looked for Tyler. She spotted him talking with Aaron and Brandon. He had a fresh Tiki-Tini in one hand and his other hand rested on Brandon's shoulder affectionately. He was clearly intoxicated and seemed way too comfortable chatting with gay men.

She hurried up to Tyler and grabbed his wrist, nearly spilling his drink. "It's time to go."

Tyler turned and looked at his wife incredulously. "What do you mean? The party's still going strong."

"You heard me. It's time to go." She said to Aaron and Brandon. "It was nice to meet you." She tugged on his wrist and led him away.

Once they were in the hallway, Tyler shook his hand free of Chloe's grasp. "What the hell is wrong with you?"

Chloe snarled, "What is wrong with *you*? You're drunk and you're spending all your time with the homosexuals."

"Ninety percent of the people here are gay. It's a gay wedding! Duh! Why shouldn't I talk with them?"

"It's not just that. You were looking a bit too ... *comfortable* with them. And it got worse the more you had to drink."

"Of course, I'm comfortable with them. My brother's gay! Maybe if you put forth a little effort to talk with them and get to know them, you'd be more comfortable with them."

"I do not choose to associate with people like that. They're welcome to make their own lifestyle choices and do as they see fit, but I don't have to like or approve of it. I think I've been a pretty good sport about accepting your brother, and I agreed to come to his ... whatever that was. But it's over now, and I've had enough gay thrown in my face to last me for the next ten years. And you've had too much to drink."

"Who cares? We're not driving. We don't have any place to go tomorrow morning."

"That's no reason to act like a drunk fool. The way you were carrying on, people might think you're one of *them*."

"Who cares what people think?"

"I do. Come on, we're going back to the room."

Tyler reluctantly followed Chloe back to their room. As she fumbled for the key card in her purse, he exclaimed, "NO! I am not done for the evening! It's my brother's wedding, dammit, and I'm going to celebrate!" He turned and stomped back down the hallway.

"Tyler Thomas Robertson! You come back here this instant."

Tyler spun on his heels. "Bitch! You can't order me around. I'll stay out and party if I damn well please. You can stay in the room and wallow in your self-righteousness if you want, but I'm having fun for a change."

When Tyler returned to the ballroom, he passed Rocket Crockett in the hallway. He was talking on his phone, but they nodded to each other as Tyler passed.

Rocket spoke into the phone, "Catie? Hi, Honey, it's me. How are you doing?"

Catie replied, "Fine. I finally got Caleb to sleep about an hour ago. He was full of questions about where you are and what weddings are like and where Scottsdale is and everything else he could think of. Now I'm relaxing with a glass of wine and catching up on Facebook. I'll probably go to bed in a few minutes."

Rocket chuckled. "He's an inquisitive kid, that's for sure. Anyway, I'm glad you're still up. I know it's two hours later there, but I wanted to say hi and hear your voice."

"Awww, that's sweet. I'm glad you called. How was the wedding?"

"Oh, it was awesome! It was kinda different because it was two guys, but it was really nice. And the reception has been fun. The jazz band Ryan and Chris belong to was there, and they played with them for a few songs and each did a solo. Then... get this! They had a drag queen come out and sing a few songs with the band playing behind her. It was amazing! He – er, I mean *she* – had an incredible voice!"

"You mean she wasn't lip-synching?"

"No! She was really singing! Apparently, she used to be famous. She sang all over the US and on cruise ships. Anyway, the guy was one of Ryan's housemates in college. So next time you and Patrick go to a drag show at Burger Betty's, I want to come along."

"Well, just to manage your expectations, they're probably not going to be as good as the one you saw. But it's still a lot of fun. So then, you're having a good time?"

"Yeah! Kinda. I mean, I don't know most of the people. A lot of them are their gay friends from around here. But I was sitting at a table with several people from Kansas City and Prairie Village. There were Chris's parents, his brother and his wife, and an older gay couple. One was Ryan's boss when he worked at a grocery store in high school. So I got to know them. I got to spend a little time with Ryan and Chris, but I realize they have to divide their time with everybody else. So I spent most of the time just sitting around, but that was okay."

"So you're glad you went?"

"Oh, definitely. I wish you could have been here too. The whole time during the wedding I was thinking about how I want our–" Rocket caught himself before any more words slipped out. "You know, what goes on at weddings and how much planning it must take and all that. I've only been to a few weddings, but this was definitely the best."

Rocket's little slip-up was not lost on Catie. She grinned with delight on the other end of the line. "Well, I look forward to hearing all about it when you get home."

"Okay, well, things are starting to wind down, so I'll head back to my room pretty soon. It's almost 9:00 here, so maybe I'll watch a movie for a while and then try to get some sleep."

"Thanks for calling. I'm glad you had such a good time."

For a moment, neither of them spoke. Neither of them wanted the conversation to end yet.

Rocket broke the silence. "I've been thinking about you a lot."

"I think about you a lot, too."

There was another pause. Rocket had something else he wanted to say, but he wanted the first time he said it to be in person.

Catie had something she wanted to say too, but she wanted Rocket to say it first.

Rocket said, "I can't wait to see you again."

"Me too!"

"Okay, well... good night!"

"Good night!"

Rocket lowered the phone from his ear and looked at the screen. He hesitated for a second, then pressed the hang-up button.

He walked back into the ballroom long enough to say goodnight to Ryan and Chris. They each gave him a quick hug.

He took one last look around the room. About a dozen people were still dancing. Chris's brother was sitting at a table near the bar talking to one of Ryan's housemates from LA. He didn't see the ginger guy.

At the table near the bar, Ricky asked Tyler, "So where's your wife?"

"She went back to the room. She wanted me to go with her, but the party's still going on, y'know?"

"Dude... She probably wants some! Women get all romantic and stuff at weddings ... or so I've been told. Man, you could be gettin' laid!"

"Nah... She and I kinda had a bad day. And she never puts out anymore. When I met her in college, it took me a while to get her to go all the way, but after that first time, man, it was great. I was hittin' home runs all the time! But then after we got married it kind of died down. And now, after having two kids, I can't ever get her to do it. She's all like, 'Just hold me. I just want to cuddle.' And I'm like, fuck that! I don't wanna cuddle. *I wanna fuck her brains out!*"

Ricky looked around. A few people had glanced over in their direction. "Dude, you might wanna keep your voice down a little."

Tyler was oblivious. "See, that's where gay guys have it made. With women, you've got to, you know, romance them and bring them flowers and shit, and then you get, 'I just want to cuddle.' I mean, romance is nice and everything, but sometimes you really wanna churn some butter, you know?"

Ricky said, "It's like women read romance novels and guys watch porn."

"Yeah! Exactly! That sums it up right there. So with two guys, there's a lot more times when you're both down to fuck. I mean, come on, man... You used to get laid all the time. I bet you still do."

"Well, now that I've gotten older, not so much." Ricky decided not to mention the fact that he had HIV, so getting together with guys always meant going through that awkward moment of disclosure. Tyler didn't need to know that. And in his horny, drunken state he wasn't interested in hearing about Ricky's personal life anyway.

Tyler said, "Yeah, well, I bet Chris and Ryan fuck like rabbits. And I've heard Ryan's dick is huge! Man, I'd like to be a fly on that wall."

Ricky was ready for this conversation to be over. "Well, it's been nice seeing you again, but I'm going to call it a night."

"Hey, well, before you go..." *It's now or never*, Tyler thought. "You and I had some fun times back in college. You wanna go one more round, just for old times' sake?"

"No." Ricky's firm answer left no doubt that the question wasn't open for negotiation. "I'm not some piece of ass that's available at your beck and call whenever you feel horny and your wife isn't putting out." Ricky stood up. "Besides, you're a married man now. I don't do married men. I'm not going to be a party to some guy cheating on his wife. Or husband."

Ricky left the table and circulated among the remaining crowd. He said congratulations and good night to Ryan and Chris and hugged them. He spent a few minutes chatting with Kent and Justin, whom he had met at San Diego Pride several years ago and reconnected with earlier in the evening at their table.

Tyler watched Ricky chatting with Kent and Justin. He wondered whether either of them might be interested in hooking up – or maybe both! During his experimental phase in college, he never had the opportunity to do a three-way. His hopes sank when he saw Ricky, Kent, and Justin leave the room together.

Tyler dreaded going back to his room and facing Catie. Maybe she'd already be asleep.

The last few people said congratulations and good night to the grooms. Ryan spoke to the manager for a minute, signed something, then shook his hand. The bartender and two staffers were packing up the bar. Other hotel employees were clearing the tables of the remaining glassware and tablecloths.

As they headed for the door, Chris swung by the table where Tyler sat alone. Tyler's alcohol consumption throughout the evening had caught up with him. He felt like shit and was getting drowsy.

"Are you okay?"

"Not really."

"Do you need me to help you back to your room?"

"Nah, I'll be okay."

Tyler stood up and wobbled. Chris stepped closer and put his hands on Tyler's shoulders. Normally, he'd hug his brother, but he didn't want to get any closer in case Tyler suddenly vomited. That looked like a distinct possibility. "Take care, man."

"Yeah. Oh, hey... Great wedding."

"Thanks. Are you sure I can't help you back to your room?"

"I'm sure."

Chris dropped his arms. "Okay, well, it's time to go. They need to get this place cleaned up." He turned and left.

After Chris and Ryan left, Tyler started staggering toward the door. A couple of employees paused from their duties long enough to watch him walk out, ready to run up and assist if necessary.

Once he got out into the hallway, he spotted the nearby restroom. Thankfully, he made it into a stall in the nick of time.

So Many Questions

Saturday, October 22, 2022

After Rocket left the ballroom, he decided to stop by the lobby bar for a beer before he turned in. It had been an exciting day of fun, new experiences, and a few emotions he wasn't sure how to deal with. He wanted to process some of them and try to wind down or he'd have trouble falling asleep.

He walked up to the bar, ordered a beer, then turned and looked for a place to sit. Since it was Saturday night, the room was fairly crowded. He spotted the handsome ginger from the wedding sitting at a two-seat high-top table near the window. He walked up and asked, "Mind if I join you?"

Ted motioned for him to sit in the other seat. After he sat down, Ted offered a handshake. "Ted Purcell."

Rocket shook his hand firmly. "Clay Crockett."

Ted was sipping a glass of red wine and munching from a bowl of mixed nuts. He pushed the bowl to the center of the table and said, "Help yourself."

"Thanks. Beautiful wedding, wasn't it?"

"Yep. It sure was. And I'm so happy that Ryan finally ended up with Chris."

"Yeah, me too. So, where are you from?"

"Sydney, Australia."

Rocket's eyes popped open. "You came all the way from Australia for the wedding?"

"You bet. I watched his first wedding on the livestream. That was okay, but it was nothing like being there. So this time, I wanted to be here. My company's headquarters is in LA, so I arranged a business trip for a training class and some meetings. That way the company paid for the trip. But I would have paid for it myself if I had to."

"Same here. I watched the first one on the livestream too, and I knew I wanted to attend this one in person."

"Where are you from?"

"Kansas City. Ryan, Chris, and I went to high school together in Prairie Village, Kansas. We were on the track team."

"Yeah, I remember that he ran track in high school. What do you do now?"

"I'm a police officer. So how do you know Ryan?"

"We lived together in a house near UCLA for three years while we were going to college."

"Sweet. So I bet you got to know him pretty well."

"Very well. He's my best friend in the world. So yeah, I'd travel halfway around the globe for his wedding."

Rocket wondered just how well Ryan and Ted knew each other. But he knew it would be inappropriate to ask.

Ted asked, "When we lived together, Ryan didn't want to have any contact with people from back home. He didn't want anyone to find out where he was. I practically had to force him to get back in touch with Chris. So how did you and Ryan get reconnected?"

Rocket let out a nervous chuckle. "Well, that's a funny story. Are you familiar with what happened to his father?"

Ted knew, but he decided not to let on. "Ryan said his father was an ultra-conservative paster of a right-wing church. He had to leave home in a hurry when he found out his dad was about to send him to some place for gay reparation therapy. Ryan hated his guts, and I don't blame him. It still blows my mind that his father officiated his wedding."

"I know, right? So you didn't hear what happened back in 2016?"

"I was living in Buenos Aires then."

"Okay. Well, another friend from high school is the manager of a Helton Grande Inn and Suites in Kansas City. In fact, he worked his connections and got them a nice discount here. He comped my room. He was planning to come too, but he had to cancel at the last minute. Anyway, he asked me to come to his hotel one day and showed me some security camera footage. Long story short, there was this gay group that rented one of their suites the first Friday of every month for an orgy. That wouldn't have been a problem by itself, but there was evidence of illegal drug use taking place. So I reported it to my supervisor and, well, he had me go undercover to the next event to see if they were actually using drugs. When I went, I found out they had hired male prostitutes too. So the police swept in and busted the event. As it turned out, Ryan's father was one of the men busted that night."

Ted feigned surprise. "No shit! His father, who came down on him so hard when he found out he was gay, was gay himself?"

"Yep. Anyway, that's how I got reconnected with Ryan. Actually, our friend Trevor, the hotel manager, told Chris on Facebook. Chris knew Aaron, so he told him. And that's how Ryan found out. Oh, and it led to Ryan being reunited with his brother Brandon. So anyway, Ryan and I talked on Skype not long after that and caught up. And I saw them this past December when they came to Prairie Village to spend Christmas with Chris's parents."

"Wow. That's quite a story. But let's back up a second. They sent you undercover to a gay orgy?"

Rocket nodded.

"So, pardon me for asking, but... Are you gay?"

"No, but I'm totally cool with it. Obviously, or I wouldn't have come here. There were a couple of gay guys on the force, but my boss didn't want to send one of them in case they knew anyone at the event."

"Wow. I'll be that was an eye-opening experience."

"You have no idea." Rocket glanced around the room. There were at least a dozen people within earshot. "Hey, I'd rather not talk about this around so many people. Is there somewhere else we can go?"

"We can go up to my room. Do you drink wine?"

"I'm mostly a beer guy. Or Jack and Coke. But wine's okay. What are you drinking?"

"Malbec. This one's pretty decent. It's from Argentina. I got turned on to Malbec when I lived in Buenos Aries. Anyway, how about if I order a bottle and we can enjoy it while we talk some more?"

"Yeah, sure. Thanks."

Ted got up and walked over to the bar. "I'd like a full bottle of that Malbec I was drinking and another wine glass. Can I take it up to my room?"

The bartender shook his head. "You're not allowed to remove alcohol from the bar area. Sorry, state law. But I can have Room Service deliver it to your room."

"Okay. Room 326."

"Would you like anything to go with that? A cheese board or something?" He handed Ted a menu.

Ted scanned it and said, "The cheese trio with the crackers, olives, and nuts looks good."

"Excellent choice. I'll send it right up."

Ted returned to their table and said, "Okay, let's go. They have to send the wine up using Room Service."

Rocket followed Ted up to room 326. As Ted unlocked the door, it occurred to Rocket that he was about to enter a hotel room with a gay guy he had just met. But Ted seemed nice and he was enjoying talking with him. He probably had some good stories to tell about Ryan.

Once they were inside, Ted took off his jacket and hung it on one of the hotel hangers. He kicked off his shoes.

Rocket hung his jacket up and followed Ted to a round table with two chairs. "These rooms are so nice! Man, if Trevor hadn't comped my room, I'd probably be staying at some budget motel. I can't afford this shit."

Ted said, "Helton is one of my company's preferred vendors, so I got the corporate rate."

There was a knock on the door. A young man called out, "Room Service."

Ted walked over to the door and opened it. A uniformed waiter rolled a small cart into the room. He placed the perfectly arranged cheese assortment in the middle of the table, then put a small plate, napkin, and silverware in front of each chair. He placed two wine glasses on the table and showed the wine bottle to Ted.

Ted nodded. "That's the one."

The waiter expertly wielded his corkscrew and opened the wine. He poured a small amount into Ted's glass to taste.

Ted swirled the glass, inhaled the aroma, and took a sip. "Yes. That will do nicely."

The waiter poured five ounces into each glass and set the wine bottle next to the cheese plate. He went about his tasks with polite enthusiasm. He seemed excited that he was setting up this spread for two men. "Were you two here for the wedding?"

"Yes." Ted wasn't interested in engaging the waiter in conversation.

When the waiter finished, he stood upright, smiled, and winked. "Is there anything else I can do for you gentlemen this evening?"

The underlying meaning of the waiter's question was not lost on Ted. "No thank you, that will be all." Under different circumstances, he might have answered differently. He walked to the door and held it open. The waiter's smile disappeared and he pushed his cart out the door. Ted dropped a $5 bill on the cart as he passed.

Ted closed the door, locked and chained it, and turned back toward the table. "Man, I've been sweating in these clothes all night. I don't care what they say about dry heat, it's still hot here. Mind if I get more comfortable?" He unbuttoned and removed his dress shirt, revealing a V-neck white undershirt stretched across his impressively sculpted chest. Then he unbuckled his belt and pants, stepped out of them, and laid his pants carefully on the bed. "Feels great to get some of that stuffy clothing off. I'm gonna go take a leak. Make yourself at home."

Rocket took off his shoes. He decided to go ahead and remove his shirt and pants. He'd still be in his underwear. He was comfortable being naked around men in a locker room shower, so there was no reason he should be uncomfortable hanging around with another guy in his underwear.

When Ted emerged from the bathroom and walked toward the table, Rocket couldn't help but notice how his arms bulged out from the undershirt sleeves, how his chest stretched the fabric, and how his torso tapered perfectly down to his trim waist. He also couldn't help but notice the full bulge in his underpants.

Ted noticed where Rocket's eyes went.

Rocket said, "Dude, your physique is amazing. How often do you work out?"

Ted smiled as he sat down and took a sip of wine. "Thanks. Usually just three times a week. Not as much as I'd like. When I was in high school, in the Marines, and in college, I used to work out almost every day. Back in high school, I was a scrawny little kid. Some of the other guys suspected I was gay, so I got picked on a lot. I went to the gym to build myself up. Plus, it got me out of the house. My dad and I didn't get along very well. I think he suspected I was gay too. The gym was my escape. It did a lot of good for my self-esteem."

"Man, I can so relate! My dad was a real asshole. He was drunk all the time and he had a hard time keeping a job. He thought I was worthless and he said I'd never amount to anything. So one of the reasons I got good at football was to prove to him – and myself – that I could be good at something and I wasn't worthless. Plus, I wanted to be more popular at school. I kinda was ... people wanted to hang out with me because I was the star of the football team. But I never really had any close friends. That's one thing I admired about Ryan and Chris. They were each other's best friends. I figured they were probably gay, but that didn't matter. They had the kind of friendship I wished I had."

"I know what you mean. He and I were that close. As I said earlier, he's the best friend I've ever had."

For a moment, neither of them said anything. Then Ted asked, "So what about your mom? Surely she must have been more supportive than your father."

Rocket sighed and looked down. "My mom wasn't around when I was a teenager. When I was twelve, she got caught embezzling money from the company she worked for and got sent to prison."

"Oh, man, I'm so sorry."

"What about your mom?"

"Well, as it turns out, my mom is a lesbian. I guess she figured it out when she fell in love with one of the other housewives in the neighborhood. I don't know, maybe she knew all along and just got married because she was supposed to. Anyway, when I was ten my dad found out, so of course they got a divorce. Dad got custody of me because he could afford a better attorney and the judge was a homophobe. Anyway, my mom and the other woman – who's now her wife – moved to Northampton, Massachusetts. It was a lot more welcoming for gays and lesbians than bumfuck, Pennsylvania. I understand a lot of lesbians live there."

"So you never got to see her?"

"Once in a while. I got to go up there for a couple of weeks during the summer. But she and her wife adopted two kids and were raising them, so I kind of felt like an intruder. I mean, my mom and I love each other and we get along fine, and her wife's really nice and we get along well too. But it's like her life went off in one direction and mine went in another. After my training classes and meetings, I'll fly to Massachusetts to visit them for a few days. I haven't seen them since before COVID."

"That'll be nice. I don't have any contact with my mom or dad anymore. I don't want to. I'm not even sure where they are. But anyway... You said you were in the Marines."

"Yeah. I went in right after high school. I wanted to get out of Allentown and my dad had no money to send me to college. I figured I'd put in my four years, then go to college on the GI Bill."

"What was it like?"

"It was hell. It was a living hell. I got sent to Afghanistan, and I got to see all the horror and inhumanity of war first-hand. It really fucked me up. I carried a lot of baggage around for years. Ryan and I talked about it once in a while, but I needed professional help. My company has excellent benefits, so

I finally got counseling. It really helped."

"I know what you mean. After I went to that orgy, I got kinda shaken up about some of the things I saw there. The police force offers counseling too. Being a cop is stressful. Sometimes you see some pretty gross things, like people who have been shot or badly injured in a car wreck. So I got counseling, and it did me so much good. It helped me deal with a lot of stuff from my childhood too, and some other issues I had."

"I wish I had gotten counseling years earlier."

"Me too. Man, you and I have so much in common! I'm really enjoying talking to you!"

"Yeah, me too. But let's stop talking about depressing shit. Tell me more about football."

Rocket perked up. "I was a running back. A damn good one, too. When I was in high school, our team won our conference every year. I did track in the spring to stay in shape and run faster. That's where I met Ryan and Chris."

"You guys went to the state championships, right?"

"Yeah. We didn't do as well as we could have, but... that's another story. Anyway, then I got a scholarship to play for TCU. We went to the Fiesta Bowl after my sophomore year and the Rose Bowl after my junior year."

"Nice! Yeah, I remember that TCU played in the Rose Bowl while I was living in LA."

"We went undefeated that year and beat Wisconsin in the Rose Bowl. But we were still only ranked #2, behind Auburn. The year before, we went undefeated during the regular season but we lost the Fiesta Bowl. But anyway, TCU switched from the Southwest Conference to the Big 12 for my senior year and went 7-6. None of the pro teams were interested in me, so I got a job as a police officer in Kansas City. I majored in Criminal Justice. So that's where I am today."

"Do you still run?"

Rocket shook his head. "I need to get back into it. I've put on 20 pounds since I stopped playing football."

"People expect football players to be a little beefy."

"Beefy is one thing. Soft is another."

"I don't run every day like I used to, but I still run three or four times a week. I try to run on the days I don't work out."

"Well, it shows. You look great. I'd kill to be cut like you."

Tell stood up and peeled off his undershirt to show off his chest and six-pack abs. "I'm not interested in getting bulked up like a body-builder. I just want to have some good definition."

Rocket stood and cautiously took a few steps forward. "Do you mind?"

"Not at all." Ted raised his arms and flexed his biceps.

Rocket wrapped his hand around Ted's right bicep and squeezed it. "Nice." He scanned Ted's chest and abs. "Dude, you're totally ripped. You must have, like, 2% body fat."

"Well, not quite. But I'm careful about what I eat. I try to avoid as much saturated fat and sugar as I can. I love a good steak, but I've had to cut way back on that. That was tough in Argentina. They have, like, the best beef in the world there."

"Yeah, there's no shortage of steaks around Kansas City either. That and barbecued pork."

Rocket wondered what he should do, with Ted standing in front of him shirtless. He was reluctant to take his undershirt off because, well, those 20 pounds. He didn't have anything to show off and it might seem weird for two guys to sit around in only their underpants. He felt kind of awkward but ... kind of not. He wasn't sure. He decided to leave it on.

They sat down. Ted placed a square slice of cheese on a cracker and took a bite. "I probably shouldn't be eating this cheese either. But it's a special day, you know? Anyway, I think staying in shape is more about diet than exercise. I mean, exercise is important, but we can't eat like we did in college. It's like our metabolism grinds to a screeching halt when we turn 30. We can't keep eating pizza and drinking beer and expect not to gain weight."

"Guilty on both counts. You should have seen the training table for the football players at TCU! Man, I'll never be able to eat like that again."

"I know, right? How old are you now?"

"Thirty-two."

"I just turned 40."

"You're 40? No fuckin' way, dude! I thought you were around my age. Thirty-five, tops."

Ted smiled. "Thanks. Sometimes I feel 40, though. Anyway, if you're serious about losing weight, you have to cut back on the beer. It's nothing but empty calories. It'll give you a beer gut in no time. That's why I drink red wine. If you're going to drink – and let's be honest, I love my alcohol – red wine is the way to go. Only one or two glasses a day, though. It still has calories, but it has antioxidants. It helps lower your bad cholesterol and relieves stress."

"You're probably right. I don't know much about wine. This Malbec is good, though."

"Just try this and that until you find what you like. You don't have to buy expensive wine but don't buy the cheapest stuff either. Eight or ten bucks will get you a decent bottle of wine." Ted noticed that both glasses were almost empty, so he picked up the bottle and replenished them. He smiled. "I remember when Ryan first came to live with us. I don't think he had ever drunk alcohol before."

Rocket chuckled. "Yeah, he was real straight-laced back in high school. I used to call him PK 'cause, you know, he was a preacher's kid. One night when the guys on the track team were having a party I got him to drink a little Jack Daniels." Rocket paused. "I probably shouldn't have done that, but oh well."

Ted continued. "Anyway, one night – it was probably less than a week after he started living with us – he and I were out in the pool. That was one thing I loved to do – sit outside late at night in the pool or the hot tub, depending on what time of year it was, and sip wine and enjoy the peacefulness. It was so relaxing. He and I spent so many nights out there talking and drinking wine. That's how I got to know him so well. Anyway, I offered him a glass of wine. That was totally new to him. First, he looked at me funny, like why did I only pour a few ounces into the glass instead of filling it up? Then he picked up the glass and took a big chug like it was water or soda. I had to explain that first you swirl the wine in the glass, then savor the bouquet, then sip it slowly and roll it around on your tongue. But he got the hang of it. Before too long, he was as much of a wine connoisseur as I was."

"Wow. It still blows my mind that Ryan started drinking back when he was in high school. He was the most wholesome, clean-cut kid around."

"Well, after everything that happened to him, he was more than ready to dump the whole religion thing. I don't think he was that bought-in anyway, but he had to go along."

"Kinda like he was rebelling."

"Yeah. Either that, or after being in the big city and living with us for a while he got a more realistic view of life. We were all a few years older than him. When he first arrived he was pretty naïve, but he grew up fast. He had to."

Rocket was keenly interested in all this new information he was learning about Ryan. He had so many questions he wanted to ask. "So... you said you and he spent a lot of time in the pool together. Did you ever go skinny-dipping?"

Ted laughed. "Oh, we never wore swimsuits. I don't think he even had one when he first moved out there."

"So... you got to see it."

"Oh, yeah. All the time. And yes, it was quite an eyeful."

"No shit, man. God, I remember when I first saw it... I mean, I see dicks in the shower room all the time. Doesn't bother me at all. And come on – you know everyone's checkin' out everyone else's junk, even if nobody will admit it."

"Right. The only guys who aren't checking out other guys' dicks are the liars."

Rocket chuckled. "Good one. Anyway, the first time I saw Ryan's dong, I was like, 'Oh my God!' I had never seen anything like it. I couldn't stop looking at it. He probably noticed."

"He was probably used to it."

"I don't know. But after a few days, he started hanging back to let everyone else get done in the shower before he came in. Like he'd run a few extra laps or talk to the coach or something."

"Yeah, I can relate. I know all about gym locker rooms. I don't wanna brag, but I'm fairly well off in that department – I mean, not like Ryan, but still – guys check me out all the time. I got over it a long time ago. Now I don't care. If they want to look, let them look."

Rocket flashed back to when he saw Ted in his underwear earlier. Now his view was blocked by the table, and he sure as hell wasn't going to lean forward to get another look. "Well, you've got a great body. They're probably checking out your chest and your abs and everything else."

"Yeah, maybe. But they can see that out on the floor."

"So... I know I probably shouldn't ask this, but... since you guys spent so much time together in the pool naked, did you... you know... do stuff?"

"Actually, no. And believe me, he really wanted to at first." Ted smiled as a fond memory returned. "I remember the first time we went running together. It was like his third or fourth day there. It was like 8:00 in the morning and I was leaving my bedroom to go for a run. He happened to come out of his room at the same time and asked if he could join me. So we went to the track at UCLA and ran four or five miles. Anyway, when we stopped to take a break, I took my shirt off. And I could see him gawking at me. It was that obvious. When we took off running again, it's like he was practically tripping on his tongue."

Rocket laughed at the mental image. "Dude, you're funny!"

"So I think it was that night when we got in the pool together for the first time. That was also the first time he tried wine, as I was saying. Anyway, it was obvious he was a little too interested in me – not only for sex but also romantically. So we talked about it. I made it clear that nothing would happen between us. I said I'd love to become friends, but that would be all."

"Really? How come? Man, if you guys were naked in the pool or the hot tub all the time, I figured you'd be fucking constantly!"

"Yeah, well, there were a couple of things. First, he was only 17 at the time. I'm eight years older, so I was 25. That's a big age gap. And a maturity gap. He had only been out of the closet a couple of months at the time, and I wasn't interested in dealing with all that. Plus, we had an unwritten rule at the house that we wouldn't screw or get involved with our housemates. There would be too much drama if things didn't work out."

"Yeah, I guess there's that."

"Besides, I think knowing that we weren't going to have sex or be in a relationship allowed us to become such good friends. We could stop worrying about whether tonight would be the night or who was going to make the first move or whatever. We could just talk. And we really opened up to each other. He had a lot of stuff to work through after what his dad did to him and coming out and being out on his own and all that stuff. And I had a lot of stuff bottled up inside that I never felt comfortable talking about until he came along. I'm pretty introverted. And for most of my life, I've been a loner. And I'm okay with that. But he and I connected. I could talk to him about anything."

Rocket looked surprised. "Really? 'Cause it doesn't seem like you're having any trouble talking now. And you're so easy to talk to. I'm enjoying this."

"Thanks. Me too. I guess I feel comfortable enough around you. And you know, I think sitting here in our underwear helps. It's like we've let down some barriers and we can be more comfortable."

"Yeah, I know what you mean. I think that's why I have no problem being naked in the shower room. It's like, when you're naked with other guys, you're not hiding anything. It's like everyone lets their guard down a little."

Ted said, "It's a male bonding experience."

"Yeah, that's it! Male bonding. That's a good way to put it. Anyway, I'm pretty average down there, and I used to be kind of bashful about being in the shower. You know, like other guys would be checking me out and comparing. But I got over that and now I don't care. I mean, I'm me. That's what I've got, like it or not. And it's not like I'm going be fucking them anyway."

"Even if you were, it's not like you're going decide whether to have sex with a guy based on the size of his dick. You're going to do it if you're attracted to him. And if he's gay, of course."

"Yeah, that would help. But anyway... So you guys you never did it?"

"I didn't say that. After I graduated, I moved out of the house and into an apartment in Redondo Beach. Let's see... that would have been at the end of his sophomore year. Later that year, he turned 21. I invited him over and took him to a nice restaurant for dinner. It was right on the beach. We watched the sunset over the ocean and went for a nice walk on the beach afterward. When we got back to my place we agreed he should spend the night, since we had both been drinking plenty of wine. So, we celebrated his 21st birthday in the best possible way."

Rocket smiled. "Sounds like you planned for it to happen that way."

"I hoped it would, no question. But if it didn't, that would have been fine too. I mean, we had a very close platonic friendship. After three years, it was kind of hard to turn that into a friends-with-benefits kind of thing. But the time was right, and we did it."

"Cool! Wow." Rocket couldn't help but imagine Ryan and Ted having sex. "So... How do I say this? ... On that night when I worked undercover at that orgy, they had pornos playing on the TV screens. And one of them had Ryan in it."

"I bet that was an eye-opener."

"I was stunned. I mean, I had no idea what happened to him after he disappeared. I didn't know where he was or what happened to him or even if he was still alive. And then to see him in a porno nailing another guy – I almost lost it. Anyway, that was the first time I ever saw it hard. Every time I saw it in the shower, it was always soft. And God, it was huge even when it was soft! But anyway, as I was watching him fuck that guy I was wondering, how do guys even take that much cock in their ass? Wouldn't it hurt?"

"Well, keep in mind that those guys get hired to be in those videos because they can take large cocks."

"Yeah, I guess." Rocket hesitated. "So... Did he... Did you..."

"Did he fuck me? Yes. And to answer your next question, yes, it was a challenge to take it all. It took a lot of relaxation and deep breathing. And yes, it was totally worth it. It was amazing!"

"So it actually feels good to have that much cock in your ass?"

"In his case, yes. But look. The size of his cock had nothing to do with it. I didn't care whether his cock was ten inches, or eight, or six, or four. I wasn't having sex with a big cock. I was having sex with Ryan. Or more accurately, making love. And that's what made it so beautiful. It wasn't just the physical stuff we did with each other, it was the emotional connection. After three years, we had a lot of feelings for each other stored up – sexually, romantically, and everything else. It all came pouring out that night." Ted grinned. "And the next morning."

"So, did you get to..."

"Yes, I fucked him too. And that was another reason that evening was so special. I didn't know until he told me the next morning, but that was the first time he had ever bottomed. He gave up his ass cherry for me."

"What? No way!"

"I couldn't believe it either, especially after all the porn he had done up to that point. But in porn, he was always cast as the top, for obvious reasons."

"But I thought he and Chris would have..."

"Apparently not. He told me they only went all the way once before he was outed to his father. I guess he topped Chris but not the other way around. His father grounded him, so they never got to be together again – until last year."

Rocket took a moment to process all that information. Ted reached for the wine bottle. Only a few ounces remained, so he divided it between their two glasses.

"Okay, so... God, I can't believe I'm asking you all these questions, but..."

"That's okay."

"So... When two guys get together, how do they decide who does what?"

"I don't know. I guess it depends on the guys and the situation. Some guys only want to be bottoms and some guys only want to be tops. If they're just hooking up, like on Grindr or something, that's usually stated upfront. A lot of guys are willing to do either or both. They're called 'versatile.' Then, they just go with the flow and see where things lead. It helps to speak up and tell the other guy what you want."

"So since you and Ryan fucked each other, that means you're both versatile."

"That's right. Even though he was only cast as a top in porn, in real life he likes to go both ways. And so do I. I figure, hell, it's all so good, why limit myself to one or the other? That's one of the great things about being gay. You can have it both ways."

"So it actually feels good to get it in the ass?"

"Oh, it's amazing! You know, I'm convinced most men, straight or gay, would enjoy getting fucked. Or at least, like, having a couple of fingers or a dildo in their ass. But they're too hung up about it. Like, if they enjoy it, does that mean they're gay? No, it just means they enjoy the sensation of having something in their ass."

There was so much more Rocket wanted to ask, but he knew he had already asked way too many personal questions. Their wine glasses were empty and the cheese board had been polished off twenty minutes ago. He could tell Ted was through answering questions and was ready to call it a night.

Ted stood up. "Well, Clay, it's been great hanging out with you, but I think I'm all talked out."

Rocket stood up. "Yeah, me too. But I really enjoyed our conversation. I know I asked a lot of questions, and some of them were kinda personal."

"No problem."

They stood facing each other. Rocket took one last look at Ted's perfectly-defined body. After admiring his chest and abs, he glanced downward for only a second. He wondered how much Ted had. He said it wasn't as big as Ryan's, but he looked pretty well-hung nevertheless.

Ted knew Rocket was checking him out all over. "I think you have a few more questions."

Ted moved closer to Rocket and stopped when their faces were only inches apart. Rocket felt his space being invaded but he didn't move.

Ted peered deep into Rocket's eyes. "Let's get them answered, shall we?"

Ted grabbed Rocket's shoulders and kissed him. Instinctively, Rocket opened his mouth and allowed Ted's tongue inside.

Ted wrapped his arms around Rocket and pulled him closer until their chests pressed against each other. Rocket reached around and placed his hands on Ted's back.

Rocket's brain swirled with confusion and desire. He tried to tell himself he shouldn't be doing this, but his lips were locked with Ted's, his tongue was probing Ted's mouth, and his hands were caressing Ted's back. His feet weren't moving. Since Ted was a few inches taller, his growing cock pressed against Rocket through the fabric of his underwear, just below his navel. Rocket realized his cock was tenting his underwear, growing into the space below Ted's balls. His hardening cock settled the matter.

Their hugging and kissing grew more passionate and urgent. Ted stopped kissing Rocket long enough to peel his undershirt upward. Rocket raised his arms without being asked, and Ted pulled his undershirt off and flung it aside. They wrapped their arms around each other and pulled their bodies together tightly. Rocket savored the feeling of Ted's skin pressed against his. Ted squeezed Rocket's buns as they slid their bodies up and down against each other. The warm, soft touch of Ted's skin against his sent waves of pleasure coursing throughout Rocket's body.

Ted stepped back and pushed his underwear down past his three-quarter erect cock. Once freed, it sprang up and continued growing. Ted shook his legs slightly and the underwear fell to his ankles. He stepped out of them.

Rocket's mouth dropped open as he gazed in awe at Ted's bright orange pubes and his fully-hard eight-inch cock, pointing proudly toward Rocket with a slight upward curve.

Ted dropped to his knees in front of Rocket. "Let's get this off you." It wasn't a question and he didn't wait for an answer. An instant later, Rocket felt his underwear at his ankles and his cock inside Ted's warm, moist mouth.

Rocket had no idea where this would lead, but he sure as hell wanted to find out. If it was true that 37% of all men have at least one sexual experience with another man sometime between adolescence and old age, he figured he was hardly alone.

All Good Things Must Come to an End

Saturday, November 26, 2022

Ryan and Chris sat in the Air New Zealand lounge at the Dunedin airport, sipping cocktails and eating fancy nibbles while they waited for their flight back to the US. They had a 26-hour journey ahead of them, with lengthy layovers in Auckland and Los Angeles.

Chris's mood was upbeat as he flipped through all the pictures he had taken on his phone. "Man, this has been a great trip! We did so much cool stuff. I still can't get over how beautiful New Zealand is."

"Yeah. It's my favorite place on earth."

"I have to admit when you suggested that we spend our honeymoon driving all over New Zealand in a camper van for four weeks, I was skeptical. I imagined we'd go to a fabulous resort in Maui, lay in lounge chairs by a beautiful pool, and sip fancy cocktails. And of course, fuck three times a day."

Ryan cut in. "Only three?"

Chris grinned. "Whatever. I'm sure we would have lost count."

"Well, I'm sorry if the frequency of lovemaking on our honeymoon did not live up to your expectations."

Chris chuckled. "This was different. At a resort, we would have been lying around all day. Here, we were constantly going places and doing things. But seriously, this has totally been, like, the best honeymoon ever."

"What was your favorite part?"

"I don't know. It's hard to pick only one thing. The cruise on Milford Sound was amazing. The Waitomo Glowworm Caves was definitely a highlight. Sailing in Auckland Harbor was great. It was a perfect day and the skyline was beautiful. I enjoyed meeting your friends. It was nice of Gavin and Reed to host that party on their boat and for Michael to bring a decorated cake. It was like a mini-wedding reception."

"Yeah, they're great guys. I wish I could see them more often."

"What was your favorite part?"

"All the places we went were nice, but the best part for me was just being here. That, and seeing my friends again."

Chris nodded. "We should definitely come back every few years. Of course, there are plenty of other places I'd like to travel to as well. But after four weeks away, I'm looking forward to being home again."

Ryan said nothing. Chris looked at a few more pictures on his phone, then looked up at Ryan, who was staring into space. He looked sad.

Ryan sensed Chris's gaze, so he turned to look at him. "I wish we didn't have to leave. I really wish we could live here."

"Well... okay... But what about Brandon and Aaron? Remember right after you and Aaron broke up, you said you never wanted to be separated from them again? And what about my family? What about our jobs? You could probably get a transfer, but what about me? I'm not licensed to practice law in New Zealand."

"Yeah, Aaron and I talked about the same thing when I took the assignment here. He wasn't licensed as a pharmacist here, and it wouldn't have been worth it for him to go through that whole process for only a year. But in our case, we'd move here permanently. Maybe we could look into how you'd go about getting licensed. Maybe you could still work for Technovations."

"And what about the Hal Morris Project? And the bands and our friends in them? I wonder if they even have a gay band in Auckland. And think about all the jazz concerts in Phoenix. Would you be able to see your favorite bands if we lived in Auckland?"

Ryan sighed. "Yeah, I guess it's not really practical. But you met my friends. We'd have a good social network. There's a good cultural scene in Auckland. And if there isn't a gay band, we could start one!"

"You're serious about this, aren't you?"

"I'm giving it a lot of thought. But you're right. There would be downsides."

"It would disrupt practically everything in our lives. It's fun to fantasize about the possibilities and wonder 'What if?' but I think we'd lose at least as much as we'd gain. And everything's a lot more expensive here. Honestly, I'm not really bought into this."

"Okay, but remember when Aaron and I broke up and we promised each other we'd spend the rest of our lives together? You said, 'I want nothing more than to spend the rest of my life with you. I don't care where – here, or back in DC, or in New Zealand, or wherever. As long as I'm with you.'"

"Yeah, I guess I did say that. Damn, you have a good memory!"

"It was one of the best moments of my life. I remember it vividly."

"Well, I can't back away from that, can I? Especially at the end of this wonderful honeymoon." Chris's mood sank. "You're going to hold me to that, aren't you?"

Ryan reached out and held Chris's hand. "No. At least not right away. I need to take my vacation goggles off and consider this more realistically. Maybe sometime in the future. But for now, let's build our life together in Scottsdale."

Then Ryan added, "But I'll tell you this. If He Who Shall Not Be Named somehow gets back into the White House, start packing!"

"If that happens, God forbid, you won't get any argument from me."

They gazed fondly at each other and smiled. Ryan said, "I love you."

"I love you too." Chris glanced at his watch. "We should probably finish up here and head to the gate. It's about time for them to start boarding."

Ryan nodded.

As they finished the last few bites of their food, Chris said, "I'm glad we sprung for business class tickets. I could sure get used to hanging out in airport lounges. It's so much more civilized."

Ryan raised what was left of his cocktail and said, "To civilized traveling!" They clinked their glasses and swigged the remainder of their cocktails. "We're worth it."

They leaned into each other and kissed.

Afterword

Thank you for purchasing and reading this book. I hope you enjoyed it.

This is the final book in a series called "Gay Tales for the New Millennium" that follows Ryan as he finishes high school, goes to college, launches his career, forms relationships, and comes to terms with his past.

I invite you to subscribe to my newsletter. I'll keep you informed about my future books and offer them to you at a discount. I'll share background information about the stories and the writing process. Occasionally, I may solicit your input which will help make the books even better! To subscribe, visit my website: AuthorDaveHughes.com.

To thank you for subscribing, I will send my short story, *Cruise Virgins.* In it, Ryan (as a young adult) and Ted experience their first gay cruise – and confront their feelings for one another.

Now, I have a small favor to ask.

As a self-published author, it's incredibly difficult to get my books noticed in a world where hundreds, if not thousands, of new books are released daily. It's challenging to build an audience for my work. If you enjoyed this book, please consider posting something about it on your social media platform of choice. All it takes is something simple, like 'I thoroughly enjoyed reading *Maybe Now,* by Dave Hughes. Check it out.' Also, please consider leaving an honest review on the website where you purchased this book. And tell your friends!

Thanks! I truly appreciate it.

I would like to thank my launch team for their thoughtful reviews, feedback, and support of my books: Tom Bogardus, Gary Brenkman, Aaron Chavez, Jeff McKeehan, Paul Phillips, and Mike Triggs.

Thanks to my email subscribers for their loyalty and support. I've made numerous decisions based on their feedback. And thanks to the Chandler Public Library Downtown Writers Group, led by Andrew Flynn, for their encouragement, support, and constructive feedback.

Special thanks to Gregg Edelman of Exposed Studio & Gallery. His charming art gallery is the perfect location for my book signing events. Thanks for all you do for the community!

Very special thanks to Mark McNease, prolific author of LGBT-themed mysteries and short stories (see MarkMcNease.com), for his priceless support and friendship. Mark hosts podcasts, writes on Substack, runs a website and Facebook group called LGBTSr, and promotes my work through all those avenues.

Most importantly, I would like to thank my husband, Jeff McKeehan, who has supported and encouraged me every step of the way, provided great ideas and valuable feedback, and tolerated all those times when my mind was immersed in the world of my characters. Every spouse of an author knows exactly what I'm talking about.

Other Books by Dave Hughes

Fiction
Gay Tales for the New Millennium
Maybe Next Year
Instant Adult
Open Books, Closed Sets
If I Seem Quiet...
Karma Train from Kansas

Retirement Lifestyle
Design Your Dream Retirement
Smooth Sailing into Retirement
The Quest for Retirement Utopia

AuthorDaveHughes.com

About the Author

This is Dave Hughes' sixth novel in the "Gay Tales for the New Millennium" series.

Before writing fiction, Dave wrote three retirement lifestyle planning books, *Design Your Dream Retirement, Smooth Sailing Into Retirement,* and *The Quest for Retirement Utopia.* Dave created the website RetireFabulously.com, which enables readers to envision, plan for, and enjoy the best retirement possible. In addition to writing hundreds of articles for RetireFabulously.com, Dave's writing has appeared on US News & World Report, LGBTSr.com, Medium, Yahoo! Finance, CNN/Money, Next Avenue, Tiny Buddha, and others.

Aside from his writing, Dave is also a jazz musician. He plays trombone and steelpan in various bands in the Phoenix area. He owns an embarrassingly large collection of jazz, Brazilian, exotica, steel band, jazz/rock, and vocal ensemble CDs and videos.

Before retiring early at age 56, Dave was a software engineer for 34 years, working for companies such as Intel, Computer Sciences Corporation, McDonnell Douglas Space Systems, and NCR. Throughout his career, his assignments included software development, customer support, training, course development, and management.

Dave resides in Chandler, Arizona with his husband Jeff and their dog Maynard.

Dave is available for interviews, book readings/signings, speaking engagements, and panel discussions. You may contact Dave at Dave@AuthorDaveHughes.com.

Visit AuthorDaveHughes.com to learn more and subscribe to his newsletter.